## PRAISE FOR
## THIEF OF SOULS

"Terrifying—emotionally as well as physically. . . .
No one will be able to resist rooting for [Dan Behr]
as he fights for his wife, his daughter, and
ultimately, his own soul."
—*Minneapolis Star-Tribune*

"Taut suspense and believable
psychological insight mark this thriller."
—*Library Journal*

"North's depiction of ritualistic secret evils is scary,
even fascinating. Brisk pacing will tug
readers along."
—*Publishers Weekly*

"Takes the readers into the darkest recesses of the
human heart and mind. Its characters are totally
credible and fully developed. . . . Should find a home
on every bestseller list in the world."
—*Tulsa World*

"Boy, is this powerful stuff. I was enthralled."
—*Poisoned Pen*

"An absolutely terrific chiller."
—*I Love a Mystery*

# Darian North

# THIEF
# OF
# SOULS

A SIGNET BOOK

SIGNET
Published by the Penguin Group
Penguin Putnam Inc., 375 Hudson Street,
New York, New York 10014, U.S.A.
Penguin Books Ltd, 27 Wrights Lane,
London W8 5TZ, England
Penguin Books Australia Ltd, Ringwood,
Victoria, Australia
Penguin Books Canada Ltd, 10 Alcorn Avenue,
Toronto, Ontario, Canada M4V 3B2
Penguin Books (N.Z.) Ltd, 182–190 Wairau Road,
Auckland 10, New Zealand

Penguin Books Ltd, Registered Offices:
Harmondsworth, Middlesex, England

Published by Signet, an imprint of Dutton NAL,
a member of Penguin Putnam Inc.
Previously published in a Dutton edition.

First Signet Printing, August, 1998
10  9  8  7  6  5  4  3  2  1

Ⓢ  REGISTERED TRADEMARK—MARCA REGISTRADA

Printed in the United States of America

PUBLISHER'S NOTE
This is a work of fiction. Names, characters, places, and incidents either are the
product of the author's imagination or are used fictitiously, and any resemblance to
actual persons, living or dead, events, or locales is entirely coincidental.

To
My Beloved Children

*Jennings*
*Brienna*
*Catanna*
&
*Connor*

Instead of being at the mercy of wild beasts, earthquakes, landslides, and inundations, modern man is battered by the elemental forces of his own psyche. This is the World Power that vastly exceeds all other powers on earth. The Age of Enlightenment, which stripped nature and human institutions of gods, overlooked the God of Terror who dwells in the human soul.

—Carl Jung

# PART
# ONE

# Chapter 1

On the day that he lost his wife, Daniel Behr awakened to the melancholy lowing of a ship's horn signaling fog in the harbor. No dark forebodings or premonitions of evil struck him. The morning seemed completely ordinary except for the fact that he was alone.

He hurried through his shower and into blue jeans and a crisp white shirt. Passing through the kitchen, he grabbed orange juice and an English muffin, then carried them to the living room, where he stood at the window and looked out as he ate. Though he was on the fourth floor and usually had a spectacular view, all that was visible through the fog was the uppermost tracery of the Verrazano Bridge, caution lights winking like stars through the overcast.

The day was made for dreaming, for reflecting, and for questioning, but Dan Behr did not stare into the fog and think about his unfullfilled youthful ambitions or his discontent with his work. He did not consider his five-year-old daughter's future, or marvel at the passionate and consuming love he had for his wife. He avoided such personal contemplation. Instead, he tried to keep his focus on the physical world. Things he could study and understand. Things that were logical and quantifiable. This approach had enabled him to construct a life in which he worked hard, did what he thought was right, and slept well at night. A safe life. Or so he still believed on this one last morning.

Chimes began as the hands on the grandmother clock reached the half hour. He picked up his briefcase, slung his battered leather flight jacket over his shoulder, and let himself out of the apartment. The sound of his door closing triggered the appearance of Mrs. Svensen, who lived across the hall in 4F. She stood in her doorway, a frail, hunched figure in a pink flannel bathrobe and yellow woolen socks, holding a small bag of trash in her gnarled hand.

"Hello, Mrs. Svensen," he called, pulling on his jacket. "I'm going down now, so I can take that for you."

"Since you're going down . . ." she said in her customary tone of vague annoyance. "I guess you might as well."

She thrust the neat bundle at him. Always triple-bagged and tightly tied because she was worried about people "snooping" through her castoffs.

"It's regular," she said. "No recycles."

Some time ago he had suggested that she leave her trash outside her door and he would automatically take down whatever he saw there without her having to ask. The suggestion had offended her. "Do you think I'm an invalid?" she'd demanded. "Do you think I can't take care of myself?" Since then he had played out the charade, pretending that she was actually on her way downstairs in her bathrobe and socks, and that his offers were spontaneous.

"You've got your briefcase!" she declared accusingly. "You're working today."

He shrugged and she glowered.

"My husband never would have worked on a Sunday. That was a sacred day. And I don't mean for religion . . . though he was a good Lutheran. Sundays are for family." Her eyes narrowed. "Your wife and daughter are gone, aren't they? That's why you're sneaking off to work."

He smiled. "Alex and Hana are indeed away for the weekend. But I promise you—Alex knows. I'm not slipping to the office behind her back."

Mrs. Svensen shook a bony finger at him. "She left because she didn't want you to work on Sunday!"

"No. Alex went to a retreat, and Hana is staying with a friend. So it's a good thing I have to go to work. Keeps me out of trouble."

"A retreat?" the old woman said as though this was a preposterous idea.

"I've got to run now." He began backing away, making

his escape before she could launch into one of her paranoid diatribes on spy satellites or government eavesdropping on her telephone.

Bypassing the elevator, he took the wide marble steps two at a time to the Art Deco lobby, went through the service door at the side and down the concrete stairs to the basement. He threw Mrs. Svensen's tidy bundle into a trash can with a feinting overhand shot, then went to his workshop in one of the basement service rooms. The building's owner, Petrous, had given him permission for a workshop in exchange for his performing minor carpentry work around the building. Petrous had been surprised both by the request for work space and by the offer of carpentry. "But you are a professional," Petrous had said, implying that a professional should not stoop to manual labor. Dan Behr had not enlightened the man as to just how low a young architect was in the professional scheme of things. Nor had he tried to explain that even if he did achieve a position in the professional stratosphere, he would still do as much woodworking and carpentry as his schedule allowed. He had chosen a career wielding a pencil, but his first love had been the tools of a carpenter.

He unlocked the service room. Inside he had fashioned a simple arrangement of rough shelves and pegboard surrounding a workbench and stool. His current project, a dollhouse for his daughter, sat on the bench. He studied it for a moment, pleased with his creation. The exterior was a scale replica of the Morris-Jumel house, a historic New York City landmark that was just one of the city's many architecture and art offerings that he never had the time to see anymore. The Morris-Jumel made a perfect dollhouse, a white Georgian wedding cake of a building with a two-story portico, dentiled cornices, and a balustraded roof. And columns. Four tall white columns. No glass boxes or less-is-more for Hana. He wanted the dollhouse to be a delight rather than a flexing of architecture's ego.

He had been working on the project for months and was down to the last of the inside details, reaching through the open back to craft an interior that was practical for play while somewhat in keeping with the style of the period.

The night before, he had used strips of balsa wood to create tiny crown moldings for the rooms, and this morning he wanted to paint the ceilings and moldings before he left for work. It was frustrating, having only stolen bits of time to spend on the house, but even with his slow progress he thought he could be done with it by Hana's sixth birthday.

Quickly, he applied a coat of white in even strokes. When he was finished, he relocked the workshop and left the building through the basement access door, stepping out into moisture-laden air. He smelled wet pavement and decaying leaves, and beneath the stronger scents was the subtle presence of the sea. Alex loved being so close to the water. They had chosen their apartment so she could look out over the Narrows.

Alexandra.

He drew in a deep breath.

Though he tried not to dwell on it, Dan Behr had missed his wife acutely. Three days without her had disconcerted him and left him vaguely distracted, with a persistent tug in his chest that was not quite an ache but close to it. He smiled to himself. All that would be cured soon. She had said to pick her up at five o'clock. He started down the block toward his car. Only nine hours to go.

After driving into a Sunday-quiet Manhattan, Dan entered the cavernous marble lobby of the office building that housed his company and got on an elevator with several sleep-stunned colleagues clutching take-out coffee.

"Good morning," he said, receiving a nod, a grunt, and one grumbled "Morning" in return.

At their floor, he led the way through the reception area, waved at the man behind the desk, a guard rather than a receptionist since it was the weekend, then held open the heavy door leading into the inner warren of offices and work spaces so that his fellow arrivals could file through without jostling their coffee.

"How can you be so cheery?" one of them asked.

"I like the Sunday morning energy level," he teased, and got groaning laughter in response.

"Morning," he called as he stepped into his assigned

area. Two of his colleagues were present and silently eating doughnuts at opposite ends of the long worktable.

"It's the Behr-man," Rich Medford said with his usual morning grouchiness. "How'd the bachelor Saturday night go? Been out running after bear-ettes?"

The other man, Wendell Crispin, looked at Medford with distaste. "You are such an idiot, Medford. You've seen his wife. He'd have to be brain dead to chase after other women and jeopardize his marriage."

Shaking his head in good-natured exasperation, Dan tuned out their conversation and hung his jacket on a peg. Including himself, there were four in his working group. Each of them had a drawing board. They shared two computer stations, the table, the shelving, and the storage cabinet. Beyond the three-quarter walls that defined their work space were other three-quarter walls and other small groups of workers.

The highly paid consultant who had created the arrangement had termed it "nesting." Each little nest of workers was supposed to bond, nurturing each other's ideas at the same time that they were sharing equipment and conserving floor space. The partners and supervisors did not nest. They had individual offices with windows to look out of and doors to close. This disparity, even more than the huge difference in salaries, was a constant source of grumbling, but Dan never took part in the complaints. All things considered, he thought that Hodder, Tang, and Orloff Architectural and Engineering Associates, or HTO, was a decent place to work and probably not much different from any other big firm in New York City. And it *was* a job in architecture. Which said a lot at a time when so many licensed architects were selling insurance or trying to break into the carpet-cleaning business.

Dan Behr's dissatisfactions, which he seldom allowed himself to consider and which he never voiced, were not with his employer but with the nature of his work. It was not what he wanted to do. It did not engage his passions or fill him with pride. Though within his field, the work he did for HTO was without meaning for him. But, being barely thirty years old, he believed he had a boundless future in which to remedy this, and so he was happy with the chance to gain experience while earning a living, happy with the savings account that was growing in preparation for the change he would make one day, and, most of all, happy with being a productive man, a family man, a man just like his father before him.

"Hey, Behr!" Medford boomed, demanding Dan's attention. "Do you believe this guy?" Medford was staring at Crispin in an exaggerated show of incredulity and skepticism. "Tell me, Crispy, how'd you become the voice of experience on women and marriage? You haven't even had a date this year."

Wendell Crispin, a washed-out, bony, Ichabod Crane of a man who appeared older than his thirty-odd years, turned bright red. "What's that got to do with anything? I'll tell you, Medford—when I do find the right woman, I'm going to have a mature attitude. I'll know how to be a good husband."

Medford moaned. "I think I might puke."

Richard Medford was a former college wrestling star who was still proud of his strength and physique. At first he had been wary and challenging, set off, perhaps, by Dan Behr's greater height, but Dan had ignored the macho posturing and gradually it evaporated. Always expensively dressed, Medford got his hair styled instead of cut, and he wore a diamond pinkie ring. His wife's family had money and influence, and it was whispered that he was guaranteed an eventual partnership at HTO. It was also whispered that he was sleeping with the nineteen-year-old receptionist.

The fourth in their nest was a petite, quiet young woman named Karen Lai, who managed to be stylishly attractive and unassuming at the same time. Theirs was an ill-matched group that had been forced into constant togetherness and into tolerating one another, yet somehow they had managed to form a unit and to become a part of each other's lives. In that way they were very much like an extended family.

"Where's Karen?" Dan asked as he settled in at his drawing board. Their sole female colleague was usually the first one at work every morning.

Medford shrugged.

Crispin dabbed his mouth with a paper napkin and said, "She hasn't called or anything. Think we should try her home number?"

"Let's give her a little more time," Dan suggested as he smoothed out a drawing and began to study it.

"Wait! Before you get started . . ." Medford jumped from his chair and leaned his elbows on Behr's drawing board. "I'm putting together a group for billiards on Thursday nights. We'll go straight from work, grab a burger, then go to this great place where tables will be reserved for us."

"I can't. Sorry."

"Ah, come on, Behr-man. We need you."

Dan smiled. "Thanks, but I just can't do it."

"You didn't play softball this summer either. What's wrong with you? I know you like sports."

"He lives way down in Brooklyn," Crispin said. "It's a long commute. Maybe he doesn't want to stay out with a bunch of assholes and then have to take the train home so late."

"How about every other Thursday?"

"It sounds like fun . . . but really . . . no."

"Once a month?"

"Maybe. I'll have to see."

Medford snorted sarcastically. "You mean you'll have to get permission from your wife."

Crispin crumpled up his doughnut bag. "Jesus, Medford. We work ten- and eleven-hour days here plus weekend time."

"So. . . ?" Medford swung toward the other man defensively. "What's that got to do with playing pool?"

"I have to leave at four-thirty," Dan reminded them. "So I'd appreciate it if you two would let me get some work done."

"Sure!" both men agreed quickly.

This was a pattern that had emerged. Crispin and Medford nipped and nagged and tortured each other, neither one willing to back down or put an end to it, but at the first word from Behr it was over. He had somehow come to be the referee and peacemaker of the group.

Nearly an hour of quiet passed before Karen Lai finally walked in.

"Karen!" Medford blurted. "Where in the hell have you been?"

"Personal business," the woman said shyly, head down and geometrically cut black hair falling forward to obscure her face as she sat down at her board.

"Is everything okay?" Crispin asked.

"You shoulda called in," Medford said.

Karen mumbled an apology without explanation and kept her head down.

"What—" Crispin began. "You owe—" Medford started to say.

Cutting them both off, Dan threw up his hands. "We don't have time for this! I don't know about the rest of you, but on my end that Brunner project is a long way from done, so . . . how about we get down to business here?"

The two men mumbled in agreement, and Karen Lai shot him a grateful look.

Another day, another dollar, Dan thought to himself, amused at having had the thought, but also touched by a wave of poignancy. How well he remembered that phrase. Every morning as his father had headed out for his assembly line job, he had paused to grip Dan's chin and fiercely lock eyes. "You learn a lot today, son, so's you can do better than your dad." Then, with a sigh, he would pick up his lunch box and go out the door, saying, "Another day, another dollar."

Pushing the memory away, Dan bent to study his in-progress drawing. He was part of a team working on the interior renovation of a major corporation's building. The task was to sandwich the mid- and lower-level employees into ten floors rather than fourteen so that the other four floors could be leased out and make a profit for the investors. Beneath the talk about spatial economizing and maximization of power delivery, what the job really amounted to was designing generous windowed perimeter offices for executives while the center of each floor was converted into a warren of cubicles with chest-high walls. The early sketches had reminded him of rat mazes.

He sighed. A sigh not unlike those of his father's that he remembered. Another day, another dollar. Then he shook off the mood by visualizing Alex. Tonight she would be back. Tonight. A frisson of sexual excitement ran through him, and he smiled to himself as he worked.

At twenty minutes past four Dan began the process of cleaning up and packing his take-home work into his brief-case. Sundays were loose. Everyone stayed until four on weekends, but beyond that it was up to the individual.

"You're leaving, Dan?" Karen asked, pencil poised over her drawing.

"He's going to pick up his wife," Crispin supplied before Behr could answer for himself.

"Yeah, remember she went to that woo-woo convention in the Village," Medford added.

"A retreat," Dan said. "It's just a retreat."

"I don't care what you call it," Medford insisted. "It's all a lot of nutty New Age millennium crap."

"Lots of groups have retreats," Crispin quickly retorted. "You're so ill informed, Medford."

"Is there anything else about the Brunner project that we should discuss?" Dan asked them all. "Or are we set for now?"

"We're fine," Medford said.

"Just behind," Crispin added.

Karen nodded in agreement.

"See you in the morning, then." Dan fished his car keys out of his briefcase before closing it.

"You're driving?" Crispin asked in surprise.

"You have a car!" Medford exclaimed. "I thought you were so into doing your duty to the environment and the city by using public transportation."

"I have a car," Dan said, without explaining that he had needed it for late-night car-service jobs at the beginning of his marriage when money was so tight. "I usually take the subway in, but Alex will have a suitcase and things, so I wanted to pick her up in the car."

"What do you drive?" Medford asked, craning his neck to look at the keys. His own keys with their prominent

Mercedes symbol had been flaunted ever since he received the vehicle as a gift from his wife.

"Just an old Chevy. Nothing fancy."

Medford laughed. "I knew it! What else would the Behrman drive?"

Dan laughed and walked out without responding. He was nearly to the elevator when he heard his name called and turned to see Karen hurrying after him.

"Sorry, Dan," she whispered. "I know you're in a hurry, but I need to ask you something."

"That's okay. I've got a few minutes."

She compressed her lips, drew in a deep breath, and lowered her eyes.

Dan waited, concerned but not at all apprehensive.

She glanced around, checking for eavesdroppers, then said, in a very low voice, "One time you said something about having an alcoholic mother, and I wanted to know . . . how did your father deal with it?"

The question hit him like a surprise punch. He had the urge to argue with her, insist that he had never mentioned his mother's drinking, but of course the fact of her knowing meant that he must have said something.

He shrugged. "My dad tried hiding bottles. He tried keeping money away from her. He put up with a lot of broken promises."

"Did he get her into programs or counseling?"

"He tried. She'd always quit."

"But he stayed with her?"

"She wouldn't have survived otherwise."

"Did he still love her? I mean . . . did he grow to hate her for what she was doing?"

"He loved her very much. But why are you asking me all this, Karen?"

She hesitated. "Because I don't know what to do."

"Is your husband drinking?"

"No. It's drugs." A heavy sigh came from deep in her chest. "He says it's no problem. He says all the interns do it. But it's getting worse and it's changing him. Last night we had a bad fight, and he locked me in the bathroom." She bit her top lip. "This morning he had no memory of it."

Behr felt completely at a loss. He'd had no idea that Karen had any problems whatsoever.

"I'm sorry," she said quickly. "I shouldn't have dumped on you like this. It's just . . . I'm confused and my husband refuses to take it seriously and you're so nice and I thought . . . since you'd had experience with something similar . . ."

"Don't apologize. Tell me what I can do to help."

"Nothing." She started backing away. "Nothing. I'm probably just being hysterical or something. It's probably just a phase. Forget it, okay? Please . . . Can we just forget it?"

The earlier fog had evolved into a threatening overcast, and the air smelled like rain. Putting the puzzle of Karen's revelation aside, Behr took the West Side Highway north, turned into the Village, and attempted to follow the scribbled directions in the note Alexandra had left him. When she wrote "Greenwich," had she meant Greenwich Street or Greenwich Avenue? When she wrote "the square" had she meant Sheridan Square or Abingdon Square? He knew that she herself had never been to the location and that she had been relaying secondhand information. Add to that her dislike of what she referred to as "trivia," a category in which she placed street names and the four points of the compass, and he had little faith in her directions

As he wound through the convoluted Village streets he wondered if Vanzant existed at all. He could not recall seeing a Vanzant Street. But that didn't mean anything. He had never become familiar with all the crisscrossing byways of the West Village. Unlike the straight numbered grids that the founding fathers had forged in uptown Manhattan, this area was a warren of narrow, haphazardly aimed, and oddly named little streets—quaint and charming, but impossible to navigate. He drove up and down, back and forth, determined not to stop and ask for help. Finally he found it. Vanzant. A picturesque block of three-story bow-fronted brownstones. Traffic was a single lane one way, and parallel parking was tight.

He drove slowly, leaning forward to read the house

numbers. The buildings were probably not quite a hundred
years old yet, which was young compared to much of the
Village. They were row houses, typical of their era, all attached and all identical so that they repeated from one end
of the block to the other in a unified exterior, each with
stone steps leading up from the sidewalk to the front door.
Number 44 was mid-block. A fire hydrant squatted in front
of the house. "Parking pumps" Alex called them. He
pulled in at the hydrant illegally, expecting to leave in minutes. Since it was past five, Alex was probably waiting just
inside the door for him. He took the steps two at a time,
excited and eager, feeling a rush of anticipation. This was
the longest they had ever been apart.

There was no bell or knocker. Just an intercom. He
pressed the button, then waited. A car went by. A dalma-
tion dragged its owner past.

Dan shifted. From the sidewalk, the front door had appeared to be an original, but a closer look revealed that it
was not only a reproduction but a repro-replacement that
was actually a cleverly crafted steel-jacketed security door.
He stared at the silent intercom speaker, then glanced up
and saw the tiny eye of a surveillance camera staring down
at him. Someone was very conscious of security, but then,
many New Yorkers were. He stabbed the intercom button
again. Twice. Three times. Still no response. He leaned
close to the mute speaker.

"Excuse me . . . this is Dan Behr, and I've come for my
wife, Alexandra."

He waited. The faint hum of electrical connections
buzzed in the speaker, and he knew that the intercom
was on.

"Hello? Can anyone hear me?"

Nothing.

He took a step back, pulled her note from his pocket,
and checked the address—"44 Vanzant." The fours could
have been nines, but when he looked up the street he
saw that there was no 99. He rang the bell again without
an answering response. Finally, he went back down the
steps, resigned to waiting. It wouldn't be the first time

he had waited for her, and he was sure it wouldn't be the last.

At his car, he leaned against the fender and scanned the unbroken line of houses. Though they had not been built for grandness, their facades had a grace and grandeur that had endured. He was pleased to see that they were being maintained. Judging from the frequency of window boxes and restored details on the block, there were a lot of proud, appreciative residents in the buildings. No doubt the exteriors had some measure of historical protection. Or at least he hoped they did. He wondered about the interiors. How many had been carved up into tiny rental units?

A drop of rain fell on his hand. He squinted up at the overcast, hoping that Alex would come out soon so they could make it to a restaurant before the threatened downpour occurred. There was no umbrella in the car. He glanced down at the watch Alex had given him for his birthday, then looked back up, and realized that 44 was the only house on the block that was completely devoid of ornament—no shrubs in planters or flowers in pots or enameled railings. Not even a nice mailbox. And it struck him that 44 was the only house on the block with security bars at all the windows, even those on the third level. A thread of unease wound through his gut, but he dismissed it.

A legal parking spot opened up and he moved his car, even though it was probably a waste of time because Alex would surely appear at any minute. The thing had to be over soon. Dinnertime was approaching, and people would have obligations and plans. He thought about how long it had been since he had had an adult dinner in a restaurant with his wife. Especially in Manhattan.

Another ten minutes passed, and he went back up the steps and pressed the intercom button again. Nothing. He sighed in annoyance, then pushed the button steadily for several seconds.

Maybe the retreat activities were simply running late, assuming there were activities in a retreat. Or maybe she had given him the wrong time. He turned away from the door and scanned the block. Maybe this wasn't even the right

house. Or the right street. He wished that he could go to a
pay phone and call, but he didn't have a number. She had
told him it was unlisted, kept secret so that the tranquillity
of the retreat would not be disturbed. He just had to wait.
When Alex was finished she would probably come outside
looking for him.

Slowly he went back down the steps. Neighbors might
be able to confirm whether 44 was the right house, but he
was not about to ring a stranger's bell in Manhattan. The
rain started, light but steady, and he sprinted to his car and
slid behind the wheel. He turned on the radio. Only the
AM band worked, and the push buttons had frozen in place
so he had to dial in the stations with the turner knob. That
didn't faze him, but it bothered Alex. She was more concerned with the radio than with the general health of the
vehicle.

He flipped through the stations on the dial, hearing snip-
pets of Spanish and country music, angry talk show voices,
and abbreviated news flashes before finally finding the
public radio station he preferred. He peered closer at the
numbered readout. The station was at eight-twenty. Why
couldn't he ever remember that?

The afternoon's program featured a man who was explaining that the members of the Ku Klux Klan and the
Aryan Nations had not disappeared. They had simply
melted into other groups and cults that were active today.
Dan listened for a few minutes, but the facts were disturbing and the situations seemed so completely remote from
his own life as to be irrelevant. He turned off the radio and
checked his watch. Fifteen minutes had passed. He would
wait five more and then try the intercom again. What a
waste of time. He could have stayed in the office another
hour. Instead he was trapped in the car without enough
room to spread out and work, and without anything to do.
Not even a newspaper to read.

He switched on the dome light and opened the glove
compartment to rummage. Buried beneath maps and mis-
cellany was an envelope of photographs. Smiling, he
looked at pose after pose of Hana smelling flowers, holding a balloon, riding on a carousel, her sweet solemn face

dutifully turned toward the camera. Then suddenly there was a picture of Alex straightening Hana's dress and glaring over her shoulder with her usual "Don't point that thing at me" expression. And he remembered that he had hidden this group of photographs in the car to keep Alex from throwing away one particular shot.

A small knot of excitement tightened within him as he flipped through in search of that one special picture, remembering that he had intended to have it enlarged and framed to take to his office, remembering every detail of the photo now. Remembering how very stunning it was. But still, even though he knew exactly what he was going to find, when he finally came to it, he was caught. Nailed through the heart by her image. He drew a deep breath and held up the picture.

Through a miracle of timing he had managed to steal this one click of the shutter while her attention was on Hana. Her expression was natural, showing neither tense resignation nor annoyance at being the focus of his lens. This one chance shot captured her fully for him. The contradictions. The hopefulness beneath the careless, challenging posture. The vulnerability beneath the confidence. The illusive wildness that ran like a dark undertow within her.

But the shot did more than reveal her nature. He tilted the photograph toward the light and remembered why he had delayed taking it to the office. After his initial awe, the picture had begun to disturb him.

On paper, gently side-lit by the sun, her too-sharp cheekbones were softened and her lovely-but-not-perfect skin was transformed into the purity of honeyed velvet. Her dark red hair gleamed like antique polished mahogany. The green-gold of her eyes was magnetic. She was, through the alchemy of lens and light, so breathtaking that she made his chest ache. So breathtaking that the reality of her as a flesh-and-blood human being was obliterated. She was not just beautiful. That would have been too pallid a description for her. She was . . . striking. She was a lightning bolt.

Slowly, sitting there in the dimming car light, he allowed himself to consider why the picture disturbed him.

It reminded him that his wife, whom he loved and cherished, the person he ate with and sorted laundry with and held close each night, was not just his wife and partner and companion. Not just a devoted mother and new member of the PTA. She was a woman possessed by a devastating, consuming beauty. A woman who was seductive and irresistible to others whether she wanted to be or not. A woman who had been haunted all her life by her own image. And he realized that framing such a picture, displaying it on the office shelf, would have been a betrayal of all they had together and of what they were to each other. Crispin and Medford would have gawked at it constantly. Casual visitors would have commented on it. And somehow his display of this particular picture when he could have chosen from other more mundane snapshots of Alex and Hana together would have been akin to Medford's continual showing of his Mercedes keys. It would have made Alex seem like a trophy.

He turned the picture facedown and stuffed it back into the envelope. No. He would never frame it. But he couldn't let her tear it into pieces either. The glove compartment was the perfect place for it.

He turned to look out at 44 again. What did people do at a retreat anyway? What had she been doing inside that house all weekend?

When the hands of his watch reached six-thirty he lost all patience. Resolutely, he got out of his car and went back up the steps to hit the intercom button again. The dark eye of the security camera glared down at him as he waited. He pressed the button again. And again. Pausing briefly between each try. Eight times. Twelve times. Eighteen times.

Suddenly there was a sharp crackle of static.

"Stop buzzing!" a voice shouted.

Startled, he jerked back. "Sorry," he said. Then, leaning in toward the intercom, "This is the place where the weekend retreats are held, isn't it?"

"If you continue harassing us we'll call the police!"

"No! Please . . . You don't understand. I was supposed to pick up my wife from a retreat. At five o'clock. If I'm not at the right place, then just say so."

"Get away from the door and get off the premises! Now."

Dan stared, dumbfounded, at the intercom. Was his wife inside or not? Why was the speaker so hostile? What in the hell was going on here?

# Chapter 2

Dan went back down to the sidewalk, stood a moment, then turned and walked toward the avenue and the commercial areas in search of a pay phone. Clearly he had misunderstood something. Maybe the plans had changed and the retreat had ended early. Maybe Alex had tried to reach him at work but had missed him by a few minutes. Maybe she was already at home.

When he finally found a working street phone he called their apartment number. The line rang and rang. She was not there. He cradled the receiver, considered his options, then dialed Felice Navarre's, where his daughter was staying. The woman answered with a bright hello.

"Hello, Felice . . . it's Dan Behr. Have you heard from Alex?"

"No. Was I supposed to?"

"No." He sighed involuntarily. "I'm here in the Village and I can't find her and I'm not sure if the address she gave me is even right."

Felice laughed. "I swear, you two need a keeper. If she calls here I'll tell her you're looking for her."

"Tell her I'm parked near 44 Vanzant in the West Village."

"One minute. Let me write that down."

He waited. Hana said something in the background, making Felice laugh again. "Your daughter is worried that you both might get lost and not be able to find your way home."

"Put her on, please."

After much banging and shuffling a small voice said, "Hi, Daddy."

"Hi, punkin. Don't you worry. We can find our way home."

Instantly reassured, Hana switched to a different subject. "Felice let me hold the leash when we walked Peppy and I got to go to sleep with Peppy. Not for all night, but just for snuggling."

"Good," he said, though certain that Alex would not approve of her daughter snuggling with the dog.

"Tomorrow is school and we're making our room all decorated up for the open house. Felice read a note from my teacher about it."

"Okay, sweetie. You can tell me more later. Now, put Felice back on, please."

"The open house is tomorrow night at seven," Felice said as soon as she had the phone back. "When we got her weekend homework out of her book bag, I found the note."

"Okay. I'm sure Alex is aware." He hesitated. "This looks like it could take awhile. I mean, we aren't even on our way to a restaurant yet. Maybe we should just skip dinner and—"

"No, no, no. Go out. Have fun. If it gets late I'll tuck Hana in on the couch and you can carry her home asleep."

"And if Alex calls there—"

"Got it. Wow, Dan, I'm not used to you sounding so stressed. Loosen up, man. It will all be fine."

As he headed back toward Vanzant, he took Alex's note from his pocket and reread it. "Don't forget to pick me up," she had written. "Five o'clock on Sunday. 44 Vanzant. Love, A." And then she had added the few lines of directions.

He reached number 44 and stood on the sidewalk in front of the house, frustrated and uncertain. Hovering on the edge of a nonspecific anger that was directed at the situation in general. What now? Should he get back into his car and sit there? Should he leave and come back later? Should he buzz the intercom until someone reasonable answered the door?

Two men stepped out of the house next door. They were dressed in identical jogging suits and absorbed in conversation, heads tilted together. Dan hurried toward them but was not noticed until he called out, "Excuse me!"

The two stopped and cautiously watched his approach. "Yes?" the older, smaller man said.

"I'm sorry to bother you, but I'm trying to find someone on this street and I'm not sure I have the right address."

The smaller man shrugged. "We don't know many of the neighbors."

The second man was in his mid-thirties, and was powerfully built. He smiled. "Who are you looking for?"

"I don't actually have a person's name," Dan admitted. "But it's a place where they have weekend retreats. I thought the address was forty-four."

The smile faded, and the two men exchanged wary looks.

"You've got it right, forty-four," the smaller man said, and the two quickly started to move away.

"Wait! Please . . . Do you know them? Do you have the phone number? My wife is in there but no one will open the door."

"If I was you," the bigger man called back over his shoulder as they jogged away, "I'd go straight to the police."

The words hit Dan like a fist. Pulse escalating and belly clutching, he turned to look up at the house. It no longer blended in with the rest of the block. Now it loomed over him, full of menace. Something was very wrong in that house. As he stared up at the age-darkened brown facade, there was a movement in the heavy curtains behind a barred window, and he realized he was being watched.

Alexandra was in there. He was suddenly sure of that. His wife was in there. And he knew, deep in his gut, that he had to get her out. He had to get her out fast.

The police station was only blocks away. During his search for Vanzant Street, he could not help but notice the Sixth Precinct House because it was so out of character in the quaint atmosphere of the Village. It was, he suspected, a product of the seventies—an era of relentlessly undistinguished public building design—and he'd found it ironic that the city had committed an architectural crime against a historic area in the effort to fight crime there.

He rushed through the doors on Tenth Street, then through another set of doors. Having never been inside a police station before, he was seized with utter dismay. It was the complete antithesis of the high-tech, sharp-edged scene portrayed in so many crime dramas. Ceiling tiles sagged and the aggregate floor looked as though it had gone through an earthquake. The gray metal desks and file cabinets were as dented and scratched as if they'd been rescued from a junkyard. And over it all—over the ceiling and floor, over the furniture, over the cocoa-tiled walls and the robin's-egg-blue concrete block wall—was a pervasive weariness. That weariness was echoed in the postures and mannerisms of the uniformed officers behind the battered desks and fogged Plexiglas partitions.

Dan reined in his panic and stood in the knot of civilians clustered at the front desk, waiting his turn. He waited through tales of stolen purses and missing ATM cards. A young Wall Street turk demanded to see a detective. A woman with a black eye wanted to talk about her mugging. An elderly man whined about the patrolman not taking his cousin to jail. In an open area behind the desk, a typist was plodding away, transforming handwritten reports into typed complaints.

"Who's next?"

Dan stepped forward.

"My wife is being held at a house on Vanzant Street."

The thick-chested officer behind the desk looked up at him with a carefully neutral expression. "Held how? What do you mean held?"

Dan went through the story. He was handed over to another officer, who was armed with a pen and a form, and he went through the story again. With the retelling he realized that the whole thing sounded flimsy and perhaps even trivial. He was not conveying the ominous character of the experience at all. And he had neither proof nor eyewitness knowledge that a crime was indeed being perpetrated.

"Is this a domestic dispute, sir?" the young officer finally asked.

"No. Not at all."

"Drugs involved?"

"Not to my knowledge."

"Robbery?"

"No! They've just . . . got her there. Listen"—he straightened and followed the example of the Wall Streeter whose performance he had witnessed earlier—"I want to see a detective. Right now. My wife is in danger and . . . and one of the neighbors said there'd been trouble at that house before." Just a slight embroidery of the truth. "I want to talk to a detective," he insisted.

"I'll see if there's a detective free, sir. Have a seat."

"Could I call and check on my daughter first . . . to make sure that nothing has changed and . . ."

"Come this way. I've got a phone over here you can use."

After Dan had checked with Felice again he sat down in one of the molded plastic chairs that lined the wall opposite the desk. It was an orange chair with chrome legs, so much grime rubbed into the plastic over the years that the orange was muted. When he could sit no longer he moved aimlessly between the front door and the line of chairs, keeping his attention on the desk, waiting to be called. The barrel-chested man was replaced by two women, one uniformed and one not. When he could wait no longer he approached them from the side, ignoring the clustered complainants grumbling about him jumping the line.

"What is going on?" he demanded.

The uniformed officer straightened and glared at him. "Keep it down," she ordered. In contrast to her fashionably feminine haircut, her demeanor was tough and bullying.

"My wife is in danger! Doesn't that mean anything? Isn't there someone in here who does more than ask questions and fill out forms?"

She puffed up and fixed him with a warning stare.

"I think one of the detectives is coming down for him," the woman in civilian clothes said.

"When?" he demanded.

There was a tense moment, with the puffed-up female officer glaring at him, and the other woman calling upstairs, and the crowd around the desk watching the drama expectantly.

"Yeah," the woman said into the phone, her eyes fixed on Dan. "Yeah. Yeah. Yeah. How about somebody walks him up, then?"

\* \* \*

The detective squad was up one flight of concrete and metal stairs, through a short hallway, and behind a metal door. Dan was parked on a backless wooden bench just inside the door. There were open doors to small offices, but the majority of the floor space was given to a large room full of desks. It had generous windows and would have been filled with natural light in the daytime. He took in shades of beige and brown, the standard gray metal desks, a shelf unit packed with telephone books, metal file cabinets, and in the far corner the black bars of a holding cell. Utilitarian but not unpleasant. There was a fairly fresh coat of paint on the walls, and there were personal touches here—snapshots of smiling detectives pinned on a board, a handmade key hanger, knickknacks on some of the desks. Dan felt better. This was more human and more reassuring than the scene downstairs.

"Be with you in a minute," a man said from a desk. He was dressed like a businessman: dress shirt and tie, black wing tip shoes, suit jacket over the back of his chair.

Dan drew in a deep breath. A half dozen men were seated at the assemblage of desks, talking on phones or doing paperwork. The room was a blizzard of paperwork—piles of forms on the desks, posters and announcements and notices taped on the walls, lists and reminders and internal squad memos tacked to the bulletin boards. He watched the men work. There were dark faces and light faces. He heard a musical island accent from one and a pure Bronx accent from another. They were all different, and yet they were alike in their dress and their projection of businesslike efficiency. Hope filled him. These were people who could help. These were men who would know what to do.

The detective who had spoken to him rose and crossed to the waist-high divider that separated the waiting area from the main room. "You're Mr. . . ." He glanced down at a piece of paper. "Is it pronounced like the animal or the brew?"

"The animal."

"I'm Detective Gasparino," the man said. "Come on over to my desk."

The detective dropped back into his desk chair and immediately began studying the complaint form that had been sent from downstairs. Dan sat down. The chair for Gasparino's "visitors" faced the desk and was pulled up so close that Dan's knees bumped against the metal front. He watched the detective read. The man was around fifty, solidly built and ruddy-cheeked, with thinning red-blond hair. In spite of the Italian-sounding name he looked as though he played in a bagpipe band on Saint Patrick's Day.

"Okay . . ." The detective sighed, lowering the report and making eye contact.

"It's hard to explain," Dan admitted. "It's a very strange situation."

Gasparino's mouth and chin did a series of exercises while his eyes scrutinized Dan intently.

"You seem like a regular guy, Mr. Behr." He glanced down the form. "Daniel? Danny is it, or Dan?"

"Dan."

He lifted off his chair slightly and leaned over the desk to shake hands. "I'm Jimmy."

Dan shook the hand and nodded.

"So, Dan . . . You seem like a nice guy. A smart young man." He shifted in his chair, stretching back and hooking his hands behind his neck. "What is it you do? What kind of work?"

"I work for an architectural and engineering firm."

"Yeah? You an architect or an engineer or what?"

"Architect."

"Got a card?"

Dan fished one out of his wallet and handed it over.

"Hmmm." Gasparino chuckled. "My wife always says she should have married a doctor or an architect. Least she didn't rate me below lawyers, huh?"

Dan could not make himself smile.

The detective cleared his throat, then straightened and crossed his arms. "Okay. You think your wife is being held prisoner on Vanzant Street."

"I know that sounds a little hard to believe . . ."

"Yeah," the detective agreed. He tugged on his ear. "Has she done this before?"

"What?"

"Not been somewhere when you went to pick her up."

"No."

"Does she go away a lot on weekends?"

"Never. And she's never been to a retreat before."

"Who runs the retreat?"

"I don't know."

"Is it a church thing, or is it connected to a group she's in?"

"It's connected to some meetings she's been going to."

"Are you sure this isn't a shelter or a safe house?"

"What do you mean?"

Gasparino studied him as though gauging his sincerity. "A place for abused women to get away from their abusers."

Dan shook his head, partly in denial, partly in disbelief. "You think that I . . . ?"

"We've gotta look at all the possibilities."

"I love my wife."

Gasparino nodded. "Any fights lately? Any reason she might want to duck out for a while?"

"No. Everything was fine. And even if she was upset for some reason—we have a five-year-old daughter. She wouldn't just leave Hana."

"Where is your daughter?"

"At a friend's house."

"You sure she's there?"

"Yes. They let me call from downstairs and I spoke to her."

Gasparino frowned. "You got any proof that your wife was planning on coming home?"

Dan thought a moment. "I have the note she left me saying when and where to pick her up."

He pulled the paper from his pocket and passed it over to Gasparino. The detective examined the note, worked his mouth, blew out a deep breath, then met Dan's eyes. Weighing and deciding.

"Greenberg," Gasparino called to a man at a desk across the room, "let's run over to Vanzant and check this out."

The man called Greenberg looked up as though surprised,

then quickly gave a professional nod and closed the file he had been reading.

Gasparino stood, grabbed his suit jacket and slipped it on. "Are Thelma and Lynn both out of the building?"

"Yeah," Greenberg answered as he too stood and put on his jacket. "Think we need a female along?"

"Might be a good idea."

"That uniform . . . what's her name . . . Brown . . . is downstairs working with Domestic Violence," Greenberg offered, already dialing the phone as he spoke.

"Detective Greenberg is my partner," Gasparino told Dan. "Did you walk here or what?"

"I walked."

"You can ride with us, but you've gotta stay out of the way and let us do our job. Understand?"

Dan nodded.

It was nearly eight by the time they arrived at 44 Vanzant. The old-fashioned streetlights reflected on the wet sidewalks but the rain had stopped.

"Wait here," Gasparino said, pointing to a spot on the sidewalk. "Don't move. Don't cause any trouble."

Brown's eyes flicked briefly to Dan, as though he were a curiosity. Then she turned and followed the detectives up the steps, keeping slightly behind them. She was an average-size woman with intelligent eyes and tightly ringleted black hair that hung around her face and stuck out from her head in little springs. Dan had not heard her say a word. He had seen her smile, though—a genuinely sweet smile—and somehow that smile had made him trust her.

Dan watched them, Gasparino looking formidable in his brown suit, the stoop-shouldered Greenberg not quite as impressive but still a comforting sight as he mounted the stairs, and Brown in her uniform and heavy black belt with the gun and stick and flashlight bumping against her hips. He felt an overwhelming relief and gratitude, but it was accompanied by a sense of helplessness, as though he were a child waiting for the adults to go settle a dispute for him. He turned away and saw faces at the window of a nearby house. It was the two men he had spoken to earlier. They were watching the show. He turned back. Gasparino was talking into the intercom. Dan couldn't hear the words.

Suddenly the heavy door opened. All three of them went in, and the door closed. Dan stared up at the empty space where they had stood. He stared at the door. He clenched his fists and unclenched them. He paced in a tight pattern, back and forth on the sidewalk. He went up two steps, then, dutifully, returned to the sidewalk.

Just when he thought he could stand it no longer, the two detectives emerged from the house. Dan started up the steps.

"Stay there!" Gasparino called, and headed down to meet him.

"What's happening? Where is she?"

"Everything's under control," Gasparino said, taking Dan's arm and steering him toward the unmarked car.

"She's there?"

"Yeah. She's inside. She's a real looker, right? Tall . . . with dark reddish hair?"

"Yes. Yes. That's Alexandra. She's all right? She's safe?"

"Seemed fine to me."

An involuntary sigh escaped Dan's lungs and his knees went wobbly. He leaned against the car for support and attempted a smile. "Damn . . . Thanks for going in there. I don't know what I'd have done." He shook his head. "What happens now? Can we go home or does she need to go back to the station and make a statement?"

Gasparino squinted up at the moonless night sky. He squinted down at the dark pavement. When he finally looked at Dan he was still squinting.

"She's not going home."

"What?"

"She wants to stay there."

Dan searched the man's face, trying to make sense of the words. "She wants to stay there?" he repeated dumbly.

Gasparino nodded.

"How much longer?"

The detective's squint became a wince.

"She didn't say."

"I need to talk to her," Dan said, starting forward.

Greenberg sidestepped neatly to block his path.

"They won't let you talk to her," Gasparino said sadly.

"She's my wife! I need to find out how she thinks this is going to work if she stays longer. What does she want me to do with our daughter? Who's going to pick her up from school? And what about the school open house tomorrow night? Will she be home in time to go?"

"Dan—"

"She's my wife! They're keeping my wife from me! She doesn't understand what they're doing."

"Take it easy, Dan. Brown is trying to have a word with her right now, you know . . . female to female."

Dan studied the solid door and the barred windows. His father had taught him from infancy that violence was never the answer, and he had taken that lesson to heart with ease because he'd been a relatively good-natured child, seldom angry, and never using his greater size against the bullies who called him a math nerd or made fun of his preoccupation with building things. He had taken that lesson to heart and he had grown into an even-tempered man who saw any expression of violence as a terrible character flaw. But now, suddenly, Dan Behr was consumed by rage. He wanted to break open the door and rip off the bars that guarded the windows. He wanted to tear the place down. He wanted to get his hands around the throat of whoever was holding his wife.

"Take it easy," Gasparino cautioned again, resting his palm against Dan's chest.

Dan unclenched his fists and scrubbed his face with his hands. "Who are these people? What do they want?"

"It's a group. That's all I know." The detective's sigh was tinged with anger. "The property is leased to them."

Brown came out of the house. Her expression was grim as she hurried down the steps.

"What did she say?" Dan called. He took a step forward, but Greenberg's arm shot out to hold him back.

Brown's eyes were fixed on Gasparino. The detective nodded at her and she turned to Dan. "I told your wife you were out here. I told her about you being upset and worried. She said she was sorry, but she needed to stay."

A strange numbness crept over Dan, and all the rage evaporated. "You mean . . . they aren't keeping her from leaving?"

Brown's professional demeanor softened. "We all need a break sometimes. You know . . . just a little breathing space."

"She told you she wanted breathing space?"

"No. I'm just guessing at what she's thinking . . . from my own experience."

Dan shook his head. "When is she coming home?"

"She—" Brown's eyes flicked to Gasparino before she continued speaking. "I don't know. I don't think she knows."

"This is crazy," Dan said, without conviction. "This is crazy."

He repeated those words to himself all the way to Bay Ridge and was still repeating them when he knocked on Felice Navarre's apartment door.

"Where's Alex?" Felice said as soon as she opened her door and saw that only Dan was standing there.

She was so small and slight that, from a distance, she could have been mistaken for an adolescent girl. Dan looked down at her, this woman who was his wife's best friend, and it was clear to him from the pleasant curve of her mouth and the questions in her dark eyes that she had no knowledge of whatever was going on with Alex. And he could not find a suitable answer for her. When he called her from the police station he had not said where he was. He had told her only that Alex was still inside the retreat and he was having trouble communicating with her because it was sealed up like a convent.

"So, where is she?" Felice repeated as she led Dan into her cluttered apartment, fashion sketches pinned to the walls and colorfully draped dressmaker's forms lined up like mute party guests.

He could not bring himself to recount the entire story, so he reduced it to the simplest and most optimistic form. "She decided to stay another night."

"You're kidding! And she's trusting you to take over

with Hana?" Felice's dark-winged eyebrows lifted in amused disbelief. "This retreat thing must have really mellowed her out. Maybe I should join up, huh? Get the workaholic's cure." She shook her head. "Nah. I'm terminal. Let's face it. Well, tell her to call me tomorrow when she gets home."

Tomorrow. The word flashed red in Dan Behr's numb consciousness as he crossed the room to look down at his daughter, sleeping sweetly in her pink-ribboned nightgown, snug beneath a comforter on Felice's couch. Tomorrow. Tomorrow. What would he do tomorrow? He couldn't miss work altogether. Not with the Brunner project behind. He couldn't take Hana to school because that would make him late for the department meeting. And he certainly couldn't cut his day short to pick her up at three o'clock.

Felice was finishing a sentence and he realized he'd missed the point of it.

"Hello . . ." she said, waving her hand in front of his eyes. "Are you in there?"

"Yes."

"Okay, well, just remember to tell Alex to call. Any time tomorrow. I'm working at home all day."

"You're working at home tomorrow?"

"Yes."

"Felice . . . I hate to ask, but things are tense at my job and I can't take any time off, and with Alex staying over, I was wondering . . . Could you . . ."

She grimaced, then shrugged. "Okay," she said, "I'll just turn on a kiddy video after school. But you guys owe me big."

"Thanks," Dan said, feeling a sudden warmth for her, thinking that he liked her. Felice was Alex's best friend, and he felt as though he knew her well, but he had not actually had much contact with her himself. She was never around when he got home at night or when he had a weekend day off.

He bent to scoop Hana into his arms.

"Leave her, Dan. It doesn't make sense for you to pack her home. She's already tucked in here, and you'll just have to drag her back in the morning."

He hesitated.

"Don't worry. I've got everything she needs. Alex brought enough clothes and toys to last a week. Go on. You look exhausted."

Dan let himself into his silent apartment and went through the motions of hanging his jacket in the closet, stashing his briefcase, dropping his keys in the basket on the kitchen counter. Mechanical actions. With only the hall light for illumination he went into the living room and opened the blinds. Tomorrow was arranged. He would go to work and Hana would go to school and everything would progress normally. Except that Alex would still be at that place.

The rain had stopped and a few stars showed. Across the wide black mouth of the harbor he could see the distant shimmer of Manhattan. Where Alex was. Where she had chosen to stay.

Why?

He didn't understand. But then he hadn't understood why she was interested in the retreat in the first place. And way back in the beginning, when she had started going to the weekly meetings, he hadn't understood what the attraction was. He had listened to her glowing reports on the espoused philosophies and found it difficult to keep from telling her just how trite and sophomoric they sounded. She had asked him repeatedly to go with her, and he had not found the time. When the group's leaders extended personal invitations to him and she pleaded for him to go just once, he was in the middle of a big project at work. A legitimate excuse, but nonetheless an excuse. He had ignored it all, believing she would eventually tire of the group just as she'd tired of poetry appreciation and quilting and holistic living class.

Should he have vocalized his criticisms? Should he have gone with her and ridiculed all the absurdities they were spouting? Should he have told her that it reminded him of the naive idealism and flaky notions that college freshmen fall prey to? Should he have told her just how foolish it all appeared to him? So foolish. But not threatening at all. It had never struck him as a threat. Foolish but harmless. Certainly less extreme than much of what he saw being routinely dished out by enlightenment gurus on television or through the media.

Now he didn't know what to think.

He knew his wife so well. How was it possible that this group could have had such a profound effect on her without his awareness? Could she have undergone some kind of spiritual shift without his noticing? Was she unhappy? Or tired? Was she, as Officer Brown had suggested, simply in need of a longer break?

And, assuming it was all possible . . . why wouldn't she have been open with him about it? He'd always been supportive of her, or at least tolerant. He could have accepted change or unhappiness or dissatisfaction. What he could not accept was the secrecy. The deception. The sneaky underhanded hiding behind a door. Letting strangers come between them. Refusing to see him or talk to him.

He rested his forehead against the cool glass of the window and squeezed his eyes shut. What the hell was happening? The woman he had loved and lived with would not hide behind a door and send him away.

She wouldn't.

And she wouldn't turn so blithely from her responsibility to her daughter. If anything, Alex had always been overly involved with Hana. Overly protective. Worrying constantly and trying to manage the smallest details of Hana's life. She wouldn't stay away longer without issuing lengthy instructions for Hana's care and scheduling.

She wouldn't.

And she wouldn't miss Hana's school open house. The very first open house of Hana's very first year in real school. She wouldn't.

Which opened it right back up to the terrifying possibility that his wife was being held prisoner there. That for some unfathomable reason the people in that house were keeping her against her will.

But she had spoken to the detectives and Officer Brown, hadn't she? She had told them she wanted to stay.

But . . . had she been alone with them? Maybe the people in the house had stayed close to her, threatening to hurt her, or the officers, if she said anything wrong.

Or maybe she'd been drugged. Or hypnotized. God, he was sounding like old Mrs. Svensen with her conspiracy theories. He gripped the top of his head in his hands, squeezing hard. This was crazy. Too weird to be real. There had to be a sane and reasonable explanation.

He dropped his hands.

Yes.

There had to be a reasonable explanation. This was the modern world. This was the United States of America. There had to be a reasonable explanation.

"Yes," he repeated aloud.

It was all miscommunication. Just an overinflated series of miscommunications.

Tomorrow she would call . . . probably even come home. The certainty of that settled in and took root. Tomorrow night she would be in the kitchen making a cup of tea and worrying over whether Hana's teacher was concentrating on the right lessons. And someday this would probably all be funny. Someday.

After a sleepless and miserable night, Dan showered, dressed in his weekday uniform of slacks, pinstriped shirt, and sports jacket, and paced in his apartment. He needed to take action. He needed to do something. He called the Sixth Precinct to ask if there had been any new developments. Gasparino was not there, and Dan was told that the detective did not go on duty until four in the afternoon. The news sent Dan's spirits plummeting. If something did change—if there was a disturbance at the house on Vanzant or if Alex tried to contact Gasparino or Brown—they were not on the job to handle it.

Dan agonized over what to do. But in the end he realized that there was nothing he could do except go to work and keep his normal everyday life from falling apart. He pulled on his tan trench coat, picked up his briefcase, and headed for the subway. En route he mechanically made his routine stops for a morning paper at Mr. Chin's and a take-out coffee at Sally's. He went downstairs to wait for the

Manhattan-bound R train, sat on the bench at the far end of the platform, and put the paper and coffee down beside him, both untouched. When the train came, he got up and absently left them behind on the bench.

The car was nearly empty, a benefit of living close to the beginning of the R line, and so he got a seat, as he usually did. He stared at the overhead advertisements for dermatologists and trade schools and safe sex. As the train progressed, more and more riders boarded, and eventually he could not see beyond the people who were squeezed into the standing room directly in front of him. He continued to stare without seeing anything.

"We're at Union Square anyway," a nearby woman argued to her companion. "We could just get off and go to the Barnes and Noble. We have time."

Union Square? The train stopped and the doors slid open and Dan jumped from his seat and threaded his way to the door, muttering "Excuse me" as he went. He made it onto the platform and stood, trying to blink away his confusion as crowds of hurrying commuters surged around him. How had he ridden all the way to Union Square? He always got off at Pacific, walked through to Atlantic, and took the 4/5. But he had somehow missed Pacific Street. It was way back in Brooklyn. He was already in Manhattan and well north of the Financial District.

Agitated, and annoyed with himself, he hurried through the labyrinthine station until he found a wall map, then he studied it for the fastest way to his office. But the colored lines of the train routes seemed to tangle together, and his gaze kept sliding to the West Village, where Alex was.

The crowded underground station suddenly felt stuffy and claustrophobic. He had to get out. There would be buses he could take downtown to his office. He went toward the nearest exit, battling like a salmon going upstream against the flow of commuters pouring down the stairs. Finally he reached street level and fresh air.

A chilly breeze nipped at the hem of his trench coat. Billowy white clouds moved against the pale sky and fast-food wrappers swirled in little eddies over the gutter grates. He went to the corner to stand with the huddle of pedestrians facing south, waiting for the light. If he hurried and had luck with the bus he could still make it to work on time. He stared at the orange Don't Walk sign until the words wavered and melted together. Around him people stirred and edged forward, anticipating the light change. Suddenly, without a conscious decision, he wheeled and sprinted in the other direction. West. Toward Vanzant.

# Chapter 3

The avenues in the Village were crowded with professionally dressed men and women walking briskly, carrying their briefcases toward another day of work. But when he reached Vanzant the street was quiet. It seemed impossible that his wife had been swallowed up in such a familiar, benign setting. And once again he was flooded with hope. This had to be a misunderstanding.

He crossed the street, went up the stone steps, and stood beneath the security camera in front of the maddeningly solid door that separated him from her. He pressed the intercom button twice, then cleared his throat and leaned close.

"Hello. This is Dan Behr."

Nothing. He listened to the faint hum of an open connection.

"I know someone can hear me, so—I just wanted to say that I'd like to clear things up. I mean . . . I think we must have gotten off to a bad start yesterday. I certainly didn't intend to sound angry or threatening when I first asked for my wife, but maybe someone thought I did. And I can understand . . . If everyone thought I was out here looking for trouble . . . I can understand why you didn't want her to talk to me. But I'm not angry. And it's all right with me if she wants to stay a little longer. I just . . . I just need to talk to her. To know that she's okay. And to work out some arrangements." He chuckled, more from nerves than from the rueful amusement he'd intended. "I've never taken care of our daughter by myself and I guess I need some guidance."

Several seconds ticked by.

Suddenly he was startled by a loud voice. "Stop harassing us."

"Wait! Who is this? Please . . . I only want to talk to her. I just need to ask her—"

"Your harassment is being reported to the police."

"Wait! She's my wife, dammit! I—"

But then there was a crackle of static and the intercom went dead. They were not listening anymore. He pressed the button several times without response. Then he pounded on the door with his fists. What could he do? He wished he had a hammer or an ax. He went down the steps, ran to the pay phone on the avenue, and called the number for the detective squad.

"Detective Pell," a female voice said.

Briefly, Dan explained his situation. "Someone has to go back to Vanzant," he said in conclusion. "Right away. There's no time to wait for Detective Gasparino to come on duty. Something bad is going on in that house. Maybe drugs. Maybe they have my wife strung out on drugs."

Pell was silent for a moment. When she spoke it was with the exaggerated patience of a teacher going over a lesson for a slow learner. "Mr. Behr . . . do you have any new evidence of a crime being committed at that location?"

"It's common sense!" he insisted. "Don't you think it's suspicious, Detective, the way they have that place fixed up like a fortress? And all that nonsense with the intercom and the security camera and refusing to answer the door . . . If it's legitimate then why are they so afraid to let me speak to my wife? I'll tell you why—because I *know* her and I'd know in an instant whether she was completely herself or not."

"I'm sorry, Mr. Behr. I wish we could help, but there is really nothing more we can do. Suspicions are not enough. When Detective Gasparino comes in I'll tell him you called, but without additional evidence of criminal activity there's nothing he can do either."

Dan hung up the receiver. In the telephone's polished metal face plate, his fractured reflection stared back at him. He met the stare for a moment. What could he do? He stood on the sidewalk, heart hammering, filled with both rage and helplessness. Then he ran back to Vanzant.

He was just approaching the house when a man lunged from between parked cars and knocked him to the pavement.

"Where is she!" the man demanded, face red and fists clenched.

Slowly, Dan got to his feet, crouching, ready for the man to attack again.

"Where is she?" the man cried again, this time sounding more distraught than threatening.

"Who?" Dan asked.

"You know who. My daughter, Bibi! Bibi Khadra. You took her into that house and I want her back!"

"I'm not one of those people," Dan said.

"I saw you come out of there and run away a few minutes ago! I would have caught you then but you were too fast for me."

"I wasn't coming out of there. I was just coming down the steps. They've got my wife inside."

The man's anger evaporated and his entire body sagged. He was a short but stocky man with wide, hardened hands. Now he held those hands out and stared at them as though they had failed him.

"I don't know what to do," he said. "My wife's heart is breaking. She's our only daughter."

"I don't know what to do either," Dan said. "I've been to the police—"

"Hah! The police won't even talk to me. They say there's no crime. They keep telling me how nineteen-year-old girls don't stay home like they used to. They won't listen when I try to explain how Bibi is. She's special. Never in any trouble. Very thoughtful and quiet and sensitive."

"They talked to me," Dan told him. "They even went inside there and talked to my wife. But it did no good."

The man held out his arms and looked toward the heavens. "What's happening? I don't understand nothing. How can these kinda people be free to do these things? How can the police look the other way?"

"I don't know," Dan said. "I don't understand what their object is. Are they kidnappers? What are they?"

The man nodded sadly. "This I can answer. It's a cult. Just like you read about in the newspapers. Didn't you see that poster they used to advertise? 'Meaning and Moment,' it said big at the top. Then at the bottom in tiny letters it said 'First Light.' That's it. First Light. It's a cult that turns people crazy."

A cult. A cult. A cult. The words echoed in Dan's brain as he rode the train back to Brooklyn, all thoughts of going to work discarded. His wife was being held by a cult. First Light. A cult.

Newspaper headlines haunted him. The Branch Davidians at Waco. That nutty Swiss cult with the mass suicides in several countries. The crazed Japanese guru Aum Shinrikyo who enslaved his followers and assassinated his enemies and dropped nerve gas in the subway. And, of course, Jonestown. Drink your poison now, Jim Jones had told his followers. Give it to your babies first. Nearly a thousand people died there. With bullets for the ones who wouldn't drink.

A cult.

His instincts had been right from the beginning.

A cult. And the police could do nothing because cults were perfectly legal.

A cult.

He had to get her out himself. He had to save her.

He hunched forward, leaned his elbows on his thighs, and buried his face in his hands. He had saved her before. Her hair had been long then. Long enough to stream out in the water like silken sea kelp. Long enough to wind around his hand. So long. And so long ago. Not in years but in living.

They hadn't known each other yet. They hadn't even suspected the possibility of each other.

He had been on top of the world, having just won a grant and acceptance to Columbia University's graduate architecture program. It was late May. He had gotten his diploma from Georgia Tech, packed up, and taken the bus to New York City, the architect's Mecca, ready to spend the summer absorbing Manhattan before he started at Columbia in the fall.

The day had been warm, but with a capricious wind that was gentle one moment and snatching hats the next. He went to the East River just before dusk. Only an occasional jogger or strolling couple joined him on the walkway, making it so quiet and pleasant that he wandered farther than he'd intended, hands stuffed in his jeans pockets, watching the wind play in the water as the shadows lengthened.

He saw her up ahead, leaning against the low fence, gripping the iron spikes in her hands and staring down into the water. She was wearing a white dress so delicate and old-fashioned that he thought at first she might be posing for a photo shoot—a sight he'd already come across once during his week in the city. But there was no camera crew. She was alone.

Looking back, he knew that that was the point where everything converged—his life and her life, past, present, and future. All lines forward and back meeting at that tiny point in time as if it were the pinhole in a Vermeer canvas.

He had veered to the side and stopped in the shelter of a tree, a position that allowed him to watch without disturbing her reverie. She continued to stare down into the inky water with complete absorption, heedless of the approach of night. Fine spray dampened the front of her dress every time a wave crashed against the retaining wall, but she made no attempt to pull back. Wind teased the long, dark red strands of her hair, lifting and tangling them, lashing her cheeks. She kept her hands on the fence and her eyes on the water.

He was fascinated. New York women in general had been a revelation to him. So many glamorous and sophisticated and sexy females all packed into one place. And this particular woman at this particular time was to him a culmination of fantasy creatures. She was every mystery and every myth, every adolescent dream.

Lights winked on in the distance across the river, and the full moon showed itself, pale and luminous, stunning in its sadness. He looked up at the moon, caught a flicker of movement from the corner of his eye, and looked back toward the woman, but she was gone. Vanished.

He stood for an instant, frozen in disbelief, his eyes riveted to where she had been, where now there was only a flutter of white fabric impaled on an iron spike. Then he ran, shedding his shoes as he vaulted into the water after her.

The shocking cold registered first. Then the power. The grinding, pulsing, surging power of the treacherous ancient river. He fought against the sucking currents, muscling his way to the surface with lungs bursting. Frantically he searched for her. Saw a gleam like a silvery fish in the moonlight. Her dress. Swam forward. Lost her. Then saw her face tilted upward in the waves. She was not more than ten feet from him, but—though he had always been a strong swimmer and was physically fit—the river battled him for every inch of those ten feet.

"I'm coming!" he shouted, gagging on the oily water.

Her eyes were closed. Her skin was ghostly pale. And just as he reached her the waves closed over her and she vanished. With a burst of effort he lunged and dove. Blindly he groped in the blackness, and he caught her by her long streaming hair, pulled her up with him by her dark red hair.

The rest was a blur. He had no idea how long he struggled, playing tug-of-war against the river for her limp body.

When the rescue unit finally pulled them out, his muscles and heart and lungs were burning but on the outside he was icy numb and barely able to respond. They had to pry her loose from him. He remembered them doing that. His arm was locked around her and he could not let go.

She had no vital signs. He watched the paramedics work on her. They restored her heartbeat and her breathing, but she was still unconscious when they loaded her into the ambulance beside him.

At the hospital, they warmed and prodded and poked him, gave him shots to ward off the evils that lurked in the polluted waters, and released him just before dawn. He could not leave. He found a couch in the waiting room outside the intensive care unit, and he fell asleep there.

When Dan came out of his reverie to get off the train at Bay Ridge he realized that he no longer had his briefcase. He had no idea when he'd lost it. Most of his Brunner work had been inside. It was gone for good. He had no illusions about someone turning in the case to a lost and found. But work was not important now. He had to get his wife out of that house. He had to make a plan. He had to get organized. He had to be very clever.

It was midafternoon by the time he drove back into the Village. He was dressed in coveralls that he had bought in a Bay Ridge uniform outlet, and on his head he wore an A1 PLUMBING AND HEATING baseball cap that had been in their apartment when they moved in. Next to him on the seat was a clipboard stuffed with generic-looking forms that were actually used for scrap paper at his office. On the floor was a large workman's satchel that he had stocked at the hardware store with an ax, an oversize hammer, a glass cutter, and assorted miscellaneous tools.

He did not drive by number 44, just in case they were watching the street. Instead he waited for a parking spot around the corner so that there was no possibility of his car's being seen from the house. He had no definite plan, rather he had a mental list of approaches that he had ruled out.

Clipboard in one hand and satchel in the other, he stood on the corner and looked down Vanzant. The brownstones presented an unbroken fortress from the front. No side windows to explore. Nothing but a head-on attack possible there. And he doubted that he could get inside that steel-jacketed front door before the police arrived to haul him away. He turned and walked along the north-south avenue, then circled the block until he was in sight of number 44 again. From sidewalk level the backs of the houses on one street appeared to be built right up against the backs of the houses on the next street, so that the entire block was a solid rectangle of adjoining walls. He retraced his steps and walked back around the long way to his car so he wouldn't pass number 44.

As he turned onto the avenue at the end of the block he realized that there was a treetop visible behind the row of two-story commercial buildings facing the avenue. A tree meant there had to be an alley or open space. Maybe access to the backs of the houses. Maybe unbarred windows. Maybe even back doors.

A knot formed in his gut as he walked into a little bakery shop that sat in the center of that block of the avenue's small businesses. He wished he knew something about plumbing and heating.

"Hi," he said to the balding man behind the counter. "I'm with the ah . . . A1 Plumbing and Heating, and we got a call that there's pipe trouble out in back somewhere. Have you got a back door?"

"Yeah, but I didn't make the call," the man protested.

"No? Well, I'll have to straighten that out with the dispatcher later. But I'd better go out and look things over first."

"I didn't make the call and I ain't payin' for nothin'," the man said.

"No problem," Dan assured him. He stared down at the pad on his clipboard and made some random checkmarks so that he wouldn't have to meet the man's eyes. "You aren't the responsible party. But I can't waste time finding out who is because things could get dangerous. Leaking gas could cause an explosion."

"Shit," the man grumbled. "That's all I need. Shouldn't the gas company be here, too?"

"They're probably on their way," Dan improvised.

The back door to the shop opened with a jarring scrape of metal against metal and Dan saw an oasis of green. There was a narrow open patch that ran behind several of the shops with a boundary marked by a decaying six-foot-tall wooden fence. Beyond that were postage-stamp-size backyards for the brownstones. And backyards meant back doors.

He stepped over scattered soda cans and drifts of cigarette butts indicating that this was the preferred employee break area for the line of shops. But no one was out smoking on this Monday afternoon. He pulled himself up on the first fence, looked around, then went over. No challenging shouts came. He went on, scaling fence after fence, counting as he went so he would know when he came to the back of number 44. Most of the tiny yards were neat and well cared for. He tried not to disturb any of the plantings. Finally, he came to a taller, newer fence of solid wood with a pointed stockade top, and he knew that the cult had built this barrier.

He scanned the fence for a crack or knothole that he could look through, but the wood was doubled and overlapped. He listened but could hear nothing.

He boosted himself up on the adjoining yard's shorter fence and looked down into number 44's backyard. It was covered with paving stones and lined with rows of cast concrete benches. A woman in a long white robe knelt on the stones beside one of the benches, head bowed and partially covered by a hood. His heart lurched.

But it wasn't Alex. It clearly wasn't Alex.

Determined to carry through, he grabbed hold of the stockade top and swung over. Too late, he saw that each wooden point had tiny metal spikes embedded in it. He thudded onto the paving stones with a searing pain in the palms of his hands. The kneeling woman screamed.

"Please . . ." He held up his blood-dotted hands in appeal. "I'm looking for my wife . . . Alexandra. Do you know her? Alexandra Behr?"

The woman stared at him with wide, affectless eyes, and he saw that her wrists were tied and somehow shackled to a metal ring in the end of the bench.

"Are you all right?" He moved forward to see if he could free her, and she screamed again, then cowered into a semi-fetal position.

"Shhh. Please. I want to help you. I'll take you with us. I'll find my wife and I'll get you out, too."

The back door banged open and a young man stepped out. He was holding a very large, very menacing gun.

"On the ground," he shouted. "Face down and spread 'em."

Dan stared at him, stared at the round mouth of the gun barrel.

"Now!" The man waved the weapon. "Or I'll blow your head off."

Dan drew a deep breath and lowered himself.

The man squatted just out of arm's reach and pointed the gun at Dan's face.

Swallowing hard, with the rough paving stones cutting into his cheek and the punctures in his hands burning, Dan said, "I just want my wife."

"Shut up! The police are on their way. But I could still shoot you." The man clicked his tongue in a scold. "Breaking in and attacking that poor girl . . . You're lucky I'm waiting for the police."

Dan closed his eyes to shut out the gun. It was a real gun. He was certain of it. And he knew he ought to be terrified, yet everything seemed disconnected and unreal. And he felt careless. Heedless. As though he were no longer responsible for his own safety.

Did Alex know what they were doing to him? Did Alex know about the gun? Maybe she was chained somewhere like the poor girl kneeling on the paving stones. Maybe she was drugged. Hadn't the girl's eyes looked oddly vacant? That was probably a common method of controlling people.

The thought of his wife drugged and chained filled him with such rage that he was suddenly afraid. Not of the gun but of himself. Of what he might do. He concentrated on the burning in his hands. That was real. And he concentrated on the cold weight of the gun barrel pressing against his temple. That was very real. And it would be real if he died there on that little patio. It would be real and it would solve nothing.

"Mr. Behr . . ."

He opened his eyes and saw that the kneeling girl was gone and the yard had filled with police. Gasparino was looking down at him with a regretful, resigned expression. He sighed heavily.

"This call came in and I knew it was you," the detective said, shaking his head. "Here you've got a good job and a kid and a nice life but you're fucking it all up by going off the deep end. Couldn't you just let it ride? Give her a chance to come home?"

"They won't let her come home. Don't you see? It's a cult. They don't let people go."

Two uniformed officers jerked Dan to his feet and handcuffed him. The armed young man, who was seated on a bench and giving a statement, smirked as Dan was led past him toward the back door. Dan suddenly realized that the only passage out of the yard was through the house. He was going inside. Into Alex's prison.

He stepped through the door. The interior was cool and dimly lit and smelled of cleaning products. Like so many houses of the era, it had a straight hallway that went from front to back. He tried to look into other rooms as they

passed doorways. The woodwork gleamed. The walls had
fresh paint. There were framed photographs of people
gathered in a green mountainous location. Everything had
a patina of normalcy.

When they reached the stairway and the arched entrance
to the living area Dan jerked free of his escorts.

"Alex!" he shouted. "Alex! It's Dan!"

He lunged for the stairs. Something hit his back. He piv-
oted to escape. Something struck his chest and he dropped,
struggling for breath.

"Jesus, Behr . . ." Gasparino squatted beside him. "Why
are you making it so hard on yourself?"

"My wife," Dan gasped. "Where is she? Can you find
her?"

"I've already got Brown looking for her," Gasparino
said. "Now you've got to let these officers do their job."

Once again Dan was hauled to his feet.

"I don't want to see you get hurt," Gasparino said
gruffly.

As soon as they were out on the sidewalk Dan's hands
were freed and then recuffed in the front. It was just as humiliating but a lot more comfortable.

"Watch your head," someone said as he was put into the
back of a patrol car.

People spoke. He answered. They read him his rights
and asked if he wanted a lawyer. But as time progressed it
all became a blur.

"Are you with us, Dan?"

"Yes. Did I tell you about Khadra? They took his daughter. They . . . they . . ."

The handcuffs were off. He was at the precinct house.
Gasparino was there. And Greenberg. He felt sick. Sweaty
and cold and weak. And he was having trouble organizing
his thoughts.

"Let's go over this again, Dan. You say you jumped the
fence to look for your wife, and the girl was in the yard."

He nodded. "She was kneeling, on those hard stones,
and then I saw that her wrists were tied . . . chained to a
ring in the bench . . . so I was going to try to get it off . . .
but she screamed."

"She says there were no restraints. And Mr. Carle—"

"Is that the guy with the gun?"

"Yeah. He says the rings in the benches are just for decoration. He says no one gets tied up and there's never been chains."

"She was drugged or something. Those stones would have hurt her knees otherwise."

"What makes you think she was drugged?"

"Her eyes. Didn't you see her eyes?"

"She says she was kneeling out there for some kind of penance."

"She was chained."

"How'd her robe get torn?"

"I don't know. It didn't look torn to me."

"We've got it. It's torn. She says you tore it."

"I didn't touch her."

"She says different."

"I was going to try to free her, but she screamed and hunched down on the ground. Then the guy came out with the gun. How can that be legal . . . having a gun like that in the city? Threatening someone with it."

"It's registered. And you were an intruder attacking a woman in the backyard. He did everything right."

"He threatened to blow my head off and not wait for you to come."

"But he didn't, did he?"

"I didn't attack anyone. I was looking for my wife."

Brown arrived then and had a whispered conversation with Gasparino.

"Did you talk to my wife?" Dan asked her.

Brown looked at Gasparino, and the detective gave a tiny nod.

"She's not there anymore," Brown said.

"What? What do you mean? Has she gone home? Is she—"

"Take it easy, Dan," Gasparino cautioned.

Dan stared at Brown. He couldn't focus. Everything about her was blurry.

"They told me that your wife went to a different location. In another state. That's all I could find out."

Dan covered his face with his hands. A sob tore through

his chest. It was a wrenching, agonized sound. A sound that embarrassed him. He dropped his hands to his lap and stared at the little puncture wounds in his palms. There was a long silence.

"Do you want to call a lawyer now?" Gasparino finally asked.

"I don't know any lawyers," Dan told him, and the detective repeated a line about how a lawyer would be provided for him if he wanted.

"What happens to me next?" Dan asked. "I can't stay here. My God." He gripped his forehead and tried to clear his thoughts. "Hana. My daughter . . . I should call Felice . . . I should . . ."

"You already called," the detective said.

"I did?" He squinted and shook his head at the confusion invading his brain. His stomach rocked as though he were in a small boat on a rough sea.

"Are you all right?" he heard a voice ask.

He tried to stand, but the floor rushed toward him and smacked him in the face.

# Chapter 4

Dan woke up in a hospital room. It was night but a light was on. Hurting his eyes. He turned his head. There was a patient in the other bed. He was very old and his lips moved as if he were snoring, but only a soft hiss emerged. Why was he in the hospital?

He had a dim memory of an ambulance ride and of being in the emergency room beneath a flurry of scrub suits and lab coats and eyes staring at him over surgical masks. He remembered that it had seemed curious to him at the time. As though he were an observer rather than a participant.

He tried to move, but he was connected to wires and tubes. Moving was too much trouble. And he was so tired. He closed his eyes for a minute. When he opened them again it was daylight. He was still in the hospital. The wires and tubes were gone. The old man was gone, too, but it looked as thought his absence was temporary.

Why was he in the hospital? Other than having a few sore spots and an odd taste in his mouth he felt fairly normal. He sat up and swung his legs over the edge of the bed. Pain shot through his head and his stomach heaved a warning. Maybe he didn't feel so normal.

He surveyed the room. The old man's bedside stand held a telephone and a box of tissues. His own held only a pitcher of water. He opened his drawer. Inside was a letter of welcome to the hospital and a pair of disposable paper slippers. He put the slippers on his feet, held the back of his cotton gown closed, and shuffled to the small closet near the door. One side of the closet was empty. The other held a small worn suit that he supposed belonged to the old man.

He looked into the bathroom. He peeked out the room's door into an empty hallway. He went back to his bed and pushed the call button.

"Can I help you?" a voice asked through a speaker in the wall over his bed.

"What day is it?"

"Tuesday."

"I can't find my clothes," Dan said.

"I'll send someone to your room."

"What's wrong with me?"

"The doctors are on rounds right now. You'll be able to ask them."

He drank some water and used the bathroom. Tuesday. Twenty-four hours had vanished. He regarded the phone at the old man's bedside for several minutes before deciding that there was no reason he shouldn't use it.

Quietly, he dialed his home number. It rang unanswered. Then he dialed Felice's number. It too rang unanswered. His watch was gone, and he wasn't sure of the time. He walked to the window and looked out. There was no view except a patch of tar roof on a lower section of the building, but he could see the sky, and from the position of the sun he thought it was afternoon. Maybe Felice was picking up Hana from school.

A nurse's aide came in and he asked her about his clothes. She said something vague about checking on it, then ordered him back to bed. She left without watching to see that he complied.

He sat in a turquoise vinyl-covered chair. The cushion expelled air as his weight hit, and the plastic was unpleasant beneath his barely covered back and buttocks, but he didn't want to get into the bed again. He recalled the gun pointing at his face and the handcuffs and the police car and the interrogation. Wasn't he supposed to be in jail?

Jail.

How bizarre. He was a criminal now. A criminal with no regrets. He would break the law again if there was a chance of saving Alex.

Alex. Alex. Alex.

He had pulled her from the water, so pale and lifeless. Saved her from the water.

Razor-edged memories sliced through him. The endless hours waiting to hear that she would live. That she was conscious. Then the continued waiting, stubbornly refusing to leave until he saw her, bothering the nurses, hovering outside her door, asking the doctors to intercede for him. And then, finally, being admitted to her bedside.

Her face had been white against the pillow. Her eyes shadowed. Her long hair limp and snarled.

During the waiting he had thought of so many things he wanted to say to her, but in facing her he was struck nearly mute.

"I'm Dan Behr," he had managed after an uncomfortable silence. "I'm . . . I'm glad I was there the other night."

"You don't talk like a New Yorker," she said.

"I'm not. I'm new here. From Georgia."

"You don't sound much like a Southerner either."

"Well, I was raised in Sacramento, California. I didn't move to the South till I was sixteen."

"I hate California," she said vehemently.

Then she turned her head away, making it clear that she was no longer interested in him. He thought he should probably leave, but instead he pulled a chair up beside the bed. And he sat there for the allotted hour, speaking occasionally but mostly just filling the silence with his presence. At the end of visiting hours, he got up from the chair.

"I'll be back tomorrow," he said.

And she'd looked at him, bored a hole through him with those gold-green-starred eyes, and she'd said, "Why?"

He'd had no answer that he could adequately explain, so he'd simply repeated, "I'll be back tomorrow."

Alexandra.

This time he hadn't been able to save her.

Something started in his chest. He crossed his arms and hunched forward in his chair, trying to contain it, but the sobs came anyway.

Dan had regained emotional control by the time the doctors arrived. He'd also pulled the white cotton blanket off the bed and wrapped it around himself to combat the effects of the chair and to restore some of his dignity. The flock of white coats swarmed into the room like seagulls descending on a discarded sandwich at the beach.

A very officious man of about Dan's age appeared to be in charge, and he began discussing the case in technical terms, addressing the residents as though Dan were not present.

"Excuse me," Dan said.

The young doctor flashed him a perfunctory smile but continued his speech.

"I want to know why I'm here," Dan insisted.

With an exasperated sigh the man turned and said, "Mr. Behr appears to be fully alert now."

"Mr. Behr is fully alert," Dan said, "and Mr. Behr wants to know what the hell happened."

"You ingested a toxic substance. It wasn't identified."

"You mean I was poisoned?"

"Basically. Yes."

"Food poisoning?"

"No. No. Something chemical and very unusual. All we could do was sustain your system while your body fought it. Luckily you were strong and healthy."

"But how . . ." Dan extended his hands in a gesture of confusion, revealing the puncture marks. "Could it have been on the spikes that went into my hands?"

The doctor bent to examine Dan's hands. "It could have been."

There was no doubt in Dan's mind. The people who were holding Alex had tried to poison him.

"Can I go now?" he asked.

"How do you feel?"

"Fine," he lied.

"I'll sign the discharge. But I believe the police want to talk to you first."

Gasparino came in with both Greenberg and Brown in tow. Dan was embarrassed, sitting there in the scanty hospital gown with the blanket wrapped around his shoulders. They did not seem to notice.

"So—you lived," Gasparino said.

Dan nodded.

The detective prowled around the room for several minutes, then turned abruptly toward Dan. "The charges have been dropped."

"What?"

"As soon as you got hauled off to the hospital everyone changed their tune. The girl said that she'd had a chance to think it through and she realized you didn't attack her. She tripped and tore her own robe. And their lawyer has come up with some kind of line about how they understand your being distraught and they don't want any trouble about you jumping the fence."

Dan thought a moment. He looked down at his hands. "They had poison on the metal fence spikes."

Gasparino frowned. "I sent a tech over this morning to check those spikes. There was no trace of anything toxic."

"They cleaned it off! Can't we have tests done on my hands?"

The detective blew out an exasperated burst of air. "Danny . . . Danny . . . Danny . . . Stop playing James Bond. You came out okay on this one. Don't push your luck."

"And what about my wife? Am I supposed to just forget about her? Forget that she's in trouble?"

"I don't know what to tell you, guy. Except that you can't let this wreck your life. You don't wanna make things worse than they already are. Not for yourself or your kid. All you can do is pray that she wakes up and comes home."

Dan shook his head. "I can't believe this is happening. A woman has been taken. She's been drugged or brainwashed or something. . . . And no one cares."

"We don't *care*? We're not *caring* enough? Wise up, Danny boy. We're here to uphold the law. And so far nobody's broken the law except you."

"It's a cult called First Light," Dan said. "And they've done this before. There's a man—Ben Khadra. They have his daughter, and he can verify everything I'm telling you."

"So what!" Gasparino threw his hands into the air. "So it's a cult. That's not illegal. The world is full of nuts and weirdos and wackos—cults and groups and groupies. And this city gets more than its share. We've got a history of loony groups here. But so long as they don't break the law it's not police business."

Dan cradled his forehead in his hand.

"Count yourself lucky not to be in jail, Dan, and get on with your life. And you oughtta call an attorney."

As soon as he had his clothes, Dan dressed and left without waiting for paperwork. He went out the front doors of the hospital, got his bearings, and started walking to where he had left his car, just around the block from Vanzant, maybe nine or ten blocks from the hospital. The distance seemed short when he set out, but the exertion made him feel worse. By the time he reached his car he was admitting to himself that walking had not been a good idea.

Only he didn't actually reach his car, because it wasn't there. He stood on the corner, disoriented and shaky, thinking that the toxin must still be making his brain foggy. He checked the signs. He looked up and down the converging streets. He took note of the bakery and caught a glimpse of the same plump balding man inside. This was the right place. But the car was no longer in the spot where he had parked it. The car was gone. Truly gone.

He sagged against a light pole. The car had probably been ticketed several times during his hospital stay. According to the signs, it would have been there through two no-parking periods. And that was the one efficient government function in the city of New York—patrolling for parking violations. And towing. Yes. Good old city government on the job. No doubt he would have to pay hundreds of dollars and go through endless bureaucracy to reclaim the vehicle.

But he was too sick to deal with it now. He closed his eyes for a moment and considered how to get home. The thought of a long subway ordeal made his stomach turn over, but a taxi to Brooklyn was expensive, and he had very little cash in his wallet. He looked up the avenue. Surely there was an ATM nearby.

He walked three blocks without seeing a bank machine.

The nausea and shakiness progressed to a point where he was afraid he might collapse in the middle of the sidewalk and be dragged back to the hospital. All he could think about was lying down. Anyplace. A homeless man's cardboard bed in a doorway looked inviting. Dan decided to forget the ATM and use what little energy he had left to hail a taxi. One stopped almost immediately.

"Bay Ridge, Brooklyn," he said as he opened the back door.

The driver sped away with the door half open. When the next taxi stopped, Dan climbed inside before he told the driver his destination, recalling that cabbies hated long one-way fares to the outer boroughs.

"No Brooklyn!" the driver said. "Out! Out! No Brooklyn."

"Yes Brooklyn!" Dan shouted back at him. "I see your name and number. I'll report you."

The driver strung together a creative multicultural litany of obscenities.

"Bay Ridge, Brooklyn," Dan said again. "Take the bridge to the BQE. Go toward Staten Island. Get off at Eighty-sixth Street." Then he sagged down onto the lumpy backseat and fell into a fitful sleep.

"Eighty-sixth Street!" the driver barked some time later.

Dan sat up. He felt marginally better. "Turn right at that next light and stop at the ATM."

The driver scowled and muttered under his breath, but made the turn.

Dan dragged himself out of the car and up to the automatic bank teller. He put his card into the slot, entered his identification number and his checking account information, then the cash withdrawal request. ONE MOMENT PLEASE, the screen flashed. The machine whirred, and he leaned sideways against the cool metal while he waited for the characteristic sound of the money falling into place. But the money did not drop. Instead a new message appeared on the screen. YOUR REQUEST CANNOT BE PROCESSED DUE TO AN INSUFFICIENT BALANCE IN THIS ACCOUNT. FOR FURTHER ASSISTANCE USE THE CUSTOMER SERVICE PHONE.

Dan shook his head. Obviously he had made a wrong

entry somewhere. Slowly, laboriously, he repeated the procedure, saying each number to himself before he touched it. Again the insufficient balance message appeared.

Something was wrong. The bank computer was having a bad day or someone somewhere had fouled up his checking account. But he did not feel up to the hassle of using the customer service phone, so he began again, this time keying in the number for his savings account.

YOUR REQUEST CANNOT BE PROCESSED DUE TO AN INSUFFICIENT BALANCE IN THIS ACCOUNT. FOR FURTHER ASSISTANCE USE THE CUSTOMER SERVICE PHONE.

He stared at the words in disbelief. Outside, the taxi's horn beeped impatiently.

He gripped his head with his hands and squeezed against the ache at his temples. This wasn't happening. First his car had disappeared and now his money? He picked up the black handset of the customer service phone and listened to the ringing at the other end. This was not happening.

But then he realized that his car hadn't been first to vanish. His wife had been first.

"Hello, may I help you?"

"There's something wrong," Dan said, and then added, "with my accounts."

She asked him for all the numbers and bits of information that identified him. He listened to the faint click of her fingers on a computer keyboard.

"Mr. Behr ..." she said finally, "I've checked the records and there is no mistake. Both your savings and checking accounts have a balance of zero."

"That's impossible," Dan told her, covering his free ear against the honking from the taxi outside.

"The withdrawals were made at a teller's window."

"I haven't made any withdrawals."

"But you do have a co-signer on the accounts," the woman reminded him.

"Yes, my wife, but—"

The realization hit him like a brick to the head. The cult had forced her to give them everything. Their living money for the month—every penny of it budgeted for rent and groceries and gasoline and credit payments. The savings that had been so carefully accumulated. All of it had been stolen.

"Thanks," he mumbled, and hung up the phone.

He must have looked terrible as he left the ATM, because the taxi driver stopped honking and stared at him in alarm.

"Doctor?" the driver asked. "Hospital?"

"No. Just take me home. But . . . I'm sorry . . . I couldn't get money. I'll have to look for cash at home. Or write you a check."

A bad check, Dan realized as he let his head fall back against the seat.


"Gasparino here."

"Hello, this is Dan Behr."

"Behr? You're supposed to be in bed. Didn't the doctor say you should go home and sleep the rest of it off?"

Dan shifted the phone to his other ear. He had taken medication, sipped ice water, and propped himself up on the couch. He didn't feel great, but he felt better. And the knot of hope in his stomach was pumping him with energy.

He took a deep breath, wanting to sound calm and rational. "There's new evidence. Proof that my wife is being held against her will."

"Yeah? Like what?"

"Both our bank accounts have been emptied."

"Jesus! Haven't you heard divorce horror stories before? Those accounts should have been frozen immediately."

"This is not a horror story about divorce! Can't you see what's happening? We have a good marriage. She was coerced into withdrawing that money. So now you've got something to charge them with. Now you can—"

"Hold it!" Gasparino ordered. "She was a joint signer on the accounts, right?"

"Yes, but—"

"No buts. Under the law you've still got nothing unless you can prove force or coercion. She had every right to that money, and I don't hear her complaining about somebody taking it away from her."

"She never would have—"

"We've got no proof. Hear me? No proof of intimidation or harassment or force of any kind. All we got here is an adult who says she doesn't want to go home and a bank withdrawal by a legally entitled account holder."

"So you won't help me."

"We *can't* help you. When will you get that through your head? Personally, I think you're being screwed, but that doesn't mean a damn thing. There's nothing the law can do."

Dan stared across his living room. Everything so neat and normal. He wanted to smash it all.

"Listen, you've gotta start watching out for yourself and your kid. Talk to an attorney. Get one from the yellow pages if you have to, but do it as soon as you hang up. And if you've got any other assets you better nail them down quick."

"There isn't anything else. Except the car—and that's missing in action."

"What do you mean, missing in action?"

"Towed. While I was in the hospital."

"Have you called about the car?"

"Not yet. But—"

"Do it. There's a number listed under 'Traffic Violations.' Call it. Then call an attorney."

There was a click, followed by the dial tone. He held on, listening to the empty mechanical buzz, absorbing the impersonal deadness of it. When he finally put the receiver back in the cradle the buzz still sounded in his head.

He glanced at the clock. It was five. He had been home for nearly an hour and still had not called Felice to check on his daughter or let her know that he was out of the hospital. He stared at the phone, knowing he ought to make the call but dreading any contact with his daughter. It was so much better for her to be in Felice's living room, playing with her dolls or practicing her reading, happy and safe and insulated from the mess that her parents' lives had become. What would he say to her? How could he possibly explain any of this?

So he put aside calling Felice and dialed the number for

Traffic Violations. The young woman who answered informed him that there was no record of the city's towing his car. She assured him that the system was very efficient and that the computer records were rarely wrong and that he ought to take his registration and title to the police precinct and report the car stolen because that was undoubtedly what had happened to it. All of this she went over with exaggerated patience, as though he were disturbed. As though he sounded on the edge of a breakdown.

No record of the car being towed. A dark resignation settled over him. The car had been parked just around the corner when he was hauled away from 44 Vanzant by the police. Alex's captors could have spotted it easily. And Alex had had a set of keys in her purse. If they had stolen the money, why should he be surprised that they would also take the car? He looked around the apartment. Nothing had been touched or taken there. He wondered why they hadn't used Alex's keys to clean it out while he was in the hospital. But then maybe miscellaneous personal possessions were not worth the effort. It wasn't as though the apartment contained expensive jewels or rare coins.

He thought of Ben Khadra, the grieving father who had attacked him on the sidewalk. A daughter would have far less access to her family's assets. Khadra might have escaped this part of the torture. On impulse, he rummaged in his coat pocket for the card Khadra had given him, and he dialed the man's number.

Khadra picked up on the second ring. Dan recognized the desperate hope in the man's voice as he answered.

"I'm sorry, Ben. It's not Bibi. It's Dan Behr."

"Dan," Khadra said quietly. "I always think . . . every time the phone rings . . . just maybe . . ."

"I know."

"Where you been, Dan? I tried to call you."

"I was sick. Poisoned by those people."

"What!"

Dan told him the whole story.

When he finished, Khadra said, "And you just got home from the hospital?"

"Yes."

"Then you don't know."

"Know what?"

"They're gone. They packed up and left sometime in the night."

"They left Vanzant?"

"The house is empty." Khadra hesitated a moment. "I talked to a man. A cult deprogrammer. My sister read about him in a magazine a long time ago, and she went to the library and found the story and got his name . . . and I finally found a way to talk to him."

"What does he do?"

"He gets people back."

"How?"

"He does whatever he has to. We made a copy of the magazine story, and I mailed it to you already. Are you interested?"

"Yes."

"It costs a lot of money, but he said it would be cheaper if he was working for me and you both."

"Would he get them back together?"

"Probably not. But there's a lot of expense in just tracking them down and figuring out what's going on with the cult. We could share those costs if he was finding Bibi and your wife at the same time."

"How much money will I need?"

"Between fifteen and twenty thousand."

Dan sighed wearily.

"That's a cheap price to get someone you love back."

"I'm not worried about cost, Ben. I'd pay anything. But I'm worried about where I'll get the money. They used my wife to empty our bank accounts."

"That's bad. Very bad. We're borrowing most of it from family. Everyone is sending what they can."

"Give me his number," Dan said. "Maybe I'll think of something."

After he said good-bye he felt drained. He stared at the name and number he'd written on the reverse of Khadra's card. Everett May. In the 520 area code.

Deprogramming. Though he couldn't say exactly what he knew about deprogramming, the thought of it chilled him. There was something ominous and ugly about the very word.

And the money. Where was he going to get that much money? Maybe the deprogrammer would take a down payment to start. Then maybe he could get an advance on his salary. And sell some things . . . his father's antique grandmother clock and his great-grandfather's pocket watch. And there were the savings bonds that had been baby gifts to Hana. He could cash those in. But who was he kidding? Even if he got full value for the clock and watch—which was doubtful in a quick sale situation—he would still be a long way from the amount he needed.

Somehow he would have to borrow money. Other than a student loan for college, he had never applied for bank loans, so he wasn't experienced with them, but he was reasonably certain he would need collateral to qualify for one. And he had no collateral. Suddenly he thought of the credit card. Their emergency credit card. He had charged on it only once, for a flat tire repair when they were taking a weekend drive.

He fumbled for his wallet and searched the various compartments, remembering that he had purposely tucked the card out of sight to avoid temptation. And there it was, a shiny silver rectangle that lifted his hopes immediately. He read the fine print on the back. There was nothing about cash advances, but he knew that the card had that capability. How much could he get?

He dialed the customer service 800 number on the back of the card. After the recorded menu a human voice finally answered, and he gave his information and asked what the procedure was for getting a cash advance of his entire available credit.

The man at the other end of the line asked him to wait please while the computer accessed the account. Then, somewhat apologetically, he said, "Mr. Behr, that account had a seven-thousand-dollar cash advance drawn against it two days ago. You have no available credit."

Dan laughed bitterly. They were smarter than he was. They'd thought of everything. He realized that he sounded completely unhinged to the customer service man on the other end of the line, but he didn't care. Face it—he *was* unhinged.

Feeling drained, he sank sideways, then gave in to stretching out, with his head high on the padded arm so that the couch would accommodate his length. A lawyer. He had to find a lawyer. Not that it mattered anymore. What was there left to protect?

The phone rang. He rose up on one elbow and jerked the receiver to his ear.

"Hello! Alex?"

"Behr, is that you?"

He recognized the voice and said, with a sigh of disappointment, "Hello, Medford."

"We've been trying to reach you. Why in the hell don't you have an answering machine?"

"I should, shouldn't I," Dan said, thinking immediately about the calls he'd missed that could have been calls from Alex.

"So, what's wrong? Where've you been?"

"I'm . . . I was sick. I just got out of the hospital."

"No shit! Jeez!"

There was a moment of fumbling and whispers. Dan could tell that Medford had shifted the receiver away from his mouth and was reporting the news to Wendel Crispin and Karen Lai.

Suddenly Karen's voice came on. "Dan, are you all right? What happened? Were you in an accident?"

"I'm fine now. It was some kind of strange poisoning, but it's over."

"You mean like food poisoning?"

"Maybe . . . Listen, I—"

But then there was more fumbling, and Crispin's voice spoke. "This is unbelievable! I swear. It's the downfall of civilization. Our health is being compromised in a hundred ways what with pollution and corporate greed and no services for our tax dollars. Our food supply should be a major priority, but it's not. I'm telling you—"

There was a series of bumps and bangs, and Dan heard Crispin arguing with Medford, insisting that it was still his turn and what he had to say was too relevant. Then Medford was on the phone again.

"So Behr-buddy, we covered for you with the big cheese. Told him you'd called in with the flu. 'Course, this is a lot worse. I mean, it's really a lot better excuse."

"Thanks."

"I hope you're well quick because this is a bad time to be away from the office. They announced a reduction in force this morning and you can bet they're looking for reasons to RIF people."

"Damn . . ." Dan breathed.

Why now? Rumors about impending reductions had floated around for a year. Why did it have to happen now?

"So," Medford continued. "You're coming in tomorrow?"

"I don't . . . I . . . Yes. Yes. I should come in." He needed the money. He had to keep working.

"Whoa . . . You don't sound like yourself at all. Are you sure you'll make it tomorrow, because if you can't we need to do some serious reorganizing of our projects here."

"I'll be in."

"Okay. And how's it going with the Brunner stuff? Did you make any more progress before you got sick?"

Dan winced, remembering his briefcase. "It's gone."

"Gone?"

"With my briefcase. In the subway, I think. But I'm not sure."

There was a long silence.

"What are we supposed to do now?" Medford finally asked.

"I don't know," Dan admitted. "I'll have to think about it. Say . . . do any of you know a good lawyer?"

"Hey, hey! That's the spirit, Behr-man. The bastards damn well deserve a lawsuit—putting you in the hospital and jeopardizing your position at work. This was real solid-gold food poisoning and you should be able to collect big bucks in compensation. Was it a famous restaurant? One with some money behind it?"

"I just got home and I'm supposed to go to bed," Dan said in an effort to avoid further questioning. "If you don't have the lawyer's name right now I could—"

"I've got it right here. And he's great, too. My wife's family uses him for everything."

When he was finally off the phone, Dan looked at the clock again. He had to call Felice. But first he should contact the lawyer. He dialed the number Medford had supplied. There was a recorded voice that said the office was closed for the day and would reopen in the morning. Messages could be left after the tone. Dan waited through the tone but then couldn't decide how much to say. Finally, he gave his name and number, said he'd been referred by Richard Medford, and hung up.

Now there were no more excuses. He had to call about Hana. He had to reclaim his daughter. He had to drag her into this hellish torment with him.

With a jolt he realized that he was solely responsible for Hana until Alex returned. Just him. Not Felice. Not the kindergarten teacher. He alone was in charge. Hana's very survival and emotional health would be completely in his hands. His decisions would shape her life. His mistakes would probably traumatize her for life.

He had the urge to laugh and cry at once. Hadn't he felt a wistful longing at times? Hadn't he experienced moments of regret? Hadn't he wished that he could be a more involved father? Hadn't he looked forward to a future when his work schedule allowed him to spend more time with his daughter and when Hana was old enough that her mother no longer felt so protective and possessive of her? Hadn't he yearned for the day when Hana would be as much his as she was Alex's? *Be careful what you wish for,* he reminded himself ruefully as he gritted his teeth against the sick clammy shakiness that was returning in waves.

Damn Alex! How could she have let this happen? Hadn't she seen the danger? Hadn't she had some clue or warning?

What was he supposed to do now? Tell Hana that her mother was a prisoner and possibly a victim of something awful? Tell the child that her mother had *chosen* to go away and leave them?

And how was he supposed to take proper care of a five-year-old? Alex, who had always been the most concerned and careful of mothers—the perfect mother, goddamn it— had never deemed him capable of anything but support services. Whatever parenting he'd initiated on his own had always been wrong, and he'd long ago given up, accepting that he did not know the safe way to supervise a small child at a playground or the right way to put socks on little feet or the appropriate way to instill discipline. Now he was suddenly supposed to be capable? Now, when he felt like he was coming apart? And, most daunting of all—now, when he could not afford to make one more slip at work?

He looked at the phone. One call and Hana would be home with him. What a coward he was not to make it. He wiped his damp forehead with his shirtsleeve, held on through a wave of nausea, then lay back and closed his eyes. Just for a minute. In his dreams the phone rang but he couldn't move to answer it. When he opened his eyes again it was nine o'clock and the buzzer was sounding. He stumbled across the room to the intercom.

"Hello."

"I knew you were in there! Hana, your daddy's home!"

"I'm home," he said, and pressed the release button to admit them through the building's locked front door.

He splashed cold water on his face, scrubbed it dry with a towel, and then unlocked his front door and stepped out into the quiet hallway to wait for them. After several minutes the narrow brass elevator pinged open.

"There you are!" Felice called.

She stalked down the hall toward him, long dark hair swinging in braids as she pulled Hana in her wake. Everything about Felice Navarre was delicate, almost childlike, from her petite size to her pixyish oval face, but she carried herself with the fierceness of an Amazon warrior. He suspected she had Cuban freedom fighters in her ancestry.

"You owe me some straight talk, man, and it better be good."

"Want to come in?" Dan asked.

"You bet your ass I'll come in. And don't think that I—" Felice stopped herself and focused on Hana. "Look here," she said gently. "Your daddy is just fine. You did all that worrying for nothing."

The child clung to the woman's leg and peered up at Dan as though he were a stranger.

"She's been very worried about her mommy and daddy," Felice said sweetly while her dark eyes continued to shoot darts at him. "She even had nightmares."

"Well, I'm home," Dan said, bending stiffly to pat Hana's head. "Home safe and sound." He was afraid to try to hug her. Afraid that she would not be receptive and afraid that too much jostling would make him feel sick again.

"Is my mommy home?" Hana asked.

"No," Dan said, holding the door open. Hana continued to cling to Felice's leg.

"Go on, *bonita*," Felice coaxed. "Go into your house with your daddy."

"I want my mommy."

"Haven't you missed all your toys? I'll bet they've missed you."

"Are you coming, too?" Hana whispered to Felice.

"I'm coming. But only if you promise to go into your room and say hi to all your stuffed animals while I talk to your daddy."

Hana considered the terms, then nodded solemnly.

When they were all inside the apartment Felice had to remind Hana of their deal and physically nudge the child toward her bedroom door. Dan watched, a helpless anger rising within him in the face of his daughter's suffering.

*I'm sorry!* he wanted to shout. *I wish your mother was here. I wish I knew something to do for you. I wish I could fix everything.*

Hana stopped outside her room and turned back toward them. The light caught in her hair, sparking glimmers of copper in the dark red. Just like her mother's hair. But with Dan's perpetually tanned skin and light brown eyes. A blend of them both.

"Don't leave me, Felice," she pleaded with a quivering lower lip.

"I have to go sometime," Felice told her firmly. "You live here with your daddy and mommy, and I live at my place with Peppy."

"But my mommy's not here."

"She'll be here soon." Felice glanced at Dan. "Won't she?"

"I don't know," Dan answered, and Felice's eyes betrayed alarm.

"I want to stay with you and Peppy till my mommy comes home," Hana pleaded.

"That's not possible, Hana. I told you. I have to be gone late into the night sometimes. You can't stay there alone when I'm gone."

"Peppy stays there alone."

"Dogs can stay alone. Kids can't. Besides, who would be here to keep your daddy company? Just think how lonely he'd be without you. I have Peppy, but while your mommy is gone your dad has only you."

Hana's face clouded, but before the outburst could gather any force Felice hurried toward her. "Did you hear that, Hana!" she exclaimed as she guided the child to the bedroom door. "All your friends are calling you!"

Dan watched them disappear behind the door, thinking how good Felice was with Hana, how good Alex had been with Hana. Wishing that he had that nurturing ability that seemed to come so naturally to others.

Felice stepped out of the room and carefully closed the door.

"All right," she announced, stalking back across the room. "Hana's set for a while. So I want the straight story here. What the fuck is going on? Jesus! I turn on my machine and I hear a message that you won't be on time to get Hana because you're at a police station. Okay. But that was yesterday afternoon, Dan! I've been going crazy— calling your work and calling around to precincts."

Dan looked at his hands, not sure where or how to begin. He looked at the moon face of the grandmother clock in the corner. The clock his father had so lovingly restored. What would his father do now? How would his father handle this?

"Just spit it out! Say something!"

"I spent the night in a hospital."

Felice's eyes widened.

"Alex is . . ." He struggled for composure.

"My God, what's happened? Was there an accident?"

"No. No." He drew in a deep breath. "I went to pick her up from the retreat, and she wouldn't come out."

"What?"

"I never saw her at all. The police came. They spoke to her." He sank down on the couch, feeling sick again, or at least sick at heart. "It's a long story. I kept going back, trying to get her out. I climbed over a fence and got some kind of poison on my hands. The police arrested me but the poison made me sick so they had to send me to the hospital."

Felice backed up until she reached a chair, then sat down.

"I don't understand. Did you two have a fight or something?"

He shook his head. "We were fine. You know that. We were fine."

"So she just, out of the blue, is refusing to come home?"

"I don't think it's like that, Felice. I never got to talk to her. Not once. I think something is wrong."

*"Dios mío,"* Felice breathed, shaking her head in disbelief. "What'd the cops do?"

"Nothing. They keep saying that legally she's an adult and she can't be forced to come out or see me."

"She wouldn't do this." Felice shook her head. "She'd never leave Hana."

"I know! But I can't make the police believe that. Even after I found out that it's a cult. They just won't do anything."

"A cult! Jesus, Dan! They've got her brainwashed or hypnotized or something. God knows what kind of weird shit is going on!"

"They took all the money out of our accounts. They took the car. They even got a cash advance on our credit card."

"And that's legal?"

"Apparently. Because I can't prove that they coerced Alex."

"This is chilling, man. Totally chilling." She scrutinized him as though just noticing his appearance. "You look bad. Are you still sick?"

"It's almost worn off. I'll be fine tomorrow."

Felice shook her head. "I'm so sorry, Dan. I'm . . . really stunned."

"So am I," he said. "Stunned."

"Jesus . . . Have you called her mother?"

"Her mother?" Dan frowned. "Alex's mother? It never occurred to me."

Alex's mother. What would he say to the woman? *Hi, this is the son-in-law you've never met. I know you and Alex hate each other and haven't spoken in years, but I thought you'd like to know . . .*

"How about McAteer's? Did you call them?"

Dan shook his head. "I didn't think of that either."

"They need to know that she won't be in to work."

"Right."

Another leaden slug of despair sank through him. Alex delighted in flowers and had taken numerous arrangement classes over the course of their marriage. As soon as Hana's kindergarten had started, Alex had promptly found a job with a friendly neighborhood florist who agreed to let her work only during school hours. She was scheduled for Thursdays and Fridays currently but had been promised a full five days as Thanksgiving approached. Felice was right. He did have to call them. But calling, telling them that she would not be in, seemed an acknowledgment of utter defeat. Almost like a notification of death.

Felice frowned and rubbed her temple with her fingertips. "I guess I can take Hana to school again tomorrow and pick her up after. Keep her till you get home. I might be able to do that for a few more days. But you've got to find someone, or maybe call one of those day-care places that picks kids up after school, because I only have a limited amount of work I can do at home."

"Okay."

"You can't afford to lose your job, Dan."

"I know."

"And you have to be careful with Hana. She's never been separated from her mother like this, and she's getting pretty upset about it."

"I know."

Felice leaned toward him, peering intently into his eyes. "You've got to get her back, Dan. Alex can't save herself."

"I know."

# Chapter 5

After Felice was gone, Dan went to his daughter's bedroom door. Somehow he had to talk to the child and make it clear that her mother wasn't coming home for a while. Admit that he didn't know when her mother was coming home. Steeling himself, he turned the knob and stepped inside. To his great relief, Hana had fallen asleep on her bed, nearly buried in a mound of stuffed animals. Quietly, he approached. She looked small and fragile to him. Heartbreakingly innocent. The curve of lashes against her skin, the sweet roundness of her cheeks, the arms outflung to hold as many animals as possible: all of it made his chest ache.

It was the same feeling he had had when he first saw her, scrawny and wet with birth fluids, a tiny alien creature come to earth. Her eyes had opened wide and she had looked straight at him.

"Do you have to put those eyedrops in?" he'd asked. "She wants to see everything."

The doctor and the nurse and Alex had all laughed at him.

The baby was placed in Alex's arms, and he had watched the miracle of their instant bonding and waited for his own turn, waited with fear and excitement and yearning, his heart swollen and tender in his chest.

"I'm tired," Alex had sighed, and Dan had taken that as his cue. Tentatively he'd reached out, his arms awkward, not sure of angles or technique.

"She's getting cold," Alex said.

The doctor, who was seated on a stool at the foot of the delivery table, looked up and frowned. The nurse swooped in and gathered the baby in a blanket.

Dan watched them all, feeling like the only person in the room with no role or purpose.

"Can't I hold her for a minute?" he asked timidly.

"She's cold, Dan," Alex said, her voice strained by exhaustion.

"We can't let her get chilled," the nurse said, smiling down into the baby's face.

"Take her to the nursery and put her under the lights," the doctor instructed.

And the next time Dan had seen his newborn daughter she was behind glass. He still thought of her that way. His precious daughter behind the glass.

He watched the soft rise and fall of her breathing. The evenness of it reassured him. She was fine. She was healthy and fine. He started out of the room, stopped, turned back to gently pull her shoes off, started out again, then turned back once more to pull a blanket over her. And suddenly he was gripped by panic. Was she supposed to sleep with so many stuffed animals? What if they covered her face and she smothered? Quickly he cleared off all but one floppy dog. Was it too hot in the room? Or too cool? Should he leave the light on or turn it off? And what if she cried out in the night and he didn't hear her?

Dan spent a restless, uncomfortable night on the couch rather than in his bed because he was afraid that Hana might wake and he would not be able to hear her from his bedroom. After he had showered and dressed he went to the kitchen. Normally he was on his way to the train in the morning before Hana was up. He wasn't sure what she ate for breakfast on school mornings, but cereal was always safe for kids, he decided. He pulled several boxes from the cupboard and set them on the table. He put toast in the toaster. He got out a bowl and a spoon and arranged them at Hana's place. Then he went to her room.

"Wake-up time." He shook her shoulder.

She sat up in the bed, a dreamy unfocused expression in her eyes. He watched her face change as she came to full awareness and remembered.

"Mommy's not home yet, is she?"

"No. But I'm here. And it's a sunny day."

"When's my mommy coming home?"

Dan swallowed hard and tried to appear confident. "I'm not sure, sweetie, but I hope it's soon."

She looked down at herself. "I slept in my clothes," she said almost fearfully. "Mommy says I always have to take a bath and put on my nightgown."

"One night in your clothes won't hurt you," Dan said, trying to keep his voice light. "Now, get up and use the bathroom. Breakfast is on the table."

She climbed out of bed and walked slowly to the bathroom, shoulders hunched as though bearing a weight. When she was finished she stood in the doorway, hugging her stuffed dog and staring up at him.

"Hungry?" he asked.

"I always get dressed before I eat."

"Okay. Get dressed and then we'll have breakfast."

She continued to stare up at him.

"What's wrong?"

"Mommy dresses me."

"Of course. I should know that, shouldn't I?" He forced a smile. "What does Hana want to wear today?" he asked the stuffed dog as he led the child back to her bedroom.

"Mommy picks out my clothes," she said, looking at him with accusing eyes.

"Okay . . . Let's see what we've got." He crossed to the narrow closet and studied the contents.

"What about this?" he said, pulling out a frilly dress.

"That's a special dress. Today's not special."

"This looks good." He held up a bright red jogging suit.

"That's too big. I'm not growed enough to fit in it."

"*Growed* isn't a word, Hana. *Grown* is the word."

She frowned. "I'm not grown into it."

Dan flipped through the hangers without bothering to explain the finer points of the usage of *grown*. There weren't a lot of choices. Mostly dresses. He didn't recall Hana's wearing dresses to school.

"Don't you have some jeans? And some little . . ." He tugged at his own shirt. "Some little tops or whatever they're called?"

"You mean my school clothes?"

"Yes." He reminded himself to be patient.

She pointed to the chest of drawers. "My school clothes are in there."

He fished in the drawers until he had underwear and socks, pants and a top.

"I don't like those socks."

He took a deep breath. "What socks do you like?"

"The socks I want are in the hamper."

"Then that means they're dirty."

"I don't want those socks! I don't want those socks!"

Her face contorted and reddened. Her hands clenched into tight fists. She screamed.

He watched her, completely at a loss. She was usually so compliant. Abnormally well behaved, he'd sometimes thought.

"Hana . . . Hana! Stop it!"

She quieted but glared at him fiercely. He had never seen her with such an expression. It reminded him of Felice.

"Now, take off the clothes you slept in."

"I can't."

He turned her, unfastened the buttons at the back of the neck, and yanked the sweater up over her head. She was stiff and unresponsive. Jaw clenched, he finished undressing her and then maneuvered each fresh article of clothing onto her body. Then he took her hand and pulled her with him to the kitchen.

"I want eggs," she said as soon as she saw the cereal and the bowl on the table.

"There's not enough time for eggs."

"That's not my bowl."

"Sit down!" he thundered, and immediately felt guilty.

She slid into the chair and stared at the empty bowl. Tears ran down her cheeks and dripped onto the table.

"I want my mommy," she whispered. "I want my mommy."

Dan lunged for the cupboard. "Which bowl do you like?" he asked, jerking out every bowl he could find.

She drew a shaky breath. "The one with Mickey on it."

He found the Mickey bowl and filled it with cereal. He went to the refrigerator for milk. There was no milk.

He closed his eyes for a moment. Then he slammed the refrigerator door and turned around.

"Let's go to Felice's," he said with false gaiety.

He zipped her into her coat. He poured the cereal back into the box, picked up box and bowl, and clamped her hand in his. She didn't exactly resist, but she didn't move along normally either.

When they stepped into the hall, Mrs. Svensen appeared. "I was just taking my recycle down," she said, gnarled hand holding a small bag of cans. "Why, hello there, Hana. You're leaving early today, aren't you?"

"Mommy's not home and Daddy is making me go without breakfast."

Mrs. Svensen's eyes shifted to Dan as her lips set into a disapproving line.

"When is your wife coming home, Mr. Behr?"

"We don't know," Hana said mournfully.

Dan released Hana's hand and hurried to take Mrs. Svensen's cans so he could escape.

"You promise your wife you won't work any more weekends and she'll come home," Mrs. Svensen whispered as she handed him her bag.

"It's not that simple," he said.

"It's always simple," Mrs. Svensen declared. "You realize that as you get older. People need certain things from each other. That's all there is to it."

Felice's building was on the way to the train station. He pulled Hana along for the entire three blocks, gritting his teeth to keep from shouting at her.

"Good morning," he said when Felice opened her door.

"Good morning." Felice scrutinized Hana. "You didn't brush her hair."

"Daddy didn't brush my teeth, either," Hana said. "Not last night and not when I woke up. And I didn't have a bath. And I didn't say my prayer last night and I slept in my clothes. And I'm hungry."

"Well, that about sums it up," Dan said.

"You didn't brush her teeth?" Felice asked, wrinkling her nose.

"I thought she did those kind of things herself," he admitted. "I guess you'll have to make me a list of instructions."

"Me? Hey, I'm not a parent. All I know is what Alex has told me to do and what common sense tells me to do." She bent, cupped Hana's chin, and rubbed noses with the child. "And what my little friend Hana tells me to do." She grinned. "Right, *chica*?"

Hana giggled. The sound of it amazed Dan. How could the child be utterly miserable one minute and giggling the next?

Felice straightened and stared intently at him. "Well?" she asked raising her eyebrows. "Any word?"

He shook his head.

"Did you call California yet?"

The meaning of the question didn't register with him.

"Her mother!" Felice said as though she couldn't believe his denseness. "In California."

"Not yet," he admitted.

"What's wrong with you, man? The woman's daughter is—" She glanced down at Hana and spelled "M-I-S-S-I-N-G!"

"Miss . . . ing," Hana said, sounding out the word. "Mommy is missing?"

"She's missing her purse," Felice said quickly. "You know how sometimes she loses her purse." Then, focusing on Dan again: "You've gotta call her."

"I will. I will."

"You could go home and call her right now."

"It's three hours earlier in California, Felice."

"Okay. So do it this afternoon from work."

"I'll try," he said.

"Wait a sec." She disappeared into her apartment for a moment and came back waving a piece of paper.

"What's this?" he asked as she handed it to him.

"A page from one of my phone bills. The number's on it. That way you won't have to go back up to your place to get it before you walk to the subway."

Dan stared down at the printed sheet. The long-distance calls were itemized. Most were to Florida, where Felice's family lived. There were two calls to a number in California. He could not think of a reasonable explanation.

"You called Alex's mother?" he asked incredulously.

"Not me. Alex."

"Alex called her mother? From your apartment?"

Felice shrugged. "Twice a month at least."

"I don't understand."

"You know . . ." Felice lowered her voice. "They don't get along so well. I think she wanted to call from my place sometimes because she was embarrassed to have you hear all the yelling."

Dan stood there for a moment, thoroughly unsettled by this news. Alex had told him that she'd had no contact with her mother since her early teens and that she didn't even know where her mother was living. Alex had lied to him.

He was embarrassed at revealing that to Felice, so he thrust the cereal and the bowl into her hand abruptly. "Here. I'm out of milk. Sorry."

"I wanted a scrambled egg," Hana said mournfully.

"No problem," Felice said. "I got eggs. I got milk." She flashed Dan a stern look. "Make that call."

When Dan arrived at the office tower where HTO leased its four floors, he was so early that there was no one except a security guard in the marble lobby. Dan stepped into an empty elevator and pushed the button for his floor. The doors slid shut and he was surrounded by polished metal surfaces, utilizing the design principle that reflective materials "open" enclosed spaces and make them feel less claustrophobic. That theory was fine when the car was crowded, but he had always disliked riding alone with all those blurry reflections of himself staring from every angle. Today he found the experience particularly disturbing. The images seemed to be accusing or questioning.

Alex had lied to him about her mother. Right from the beginning. What did that mean? What else had she lied to him about?

No. He would not fall into that trap. The lie about her mother wasn't important. He couldn't fixate on that. Maybe she was ashamed of her mother. That did not mean she had been deceptive or unfaithful in any other way.

No. She had been very determined to be a "good" wife. He had teased her about it sometimes, about her continual search for a better way to organize the apartment or a better way to communicate as a couple, but she'd always said that being married was a serious commitment and she could not take it lightly. She wanted their marriage to be perfect.

And he had worked at it, too. Not because he had illusions of perfection but because he loved her desperately.

The seeds had been sown while she was still in the hospital, lying there, so lost and alone, so unwilling to trust the doctors or him or anyone who tried to get close to her. She wouldn't even admit that she'd tried to kill herself. Instead she insisted that she had seen something in the water and climbed up on the fence for a better look, falling in purely by accident. And the fragility of her toughness had struck a deep chord. This was a woman whose life he had saved, but she was still in danger. Still close to some unknowable edge that he felt compelled to protect her from.

After the hospital moved her from intensive care to a regular room, he spent more time with her, taking advantage of the longer visiting hours and of her growing acceptance of his presence. Gradually a companionship evolved. They played card games, and he read to her from the paper or talked to her about buildings and his interest in historic preservation. He told her about his grant and the tremendous opportunities that awaited him in the Columbia graduate program. He even revealed the painful truths about his mother's alcoholism and his father's ugly death—fingers and toes turning black, heart stuttering, lungs eaten by the cancer, yet smoking his pack a day right to the end. His troubled mother. His wise and kind and talented father. And he told her about his lonely childhood and isolated adolescence, made even worse by his father's death and the move to Georgia; he and his mother retreating there to live with her brother. He couldn't recall ever having bared himself so completely to anyone.

From her he learned that she hated the fashion magazines he brought her (giving them immediately to the nurse to read), that she was fiercely unconcerned about her appearance, and that she distrusted anyone who complimented her. He pressed for more and gradually learned that her only living relative was a mother who had abandoned her years before, that she lived with roommates who were not friends, and that she had lost her job and was broke. She was guarded and wary, though, comfortable only with disclosing the superficial: her favorite color or flower or flavor of ice cream.

And through it all she continued to feign indifference to him, acting as though it did not matter to her whether he came or not. Then, one day, he had problems on the subway and was very late, and she greeted him with an inrush of breath that was part surprise and part relief, saying, with a false casualness, "Oh . . . it's you. When you didn't show up on time I thought you'd finally found something better to do." And suddenly he knew that he was as important to her as she was to him.

Because she had developed a nasty blood infection and liver complications (something the doctors suspected might have been active before the river episode), they kept her for nearly a month, hooked up to constant intravenous antibiotics. Her room became his universe. He woke each morning thinking of her, and he hurried around the city, confining his job search to mornings so that he could have the rest of the day and the evening with her.

Two nights before her release she was in a pensive, almost distant mood. The woman in the other bed had been sent home and no new patient had been installed yet, so they were alone. She switched on the television hanging at her side and asked him to pull the curtain around her bed in case another patient was brought in, and to turn out all the room's lights so they could see the tiny screen better. He complied, then pulled his chair up close to the head of the bed so he could watch with her. Only she wasn't really watching. She didn't even have the sound on. She was focused on him.

In the flickering lights and shadows from the TV screen she reached out and touched his face. The contact was electric. He froze. Except for the brushing of hands that accompanies game playing they had had no physical contact. Neither the setting nor her moods had ever seemed conducive to a testing of romance.

"I did jump into the river on purpose," she said, giving the confession a weight that was both gift and challenge.

"How could you want to die?" he asked in true bewilderment.

"Oh, I didn't think of it as dying. I thought of it as escape." She gave a tiny shrug. "I hadn't even planned it, really. I just looked down into that dark water and I thought about how we all start out as contented little fishy things floating in water, and I thought about how peaceful it must be way down on the bottom, and suddenly the river looked like a good place to me. A better place than where I've been."

"The East River is anything but peaceful," he said. "It's cold and polluted. And there are ferocious undertows . . . currents so strong that you feel like you're being pulled apart."

"That's because you were fighting it. For me it was a relief." She closed her eyes. "Like I was being taken somewhere calm and quiet. Like I was surrounded by gentleness."

"Stop. Please. I can't stand hearing you talk like that."

"Don't worry. I won't try it again. You've changed everything." She smiled a captivatingly crooked smile. "This is a strange relationship, isn't it? But I think that's a sign. Like this was meant to be. Because . . ." She looked away for a moment, almost guiltily, then met his eyes again. "Because if I'd met you some normal way I'd have just assumed I knew what you were like. I never would've believed how different you are. I never would've believed any man could be so sweet or so kind to me."

He drank in her nearness, her touch, and the faint scent of her beneath the hospital soap. He absorbed the sight of her, skin still slightly sallow and pale, face hollowed and bones too sharp under the cotton gown, unevenly chopped hair sticking out oddly from too much time against a pillow. And he felt a sudden lightness, as though all the extraneous bits of his life had suddenly dropped away and he was recast as a purer, finer being.

With his heart thumping wildly, he leaned forward and kissed her. First on the forehead. Then, ever so gently, on the lips. Softly. Tentatively.

"Get up here in bed with me," she whispered.

"But . . . I don't want to hurt you."

"You won't hurt me." She tilted her head and gave him a look that sent shock waves to his groin. "You'd never hurt me."

So he stretched out carefully beside her, almost dizzy from the sheer mad fantasy of it, and she kissed him hard, pressing herself against him, igniting his blood, burning his skin at every point of contact.

"Undo my gown," she said, and he fumbled with the ties at her back.

She shrugged out of one arm, the other trapped because of the IV hookup, and she let the gown fall. Her breasts were small and firm and perfect, like exotic fruit, with ripe deep-rose nipples. He ran his fingers lightly over the creamy skin, the porcelain velvet skin, so delicate that he could see the traceries of blue veins lying just beneath. He brushed the taut nipples with his palms.

"You are so—"

Her hand shot to his mouth.

"Don't ever tell me I'm beautiful," she said, her eyes locked fiercely onto his. "Never. Promise me you'll never say any of that garbage."

He had the urge to protest but the good sense not to argue, so he nodded, mutely.

She lowered her hand.

"You don't look comfortable," she said with a suggestive smile as she began unbuttoning his shirt.

When the shirt was open and pulled out she went straight for the snap on his jeans.

"What if someone comes in?" he asked, grinning.

She shrugged. "They don't usually until visiting hours are over. And if they do—so what?"

Then his pants zipper was all the way down, and she molded herself to him, her meltingly soft breasts against the skin of his chest, the mound of her pubis thrust against the length of his erection, body heat searing even where there were layers of cloth in the way. He gasped and she covered his mouth with hers, tongue searching and demanding.

He thought that he might be dreaming. He thought that

he might have been having the best fantasy of his life. He thought that he might even have died and gone to heaven—or, if not, that he might yet die from the pleasure.

When he could not continue without exploding, he pulled back, drawing deep breaths. She wiggled out of her panties and the sight of her crisp dark-red triangle nearly sent him over the edge.

"Come inside me," she breathed.

"Here? Now? We don't . . . I mean, I certainly don't . . . have anything . . . And you . . ." He smiled a little, teasing. "You didn't arrive here with any birth control in your pockets, did you?"

She frowned.

"All right," she said, as though considering the obstacle.

"This doesn't have to go any further," he offered half-heartedly. "We can save the rest for better circumstances."

"No."

He was on uncertain ground, and he didn't quite know how to handle it. After all the reticence and reserve, all the unwillingness to trust him, he was afraid that he might say or do something to upset the tenuous balance.

"Could you slide up here?" she said, betraying a hint of shyness. "And lean your back against the pillows?"

He did as she wished, then tried to put his arms around her shoulders, but she slipped free. He watched, waiting for a signal from her, a sign as to what was next.

"Could you close your eyes for a minute?" she asked.

Blind, he waited, listening to the faint rustle of her movements. Then he smelled a familiar scent and she straddled him and her hands gripped his cock and they were slick and wet with lotion, sliding up and down, and he dug his fingers into the sides of the bed, every muscle in his body tight, every cell in his body owned by her hands . . . and yet ambivalent because this might somehow be wrong for her. He opened his eyes and she was looking at him, looking straight into him with so much hope and vulnerability and love, and he came in a fountain. Came all over his clothes and the bed and her thighs.

"Alex," he breathed, sinking back against the pillows for a moment. "Alexandra . . ."

He reached out to stroke her arm, but her attention was focused on the bed.

"I didn't know it would make such a mess," she said, dismayed.

"Don't worry. We'll clean it up." He shifted and attempted to pull her closer. "Tell me what you want," he said. "How can I make you come?"

She shook her head, stiffly resisting his embrace. "I can't. With the IV and all . . . It would be too uncomfortable."

"Please . . . We could try. Let me try."

"No, really. Not now. Like you said, we can save the rest."

He didn't know what to do. Should he pressure her? Was she really concerned about the IV or was she embarrassed? Maybe shy about coming while he watched?

"Alex . . ." He touched her hand. "This is supposed to be for you, too."

"No!" She crossed her arms over her breasts. "I just don't want to!"

Taken aback and somewhat hurt, he swiveled and slid off the bed. "I'm sorry. I didn't mean to push you. I'll get the towels."

He went to the bathroom, quickly cleaned himself and put his clothes back together, then took both wet and dry towels out to her. After she was finished and he had tied her gown back into place for her, he scrubbed at the sheets.

"There," he said, in an effort to lighten the mood, "it would take a keen nose and a sharp eye to detect any game but cards in here."

She smiled just a little.

"Tell me about your apartment," she said, settling back in her customary propped-up position.

He sat down in the bedside chair.

"It's a dump. A one-room studio with a two-burner stove and a refrigerator that's smaller than the average television set. I keep my clothes in cardboard boxes, and on the floor I've got a futon, which, I'm told, is the bed of choice for all grad students."

She smiled again. This time it was dreamy and inwardly focused. "I'll bet you don't have curtains or decent dishes or anything."

"You're right. It's strictly life on the cheap. Even with the grant and my savings and a part-time job, money is going to be tight. But I expected that. I'm not complaining."

"I'll put up curtains," she said. "And I'll shop around for bargains at all those funny little stores with the used furniture and stuff."

He laughed.

"How big is the futon?" she asked.

"Ah . . . I'm not sure. I had to get a bigger one than I wanted just for the length. I don't like it when my feet hang over the end."

"Good. Good." She nodded. "Then it should be big enough for both of us."

The sexual implications of that statement sent a flood of relief through him. He hadn't blown it with her. She still wanted him.

"Maybe I can find a coffee table that we could eat on, too."

"Well . . ." he said hesitantly. "I don't know how much eating you'd enjoy in that atmosphere."

"It's too expensive to eat out all the time."

"Definitely. But you'll want to eat at your own place and with your friends and . . ."

His words trailed off when he saw the look on her face. She appeared as stricken as if he'd slapped her.

"You . . . don't want me . . . to live with you?"

"Live with me? I . . . I'm not . . . It's a question of practicality."

"I thought I was important to you. I thought you wanted me."

"You are! I do! But we have to face realities, and in less than two months I am going to be a poverty-stricken and incredibly overworked full-time graduate student. You'd be miserable trying to live with me."

Two very large tears slipped from the inside corners of her eyes.

"Alex . . . sweetheart . . ." He rose and leaned over the bed to embrace her, but she turned sharply away.

"You're all I have now," she said.

"Don't cry. We'll work it out. I'll help you find a job,

and if you don't like the place where you've been living, then I'll help you find something else."

"I can't go back there—where I was before. They already gave my room to someone else."

"Oh. Well—you weren't happy with them as roommates anyway, right?"

She nodded.

"Where are your clothes? Your things?"

"Packed up and stored in the basement. They said the super will give me a month to move them out."

"Okay." He drew in a deep breath, scratched his head, and wondered what the hell he should do next. "I guess you'll have to stay with me for a while, then. Just temporarily. Until we can find you your own place."

Her own place.

Of course, that had never happened. She had become pregnant and was devastated at the thought of abortion, so he'd given up the grant and the place at Columbia and all his dreams for the future. And he'd found the job at HTO. And despite his long-held desire to live in Manhattan, they had moved to Bay Ridge because she didn't want to raise a child in the city.

And he had never looked back, never had a moment's regret, because nothing had seemed too great a price for a life with her. And she had flourished. The child had flourished. Their life together had been close to ideal.

So how had it come to this?

Dan was determined to keep his ongoing disaster private. He did not want to be the object of company gossip. He did not want pitying looks from people in other departments whose names he didn't know. And he suspected that confiding in his three immediate co-workers would bring him more regret than real comfort or solace. With all this in mind he had gone to his office abnormally early, hoping to be settled and so immersed in work before his colleagues arrived that he would be able to withstand their inevitable barrage of questions. The strategy was not successful. He found it hard to immerse himself and even harder to retain his composure under their scrutiny.

From Rich Medford: "You look terrible, Behr old buddy. How did this poison thing happen anyway?"

From Wendell Crispin: "We're your friends here, Dan, and I wish you'd tell us exactly what is going on, because I have the very deep feeling that we're hearing only a small part of your troubles."

From Karen Lai: "Do you have anything you want to talk about, Dan?"

The same general themes were pursued from every conceivable angle until he found himself weakening. Sliding closer to the edge. Ready to break down and tell them everything. When the section head sent a summons for Dan to appear in his office, it filled him with more relief than dread. He pulled on his sport jacket and headed out. As he neared Dreeson's office he felt an odd numbness. The summons was undoubtedly negative, since good news was always conveyed in groups. It was probably about the Brunner project. About his losing the work.

"Sit down, Dan," he was instructed as soon as he stepped through the doorway of Dreeson's glass-walled office.

Dan waited for the lecture and reprimand, guilt shouldering aside his numbness.

Dreeson steepled his hands, stared off, and ruminated for a moment. "I'm just a cog in the wheel here," he said finally. "Expendable, like every other cog."

"You're not expendable," Dan protested in surprise. "You built this section."

"Oh, I'm expendable, all right. All of us mid-level overeducated white males are expendable. Haven't you heard? We're redundant. Our jobs are disappearing. Our sperm can be frozen and used later. Politicians don't even care about our votes anymore—they're all playing to radicals or women or minorities or senior citizens or loggers or conservationists or the Christian right or God only knows who, but they don't give a damn about the average hard-working guy like me, and you know why? Because we don't matter anymore. We are expendable."

Dan stared at the man and waited. This was not what he had expected; it was like no other conversation he'd ever had with his boss.

"You know, Dan, I started out as a young draftsman thirty years ago. Same way you started. All I had was some basic training, a lot of enthusiasm, and a commitment . . . a dream . . . a dedication to my field, but I worked my way up over the years to the point where I could make a good life for my family."

Dreeson leaned forward slightly to peer into Dan's face.

"You'd like to do the same thing, but I can tell you right now you don't have an ice cube's chance in hell because the rules have been changed, Dan, and you, and all the young white guys just like you, are not going to make it like their fathers made it. You'd have been better off going to elevator-repair school than putting in five years of hard work to earn an architecture degree."

Dan considered Dreeson's words. He wondered if the man was ill or upset. He wondered what the hell the old guy was talking about. "About the Brunner work . . ." he began.

Dreeson gave a rueful snort.

"You don't see the bigger picture, do you? No one sees. Just like when they were taking Jews away in the night. No one imagined how big and how evil that picture was."

"Am I going to lose my job?"

"Eventually. We all are. We'll be RIFed. You know what that means? Reduction In Force. Much cleaner and neater than firing people. And then they'll hire twenty-two-year-olds for much smaller salaries and a cut in benefits."

Dan waited. When Dreeson didn't go on, he said, "I think I can reconstruct the Brunner stuff pretty quickly."

The older man nodded and sighed. "Good. But there's already been some damage done. I've got strict instructions to report any evidence of declining performance in my department, and they're busily calculating which heads to lop off."

"Why? Our department has too few employees to handle the workload as it is."

"It's about control, Dan. The middle class got too much control in this country and now it's being taken away." He seemed lost in thought for a moment. "You been to any of those pep rallies they hold for men?"

"I'm not sure what you mean."

"Oh, all those gung-ho deals where men are supposed to open up and recommit and rededicate and learn to keep promises."

"No. I never have."

"Good. They're a bunch of bull. See, men still don't get it. We were all raised to be more open and all that. From my age down we were taught to be more sensitive and committed than previous generations of men. We're better educated. We work longer hours. But . . . the problem is not that we need to open up even more and recommit and rededicate. The problem is not our behavior!" He slammed his fist against his chest. "The problem is that there's nothing left for a man to get his teeth into. There's nothing left to feel good about. Nothing out there to believe in. And now, you can't even believe in yourself."

Dreeson stood and Dan took it as a signal that the meeting was over so he, too, stood and turned toward the door.

" 'Things fall apart. The center cannot hold.' You know what that's from?"

Dan quickly turned back but Dreeson was not facing him. The older man was at the window staring out across the city.

"It's from a poem, but I'm not sure whose," Dan admitted.

"No matter. He's a cliché anyway. Just another dead white male."

"I can't afford to lose my job," Dan said, suddenly seized with the need to unburden himself before this strangely disturbed man. "My savings have been stolen and my wife has vanished into a cult. I'm . . . at the end of my rope."

Dreeson turned around and regarded him in dark silence for several long moments.

"Have you told anyone else in the company?"

"No. My co-workers know there's something wrong, but I haven't given them any specifics."

"Don't. Don't let anyone else know. The buzzards are up there circling, looking for any sign of weakness. If they see that you're down they'll go straight for your balls."

Dan nodded.

"A cult, huh?" Dreeson mused. "Maybe she knows something we don't."

After cleaning out all his pockets that morning Dan had discovered that he had exactly forty-two dollars and three subway tokens to his name, so he allowed himself one slice of pizza and a glass of water for his lunch break. Then he went to a nearby bookstore. There was nothing on the shelves about cults. Not that he would have been able to buy anything if there had been.

Where was Alex now? What were they doing to her? If he could somehow find the money to hire this deprogrammer, Everett May, would the man be able to get her out? For the first time in his life he understood why someone might want to rob a bank.

As soon as he was back in the building he thought of his promise to contact Alex's mother. He dreaded the call, but it was the right thing to do. Avoiding his own work area, he found a vacant desk, pulled out Felice's phone record sheet, and dialed the number in California. It was the first time he'd ever used the company's toll-free line for a personal call. As the connections clicked he sank lower in his chair, certain that anyone passing would know he was committing a trespass.

Four rings. Five rings. He hoped she didn't answer.

"Hello," a female voice said, and his armpits were instantly wet.

"Hello . . . may I speak to Valerie Vaughn?"

"Who's calling?"

"This is . . ." He couldn't make himself say *her son-in-law*. "This is her daughter's husband."

"You're kidding."

"No. This is Dan Behr. Alexandra's husband."

"Behr, huh? Dan Behr." A low throaty laugh came to him through the wires. "This is Valerie." She laughed again. "I never expected to be talking to you. Whose idea was it? Not Alex's, I bet."

"No."

"I knew it. So—you must be calling me on the sly for information. I'm surprised she let you know I existed."

"She didn't, actually. I . . ." He hesitated, reluctant to tell the woman about Alex's lies. "You haven't heard from Alex recently, have you?"

"Not since her last call. That was about a month ago."

Dan tried to think of a kind way to break the news, but couldn't. "She's gone. With a cult. Something called First Light."

There was a moment of silence. "Is this a joke?"

"I wish it was."

Valerie muttered something that he didn't catch, then said, "Tell me everything."

He recited the story, except for the money and the car, which he left out because they seemed like an indictment of Alex. When he was finished there was another silence.

"I don't believe this! I thought she was so fucking happy. So into being Mrs. Goodwife and a member of the PTA."

"I thought she was happy, too. I mean . . . I still believe she was happy. I think they've gotten her under their control some way. Maybe drugged her or—"

"Oh, my God!" the woman suddenly exclaimed. "She didn't take the kid, did she?"

"Hana? No, of course not."

"Oh . . . Whew . . . For a minute . . . Damn." There was the click of a lighter and then a long inhalation. "So, what now?"

"I'm going to get her out. I don't know how yet. It may take some time."

"Going to be her savior again, huh? Sounds like she's made it harder this time."

"I don't . . . I mean, I . . ."

"What about the kid?"

"What about her?"

"Alex was doing the stay-at-home mom bit, wasn't she?"

"She worked, but only during school hours."

"So, who's taking care of the kid while all this is going on?"

"A friend of Alex's is helping me temporarily."

"You got any family around?"

"No."

The woman chuckled dryly. "Alexandra really left you holding the bag, didn't she? Left you high and dry."

Dan stared up at the ceiling and tried not to let the woman's words affect him. A doorbell sounded in the background from her end of the line.

"I've gotta go. Let me think about this. I've got some ideas . . . and . . . I'll call you back, okay?"

"Okay," he agreed, wishing he didn't have to talk to her again.

"What's the number?"

He recited his home phone number for her.

"You'll be there tonight?"

He assured her that he would, then put down the receiver and cradled his head in his hands. Only then did it occur to him that she had not known his name or had their phone number. Alex had apparently kept parts of her life secret from her mother, just as she had kept her mother a secret from him.

Alex. Alex. Alex.

He felt like a traitor for having spoken to her mother without her knowledge.

Alexandra.

His left hand was on the desk in front of him. He stared down at his wedding band. Thought of her trying to slip it on his finger and dropping it. The ring rolling out of sight and everyone, even the justice of the peace, searching frantically before the ceremony could continue.

"I hope that wasn't bad luck," she'd said later, laughing.

"Don't worry," he had assured her, "I'll get a horseshoe to hang upside down over our door."

He slammed his hands down on the desk, threw back the chair, grabbed his jacket, and headed toward the elevator.

He could not stay there working on closet placement and divider design while his wife was in jeopardy. He had to do something. Anything.

# Chapter 6

The grand old Central Research Library in midtown Manhattan, with its miles of inaccessible underground stacks and its extensive offerings of periodicals and abstracts, was the place Dan headed for in a quest for information about First Light. Information was power. With information he might see the group's weakness.

He wasted some time looking up book titles, filling out call slips, and scanning pages before deciding that books were not going to help him. He then concentrated on searching through current periodicals and computer abstracts. He learned that cults were not a modern phenomenon but went back to ancient times. He learned that cults have proliferated during every uncertain period of history: after the fall of Rome, during the French Revolution, world-wide after the Industrial Revolution, in Japan after World War II, in the U.S. during the turbulent 1960s, and in Eastern Europe after communism's crash.

He read about groups that had sprung up when the U.S. was young. Groups like the Millerites, who gave up all their possessions and waited for the world to end—not once but several times—finally becoming disenchanted with their leader's prophecies. But just when it seemed to him that all cults had to be a form of induced mass psychosis, he read that the Mormons began as a cult and that the Oneida and Amana colonies—to him just makers of silverware and appliances—had actually started as cults.

He put aside the history and concentrated on recent periodicals, scanning for mentions of cults and searching for the name First Light. Even in the more comprehensive listings there was no mention of First Light.

Discouraged, he considered what to do. He wasn't interested in learning more history, and he didn't want to go any deeper into cult psychology. He wanted First Light. He wanted his wife. He flipped backward in his notes, looking for a new direction. One of the scholarly but outdated books on the subject of cults had been authored by a Columbia University professor, Dr. A. D. Joost, whose field was religious studies and who had been considered a leading cult expert twenty years before. Surely, if Joost was still teaching, he would have current knowledge on the subject. But was he still teaching? A lot could change in twenty years.

Several phone calls and a subway ride later, Dan was on the bustling, tree-shaded campus of Columbia in the upper reaches of Manhattan. Being there brought pangs of nostalgia. How desperately he had wanted to be a student among the bright-eyed swarm that surrounded him. How hard he had worked for it through those long miserable years in Georgia, doggedly pursuing his studies even as he cared for his mother, struggling to remain free of the bitterness and depression that filled their household, emanating from both his dying mother and his pathetic lonely uncle. Struggling to hold them both up while he felt that his own head was in danger of going under.

Due to his customary refusal to ask directions, Dan wandered past building after building on the campus, uncertain about his destination. He found himself at a student gathering point, the focus of which was a huge bulletin board covered with aging layers of flyers and announcements. And his attention was caught by a faded yellow corner sticking out from behind an appeal for a roommate. In large block letters, the word *meaning* leaped out at him. Quickly he moved forward, muttering apologies as he shouldered others aside. He pulled out the pushpin that secured the roommate notice, folded back a partially torn advertising for a concert, and there it was:

MEANING AND MOMENT
Enlightenment for the New Century
A Series of Lectures and Discussions
from First Light Int.

"Meaning and Moment." The words chilled him to the bone now, but when he'd first heard them they had seemed perfectly innocuous. He thought back to that night—less than two months ago yet seeming to belong to a distant past. He had come home from work to find the house empty and a note saying that Alex had gone to a floral photography demonstration at Brooklyn College. The fact that she had taken Hana was understood since she routinely took the child everywhere with her, carrying a backpack of books and crayons for amusement.

When Alex came home, she had been excited about the demonstration. As soon as Hana was in bed she had asked him if he thought she was smart enough or creative enough to become a photographer. He'd assured her that she was. Then they had gotten into a fight. He made the mistake of saying that she should be certain of her photography interest because the equipment was expensive. She'd immediately taken that as proof that he didn't think she was capable or that he didn't take her ambitions seriously. To defend himself, he had then made the even bigger mistake of pointing out that most of her enthusiasms had been very short-lived.

It was one in the morning before he had her calmed and had soothed away the hurt and anger. The alarm was set to wake him in five hours, but she had wanted to make love, as she always did after any unpleasantness, and so he'd concealed his exhaustion and summoned the energy to perform. Otherwise she would have felt rejected.

When it was over he collapsed into a comalike state with her curled up against him.

"Dan? Did you hear me? You're not asleep yet, are you?"

"What? Oh . . . no."

"Well, what do you think?"

"About what?"

She sighed. "About the poster I saw on campus. 'Meaning and Moment.' The lectures. I was thinking about signing up."

Great, he thought. Another interest to be pursued even before the photography idea was dead and buried. But he knew better than to express that thought.

"Does it sound like something you'd like?" he asked carefully.

"Well . . . I'm not sure. But a girl was there, just putting up the poster, and I heard her talking to some of the college students, telling them how this was really mind expanding. Really something to improve yourself with."

Oh, no! he'd thought. No! No! No!

"How far would you have to travel?"

"They meet in several locations. One is right over in Park Slope."

"Ummm. How often?"

"One evening a week for six weeks. Then, if you qualify, there's a retreat at the end. . . . No children allowed, but I've already asked Felice and she's okay with keeping Hana."

"That seems like a lot to ask of Felice. Maybe I could make it home from work early enough that—"

"No. I'd rather have her at Felice's, where I know she's fine."

"She wouldn't be fine with me, huh?" he'd teased. Keeping it light.

"You know what I mean," she'd said. "So you think it sounds like a good idea?"

"Well . . . I think you have to be careful about things like this. They can be run by nuts. Or they can be a scam to get money out of you."

"You're always so negative about my trying to better myself!"

"That's not true, Alex."

"No," she'd admitted. "I guess it's not." She'd sighed heavily then. "I don't know, Dan . . . sometimes I just feel so . . . unformed. Like I'm a character in one of those family television series, and each week I have a different episode, but I'm not real."

"Oh, sweetheart," he'd said, so tired that he could barely think. "You're just feeling down. Let's get some sleep and we'll talk about it tomorrow."

But, of course, they hadn't talked about it the next day. It had been forgotten. And he realized that he had been relieved to forget it because her complaint had seemed like a momentary thing. Now, he wondered . . . Had she felt some deeply rooted need that First Light had seen and exploited? Had he failed her?

\* \* \*

Clutching the First Light poster from the bulletin board, Dan stood in a narrow, inadequately lighted hallway in front of a door that bore only a set of painted-over numerals. He knocked. There were sounds from within and then the door opened just wide enough for a stocky, round-faced woman to peer out.

"I'm looking for Dr. Joost," Dan told her.

"He's not here. I'm his graduate assistant. If you want to leave a message I'll give it to him."

"When will he be here?"

"I don't know. I've been grading papers awhile, and he hasn't been in yet."

"Could I find him at a class?"

"He wouldn't like that." She pushed her oversized glasses up her nose and scrutinized him. "You're not a student of his, are you? If you were you'd know that he doesn't want to be called Dr. Joost. It's Professor Joost."

"You're right. I'm not a student."

"Then he won't see you without an appointment."

"How do I get an appointment?"

"You have to write him a letter and wait to hear whether he wants to talk to you."

"I don't have time for that. I need to see him as soon as possible."

She shrugged as if to say that it wasn't her problem. Then she closed the door.

Dan moved partway down the hall to a narrow window and leaned against the wall to wait. Eventually A. D. Joost would have to go to his office, and when he did Dan intended to talk to him. However long that took.

Not more than fifteen minutes later a thin, stooped man in a bow tie walked past him, stopped at the door to Joost's office, and fumbled with a key ring.

Dan hurried forward. "Professor Joost?"

The man dropped his keys and appeared so startled that Dan was afraid he might collapse.

"I'm sorry. I tried calling you earlier and then I talked to your graduate assistant just a few minutes ago and . . . well, I apologize for surprising you like this, but I really do need to speak to you."

"Are you one of my students?" Joost demanded.

"No, sir. I need to talk to you about a cult. I need—"

"Impossible," Joost said, recovering his composure and bending to collect his keys. "My time is valuable."

He struggled to insert the key into the knob lock, but before his palsied hands could accomplish the maneuver the door was opened by the round-faced woman. "I thought I heard—" she began, but stopped on seeing Dan. "I told you to write a letter," she said accusingly.

"I can't wait," he said. "Just a few minutes. Please."

"I'll call Security," the woman threatened.

The professor looked from Dan to his assistant as though following a tennis match.

"Please." Dan held out his hands. "They've taken my wife. I don't know who else to talk to. I don't know what to do. Please . . ."

The woman bit her lower lip and turned her dark almond-shaped eyes toward the professor. There was a tense moment of silence. Then, with a scowl that managed to signal resignation, Joost went into his office. Behr and the woman followed. It was a small room crammed with piles of papers and books, a desk, an extra chair, and several filing cabinets.

"How did you get my name?" the professor asked wearily as he edged behind his desk.

"I saw a book by you."

"Good God! Where did you see that?"

"At the Central Research Library."

"Humph." He gave his assistant a wry look. "Didn't I tell you to steal that and destroy it, Una?"

The woman chuckled softly without smiling.

"Why wouldn't you want people to read your book?"

The bushy gray eyebrows drew together. "I'll ask the questions. Your name?"

"Behr. Dan Behr."

"Bear? Are you part Native American?"

"No. It's spelled B-E-H-R."

"I warn you, Mr. Behr—I'm very good at distinguishing truth from lies, and should I get the slightest whiff of anything false from you I will have you hauled out of here and charged with trespassing."

Dan nodded, wondering if the man had become paranoid with advancing age or if he was just playing the role of eccentric growling professor. Una had taken the extra chair, and Dan looked around for a piece of floor large enough to sit on.

Joost pointed to a stack of newspapers. "You can sit on the clipping file."

"Sign in," Una instructed, handing Dan an open visitor's log with spaces for name, address, phone, and purpose of visit. As Dan filled in the information Joost pulled a pocket watch from the inside of his suit jacket and clicked open the lid. "Ten minutes," he said.

Dan put the Meaning and Moment poster on the desk in front of the professor. "She saw one of these at Brooklyn College," he said. "I found this one today. Right here at Columbia. So they apparently got around." He took a deep breath and repeated the entire story. He was beginning to feel distanced from it, as though the tale of losing his wife were something fictional that he'd been forced to memorize.

When he was finished Joost seemed lost in thought for a moment. He stared down at the poster. "First Light? Does that ring any bells with you, Una?"

The woman's glasses slipped down her nose as she shook her head. "It's probably just a front name."

The old man smiled slyly. "I think we can be certain of that."

"What do you mean?" Dan asked.

Joost leaned back in his chair as though relaxing into the role of teacher. "Cults often have front organizations. Some of the better-known cults run consciousness-raising groups at colleges and drug treatment centers in large cities."

"To raise money?"

"Oh, no. Fundraising is a separate process. As is the accumulation of assets. You'd be amazed to hear what some of the big cults own—major mainstream newspapers, dry-cleaning chains, copy centers. And, of course, they use their own members as a slave labor pool.

"No. These front organizations are purely for recruitment. Some of them are outright shams, little more than tools to lure people through a door, but others are quite elaborately designed to offer an actual service as bait. Meditation sessions, substance treatment, self-improvement courses . . . These programs attract the unwary and then give the cult an opportunity to discover a potential victim's weak points before the hook is offered."

Dan felt a deep welling of bitterness. Alex had been a victim of something terrible. Something sinister that was hiding behind a mask right in the midst of an unsuspecting public. Yet, even now that the crime was fully recognized, there were no laws to protect her, no legal means to save her.

"It's so hard to understand. Alex was never religious."

The professor shook his head impatiently. "That is a common misconception about cults. They don't necessarily have a religious aspect at all."

"But then, what makes them cults? I mean, if there are no common denominators couldn't you call the Boy Scouts a cult?"

A look of undisguised annoyance crossed the old man's face. He muttered something under his breath, jerked out his pocket watch and checked the time. "That's it, Mr. Behr."

"No! Please. I don't know anything about these groups. I need—"

"That's precisely the problem!" Joost thundered. "No one listens to the warnings. People like you—the public— keep their heads down . . . like a flock of sheep on a nice green pasture. The wolves don't exist for them. They don't want to hear about the wolves. Or if they do, they treat the whole subject like a bedtime horror story—a titillating entertainment."

Joost struck his fist on the desk. "My colleagues and I have been sounding the alert for decades. Before the Tokyo subway killings. Before Waco. Before Jonestown. But no one listens. Fools like you go on about their merry way and let these insidious cancers flourish and grow. And then you're *surprised* when something bad happens."

"There are people who listen," Una said quietly. "The bad guys are all ears."

"Yes," Joost said with a rueful smile.

"The cults pay attention to everything that's said or done," she explained to Dan. "Professor Joost has been sued and harassed so much that he stopped publishing."

"By who?" Dan asked.

"You name it. All the big cults have gone after him at one time or another."

"I don't publish anymore," Joost said shortly. "And if I could, I'd remove all my old books and articles from the library system."

"How can I find out about First Light?" Dan asked.

The old man sighed, then waved a hand at his graduate assistant. "Give him those cult reference handouts from my survey course."

Una went right to a box of folders, sorted through them, and passed several sheets of paper to Dan.

"Thank you," he said, scanning the densely typed pages. They were all headed with "Survey of the American Religious Experience."

"Every student in my course gets those," Joost said. "And you could have gathered the information yourself with some basic research."

"But you've saved me a lot of time."

"No. I'm trying to save myself time." He gestured toward the pages Dan held. "You have all that I'm willing to give you, so you can go now."

Stubbornly, Dan kept his seat on the pile of newspapers. "Is this information only for religious cults?" he asked. "It says 'The American Religious Experience.' "

"As I've tried to convey to you, Mr. Behr, cults have different themes. Some are specifically religious, some blend doctrines, and some don't use any religious terminology or symbolism at all. However, all cults share certain key characteristics, and at the core they are all religions."

"How can that be?"

"If you had ever taken my introductory religious history course, or if you had even bothered to look up the definition of *religion* in a dictionary, you would know that the word *religion* does not mean the congregation around the corner. Most commonly, *religion* does indeed refer to a belief in supernatural powers, but the term also means any system of values and beliefs—and or any system of values and beliefs based on the teachings of a spiritual leader—and or any cause pursued with zeal. To take the discussion of the term *religion* further, one might also note that organized religions usually have power structures and power struggles. They have strongly developed concepts of 'us' and 'them.' And they not only work to hold on to their members, they also seek to convert outsiders or they are receptive to conversion by outsiders.

"So"—Joost steepled his hands—"while all cults are not religious, they could all be described as religions."

Dan hesitated. "I think I see. But . . . what should I do now? How can I get my wife back? Should I try to hire a deprogrammer?"

Joost scrutinized him in silence for several long moments.

"During your library visit did you read anything about Dr. Ferren's work?" the old man asked.

"No. Dr. Ferren? Should I read about it?"

The question was ignored. "What is your occupation, Mr. Behr?"

"I'm an architect with a big architecture and engineering firm—HTO."

Joost peered at him skeptically. "If that is a falsity it will certainly be easy to uncover it."

"Why would I invent anything?" Dan demanded, suddenly losing patience with the old man. "Do you think I came here to play some weird game with you?"

"Time will tell. Now go. If you're serious about your quest you have the course notes to guide you further. Whether you're serious or not, I don't want to hear from you again. Don't return. Don't call. Don't write. As you so aptly described it, this is all part of a weird game, and I am no longer a player."

Dan took the subway to Brooklyn, reading through the professor's course notes on the way. The facts jumped out at him from the first page.

There are an estimated 5,000 cults in the United States today. The world-wide number cannot be estimated because there are so few international watch groups operating.

He flipped to the next sheet.

Primary characteristics of a cult:
1. A charismatic or somehow persuasive leader who becomes an object of worship
2. The use of coercive persuasion
3. Totalistic—requiring complete immersion and submission
4. Manipulation comes from both leader and fellow members
5. Self-serving—all activities (recruiting, fundraising, etc.) are solely to benefit the cult or the leader

He closed his eyes and clenched his jaw against the surge of fear that the professor's notes brought. There was much more, but he could not absorb it all in one sitting. It was too frightening.

When he reached Bay Ridge he went straight into an electronics store in the main commercial shopping area and bought an answering machine. Package in hand, he walked to Felice's to pick up Hana. There was no answer. He was an hour earlier than he would have been had he worked a normal day, so his arrival could not have been anticipated. He wedged a little note into the metal edge near her buzzer button, and then he walked the three blocks to his own apartment and became absorbed in setting up the answering machine.

When the building buzzer sounded he assumed that Felice had found the note and brought Hana home. Instead of pressing the intercom button and asking who it was, he simply hit the main door release for admittance to the building. He then propped his apartment door open and returned to the task of reading the "simple" instruction booklet that had been enclosed with his new purchase.

Some minutes later a female voice called a tentative "Hello."

He was on his knees behind a chair.

"I'm in here," he answered. "In the living room."

He focused his attention on attaching the machine's wires to the phone and electrical outlets. When he looked up there was an unfamiliar woman in his living room.

"I'm Laura Ferren. Where is she?"

"Who?"

"The woman leaving the cult."

"I'm sorry, I . . . Wait. What did you say your name was?"

"Laura Ferren. I got a message from Professor Joost and I came as soon as I could."

"You're the Dr. Ferren he spoke of?"

"Yes."

Dan stood, aware that he was staring at her but so surprised by her sudden appearance that he was unable to stop.

"My wife isn't here. The cult has her."

An immense sadness settled over the woman's features for a moment. Then she straightened her shoulders, assuming an air of calm purpose.

"My assistant must have misunderstood the message. I thought she was here."

He had to look away to clear his throat. "No. She's been gone since last Sunday."

"If you don't mind, I rushed here from Manhattan after my last appointment of the day and—"

"Oh, please! Have a seat. Can I get you something to drink?"

She took off her coat and folded it over the back of a chair. "Tea, thank you. Any kind."

When he returned to the room with her cup of tea she was studying a framed photograph from the bookcase. In it a younger Hana was centered and solemnly meeting the camera's gaze. Alex was holding her, but turned, face partly obscured. He put the cup on the table, then sat down opposite Laura Ferren and waited.

"Your wife—Alex, is it?—doesn't like having her picture taken, does she?"

"No. She never has."

She continued to study the picture, and he watched as she did so. Laura Ferren was close to his own age, with fair skin and light brown hair. She'd twisted her hair up at the back of her head, but curly tendrils were escaping here and there. Her clothes were nondescript and she wore no jewelry or makeup. She was not polished enough to look professional, yet she had an air of self-possession that evoked confidence. And there was something about her that he found compelling—an open acceptance that was knowing rather than naive, a kind compassion that was tough rather than soft. No, not tough. Strong. There was an inner strength that emanated from her.

"It's hard for me to believe that Professor Joost called you," Dan remarked. "He seemed so determined not to become involved."

She put the photograph down on the table and raised her eyes to his, every movement composed and steady, her focus shifting from the picture to him in a way that was both comforting and disconcerting.

"Your phrasing is charitable," she said. "I'm sure that the professor's determination verged on hostility."

"It was close," Dan admitted.

"He has his reasons. He didn't know who you were. And his past involvements have cost him a great deal."

"He mentioned lawsuits."

"Yes. He used to be a prominent figure in the war against cults. He wrote prolifically. His lectures to mental health professionals revolutionized treatment methods for cult exit therapy. He campaigned for stricter government standards on the tax-exempt status of religious cults, and he tried to expose some of the more flagrantly dangerous and illegal practices, naming cults by name and furnishing documented evidence against them."

She paused as though lost in thought for a moment. Then she sighed and her tone hardened slightly. "He was young and idealistic then, and he thought he had the right— as an American, as a dedicated scholar and educator—to comment on society and seek change. And he believed that this right also conferred safety. They almost destroyed him."

"Who is 'they'?" Dan asked.

"Various cults."

"Are you telling me that our country has a long-standing secret federation of cults waging war against whoever criticizes them?" he asked skeptically.

"No, there is no federation. They are completely separate from one another. And none of this is secret. It's known, but it's suppressed out of fear. And yes, they go after their critics. Some groups do it in a more fiercely aggressive manner than others. They're all different. There are those that retaliate only in response to direct criticism, and then there are others that can't tolerate having their operating methods so much as mentioned in the media."

"And how do cults go after critics?"

She sipped her tea. "Mmm. Thank you." She absently tucked a stray tendril of hair behind her ear, and then focused on him again.

"The methods are as varied as the groups' ideologies. The most powerful and wealthy cults like to use the law. Their lawyers file suit after suit after suit, never winning but forcing targets into financial ruin because the suits have to be defended in expensive court battles. Besides the legal venues there are the Watergate-style tactics—office break-ins and computer sabotage. And there are the dirty tricks—rumors, and even manufactured evidence, planted to destroy the professional or personal reputations of targets. And finally there are what I categorize as the straightforward methods—anonymous threats, telephone harassment, vandalism, disemboweled family pets, rattlesnakes in mailboxes . . . that sort of thing."

"And all this is happening around us?"

She smiled with a gentle irony. "You find it so hard to believe, Mr. Behr? You? A man whose wife walked into a house and never came out? A man who was poisoned climbing over one of their fences? A man who had a gun put to his head right in the middle of a tree-shaded backyard in a nice neighborhood? A law-abiding man who was nearly jailed by the very police force that should have been protecting him?

"If someone like you finds it hard to believe, then it's no wonder that the rest of the country ignores all the warnings."

"I see your point," Dan conceded. He watched her drink the tea for a moment.

"I'm embarrassed to say this, Dr. Ferren, but I don't know exactly what you do."

"I'm a doctor of psychology," she said matter-of-factly.

"My field is cults. In addition to my training I have personal knowledge because I was in a cult. My family died as a result of cult insanity. I specialize in exit counseling. Basically, that means I use therapy to help people see what has been happening to them, to understand it, and to break free of it."

"You're a deprogrammer."

"No."

"You're not?"

She hesitated. "That term refers to a process that became widely known in the sixties. I think of the early deprogrammers as the pioneers in a field that eventually grew in sophistication and knowledge and evolved into exit counseling."

"But there are still deprogrammers around, so they didn't all evolve."

"That's true there are still some around."

"So what do these nonevolved guys do that you don't do?"

"The usual is that the deprogrammer, at the behest of the cult member's family, forcibly kidnaps the cult member and subjects that person to a strenuous, highly charged, and sometimes abusive regimen that attempts to shock the cult member into snapping out of the thought control or programmed thinking. Deprogramming is based on the assumption that the cult member has been 'programmed' or coerced into a trancelike submission. *Brainwashed* is the popular term."

"That's what happened! My wife was coerced. She was brainwashed!"

Laura Ferren regarded him in silence for a moment. "There is a fine line between coercion and conversion, Mr. Behr. A sometimes invisible and wavering line."

"What is that supposed to mean? That you can't pass judgment because there are too many mitigating factors to allow distinguishing between free choice and coerced behavior . . . between right and wrong?"

"No. What I'm saying is that in treating these cult cases the struggle to make distinctions—indeed, the very notion of right and wrong—is often pointless. A person—your wife, say—might have started as a victim but gone on to become a true believer. Where does that put her? Is she a victim now or a convert?"

He buried his face in his hands for a moment, then met her eyes again. "I see what you're saying, but with a cult like this and with such a fresh situation, deprogramming sounds like it would be safer . . . more of a sure thing."

"Deprogramming is never safe, and it's not a sure thing. The process is brutal and uses many of the same techniques that the cults use. Coercion to fight coercion. And that is one of the oldest of wrongful human behaviors."

"Which is?"

"Sinking to the level of the enemy in order to win. Becoming the enemy."

"Oh, God . . ." He blinked hard against the burning in his eyes. "I don't even know where she is anymore. How can you use your civilized reasonable approach on someone you can't find?"

"Locating your wife would be the first problem."

"And then what?"

"We establish her routines, find out when she's accessible, and make approaches. Then engage her in a respectful dialogue."

"Does your method always work?"

"No. But then, deprogramming isn't failproof either. Some people are profoundly unreachable. However," she added quickly, "they're usually the ones who've been in the cult a long time and are so immersed in the cult's reality that they can no longer relate to anything outside of it. Or they're people who experienced the larger world as unfriendly and hazardous, people who were misfits or outcasts or in substance crisis when the cult targeted them."

"But my wife hasn't been with them long, and she has a good life and a loving family waiting for her."

"Exactly. That's why I'm so hopeful she can be counseled successfully. I believe that she can break free of all the deceit and manipulation but needs emotional assistance to accomplish it."

Dan sighed, shook his head, and held out his hands. "I have no money. They got everything. I know locating a person can be expensive, and I have to tell you right now: I have nothing."

"Yes, the professor told me that. I can't make any promises, but there are some resources that we may be able to draw on."

"Such as?"

"Some wealthy families whose children we've helped. They're very supportive of our work."

"Why would they help me?"

"It would be our organization they were helping."

"What organization?"

"There are a number of us who work loosely together."

"What is it called?"

"There's no official name. I have offices in Manhattan and in Los Angeles. Several colleagues with similar practices have offices in other large cities. We pool our resources, and we accept referrals from a network of mental health people who support our work."

"Sounds very vague."

"And purposely so. Exposure invites harassment from the cults."

Dan sat for a moment, considering everything she had said, his heart stone-heavy in his chest.

"If you could . . ." He struggled to maintain control. "I'm sorry. I just . . . If you bring her back to me. If you could help her find her way back to me . . ."

"I don't know yet if I can help you," Laura Ferren said. "But I'm going to do everything in my power to try."

He might have broken down then, but she saved him from that by turning brisk and announcing that she needed his help. Steno pad in hand, she led him through every detail from the moment Alex first saw the Meaning and Moment poster up to the present.

"I need everything," she insisted, "for clues about First Light, and for clues to Alex as well. We have to locate the cult and learn about it, but we have a greater mystery to unravel—the mystery of your wife. We have to find out what was in her heart and mind that found the cult attractive."

"We were happy. There was nothing wrong with our marriage."

"I'm not disputing that. And I'm not implying that your wife was unbalanced in any way. But I have to know what it was about the cult that appealed to her. I have to know as much as I can about her and her life and her state of mind when she went to that retreat or I won't be able speak to her in an immediately meaningful way. And, under these circumstances, that will be absolutely necessary if I'm to reach her and interest her in talking to me."

Laura Ferren questioned him about the state of their marriage and then took him back through their years together, all the way back to that night at the river. The session was painful and emotionally draining. When the buzzer sounded it was a welcome relief.

"Hi, Daddy. It's us and we brought a surprise!" Hana's voice shouted through the intercom.

Dan hit the door release and turned back to Laura Ferren. "That's my daughter coming up," he said. "You'll get to meet her."

The woman smiled one of those gentle smiles he associated with cinematic nuns. He wondered if she ever lost control. If she ever screamed obscenities. Standing up now, across the room from her with his arms crossed and his daughter on the way, Dan felt safer. Her too-perceptive probing would have to stop. Which was good, because he didn't think he could take much more.

"Look, Daddy!" Hana burst in waving a bag, and he smelled French fries. "McDonald's! Felice bought us all McDonald's! And I got a toy!"

Felice was immediately behind Hana, carrying two larger bags. She stepped in the door smiling, but stopped when she saw Laura Ferren.

"Dr. Ferren, this is my daughter, Hana, and our friend Felice Navarre. Felice, this is Dr. Ferren. She does exit counseling for people who have gotten into cults, and she's going to try to help us."

Felice set the bags down and rushed forward to fling her arms around Laura Ferren. "*Dios mío!* You're a saint, Doctor. A saint sent from heaven."

Dan was somewhat embarrassed by Felice's effusiveness, but Laura Ferren seemed unfazed by it.

"You're from Cuba originally, aren't you?" Laura Ferren asked.

Felice's eyes lit up. "You must know some Cubans."

"I worked with a Cuban family last year."

"Felice is my wife's best friend," Dan explained. "We're all feeling a little desperate." He glanced at Hana, who was watching the adults with curiosity and, he knew, wondering how her mother fit into the conversation.

"I'm so sorry, Doctor," Felice said suddenly. "I didn't know you were here and I might not have brought anything you like."

"Well, thank you for considering me, but I have a dinner engagement later tonight. So, please, sit down and eat before everything gets cold. And"—she focused on Hana—"maybe while you two are setting the table, Hana could show me her bedroom?"

"Is that necessary?" Dan asked, worried that Hana might be upset by talking to the woman.

"Oh, yes," Laura Ferren said, holding out her hand and smiling, "because I can't wait to see her room."

Hana glanced at Felice and then at her father. Shyly, she took the woman's hand and said, "My mommy's gone so my room is all messed up."

"That's okay," Laura Ferren assured her. "Does your mommy clean your room a lot when she's home?"

"Every day. She says things belong in their places."

"But what if you have a puzzle or a game that's not finished yet?"

"I'm not allowed to have puzzles or games. They have too many pieces."

They crossed the floor, went into Hana's room, and shut the door.

Dan's eyes met Felice's.

"I didn't know she couldn't have games or puzzles, did you?" he asked, disturbed by this revelation.

Felice nodded. "It drives Alex nuts."

They carried the bags to the table together and arranged the food.

"You didn't ask me where I was so late with Hana," Felice prompted.

"I'm sorry. Where were you?"

"I ended up having to go in to work so I had to take her with me."

"She missed school?"

"Dan! That's not a big deal. She's in kindergarten and she's already ahead of her classmates. Hana is already reading. Some of the kids in there are just learning not to bite the teacher. Her missing school is not one of your major problems right now."

"You're right."

"But I've got bad news. I called around. All the good after-school programs are full. Even the religious ones—which I didn't think you'd be too crazy about anyway. So your only option is finding an individual . . . you know . . . one of those ladies who'll pick her up from school and take her to her apartment or to your apartment or whatever until you get home. So I bought the local papers on my way to work, and when I had a minute I called some of the ads . . . and we're talking thirty bucks a day. Plus you've got to go through the hassle of interviewing and all that, because you can't let just anyone take care of Hana."

Dan sighed heavily and sat down in front of his Big Mac. "Thanks for checking it out, Felice. And for buying dinner. You've been terrific."

"Yeah, well . . . not so terrific from now on. Some problems came up with the new line and I'm going to be putting in long hours. No more working at home for a while. No more helping with Hana. Maybe that old lady down the hall could have her during the afternoon for a few days?"

"No. Poor old Mrs. Svensen is half blind, she won't leave her apartment, and she sleeps in the daytime because she says her husband's ghost nags at her all night. If Hana were older, maybe . . . but—"

"Then you're going to have to take her to your office with you, Dan, until you get this after-school care fixed up."

"I can't take her to my office!"

"Oh, but it was okay for me to take her to my office? Me! Not even a relative."

"I'm sorry. It's just that you work in a fashion house where everybody's running around and things are loose. My office is different. Bringing a child in would probably get me fired."

"So, you'll have to stay home a few days. Use some sick time."

"That would probably get me fired, too."

She threw her hands into the air. "Well, what the fuck do you want me to do about it! She's not my kid. I shouldn't have to feel guilty because *you* can't handle single parenting!"

"You're right. I'm sorry. I'm sorry. Please . . . sit down and eat." He turned his head toward Hana's door. "Dinner is on the table!" he called.

Laura Ferren was gone and Felice was on her way out when the phone rang. Dan and Felice both froze and stared at it a moment before Dan lunged to answer it.

"Is that you, Dan Behr?"

"Yes. Who's this?"

"Valerie."

"Oh . . . Hello, Valerie." He put his hand over the receiver and whispered to Felice, "It's her mother. I called her earlier."

"Who are you talking to?" Valerie asked.

"Alex's friend Felice. She's the one who gave me your number."

"Mmm. The one who's been helping you with the kid."

"Yes."

"Careful she doesn't start helping you too much."

"What?"

"Lonely men are easy targets."

"I don't . . . If what you're suggesting is—"

"Oh, don't go getting all huffy. I called to tell you something good."

"You heard from Alex?"

"No. But I've decided that I'm flying out to give you a hand. I need a break from this place and it's time I got to know the kid."

Dan was speechless for a moment. He glanced at Felice, but of course she hadn't heard what Valerie was proposing.

"What?" Felice hissed, crowding close as though she wanted to take the phone from him. "Did she hear from Alex?"

Dan shook his head and waved her away.

"That's a very generous offer, Valerie. But I need to think it over . . . figure out how it would work. I mean, this is a small apartment, and I'm not sure you'd be comfortable here."

Understanding dawned in Felice's eyes. "Say *yes*!" she whispered.

"What's to think about?" Valerie demanded. "You're stuck with a kid and a mountain of problems. I have the free time. I'm buying my own ticket. And I'll make myself comfortable, don't you worry about that. I'm good at making myself comfortable."

"Well . . ."

Felice was nodding vehemently and gesturing.

"The kid is my granddaughter. I want her to know me."

All his reservations crumbled then. How could he argue with something so simple? "Of course. And I want that for Hana, too. You're her only living grandparent. Of course you're welcome here . . . and I appreciate your coming."

Felice broke out into a wide smile and held fisted hands up in the air, gesturing victory.

"I already reserved a ticket. I'm getting in at seven tomorrow night."

"Okay. I'm sorry I can't offer to come out and pick you up. I don't have a car anymore."

"No car? I've heard that people in New York live without cars, but coming from the freeway capital of the world, that's pretty hard to imagine. Guess I'll have to learn, huh?"

"It's actually very easy," Dan said. "Speak to the cab dispatcher at the airport. Tell him where you're going."

"Gotcha. Can I talk to the kid now? Kind of meet her over the phone so that we're not complete strangers when I show up?"

"She's in bed, but she's not asleep yet. Just a minute."

He called Hana to the phone.

"Who is this?" Hana said instead of hello.

Hana listened intently, an expression of curiosity on her face. Then she smiled, said "Okay. Good-bye," and handed the phone back to Dan.

The line was dead. Valerie was gone.

"What did she say, punkin?" Dan asked immediately.

"She said she was my mommy's mommy, which means she's my grandma, but I'm not s'posed to call her

Grandma. I'm s'posed to call her Valerie. And she's coming to see me and we're going to have lots of fun."

"Good," he said, glancing up at Felice and wondering how Valerie's appearance would affect Hana. Wondering what Alex's hatred of her mother had been based on.

# Chapter 7

Valerie Vaughn arrived the following night in red high-heeled pumps and a cloud of perfume. She was not as tall as Alex, her hair was artificially blond rather than naturally dark red, and her eyes were not as exotically colored, but the facial resemblance of mother to daughter was unsettling. Dan went downstairs when she buzzed so that he could carry up her luggage, and he was immediately awkward in her presence. Looking into her face made his chest ache.

"Look at this woman!" Felice exclaimed as Dan ushered his guest through the door. "Now we know where Alex got her gorgeousness, don't we? You could be her sister instead of her mother!"

"Why, thank you," Valerie said, clearly pleased. "You must be Felice. Alex told me a lot of good things about you." She batted her eyes and feigned a pout. "What nasty things did she tell you about me?"

"Nothing specific," Felice assured her. "Just that you two have always fought. But that's not a big deal to me. My family *likes* screaming at each other."

Dan was thankful that Felice had insisted on being present for the welcome. He stayed out of the way, holding Hana's hand, as Felice asked about the flight and the taxi.

Finally, Valerie turned to Hana, cocked her head, and studied the gap-toothed five-year-old. "There's my little friend," she said, smiling. She picked up a large shopping bag that she must have carried with her onto the plane and she took the bag to the couch, sat down, and patted the spot beside her. "Come on and see what Valerie brought you."

Shyly, Hana sidled over to the couch. Instead of sitting down she stood and looked into the bag.

"Ta-dah!" With a flourish Valerie produced a cotton candy fluff of a dress, long and pink, with swirls of sparkled netting and sequins at the neckline.

Hana stared at it with a dazed expression.

"There's more!" Valerie cried, producing a rhinestone tiara and a long sequined wand and small pink open-toed high-heeled slippers. "With this getup you can be a princess or a good fairy or whatever you want."

"Thank you," Hana said, stroking the fabric of the dress.

Valerie reached inside her purse and brought out a pack of cigarettes.

"Nobody can smoke in our house," Hana said.

"Oh." Valerie hesitated, holding the pack in midair.

"It's bad for you. Daddy's daddy died from smoking cigarettes before I was ever born. Your lungs get all black inside like charcoal. We saw it in a movie at school."

"How interesting," Valerie said, forcing a smile and putting the pack away. "Do you like to play princess?"

"No. I like to play animal trainer."

Valerie frowned. "Well, I used to love to play princess, so I'll teach you how. We're going to be great friends! And I declare tomorrow our special day to get to know each other. We'll go somewhere together, just you and me. Where do you want to go?"

"The zoo," Hana said, brightening instantly.

"The zoo? With all that animal poop and hair and dust?"

Hana nodded.

"You sure you wouldn't like to go to that Bloomingdale's store? We could shop and have lunch and—"

"The zoo," Hana said firmly, then in a small wistful voice, "I've never been to the zoo."

Dan felt a pang of guilt. How had his daughter gotten to be five years old without having been taken to the zoo? But then it occurred to him that Alex's attitude would have been similar to her mother's. Alex would have worried about the dirt and the germs at a place like the zoo.

"The zoo, huh?" Valerie said as though already smelling animal dung.

Dan exchanged a glance with Felice. He was worried. She was clearly amused.

"Well . . ." The woman sighed. "I guess I'll survive a trip to the zoo. But I don't know if I have the right clothes to wear."

Within days they had settled into a routine. Valerie insisted on taking over completely with Hana as well as assuming all the domestic responsibilities, stepping into Alex's place so perfectly that the effect was eerie. Dan went to the office, performing robotically. He came home and worked every evening. He went through all the motions that were expected of him. With Valerie's presence and energy, a thin veneer of normalcy was applied over the broken mess of his life. But when he lay in bed at night (Hana's single bed so that Hana and Valerie could sleep together in his larger one), he stared at the flowers painted on his daughter's walls and that thin veneer peeled away, exposing the twisted wreckage inside him. And he questioned his sanity. He questioned his worth as a man and as a father. He questioned everything he had ever believed in. But he did not question his determination to get his wife back. That was the only right and good thing he knew. He had to save his wife. That was the solid unswerving rock he navigated by.

Laura Ferren came again on a Wednesday evening. She went to Felice's first, having asked if Felice would discuss Alex. Felice was happy to cooperate. Then she was happy to watch Hana so that Laura Ferren could speak to Dan and Valerie without worrying about what the child heard. Dan had not been looking forward to the meeting, and he said as much to Valerie just before the psychologist arrived.

"All these shrink types are full of bologna," Valerie confided to him as he opened the door to let the psychologist in.

"I'm glad this worked out," Dr. Ferren said, stepping inside and shrugging out of her coat. "I wanted to speak to everyone, and it seemed easier for me to come to Bay Ridge than for the four of you to travel to my office." She extended her hand toward Valerie Vaughn. "I've been eager to meet you, Mrs.—"

"Valerie. Just call me Valerie, Doctor."

"Fine, and I'm Laura."

"How cozy," Valerie declared sarcastically. "Dan and Laura and Valerie all having a little visit."

Dan quickly moved them into the living room and poured decaffeinated coffee. Laura settled into a chair and pulled out her steno pad. Dan and Valerie took opposite ends of the couch.

"If you don't mind, Valerie, I'd like you to tell me about your relationship with your daughter. What sort of disagreements did you have?"

"I do mind! That's none of your business. And I don't see what the hell it's got to do with getting her out of that cult."

"It's imperative that I be able to establish an instant connection with her once she's located. To do that I have to be intimately familiar with her background."

Valerie rolled her eyes. Then she looked sideways at Dan and shrugged.

"Alex was a good little kid. Never gave me a moment's trouble even though I was a woman on my own—having a hard time of it and maybe not being as motherly as I should have been. But as soon as she started getting tits and a mind of her own . . . look out! She argued with everything. Gave me grief over everything. Thought I was failing her in a hundred ways."

"Could you give me an example?" Laura asked.

"Okay . . . When she first went to New York . . . See, she'd got this modeling contract—a real break, you know. I'd busted my butt for years trying to get her the opportunities I never got, and here she finally lands this modeling contract and she goes off to earn her fortune and not three weeks later she calls me on the phone crying. She wants me to come to New York and stay with her. Says she can't do it alone. And I said, 'Honey, you've got to do it alone because I can't give up my life to come hold your hand, and besides, we've all got to learn that when it comes right down to it—we are alone. No matter whether you're posing in front of a camera or selling condoms behind a drugstore counter, you've got to learn to make your way alone. That's the way the world is.'

"Well, a couple days went by and suddenly there she was, on my doorstep, all pathetic and weepy. Telling me how mean the people were in New York and how she didn't want to go back.

"I told her she damn sure would go back. I told her she could be rich and famous if she'd just toughen up a little. Not be such a whiny little self-centered brat. But . . . I guess she got to me with all the crying, because I softened up and told her okay, she could stay a few days before I packed her back off. I called the modeling agency and got it smoothed over with them—'cause the damn fool had actually walked out on a job.

"So I thought everything was fine, and the day comes when she's leaving and I tell her to pack and then I get busy with some things. It's getting close to time to drive her to the airport, so I start looking for her and don't find her. I was living in an apartment in Hollywood then. And I looked all over and finally I went down to the apartment laundry room."

Valerie drew in a deep breath, straightened her back, and lifted her chin as though facing an enemy.

"And there she was. Crumpled on the floor like a pile of dirty laundry. Bleeding all over. Blood sprayed across those white walls. Blood streaked down the washing machine. The razor blade lying there right beside her.

"And I shook her and shook her. And she opened her eyes and looked at me."

Valerie's voice caught. She swallowed hard.

"And I saw that she was willing to die just to punish me."

Silence fell in the room. Valerie dabbed at tears with a tissue. Laura watched Valerie. Dan sat very still, filled with a monstrous sadness.

He closed his eyes. Alex. Alex. Alex. The river had not been the first time. She had never told him about the razor blade, though he'd asked about the faint line of a scar on her arm. She'd brushed off his questions, saying that the scar was from a bicycle accident when she was young, and he'd believed her because it was only on one arm and because it was vertical and not what he'd imagined a wrist slashing would look like. Another lie uncovered. Another painful truth exposed. Yet he couldn't fault her for it. Instead he blamed himself. He thought that he must have failed her in some way that had made her unable to fully trust him.

"How old was Alexandra when this happened?" Laura asked quietly.

"What?"

"How old was your daughter when she came by herself to New York?"

"Oh . . . fourteen, I think. That's right. Fourteen."

Dan was stunned.

"What's wrong?" Valerie demanded. "That's the way the modeling business works these days. They get 'em young and then paint them up to look older. Skinny bodies and fresh faces are what sells. And if a girl hasn't made it by the time she's eighteen, then forget about it."

"Did she have any friends or relatives in New York?" Laura asked.

"No, but let me tell you . . . the modeling world is loaded with teenage girls, and there are all kinds of things set up for them. They've got home study schooling and group apartments where the girls can stay together. Believe me, I'd have killed for a deal like that when I was a teenager."

"What happened after the suicide attempt?" Laura asked.

"I called the agency. They were terrific. Set her up with a therapist and advanced her the money to pay for it."

"So she went back to New York?"

"Of course. She was on the fast track. People predicted she'd be big. Huge, even. Her first year in the business she'd already done *Vogue, French Vogue, Elle, Harper's, Mademoiselle* . . . and she had enough catalog deals to pay all her expenses for haircuts and laser prints for her book and all the other stuff that adds up so fast—and the twenty percent to the agency . . . and still make a profit! That's amazing for a girl's first year! What kind of mother would I have been if I'd let her throw all that away?"

Valerie fumbled in her purse for her cigarettes, shook

one out, then looked up at Dan as though just remembering. Sighing, she put the box back and dropped the purse.

"So your relationship was strained from then on?" Laura asked.

"It went up and down. As she made more money I tried to manage it for her, but that was a mistake." Valerie snorted ruefully. "She hated me for that."

"Did she give up her career then? I'm unclear about what happened that led her to where she met Dan."

Leaning back, suddenly very relaxed, Valerie waved her arm dismissively. "She was big. Magazine covers. Sweetheart catalog shoots all over the world. Her pick of designers for the runway shows. She was big and made big money, and she was right on the verge of becoming huge." Valerie raised her hand and held her thumb and index finger almost together. "She was this close to exploding." Valerie let her hand fall. "And she threw it all away. She sniffed it up her nose and shot it into her arm and partied her way right out of the business. Got so strung out she couldn't remember where she was or where she was supposed to go. Started showing up in the wrong country at the wrong time. Showing up with needle tracks. Twenty years old and she was over.

"They called me. I flew out and put her in a drug treatment center. She was furious at me for it. When she finally got out she tried to work again, but she'd been blacklisted. She went through the rest of her money—which wasn't much because she'd partied it all away—and then she went to the river. And that's where she met her knight in shining armor." Valerie chuckled sarcastically.

"That's exactly what she said when she called me later. Weeks after it had happened. I hadn't even known. Hadn't been able to reach her.

"She said she'd met a real live knight in shining armor and she was changing her life. Said she was going to learn to be normal, because she'd never learned it from me.

"She wouldn't tell me his name or what her address or phone number was. And none of the modeling people knew it either. It was like she'd vanished.

"But she called me. Called me all the time. Told me things. Screamed at me. Sometimes talked nice. She said she liked it that she had all the control. That I couldn't mess with her life at all.

"After she had Hana she got nicer. Started saying that she could see why I'd done some of the things I'd done. I begged to see the baby. Begged and begged. She liked that. And then, when the baby was six months old, she had me fly into Kennedy Airport and she drove out there and picked me up. We went to some dismal, very underwhelming shopping mall and ate, and I got to play with the baby. I thought she might give in and let me stay a few days, but she wouldn't. She said she was afraid I'd ruin her new life if she let me into it. So that night she took me back to the airport and I flew home.

"She let me do that every six months or so until the baby was three. Then she said it had to stop because she was afraid Hana would start remembering me and tell her father about seeing me."

Valerie sighed. "She was calling me pretty regularly, and I had hopes of someday having a normal family—you know, all of us getting together for holidays and stuff. Then I got the news about this cult business and it was instantly clear to me what she was doing. That's it. End of story."

"What is it that you think she's doing?" Laura probed.

"Why, it's just another kind of suicide attempt. That's what it is. Another way to destroy herself. So, what I want to know, Doctor, is exactly how in the hell you think you're going to get my daughter away from those bastards."

Dan left Laura and Valerie talking and walked over to Felice's to pick up Hana.

"Hi, Daddy!" Hana called. She was sprawled on the floor putting together a puzzle of the United States.

"Can I talk to you privately a minute?" Dan asked Felice in a low voice.

"Sure. Come into my workroom."

The walls in Felice's extra bedroom were covered with pinned-up sketches of clothing and photographs of models on runways. The drawing board was cluttered with sketches. A dressmaker's model and a sewing machine filled one corner.

Felice perched on the corner of a table. Dan just stood.

"What's wrong, Dan? You seem upset."

"I just heard about the modeling. You knew her then, didn't you?"

Felice's face fell, and her gaze shifted furtively away from his.

"Tell me, Felice."

"I promised Alex."

"Tell me!"

"Ohhh," she wailed. "Is this something Laura needs to know? To help Alex?"

"Yes," he lied.

"I knew her. I was a little into partying and fun. She was a lot into it. She always made the club scene."

"She was underage. How was she getting into clubs?"

"Models are never underage for anything. I don't care how young they are. Everybody wants them—the clubs, the rich playboys, the happening restaurants—everybody rolls out the red carpet for them.

"And with Xan . . . well . . . she was wild. Everybody had crushes on her. Me, too, I guess. Everybody wanted her at their parties because she was unpredictable and crazy . . . one of those strip-naked-and-jump-in-the-fountain types. Always the center of fun. But what's weird is that when I look back I don't believe she was actually having fun."

"Xan," Dan breathed.

"That was her modeling name. You know, spelled with an *X* but pronounced with a *Z*. Very exotic."

"Were you in touch with her the whole time? While she was in drug treatment and everything?"

"No. I knew she was finished in the business, but I had no idea where she went or what happened to her. She just sort of vanished. Then I moved out here to Bay Ridge, trying to escape from an old lover who wouldn't leave me alone, and one day I was walking on Third Avenue and I saw her. I couldn't believe it! There she was, looking all healthy and happy, with a little baby in a stroller.

"She kind of panicked when she recognized me. But we talked, and I understood where she was coming from— wanting to be very private and not let anybody in the fashion world know where she was." She shrugged apologetically. "And not wanting you to know about her modeling and all.

"I promised her secret was safe with me, and I think it was a relief for her, having someone she could be perfectly straight with. We got close real fast. I swore that I'd go along with her telling you we'd just met. And I got all attached to Hana, and . . . well, you know the rest."

Dan took several breaths. Xan. His wife. Whom he hadn't known at all.

"Was she . . ." He had to clear his throat. "Did she love me?"

"Oh, yes, Dan! She worshiped you. And she said she got pregnant because she thought you would be the best father in the world."

"She 'got' pregnant?"

Felice nodded. "That's what she said."

Dan put his hand to his head. She had intentionally become pregnant? Even though she knew about his dreams of going to graduate school? She had told him it was accidental. And she had said she'd have an abortion if he didn't want to be a father. He was the one who'd insisted that he would quit school and get a job so that they could have the baby. Now he saw that she had manipulated him into that. Had she been afraid that he wouldn't marry her under other circumstances?

"Was she faithful to me, Felice?"

"Yes. She never even noticed other men." Felice hesitated and toyed with her shirtsleeve. "I think she actually kind of disliked men. Except for you, of course. She'd had some pretty bad treatment by men during the first couple of years she modeled. Ugly stuff that she never has really wanted to talk much about. Anyway, it really made her have a negative attitude about men. One time she asked me sort of jokingly if I thought it was possible to teach a little girl to become a lesbian, because she said she hated the thought of Hana growing up and being abused by men.

"I told her that I didn't think she'd have much luck with that. I told her she ought to know herself—you're either gay or you're not. You don't learn it like you learn how to ride a bike or something."

Dan regarded her for a moment but did not ask the question on his mind. What difference did it make? He turned toward the door, but then turned back.

"How could this have happened, Felice? Was she unhappy?"

"Not really. But she was always feeling like something was missing from her life. And she was always trying to figure out what it was."

Hana sang and skipped on the way home. Dan was so despondent that her singing and lighthearted behavior annoyed him. He had to remind himself not to snap at her.

When they arrived back at the apartment Laura had already gone. Valerie was waiting. Her arms crossed over her chest and a steely look in her eye.

"Go on now, Hana honey. Start getting ready for bed and Valerie will be along in a minute. You go pick out which animals get to sleep with us tonight."

As soon as Hana was out of hearing range Valerie shook her finger in the air.

"That woman has some nerve! You should have heard the things she said after you left! All kind of insinuendoes about my being a bad mother."

Dan didn't bother to point out that she could use *innuendo* or *insinuation* but they did not make a word together. "I'm sure she didn't mean—" he began but was immediately cut off.

"Don't you defend that bitch! I know her type. All saintly and goody-goody but with a knife hidden behind her back. She gets her kicks from other people's misery. And I don't see how in the hell she's going to get Alex away from those loonies. She'll never be able to do it."

"I have some doubts, too, Valerie, but she's all we've got. And she's supposed to know what she's doing."

"You mean there's no one else out there in the whole effing country who gets people out of cults?"

"There are people. In fact, there's a very famous deprogrammer whose number is right over on the counter. But it costs thousands of dollars. And I don't have thousands of dollars. The cult used Alex to take everything. Money, car, the works."

A wide smile spread across Valerie's face. "Why didn't

you say so, my dear man? I've got money. I've got plenty of money. You get on that phone and talk to that famous guy right this minute, and we'll give Miss Nosy Doctor the boot!"

The number for Everett May was answered by a recording that instructed callers to leave a detailed message with not only their number and the nature of their business but also the specifics of whoever had referred them. Dan did so, giving both his home and work numbers, and then waited anxiously for May to contact him. The call came to his office the following afternoon as he sat at his drawing board.

"It's for Dan," Wendell Crispin announced and held out the receiver.

Dan got up and went to their shared desk, turning away from them as he spoke. "Hello?"

"Dan Behr—this is Everett May."

Dan breathed out a great sigh of relief. "I'm so glad to hear from you." He glanced sideways at his colleagues. Karen Lai was working, Crispin was pretending to work, and Rich Medford was openly listening. "Could I call you back from another phone?"

"Is this one bugged?" May asked with some alarm.

"No. But I'm here at my desk and—"

"I don't want you to call me back. Just keep it simple. Don't say too much. I'll know what you mean."

Dan tried to ignore the eyes and ears that were focused on him. His three co-workers knew that strange things were going on in his life, but he had continued to evade their questions.

"Umm . . . My wife has been—"

"Yes. I know your whole situation," May said. "I'm already working with Ben Khadra."

"Have you located his daughter?"

"We've located two cult compounds, and we're observing to see which one his daughter is at. You want us to find your wife now, too, right?"

"Yes."

"Khadra said he explained the expenses to you and you had a problem with money."

"That's been solved."

"Good. We have to put this together fast, then. Let me check something here." There were rustling sounds along with the faint click of computer keys. "I need you to meet me at the St. Louis airport tomorrow. Take the seven a.m. TWA flight from La Guardia. I'll be at your gate when you get off."

"St. Louis? I don't—"

"I'm not doing this without a face-to-face meeting. St. Louis is the only place I can get to tomorrow that's also easy for you. We'll do our business and both be on flights out within a few hours."

Swallowing his uncertainty, Dan asked, "How will I know you?"

"I'll know you."

"But how? Should I wear a certain color or something?"

"I'll be able to recognize you, Dan. That's part of my business."

Dan paused to absorb this. The man sounded like a detective or someone equally resourceful. That was good.

"Bring me ten thousand for now. Cash. Hundreds are fine. And I'll need pictures of your wife. Recent ones. From different angles."

"All right."

"When we make our move—which could be soon, the way things are looking—you'll need to plan on at least a week, possibly two weeks, away from home. So start making your arrangements now. Get things set up so you can leave on a couple days' notice."

Dan's pulse escalated. "Okay."

"We can win here, Dan. This is just another megalomaniac asshole with visions of creating his own empire. We'll beat him and we'll take her back."

After Dan hung up he wanted to leap and dance around the room shouting Yes! Yes!

*We'll beat him and we'll take her back.* Those words ignited him. As much as he respected and trusted Laura Ferren, this was what he wanted. This approach inspired confidence and hope. Everett May was not proposing an attempt at quietly persuading Alex to come home. Everett

May was going to war. And that felt very good. That felt right.

He returned to sit at his board.

"I won't be in tomorrow," he said, trying to sound casual. "And I'm going to be gone for around two weeks in the near future."

All three stared at him; Karen worried, Crispy incredulous, Medford angry.

"What the fuck is going on with you?" Medford demanded. "It wouldn't be so bad if you were just sinking your own boat—but you're screwing the rest of us, too. How are we supposed to meet our project deadlines with you not carrying your weight?"

"I'm sorry," Dan said.

"We do all have vacation time that we deserve to take," Karen Lai put in timidly.

"But not in the middle of our busiest time!" Medford shouted. "And not when the whole fucking department is under the guillotine!"

Wendell Crispin stood and waved his arms like an umpire declaring a runner safe at home. "Calm down, everybody."

"I'm sorry," Dan repeated. "It's not a vacation. I wouldn't do this to you if it weren't something serious."

He looked from face to face. And suddenly he could not keep it inside any longer.

"My wife has been taken by a cult and I'm going with a deprogrammer to get her back."

Their mouths fell open. Their eyes widened. They gaped at him speechlessly.

"That's it," he said. "You'll just have to work around my absence."

Dan tried Laura Ferren several times that afternoon. He dreaded telling her his decision, but it was something that had to be done before she wasted any more of her time or resources on his behalf. Finally he caught her between patients.

"Dan? Why didn't you give my assistant a number where I could return your call?"

"Because I'm at work and I didn't want to talk to you in front of everyone."

"I see. Can you talk now?"

"Yes, I'm hiding at an empty desk."

"What is it, then? Do you have new information about Alex?"

"No." He drew in a deep breath. "I appreciate all your efforts and your concern, Laura; but Valerie has the money and she wants a deprogrammer."

"So this is all Valerie's decision?"

"Mine, too," he admitted.

"I see. Who's the deprogrammer?"

"Everett May. Do you know him?"

"I certainly know of him. He's legendary."

"Please, Laura. Try to understand. Alex was taken from me so suddenly . . . and it feels right to take her back . . . to rescue her as quickly as possible."

"Regardless of her wishes? Regardless of the trauma deprogramming can cause?"

"Her wishes! She's not functioning under her own free will. Whatever wishes she has have been planted there by the cult. And as to trauma—nothing we do to her will be any worse than what those lunatics have already done."

"Oh, Dan . . ." She hesitated a moment as though struggling with how much to argue, then, regretfully, she said, "I can tell that your mind is made up, but be very careful. For yourself as well as for her."

"I will."

"And promise me . . . if there's anything I can do . . . or even if you just want to talk . . . that you'll call me."

"Okay. Thanks."

A thin ribbon of doubt unfurled within him, but he pushed it aside. Laura's gentle tactics were not what was needed here. Everett May was the answer. This was war.

When Dan walked out of the jetway into the St. Louis airport terminal, no one waved or caught his eye. Though he did not know anything about Everett May's appearance, he scanned the faces in the crowd of people around the gate. No one seemed even remotely interested in his arrival. Nervously, he moved off to the side and waited.

Ten minutes passed and the activity around the gate calmed. The last of the passengers and then the flight crew emerged from the jetway and headed off down the bustling main corridor of the terminal. A cleaning crew went aboard the plane, and the passengers waiting to be called for the next flight out on that aircraft began stirring in their seats.

"Will Mr. Dan Behr please come to the check-in desk," the ticket agent announced over the microphone.

Dan rushed forward and identified himself. The woman smiled and handed him a small leather daybook. "Here, Mr. Behr. You left this over by the window and another passenger found it."

He thanked her and moved away. Protruding from the book was a ticket folder with his name printed prominently across the top. He pulled out the folder and opened it. Inside were instructions. May wanted him to go to a particular cocktail lounge, sit in a particular spot, and wait.

Exhilarated but slightly annoyed with all the subterfuge, he hurried toward the meeting. At least he hoped it was the meeting. In spite of his violent experience with the cult and the professor's paranoia, Everett May's secret agent maneuvers seemed excessive and slightly ridiculous to him. His annoyance built through two bowls of pretzels and a beer before a man slid into the seat beside him. The man was dark-skinned and looked like a hardworking fellow who was at the airport to pick up his wife or mother, still in his forest-green mechanic's pants and shirt, "Al's Garage" embroidered over his pocket. He carried a worn brown canvas coat and a Cardinals baseball cap.

"I'm sorry," Dan said. "I'm waiting for someone and saving that seat for him."

The man glanced sideways. "I'm Everett," he said quietly. "Sorry about the security measures, but I had to watch you for a while to make sure you weren't being followed."

"You're Everett May?"

The man nodded.

Dan absorbed this news along with May's apologies about security. "Who would follow me?" he finally asked.

"Well, it'd most likely be me they were aiming for. I'm on a lot of cult shit lists. And I've stayed ahead of them all by watching my back and never taking anything for granted."

"But no one has a reason to follow *me*."

"Could be they'd use you to find me. I don't know who you've talked to, who you've said my name to. I'm always careful. Always. Like now. I'm in disguise, and I checked to make sure you weren't tailed."

Dan studied the man. He was overweight, like an athlete who'd gone soft with age. He had a wide face with hazelnut-colored skin. His vaguely Asian eyes were a muddy green, and the shaggy ruff of hair sticking out from beneath his ball cap was a basic medium brown. What parts were real and what parts disguise?

"How do I know you're Everett May?" Dan asked.

The man chuckled softly. "You, my friend, have to trust."

Dan considered leaving. He didn't like the situation or the man's undercover game, and he had the feeling that he was being used in some way. Yet he could not make himself get up.

"You've got the money and the pictures?" May asked.

"They're in the bag between my feet."

May nodded. "I've had some more news," he said, then paused. His slow, deliberate manner of speaking was irritating for Dan after so many years in New York, the fast-talk capital of the nation. He wanted to grab May's shirt collar and shake the news out of him.

"My surveillance operative called in last night. He thinks he's seen the Khadra girl. Now, with these pictures, we can watch for your wife, and as soon as we get the fix on her, we'll take them both."

Suddenly all of Dan's misgivings were drowned by a great tide of hope. They had seen Bibi. This was his chance. This was Alex's chance.

"What do I need to do?" he asked.

"Just wait. Be ready to leave on two days' notice. My people think that all the victims from the Manhattan house were taken to the same compound."

"It's hard to believe this cult has multiple compounds." May nodded.

"Why hasn't anyone heard of First Light if it's so big?"

"Nobody ever heard of Aum Supreme Truth until the Tokyo subway was gassed."

"You think First Light is that powerful?" Dan asked in horror.

"No. I was just using the example."

May waved the bartender over, asked for a Dr Pepper, and settled for a Coke.

Dan waited. May paid for the soda and drank. He ate some pretzels.

"What do you know about these people?" Dan asked, losing patience.

"Mmmm . . ." May compressed his lips into a thoughtful, considering expression, and Dan realized that the man was deciding how much to tell him.

"I deserve some straight answers, Everett."

"First Light isn't the cult's name. That was just a shadow group created for the big membership drive. What we're dealing with here is The Ark."

"The Ark?"

"Yup. Started in the Los Angeles area around twenty years ago as Life Lessons, one of those self-help, mind-expanding EST-type deals. Life Lessons signed people up for sessions and therapies and something they called Awakening Lectures. The founder and guiding force was a charismatic guru type who called himself Noah."

May paused as though mulling over the information he possessed. "You can research this stuff yourself, but I'll give you the general picture. Life Lessons caught on with the in-crowd. It was considered legitimate and Noah was in demand as a speaker—film industry dinners, government functions, exclusive clubs, everything . . . he was a real star. And he raked in the money. He had it coming in from all directions—average citizens handing over their paychecks for his sessions, and the mega-rich naming his organization in their wills. The guy had people convinced that he had the answers to world peace, the preservation of the environment, illegal immigrants, big government, *and* constructing a workable social safety net. He was good. Real good."

May shook his head in grudging admiration. "Brilliant, in fact. And I can't get a handle on how much was calculated for show and how much was sincere. I mean, the guy actually has some interesting ideas, and I haven't been able to decide whether he's a total crook or an off-the-wall dreamer or a real visionary."

May finished his soda.

"The Ark was the spin-off, the utopian commune that grew out of Life Lessons. First it was just a couple of housefuls of people on the outskirts of L.A. Then it was an old farm. Then Noah got some rich folks to buy him a big mountain paradise and he built a real compound. But after the group moved to the mountains nobody gave it a second thought. All of the members were adults who chose to go to the mountains after a long involvement with Life Lessons. There were no surprises, no sudden conversions or rumors of force. In fact, there were people . . . druggies, hookers, gays . . . who wanted to go but were denied the privilege."

"So," Dan said, more bitterly than he'd intended, "everyone thought Noah and his bunch were perfectly harmless."

"Yup. So as far as the cult watchers knew the only complaints about The Ark were from disgruntled heirs who didn't like the fact that old Aunt Tilly had left part of her fortune to a cult, but heck, you get complaints like that about money left to the Humane Society and the Girl Scouts."

May shrugged. "The Ark was seen as a group of people who had banded together to live a simpler life and pursue the eternal questions that the rest of us don't have time for. Even the cynics kind of respected it—or at least the idea of it. Noah spent more and more of his time at The Ark's mountain compound and eventually dropped his public speaking appearances. The Life Lessons organization folded. And after a few years everybody forgot about him and the Ark. It just seemed to fade away."

"But how could they have been sucking in people through First Light without anyone realizing?"

May smiled without amusement. "They weren't. Looks like they've been busy as beavers building compounds— there's two that we know of, another we suspect—and they were taking in new members slowly . . . stragglers and relatives of existing members . . . people who showed up at the gate wanting to join after reading Noah's book."

"Book?" Dan asked in astonishment.

"Yup. *End Time.* It's a rambling lecture about humanity's future downfall, and it's an underground favorite. Attracts all kinds of nuts and would-be warrior types."

May shifted and glanced around the room, then checked his watch. "Anyway," he continued, "they apparently came to a point where they wanted more bodies or new blood or whatever, and they did this First Light business. Spent a lot of money on it, too. They set up what they called II centers, II standing for Intensive Indoctrination. Those were the retreat houses in New York City, San Francisco, and Houston. They targeted colleges, covering the three areas with a net of lectures or meditation sessions or whatever—all of it designed to identify potential converts and lure them into a weekend retreat, where they could be hit with the total immersion-in-conversion routine. They were looking for young healthy people and hoping to bag some with skills.

"For whatever reasons . . . whether there was too much heat or whether they got all the new people they wanted . . . all the First Light operations have closed down now."

Dan cradled his head in his hands. There it was. Finally. An explanation for the inexplicable. A picture of the shadowy monster that had opened its mouth and swallowed his wife.

"Do you think they're hurting her?" he asked.

May was silent for a moment. "Depends on your definition of *hurt,* I guess. But they sure aren't doing her any good."

It was late by the time Dan arrived back in New York and tiptoed through his quiet apartment. His bedroom door cracked open and Valerie stuck her head out, hair disheveled from sleeping.

"What'd the deprogrammer say?" she asked.

"He says it shouldn't be long. They think they know where she is."

"Good."

"How was Hana today?"

"Same as always. She drew a picture for you. It's on your pillow."

Pleased, he started toward Hana's room, where he was sleeping now.

"Oh, and you had a message. A woman called. Says she works with you." Valerie's emphasis on *woman* and *says* implied suspicion.

"Karen Lai?"

"Yeah. That was her name. She said to call her tonight no matter how late."

"She's a co-worker in my group. And she's married."

"Uh-huh," Valerie said. "Watch out for the married ones."

As he headed for the phone it occurred to him that Valerie's view of all females as unscrupulous predators of men was perhaps a reflection of her own nature. But he didn't dwell on the thought because he had Karen's call to worry about. He was afraid it concerned her husband's drug problem, and he felt so overwhelmed by his own disaster that he could barely face hers.

She answered on one ring, whispering in response to his greeting, "My husband is asleep, and I don't want to wake him."

That confirmed the problem for Dan. "I'm so sorry, Karen. What happened?"

"Oh . . ." She hesitated. "Actually . . . I think we're doing okay on that, Dan. I told him I couldn't live with him and watch him destroying himself, and that I would leave him if he didn't get help. That probably doesn't sound very caring to you . . . after what you watched your father go through . . . but I decided I wasn't as strong as your father was. I decided that I could easily get taken down, too, if I tried to save him. And besides, I don't think I could respect anyone who didn't at least try to save himself."

"Oh," Dan said, uncertain how to respond.

"Knowing you, you probably think that sounds cold. But my husband understood. It was hard for him and he didn't like it, but he understood. He's already started treatment."

There was an awkward silence.

"That's not what I was calling you about though, Dan. I . . . oh, shit—there's no good way to say this. You're fired. RIFed. Dreeson tried to protect you, but Medford had been whining about your plans and the grapevine carried it over Dreeson's head up to the firing squad."

"I'm fired?"

"They already sent Security to box up your stuff. When you show up you'll be held at Reception and then escorted in to get the official bullet. You won't even be allowed to say good-bye."

"I can't believe this."

"I just had to warn you. I don't know how you want to handle it, but at least now the execution won't be a surprise."

"Thanks, Karen."

"I'm going to miss you, Dan." She sniffled, and he could tell she was crying. "Crispy is pretty upset, too. We'd both like to strangle Medford, but he's feeling so guilty that he's punishing himself."

"Be careful. Hang on to your own job."

"Keep in touch, okay?"

"Sure," he said.

He put the phone down and stared at the floor. Later the outrage and anger would come. Later he would face the despair. But at the moment he felt nothing. He was completely numb.

# Chapter 8

Dan was fired by a man he had never met. Escorted by Security into a stranger's office, he was offended at first, but as he listened to the explanation of his severance package, presented with the clipped precision of a pro, he began to appreciate the cleanness of it. With a stranger there was no emotional agenda. It was all details. Sterile as a surgical procedure. After they were finished Dan asked if he could see Lester Dreeson.

"Dreeson?" the surgeon asked.

"I understand that I'm not allowed to go anywhere in the building or speak to anyone, but I thought maybe Dreeson could come here, just for a quick good-bye. The security guards can watch if you want."

"Lester Dreeson isn't with us any longer. He left this morning, just minutes before your arrival."

"You mean he was fired, too?" Dan asked in disbelief.

"No one is being fired. We're experiencing a reduction in force."

"But he didn't quit voluntarily, right?"

"That information is confidential."

Dreeson gone. Somehow that was even more devastating than his own debacle. Dan left the building and started walking with no particular destination in mind. The day was mild. He traveled six blocks, then stopped. Where was he going? What should he do? He had not told Valerie why Karen Lai had called, and so she didn't know what he had left that morning knowing. He was not ready to tell her now, either, so that meant he couldn't go home. He wondered where Dreeson had gone. Maybe there was an informal club of fired architects that met somewhere.

He stood for several minutes on the sidewalk, feeling dazed. Then, in the spirit of a drinker heading for a bar to drown in, he went uptown to the Cooper-Hewitt, a turn-of-the-century brick-and-limestone mansion that housed the National Museum of Design collections. And there he lost himself, wandering through the venerable Renaissance-Georgian building, studying the architectural drawings and browsing through 17th- and 18th-century architecture books in the reference library. For a while there was no fired architect or distraught husband or inadequate father. Then the museum closed and he was thrust back into awareness.

It occurred to him that he could go home at his usual time, just as though returning from work, and Valerie would assume that everything was normal. Then he could tell her later, when the wound wasn't so fresh. He started south on Fifth Avenue. As he walked, he tried to imagine a day, lots of days, with absolutely nothing scheduled. Unstructured days. Such a notion would have seemed preposterous to him before. His time had always been claimed by the demands of school or work or both. When he was young he had had school plus helping with his father's sideline business of furniture repair. After his father's death he had had school and part-time work plus caring for his mother. With marriage had come a heavy concentration of work and the responsibilities of being a husband and father. Schedules and routines had been the normal course of his life. Nothing to complain about. Nothing that even entered his conscious consideration. That was just the way things were. And he realized now that he had always thrived on commitment. Duty. Purpose. That was who he was.

So who was he now?

Walking down the avenue amid scores of brisk, brief-case-toting workers on their way home, he felt a sudden wave of shame. He had been rejected by his company. He had been tested and found lacking. He was a failure.

The rational part of his brain immediately countered these feelings with arguments: It was common now for Americans to lose their jobs at some point in their working lives, and there was no stigma attached. It did not mean he was a bad or worthless man. But those rational, reasonable arguments skimmed along the surface while the despair lodged deep in his heart and gut.

When he arrived home that night he worried that his expression or manner might give him away, and it was with some trepidation that he greeted his mother-in-law and hugged his daughter. But there were no questions. No suspicions. He decided to tell them the following morning, and he awoke at his usual time intending to have a serious talk with Valerie before Hana roused. But Valerie was in a bad mood, stalking around the apartment in her satin robe, her high-heeled mule slippers clicking a staccato on the hardwood floors, muttering complaints about New York and about the neighbor, Mrs. Svensen, and about the apartment's tiny kitchen and bathroom, and about the deprogrammer's taking so long to get Alex out, and he could not bring himself to interrupt her and blurt out his news. So he acted out the charade of going to work. And in the days that followed he continued the pattern, leaving in the morning as usual and returning home as usual, never lying yet living a lie, and assuaging his guilt with the thought that he was protecting them by not revealing the truth.

He left messages on both Crispin's and Medford's home answering machines. Neither man returned his call. Their shunning of him struck deeply. But then, he realized that their rebuff wasn't surprising for they had no commonality but work, no bond beyond work. He did not try to contact Karen Lai because he was afraid of intruding during a time when she had as many problems as she could handle, and he believed that if she wanted to talk to him she would call.

He read the help-wanted section of the *New York Times* without seeing anything promising, and he consoled himself with the thought that he could not take on a new job anyway—not with the deprogramming on the horizon. Once that was accomplished, once his wife was home and safe, then he would go out and find another job. He would find something. Anything. And then he would start saving again for a future in which he was able to do work that mattered to him. Though that future seemed a little less bright and a lot less certain now.

He phoned Dreeson's home repeatedly without success, finally speaking with the man's wife. Immediately he realized that Dreeson, too, had kept his job loss a secret and was pretending to go to work every day. If he ran into Lester Dreeson on the streets of Manhattan he wondered, what would happen? Would they bare their souls to each other and confess to the lies they were telling at home? Would they slap each other on the back, curse HTO's new management policies, and try to impress each other with tales of great job prospects on the horizon? Or would they stumble through an awkward exchange, shaking hands, muttering condolences, and then escaping to their separate miseries? Probably the latter. In spite of his admiration for Dreeson there was no real connection between them.

But then, who was he really connected to? Losing his job and his daily interactions with co-workers had left a void that he could not fill. Other than his fractured family, who else was there? It seemed pathetic to him that the only names that came to his mind were Felice Navarre, who was his wife's best friend, and Laura Ferren, whose only involvement was professional. He had no friends beyond work. Was this what Dreeson had meant when he'd said, "They isolate us. They rob us of any chance for meaningful companionship beyond our office or our bedroom"?

He wasn't sure he knew how to make friends anymore. Or that it was even possible. Who in his world had time for friends or community after being sucked dry by work and then exhausted by the demands of home and family? And it hit him, in a great lightninglike burst, that the perfect life he'd been leading had not been so wonderful. The man he'd become was not the man he'd aspired to be. The world he'd dreamed was not the world he'd made.

And this realization shook him and left him reeling. Hadn't he worked hard? Hadn't he strived to be a good person according to his father's teachings? Hadn't he followed the rules? Hadn't he always tried to do what was moral and right?

Yet everything had gone wrong.

He felt as though he had lost the path somewhere. He didn't know when it had happened or how to get back to the path—or whether the path had simply ended without his noticing. The territory he found himself in was foreign and threatening, and he didn't know whether to go forward or back. And he was weary enough, disheartened enough, that all he wanted to do was huddle inside himself and give up.

After his first day at the Cooper-Hewitt, he spent his "work" time wandering and sitting on park benches. He felt the seductive pull of the streets, the lure of anonymity, and he began to understand those stories about troubled people who have resources, who have family, yet who choose to be homeless. There was a dark appeal to dropping completely out of society. It harked back to that most basic of reactions: All right, then, I won't play anymore.

His bench sitting ended when it poured rain. He considered indoor options. There was nothing he wanted to do, no place he wanted to go. Even the museums he loved held no interest for him now. He was, in fact, repelled by the idea of entertainment or stimulation. The one faint beacon that still glowed for him was the rescue of his wife. The defeat of the cult. He thought of all the cult information in the library that he hadn't had time to read. Maybe he should look at it now. He would at least be dry there.

Though a weight of pessimism rode on his shoulders and he didn't believe he could learn anything significant or make a difference, he went to the Central Research Library. He forced himself through the mechanics of call slips and waited for his selections to be retrieved from the miles of sealed-off underground stacks. Then he moved to a spot in the great open cathedral of a reading room and began to read. Hours flew by. He hurried out to buy a notebook so he could record important details, then he rushed back. And so it was that the nightmare of his wife's situation became Dan Behr's salvation.

A week passed in this way. Finally, he summoned the strength to tell Valerie that he'd been fired, though without indicating exactly when, and he told her that he did not think he should look for another job until after the deprogramming. She said supportive things and agreed completely about delaying a job search, but he could not miss the note of schadenfreude. Her daughter's shining knight had been unseated, and she was glorying in the fall.

"Your daddy doesn't have a job anymore," Behr heard her saying to Hana as the beginning of any number of sentences. "Now that you don't have a job anymore . . ." she said to him at every opportunity.

Tension built between them in the confines of the apartment. Just when a blowout seemed imminent, the call came. The deprogramming was scheduled. In two days he had to be on an airplane.

He could not sleep at all that night. At dawn, he finally rose, dressed, walked to Mr. Chin's for the *Times* and then to Sally's to have breakfast and read. He had finished eating and was about to go home to see Hana before she went to school when he came across a small obituary.

### *Lester Dreeson, 54, Architect*

Lester Cobby Dreeson, formerly of Hodder, Tang, and Orloff Architectural and Engineering Associates, died Tuesday at his family vacation home in the Adirondacks. Mr. Dreeson won a number of international architecture awards and competitions in his early career working as an independent. He joined HTO at the firm's inception and was quoted in a magazine article as saying that he hoped to find a wider audience for his work through the newly formed company.

The cause of death was a gunshot wound, apparently accidentally inflicted while Mr. Dreeson was cleaning an antique pistol.

He made his home in Scarsdale and is survived by his wife, Doris; his son, Derek, a college student in Boston; his daughter Deane Hamy of Tempe, Arizona; and his daughter from a previous marriage, Mindy Dees of Las Vegas.

With Lester Dreeson heavily on his mind, Dan had followed all of Everett May's instructions. He flew to Sacramento, California, with only a carry-on bag. He was not able to rest on the long series of flights. He was not able to eat. He could not concentrate on the pages of the magazine he flipped through. Now, waiting at the luggage claim area, he was tense and edgy.

A thin man in a black cowboy hat stood at a far wall. May had said he was sending a relative from the Navajo reservation, and though Dan had never had any experience with Navajos, this man appeared promising. He had sun-leathered brown skin and sharply defined cheekbones, and he was wearing an impressive amount of silver and turquoise.

Dan approached him. "Excuse me . . ."

"Who're you looking for?" the man asked, his manner brusque and guarded, his speech toneless and lacking in normal rhythm.

"A relative from the reservation," Dan answered as he'd been instructed.

"Who're you?"

"Dan Behr."

"You don't look like your picture," the man said.

"Well, it's me."

The man nodded, then turned, indicating with a faint jerk of his head that Dan should accompany him.

As he walked to the parking lot, several steps behind Everett May's silent relative, Dan's tension expanded into a buoyant elation. This was really happening. He was going to get her back.

They drove east into a moonless night. Dan drifted off to sleep for a while and when he woke they were hugging the sides of mountains on narrow curving roads, headlights slicing through total blackness. The man was named Julian Begay. If he knew anything about the plans he wasn't saying so. He wasn't saying much of anything. He was, in fact, the epitome of the taciturn Native American.

As soon as the thought occurred to Dan he chastised himself for letting a stereotype influence him. No. He refused to accept stereotypes. There had to be other reasons for Begay's behavior. Which made Dan wonder if the man disliked him or perhaps disliked whites in general.

"I've never been in mountains like this before," Dan remarked, nervous enough to risk trying conversation again.

"Me neither," Julian Begay said, which was disconcerting because the man was negotiating the dangerous curves at a good rate of speed.

"Ah ... have you noticed that there aren't any guardrails? And that it's straight down from the edge?"

"Everett said you sleep now." Begay jerked his head toward the opening that had been fashioned from the back window of the pickup truck, connecting the cab to the attached camper shell.

Dan looked at the opening.

"Crawl through," Begay said.

Dan pulled himself into the Naugahyde tunnel, banged his shoulder, thrust forward, and fell into the dark camper. There he lay sprawled across the huge mattress, suddenly so tired that he hadn't the energy to pull the folded quilts up. The metal camper shell vibrated softly around him and the tires hummed against the road and he spiraled down into a deep bottomless sleep.

"Get on out of there. We're burning daylight."

Dan awoke, completely disoriented. A man's head was sticking in the back door of the camper. It was dawn.

"Good sleeping in there, isn't it?" the man said. "Like it myself. We've got about four hours till they come to town. You hungry?"

Dan rubbed his eyes and climbed out of the back of the camper. The truck was parked behind a stand of trees at a small roadside picnic area. There were no other vehicles and no other people. In every direction was a picture postcard vista of rugged peaks and towering pines. The man who had awakened him bore few similarities to the man he'd met in the St. Louis airport. He was of medium height and rangy. The brown skin was still the same but his eyes were black now. His kinky hair was graying and closely cropped beneath a black cowboy hat. He was no longer slumped and downtrodden. He carried himself with authority and radiated energy, rather like a business tycoon on holiday in his jeans and sheepskin coat.

"Hello, Everett," Dan said. "Where are we?"

"About halfway between the town of Calder and the cult's compound."

"Where's your car?"

"Julian stopped and picked me up some ways back. You slept through the whole thing."

Dan stretched and took a deep breath. The air was thin and crisp. Brand-new air. Tangy with the scent of pine.

"Hike on out there in the trees and take a piss," May said. "Breakfast is waiting."

When Dan returned from his nature walk he found his two companions seated on large flat rocks set well back in the trees. They were huddled together, speaking in the measured, sibilant tones of the Navajo language. Julian Begay was animated, relating something with obvious amusement, but as soon as he saw Dan his expression deadened.

May gestured toward the pile of wrapped sandwiches and three thermoses that had been arranged in the center of the flat rock. "Come and get it."

"I'll eat in the truck," Dan said, reaching for a sandwich.

"Sit down," May ordered.

They ate for a while without speaking, and Dan became aware of all the movement and sound that surrounded them. Scratching and chattering and shuffling. Calling and cawing and singing.

"How did you get into deprogramming?" Dan asked.

May glanced at Julian Begay, and the older man gave an almost imperceptible nod.

"I grew up real close to my cousin—Uncle Julian's son. After high school I went into the Marines, and Tsosie, my cousin, went away to college on a track scholarship. I was happy and a gung-ho Marine, but Tsosie hated leaving the reservation and felt like a fish out of water at that eastern college. Three years into it, when he was a junior, he went into a bad depression, and he wrote letters to me and to Uncle Julian about how he didn't want to disappoint everyone who was counting on him to get that college diploma, but he didn't know if he was going to make it. Then the letters stopped. He disappeared from campus. Nobody knew where he'd gone.

"Uncle Julian tried everything and then called me. I took a leave, and we tracked him to a cult that had been doing campus recruiting. I told Uncle Julian, no problem, I'd just go jerk him out of there and bring him home." May inhaled and exhaled in a deep sigh of regret. "I had no clue what I was up against."

"But you got him out?" Dan asked.

May's jaw hardened, and he studied the ground a moment. "I marched in there like a Marine, knocked some heads together, and dragged him out. Then I threw him into a car and started driving back to Window Rock, shouting at him and lecturing him, telling him how much he was hurting his father. He was like a walking ghost. Wouldn't speak. Didn't act like he even recognized me.

"After a day of straight driving I checked us into a nice motel. I'd stopped being mad and thought I'd try to get him to relax with me . . . eat a good meal . . . maybe take a swim in the pool. We went up to the room. Soon as I stepped into the bathroom and left him alone, he jumped out the window. We were on the third floor."

There was so much pain in Everett May's strong face that Dan had to look away.

"I blamed myself, but Julian made me see that it was the cult that was responsible. I took fighting them, fighting all cults, as my personal battle, and I saw right away that most of it had to be fought with this"—he tapped his forehead—"because that's where all the battles take place. That's the big doomsday weapon that's turned against people—their own minds. I enrolled in college and learned all I could. Took classes in religion and philosophy and psychology. Saw that all cults were just tools for tyrannical egomaniacs. And eventually decided that what I most wanted to do was help people one at a time so they wouldn't end up like my cousin."

Julian Begay said something in Navajo and May smiled sadly.

There was a long silence.

"How do cults instill their victims with such fear of being saved?" Dan asked quietly.

"By 'saved' I assume you mean saved from the cult—

and you're talking about the distress and fear that victims show when someone tries to get them out and return them to their normal lives."

"Yes."

"Some people think it's related to the Stockholm syndrome, where victims begin to identify with their kidnappers, but I see it as a lot less exotic than that. I see it as a twisting around of some basic human needs and insecurities. If you think about it, at any given time most people have something that they'd like to be saved from—unhappiness, depression, loneliness, stress, emptiness, joblessness, addiction, self-hatred, uncertainty, bad grades in school, divorce, thinning hair . . . you name it. Cults catch people during vulnerable periods and offer a sort of blanket salvation, saving people by taking control of their lives and eliminating free will. Do you follow me?"

"I'm not sure."

"It's like a return to childhood, where you're taken care of and you're not responsible for making your own decisions anymore."

"But that wouldn't necessarily cure depression or stress or thinning hair," Dan said.

"The surrender of self feels so good that it seems like the cult has taken away every burden. People feel like they've been saved because they no longer have choice or the power to change things, and so the weight of changing or curing whatever was wrong is lifted from them. And in some cases they actually have been saved. Addicts are cleaned up because they no longer have access to substances. Joblessness is cured by joining a commune-style cult because work is then assigned by the cult. Lots of psychological problems are cured because the cult keeps people so busy and exhausted and overwhelmed with rhetoric that they never have an opportunity to think or to realize that their lives still aren't perfect. Do you follow what I'm saying now?"

"Yes."

"So—it's not that people resist being returned to their normal lives because they're afraid of being saved. They believe the cult saved them from their other lives. The cult *is* the savior. And outsiders are seen as trying to rip them out of paradise. Which means that what I have to do is convince them that their cult's leader is a false savior. That the cult is based on lies and manipulations. Then I show them that true salvation is in returning to the real world and the people who love them."

"What did my wife need to be saved from? Why was she susceptible?"

"You can answer that better than me, Dan."

"I thought she was happy, but now . . . I don't know anymore."

"What's important now is that we get her out. Then you can start working together on what went wrong."

Dan nodded. He stared at the sky, wishing he could escape from the unbearable intensity. He felt as if he'd been turned inside out and scraped raw. Julian got up and wandered off through the trees. May put his cowboy hat in his lap, leaned back against a tree, and closed his eyes. Dan studied him. His skin was several shades darker than Julian's, and his close-cropped graying hair was kinky. Physically, he appeared black rather than Navajo, yet he spoke the language and called Julian his uncle. He was an intriguing man. A powerful man. The kind of man who, Dan imagined, could have been a successful cult leader.

Julian Begay reappeared from his walk and spoke to May.

May nodded, reflected for a moment, then looked at Dan. "He thinks this is a spiritually pure place. A good place to start out from.

"He also apologizes to you for speaking so much Navajo. He doesn't like to speak English because it makes him sound like a child." May cast a proud and affectionate look at Begay. "That's very humiliating for a respected man like my uncle."

Dan met Julian Begay's dark eyes. He felt a generalized shame and inadequacy far greater than anything warranted by the sum of his own behaviors.

Suddenly Begay's eyes twinkled with amusement.

"All good whites think Custer was their father," he said in his elementary toneless English.

\* \* \*

While they ate sandwiches and drank coffee, May finally explained his plans.

"She's been going into town on Fridays, usually with three other women and a male driver. Two women go to the grocery store. The third goes to either a fabric store or a drugstore. Your wife goes to a flower shop."

"A flower shop?"

"Yeah, she comes out with a couple buckets of fresh flowers every time."

"But I thought you said that this wasn't the kind of cult that sold flowers at intersections or begged at airports."

"It isn't. We don't know what they want with all those flowers. And we don't know why they picked her to be the flower lady."

"That's easy," Dan said. "She loves flowers. She worked part-time for a florist in our neighborhood."

May nodded.

"The main thing is we don't want to be seen taking her. We want it to seem more like she just didn't come back. That way nobody gets any big kidnapping ideas right away and we get a little lead time before they report us to the cops."

"You think they'll call the police?" Dan asked.

"Believe it or not, the cults yell kidnapping as soon as they smell a deprogrammer. They're not the least bit afraid to use the law when it suits them."

Dan refilled his plastic cup from the thermos. The boulder he was seated on was icy cold beneath his jeans, and the coffee burned in his gut.

"Now," May said, "this is the only road into town. We're gonna sit back out of the way and watch. Keep our fingers crossed that they haven't decided to bring along any extras and complicate matters. Especially men. We sure don't want any more weapons to deal with."

"Weapons?"

"The men all pack guns. It's part of their philosophy."

"How do you know all this, Everett?"

"You paid me to find out, boy, but you didn't pay me to tell you how I found out."

Begay gave a heh-heh of amusement.

"We'll let them go past, taking note of who's on board, then we'll ease on into town after them. You'll drive, wearing Julian's bullrider special and these . . ." He tossed a pair of sunglasses into Dan's lap.

"What's a bullrider special?"

Julian flicked the brim of his hat with thumb and forefinger and grinned.

"A nice white boy in a cowboy hat driving a pickup will fit right in here," May said. "And with the hat and specs I don't think you'll be too recognizable if your wife catches a look at you."

"Where will you two be?"

"We'll be hiding in the camper. That's why I've got those silly curtains over the windows."

"How will I know what to do?"

"I'll be talking you through everything, but it won't take a rocket scientist. You'll just cruise down Main Street and we'll watch the first two women get dropped off at the grocery store. Then the man will park the truck in a little city lot near the center of town. He'll wander off to the coffee shop, and the two remaining women will split up. One goes this way here . . ." He brushed away pine needles to expose a patch of gritty soil and used a twig to draw a crude map. "And your wife heads for the flower shop. That's our window of opportunity. That's the only time she'll be alone."

"And then what?" Dan asked. "Should I identify myself and—"

"Hell no. She'd start screaming."

Dan lowered his eyes and swallowed hard.

"Toughen up, boy. This isn't going to be pretty. Chances are they've got her convinced that you're the devil."

Dan nodded.

"You'll do the driving. That's all you've got to worry about. Me and Julian will put her into the camper. You just get us out of town."

May slapped Dan on the back. Then he rose, poured some coffee into the dirt, and stirred up a puddle of mud. He smeared it onto the license plate of the truck.

"You're going to be careful with her," Dan said. "You won't do anything rough or hurt her or . . ."

"Have faith. I'm good at what I do, and the last thing I want is for somebody to get hurt." May shielded his eyes against the bright ball of morning sun rising over the mountains and looked off into the distance. "When you start feeling weak about this . . . and you will, you will . . . what you've got to ask yourself is what's hurting her more—us taking her back or those creeps making her a slave for the rest of her life."

Dan nodded. "Are you sure this will work?"

"We have to make it work. We get one shot. If she gets away they'll be warned and she'll be moved or at least kept out of our reach. They won't give us a second chance."

The blue crew-cab pickup truck came down the road right on schedule. Dan glimpsed a driver in a baseball cap and four other heads. Then the truck was gone.

His throat went dry. His stomach clenched. His hands closed around the steering wheel so tightly that the knuckles turned white.

"Right on the money," May announced from just inside the crawl-through. "Ease on down the road after them now. Keep it casual."

"I couldn't see her," Dan said.

"You'll see her soon enough. Don't say anything more unless you have to. You're supposed to be alone."

They cruised slowly down Main Street as the blue pickup dropped two women off at the grocery store. Both women wore long loose dresses and baggy sweaters. Dan still couldn't see Alex.

The blue pickup pulled out of the grocery store parking lot and continued down the quaint little street. There were only a few people on the sidewalks. Several old men were lined up on a wooden bench watching the passing traffic. Dan pulled the cowboy hat down lower on his forehead.

"Don't follow him when he turns," May instructed. "That's the way into the parking lot."

Dan did as he was told.

"Okay, now go left at the next corner. Then make a hard left into the alley that runs behind the stores."

Dan complied. His heartbeat was becoming louder in his ears.

"Okay. Now take it all the way to the end of the alley, but keep the nose back. She'll come walking down that side street from the parking lot, and we don't want her seeing anything in the alley till she's right on top of us. And keep the engine running. Be ready to haul ass."

The alley was extremely narrow and poorly paved. Dan drove it with caution, barely breathing, trying not to think. But the thoughts were there. Just as May had warned. The questions. The weakening. Was this the right thing to do? Was this the best for Alex or was it his own selfishness that was driving him?

He pulled up with the nose of the truck just inside the alley. Immediately the two men in the camper jumped out the back. They crept around to the front of the truck, crouching low so that Dan could see only the tops of their heads.

Then it happened. In frozen frames of movement. Alex appeared on the sidewalk. Sun glinting in her dark-red hair. The two men leaped forward. Her head turned toward them. Her eyes widened in terror. Her mouth opened. And then they were upon her. And everything wound into high speed. The flailing arms. The handcuffs. The cry cut short by tape across her mouth. The cloth blindfold. Her kicking and thrashing. The folded square of cloth over her nose. Her head jerking from side to side. Then collapse. Her entire body sagging into the men's arms.

No. The word roared in his brain. *No!*

But he sat there. Silent. Unmoving. Hands clenched around the steering wheel and engine running.

There was shuffling and scraping inside the camper. The back door banged shut. He did not turn his head to look.

"Go," May ordered hoarsely. "Keep it natural, but get us out of here."

Dan pulled out of the alley and turned down Main Street

going in the opposite direction from which they had come. He drove mechanically. A nice young white man in a cowboy hat. No one to be suspicious of. Glad for the wrap-around sunglasses because they hid his eyes.

# Chapter 9

Dan drove nearly forty miles before being told to turn in at a tourist lookout point. Everett May had left a minivan there.

"Unlock it and start the engine," May ordered, thrusting his arm into the crawl-through to pass Dan the keys.

Dan went to the minivan and did as he was told. There were bucket seats, for a driver and one passenger. The other seats had been removed and there was a mattress with bedding on the floor.

Begay came around and opened the van's side door. May carried a blanket-bundled Alex from the truck and eased her onto the mattress in the van. Dan sat woodenly in the driver's seat, unable to turn or look. The two men said a few words to each other in Navajo, then Begay went back to the truck and drove away.

"I'll drive now," May said, waving Dan into the passenger seat. Dan changed seats and stared ahead. She was just behind him. Close enough to touch. But he could not turn around. He could not look at her. He felt sick.

They pulled back onto the road. May turned on the radio and worked his way through the stations. He drew in a deep satisfied breath. "I think it was clean. They don't have a clue what happened yet."

Dan had to clear his throat before he could speak.

"You said you wouldn't hurt her."

"I didn't hurt her."

"Jumping on her like that! With handcuffs and tape! You think that didn't hurt her?"

May glanced sideways at him. "We did not hurt her," he said emphatically. "What did you think was going to happen?

Did you think we'd walk up and give her a polite invitation to join us?"

"No. I just . . . God, it seemed so brutal."

May nodded agreement. "Did you know that lifeguards sometimes have to hit drowning victims before they can get enough control to save them?"

"What about the drugs? You never mentioned drugs."

"The inhaled stuff is short-acting. Just so I could get her quiet enough to give her the sedative. And the sedative is very safe. I get them both from a doctor who knows what they're being used for."

Dan scrubbed his face with his hands. "How can she ever forgive me for this? How can I forgive myself?"

May sighed. "It's tough, I know . . . seeing something like that happen to someone you love. But think about what they've been doing to her. Then think about what you're trying to do *for* her. You're trying to give her back a sane and normal life. You're trying to give her back her freedom . . . the love of her child and her husband."

Dan had no response.

"Why don't you go and sit with her? You've got your wife back, son."

She looked like she was sleeping. Resting on her side in a nest of blankets. So familiar. So very peaceful and normal and familiar that for a moment he thought everything might fade away around them and he would find himself in the apartment, beside her in their shared bed, awakening from a bad dream.

He sat down at the edge of the mattress with his back against the side of the van. The fan of her dark-red hair against the white pillow made him think of her in the hospital.

"Why do you keep coming?" she'd asked.

"I want to see you. To know you."

"You're wasting your time."

"No."

"Yes. Just because you happened to be there to pull me out of the water—that doesn't mean anything. You're not obligated to be my friend now."

He had hesitated, wondering how to explain what he felt. Wondering whether he should try.

"It's that . . . I feel a connection to you. From the moment I touched your hair in the water, I felt this connection."

"My hair?"

"Yes. It was dark. I couldn't find you. Then I felt your hair, streaming out. It's lucky that you have such long hair." He'd smiled. "Maybe I should call you Rapunzel."

She hadn't said anything more about it. When he arrived for visiting hours the next day he found that she had been moved out of intensive care. He went to the nurse's station to ask for her new room number. The nurse was one he had become friendly with, and she was eager to tell him how well the patient was doing. How she was eating better and talking more. How she'd even become concerned about her appearance and had asked them to send up the hospital beautician.

He found her sitting up, a peachy glow of color in her skin and an expression of happiness on her face. Her long hair was gone, shorn almost to the scalp. And he knew now, he could admit to himself now, that she had been making a statement.

They drove for hours before May left the highway and negotiated a series of turns that brought them into the yard of an A-frame mountain cabin. Alex had not awakened.

"Why don't you go open up and I'll bring her in," May said. Dan shook his head. "I'll bring her in."

He struggled to lift her limp body from the van. When he finally had her in his arms the physical contact nearly overwhelmed him.

"Hurry," May called from the open front door. "She'll be coming out of it soon."

The room May had prepared for her was upstairs. The walls were steeply sloped to conform to the roofline, and the peaked ceiling soared upward. There was a skylight set very high, but there were no windows. And the room was bare except for a mattress on the floor. Oddly, the mattress was covered by colorful matched bedding—piles of pillows and a thick comforter that looked as though they had been lifted from a catalog ad. High up in the peak of the roof was a light fixture covered by a pierced metal shade.

Dan lay Alex gently on the bed, covered her, then rose to face May.

"All this . . ." He gestured around him. "Is this necessary?"

"You bet it is," May assured him. "Till she calms down, anyway."

"What do you expect her to do? Smash furniture? Break windows?"

"I'm worried about her hurting herself. They're taught to attempt suicide if escape is impossible. They're told that a suicide attempt will get them to a hospital, where they'll be able to get help or get away or whatever. And if they actually do die they'll be dying as martyrs."

"That won't be true with her. She might be confused, but she'll be glad to see me."

"Don't get your expectations up," May cautioned. He bent down to check her pulse, then lifted the blanket and looked her over.

"What are you doing?"

"Checking for a belt, pantyhose, shoelaces, anything she could use to hurt herself. She looks clean."

Dan watched, throat aching and chest in a vise. "You never said what happened with Ben Khadra's daughter. Did you get her out yet?"

May shook his head. "It's frustrating as hell," he said. "We haven't been able to track her at all. Thought maybe she got sent to the other compounds, but now . . . we just don't know. Maybe Alex will be able to tell us something when she starts feeling friendly."

Sympathy for Ben Khadra's plight made Dan feel lucky. This wasn't pretty, but at least she was here. She was safe.

"I'd say we've got a little while before she comes around, Dan. Want some coffee? Soda?"

Dan shook his head. He took off his coat and sat down against the wall, facing Alex. He wanted to be immediately in her line of sight when she opened her eyes so she wouldn't be afraid. May returned, drinking a can of Dr Pepper. He settled cross-legged on the floor. "Okay now, we play by my rules. Remember? You agreed to that."

Dan nodded.

"You can speak to her. Say soothing things. But don't try to touch her until you get a signal from me."

Dan nodded again. They had been over this several times before, and he was impatient with it.

"If I start talking you follow my lead. Don't contradict or interrupt. And if I tell you to leave the room, you leave. No questions or arguments."

She moved. A hand was flung out from beneath the comforter. Her eyes fluttered. Dan's heart lurched upward in his chest and hung there, waiting.

She moaned softly and turned onto her back. Then she sat up, blinking in panicky confusion. Her eyes found May and locked on him with the terrified alertness of a trapped animal.

"Alex, Alex . . ." Dan said, edging carefully closer. "It's me. You're safe. It's me."

Her head swung toward him. She jerked up onto her knees, clutching the comforter to her chest.

"You're safe, sweetheart. You're with me now."

She closed her eyes and tilted her head back. A sound began, low and indistinct, as though starting deep inside her. It rose, gathering volume and force. Then she opened her mouth and the sound poured out in a piercing, blood-chilling wail.

Some hours later, Dan found himself completely drained and exhausted. His beloved wife was behaving like an inconsolable stranger. After the wailing subsided, she had huddled against the wall at the head of the mattress, pressing her back against the wall and hugging her knees in a defensive posture. And she had remained there, as though in a trance, neither speaking nor responding to their speech.

"Why don't you go fix us a little dinner, Dan?" May said, glancing at his watch.

Dan pulled himself to his feet.

"Are you hungry, Alex?" he asked. "I know you always did hate my cooking, but I'll try to come up with something passable."

She continued to stare straight ahead, sphinxlike in her disregard of them.

"There's a chest freezer in the washroom that's packed." May gave him an encouraging smile. "You can surprise us."

Dan felt a measure of guilt over his relief at escaping for a while. He wondered if Alex's behavior was common. Was this what May had been trying to prepare him for?

He ducked into the upstairs bathroom to wash up. May had

escorted Alex there earlier, but Dan had not gone inside. It was a small cubicle, again with a skylight but no window. There were faded marks to show where a wall mirror had hung, but it was gone. The room had a toilet, the tank's lid secured by a cable, and a pedestal sink, the drain stopper removed and no hot water handle. There was a locking device on the tub's faucets. No towels. No soap. A few tissues in lieu of toilet paper. And, of course, no lock on the door.

May had advised him to use the downstairs bath, and now he saw why.

He went down the open wooden stairs into the living area. The walls were painted white and the floors had matted brown carpeting. An eating bar separated the living area from the open kitchen. Beyond the kitchen was a hallway with doors that opened onto a normally furnished bathroom, a small bedroom, and a large utility room that was home to a washer, a dryer, a freezer, and a wall of metal shelves and racks designed to hold winter sporting equipment.

Dan opened the freezer. It was filled with food. He took out two kinds of pizza because there was some hope of interesting Alex in that and because he didn't have the energy to face preparing anything more demanding. He carried the pizzas to the kitchen and lit the gas oven. While they baked he rummaged. The kitchen was well stocked with canned, packaged, and instant foods. Enough for months. He wondered how often May used the place.

He found a cardboard carton and packed it with napkins and canned drinks. When the pizzas were done he balanced and stacked and managed to carry everything in one load.

"Dinner!" he called, tapping the closed door with the toe of his shoe. Bringing her food made him feel more positive. She had to be hungry. This was at least something he could do for her.

The door opened. "Smells good," May said, reaching out to take one of the pizzas. "Let's all eat together. Like a picnic."

They unfolded napkins and spread them over the end of the mattress. Dan sat on one corner and May sat on the other. Alex was still in her trancelike state, pressed against the wall at the head of the bed.

"What kind do you want, Alex?" May asked in the friendly

tone of voice that he had maintained since her awakening. "Let's see . . . what do we have here, Dan?"

"That one is mushroom and this one is ham, peppers, and onions."

"You like the mushroom, right, Alex?" Dan asked, following May's lead. "Here." He slid a large slice onto a plate, gathered several napkins under the plate, and set everything carefully near her right hand.

"Oh, boy. This hits the spot," May said as he ate. "You know, I don't buy those pathetic cardboard pizzas they have in the grocery stores. My favorite pizza guy makes these up for me and wraps them, then I just freeze 'em myself."

"They're pretty good," Dan agreed with a cheerfulness that sounded false even to him. "And that's a big compliment coming from me, because I live in the pizza capital of the world."

"Brooklyn is the pizza capital of the world?"

"Absolutely. Right, Alex? Within walking distance of our apartment you can get brick oven pizza, coal oven pizza, wood oven pizza, Tuscan grilled pizza, thick crust, thin crust, round pie, square pie, white pie, marinara pie, and on and on. When we first moved there we were amazed, weren't we, Alex? And remember while you were pregnant, you craved either Lento's thin crust eggplant pie or the white pies from that one little old place in Bensonhurst." He shook his head and tried to laugh, following May's instructions, keeping up a stream of conversation that was intimate yet lighthearted. "I wonder how many times I went out late at night to get you a slice of eggplant pie or white pie."

"What's white pie?" May asked.

"Mozzarella and ricotta with no red sauce."

"Hmmm. Sounds interesting."

"And this little place that Alex likes . . . I can't remember the owner's name. Alex, do you remember?" He waited several beats. "Anyway, he's this old guy who does things from scratch. Makes his own mozzarella. Uses only fresh herbs. That kind of thing. And his white pie has sautéed garlic mixed into the ricotta and fresh rosemary sprinkled over the top."

Dan forced himself to take another bite of his pizza. He was not hungry. His stomach had a sick knot in the middle of it.

"We'll go straight to Lento's or we'll order one of those white pies," Dan promised, looking at Alex. "Whichever you want. As soon as we get home." There was no response from her. Not a flicker. She had put up a wall and was shutting them out completely. Shutting him out.

"I can't—" He put his slice down. "I'm sorry. Excuse me." And he quickly left the room.

He locked himself in the downstairs bathroom, covered his face with his hands, and leaned against the wall. The sobs coming out of his chest shook his entire body as he slid down to sit on the floor.

"Hey, how are you doing?"

"I'm okay," Dan answered, surprised to see May. He had regained his composure and was in the kitchen making coffee. "I thought you said one of us should always be with her while she's awake."

May sighed. "The usual methods aren't working. This trance nonsense has to be overcome or we'll never get anywhere."

"So what are you going to do?"

"Leave her alone for a while. I'm betting she won't be able to resist exploring the room and testing her boundaries. That will at least get her up and moving. Maybe she'll even eat some of that pizza."

"And there's no way she can hurt herself or anything?"

"In that room? Guaranteed no way. That room and the upstairs bath are completely safe. Believe me, I know. I learned how to secure them after many unhappy surprises."

"People hurting themselves?" Dan said.

"Yes. Or just causing trouble. After everything breakable was removed, I had someone purposely scald himself with hot water. I turned off the hot tap, and the next time I let him into the bathroom unattended, he plugged up the sink and the toilet so that they overflowed."

"I don't understand any of this, Everett. How do normal people behave that way?"

May settled onto a stool at the bar and gazed out the window into the darkness. "I used to think I knew all the answers. I thought that the people who were vulnerable to this stuff were the young or the ones who had big problems or who'd never adjusted to life. Kind of like animals where the weak and the sick and the immature ones can't keep up with the herd so they fall easy victim to predators. And that's exactly what all these gurus and prophets and smooth talkers are— predators. Vicious, sharp-toothed, cunning, ruthless predators who get fat and powerful from sucking the life out of their victims."

May turned from the window. "Hand me a Dr Pepper, will ya?"

Dan took a can from the refrigerator and put it on the counter in front of the man. Then, pouring himself coffee, he asked, "You said you *used* to think that, but what about now?"

"I was partly right. There are people who are easier prey than others. But the scary thing is—I know now that we're all vulnerable at certain points in our lives. We all have periods when we're down or underconfident or just plain lost and our troubles seem unbearable. We all have fears and beliefs and needs that can be exploited. And if one of these cults comes along—"

"No," Dan said adamantly. "I can't agree with that. No one could ever convince me to do something that I didn't think was right."

"Oh, but that's where they get you. They mess with your mind and alter your value systems. They change your view of what's right." May took an impossibly long chugging drink from the can of soda, then cocked his head and studied Dan.

He stroked his chin as though he had a beard. "Okay. Say a co-worker you like invites you to something . . . whatever . . . a party or picnic or something . . . and you get there and find out it's more like a rally or a club meeting, because most of the people know each other. And it becomes clear that the group is organized around this one figure—let's call him John. Maybe John is presented as a potential political leader, maybe as an avant-garde religious leader, maybe simply as a common guy who wants to see a return to old-fashioned values in the community. Whatever . . . he's a charismatic fellow and you like him, and you argue with him a little or you question him some, but basically he's talking about broad easy-to-agree-with issues like family values maybe or support for the middle class, and he phrases things in a way that is interesting but not controversial.

"This John, he makes sense, and he makes you feel good about what you think and about your values, and the whole group of people is nice and fun to be with. So, of course, you'll go to more functions. And you do. And John inspires you. He fires you up. Through him you feel that you're important and that you can make a difference in the world.

"You go to the get-togethers more frequently and you look forward to them. You want other friends or family members to attend with you. If they won't go then maybe you feel a little guilty about how much time you're spending with this group, but you won't cut back because it's a good thing. A positive thing. For you personally and for the community ... world ... whatever. And you think that eventually your friends and family will realize this.

"Now John starts taking a personal interest in you, which is very flattering. The guy is wise beyond belief. He can see through all the news stories and the political posturing and the bullshit and cut right through to the heart of matters. And he has an amazing amount of quotes and facts and figures to back up everything he says.

"John tells you that he sees something special in you. He says you have the potential to do great things. And he invites you to come to a ranch retreat for a weekend. You're very honored by the invitation and you go.

"When you get there you're maybe a little disappointed to find that it's not as casual and relaxed as you'd thought it would be, or as personalized, but you're certainly not going to walk out. You can see the spirit of the place. How it's designed to give you a mental and physical tune-up. And you join in with all the other people there, adhering to the strict rules, staying up all night in intense talk sessions, sweating through punishing physical exertion during the day, eating the small meatless meals and the sugary snacks, listening to John speak every afternoon. You're never alone. What little sleep you get is communal, probably in sleeping bags on a floor. Even the bathrooms are big open spaces with no privacy. Seasoned members of the group are always with you. You're never allowed time to think for yourself. And by Sunday you're exhausted and sleep-deprived and your blood chemistry has gone haywire, and John says you need to stay longer because you're almost there. You're so close to breaking through all your old self-imposed barriers."

Dan threw his hands into the air. "All right. All right. I see where you're going with this. I really don't believe I'd let myself get sucked in by something like that, but I get your point."

"Oh, just wait. My little tale gets better. See, after you agree to stay on longer, time sort of slips away. You've been told that your family was called and your employer was called and they think it's great that you're staying longer. In reality, no one was called. Or if they were called they were lied to. But you don't know that.

"If your family is aggressive they might show up at the ranch and demand to see you. But that would be kept from you. Your family might go to the local law and complain, and the local law might come out and ask you if you want to stay at the ranch and you say sure. End of the law's interest.

"Maybe your family keeps showing up, but the ranch is like an armed camp and no one can get through to you. And you never know they're trying. You're completely isolated. All you know is what John and the group tell you. You can't leave the ranch. There's no television or newspapers. No calendars. You don't have access to a telephone. The outside world begins to fade away in importance and the group is everything. At some point you're told that you're lazy or that you're disappointing or inadequate in a number of ways and that you have to work harder to redeem yourself. To prove yourself worthy. You're given constant tasks and assignments. You focus on improving yourself. And eventually you win your way back into John's good graces.

"You're so relieved. He takes you aside. Praises you. Has heart-to-heart discussions with you again. You feel so honored. Then he tells you, sadly, that he has some bad news. The group has learned that your family is evil. They're possessed by demons. No. Sorry. Let's keep this group nonreligious. No. They've learned that everyone outside is against you. Your employer has fired you and put your name on a blacklist. Your parents think you're insane. They've signed papers and told the authorities to catch you and lock you up in an asylum. Your wife has been sleeping with other men in your bed.

"You say no, that can't be true. But John shows you evidence. Copies of papers. Photographs. Letters. Maybe he plays you a tape. They've engineered things. By this time they know you better than you know yourself, and they know exactly what it will take to convince you.

"You're despondent and confused. Maybe you say that you want to talk to your family. John agrees and says soothing things. But he tells you that too much can be concealed over the phone. You need to see your family in person. But! It's dangerous for you to leave the ranch because the place is being watched by men who want to catch you and lock you up in an asylum. For your safety John will try to convince your family to come to the ranch.

"The arrangements for your family's visit drag on and on, hitting all sorts of snags. Meanwhile, John and the group shower you with kindness and affection. You've lost all sense of how long you've been at the ranch. Then they set up the crowning blow. Your family has turned away from you completely. For proof they show you copies of your parents' wills in which they disown you and proof that your wife has filed for divorce. And you're told that your family now refuses to come.

"You're lavished with sympathy and love. Assured that the group is your family now. That the group is all you need. And you're given some major honor or privilege. Maybe a trip with John to speak to recruits at another location.

"And that's it, my friend. That's it. Maybe for the rest of your life."

Dan set his jaw and stared down at the floor. He still had doubts about his own susceptibility, but he could see the danger to others. He thought of all the dissatisfied, discontented, disaffected people out there in the world. All the sad people. The lonely people. The people who were perplexed by the difficulties and the uncertainties of life. He thought of his boss, Dreeson. He thought of the office cleaning women he'd heard whispering about the millennium and about the world ending.

"How do you explain the money?" Dan asked. "People turning over their assets."

"That's the easy part. Once they have a person's trust, the plea for funds or possessions is individually tailored. Some groups simply charge for counseling and services. But those are usually the groups that keep people out in the world, working. The cults that take over your life completely insist on a 'pooling' of assets and possessions for the communal good. Which means a person turns over everything and then is maintained at a subsistence level while the leaders enjoy the good life."

"But with Alex . . . ?"

"Could be they used a simple subterfuge with her. Told her that they needed to borrow all her available funds for a short period. Told her they needed to borrow your car. Maybe they even convinced her that they had spoken to you about it and had your permission. And then, as she was drawn deeper, loan repayments or car returns were the last thing on her mind. Or maybe they simply told her they gave it back to you. There's a lot of different possibilities. Just like there're endless possibilities for how the cult works out all the other details."

May thumbed his eyes wearily.

"Only the big picture stays the same. The cult leader takes control of every part of a person's life. Absolute physical and spiritual control. And after that anything is possible. The puppeteer pulls the strings and decent men will hand over their wives and daughters for the cult leader to fuck. Young people will submit to sterilization. Girls will prostitute themselves to earn money for the group or to attract new recruits. People will go sit on mountaintops and wait for the world to end. They'll lie, steal, and carry lethal gas into subways. They'll plant bombs. They'll shoot at the police or throw grenades at the army. They'll drink poison or burn themselves to death at the summer solstice or kill their babies to drive out demons. The true-life horror stories I have in my files would turn your hair white."

May sat for a moment, lost in thought, then he looked at Dan.

"We all think we're so tough and independent, but it's a fragile skin we wear." He eased off the stool and stretched. "I think we've given Alex enough time alone," he said. "Let's go see if she'll respond to us now."

"What if she doesn't?"

"Then we'll try something else. The woman you know is still in there. We just have to find her."

# Chapter 10

They paused for a moment at the door, listening. There was no sound from inside the room. May knocked softly, said, "I'm coming in, Alex," then gestured for Dan to follow him as he unlocked the door.

"Alex?" May called as he stepped inside.

Dan, following right behind, had a split second to see that Alex was no longer on the bed before she hurtled at May from the side. Grunting in pain, May spun away with Alex clinging to his back, her legs wrapped around him and one arm clamped on his neck in a choke hold.

"Alex! No!" Dan lunged for her, knocking them both to the floor.

She kicked and scratched and then suddenly scrambled away to the bed.

"Are you all right?" Dan asked May, helping the man to his feet.

"Yeah. Yeah." May sighed. "My own fault. I should have been more careful."

"You need to go clean those scratches on your face. One of them looks pretty deep."

"Yeah." May glanced toward Alex, who was crouched defensively near the wall at the head of the mattress. "Stay sharp. I'll be right back."

May went out and Dan heard the sound of the dead bolt being thrown from outside the door. He could not look at his wife. Instead he paced. Back and forth. Fists clenched in frustration.

"Alex. Alex. Alex." He turned toward her. "How could you do that?"

Her eyes were on him. They had a feral gleam that he had never seen before.

"I don't understand. Can't you help me to understand?"

Something faltered in her expression, and she quickly looked down.

"Please, Alex. What is going on? What has happened to you? I love you. Hana loves you. Our hearts are breaking from missing you so much. I can't believe that's what you intended. I can't believe you want to cause so much pain."

"No," she whispered. It was the first word she had spoken, and it brought a rush of hope with it.

He wanted to go to her. To gather her in his arms and bury his face in her hair. But he knew he had to be careful. One spoken word did not end the war.

"Have you missed us?" he asked.

Several moments passed before she said, "Sometimes." She continued to look down, and he could not read her face at all.

"Why haven't you called or written or something? Haven't you wanted to see us?"

She gave a tiny shrug. "My personal desires are unimportant."

"Oh, Alex . . . How can you say that? Your husband who loves you is unimportant? Your daughter who needs you is unimportant?"

"No!" She raised her eyes to his, and he saw that all the animosity was gone. "That's not what I was saying. It's not that you're unimportant—it's my reliance on you, my need for you, that's unimportant." She frowned, causing delicate lines to form across her smooth forehead. "It's hard to explain. You know I've never been good with words."

"Try, please," he urged, easing himself down to sit against the wall near her.

She fingered the comforter, thinking. He watched her hands move across the fabric. Hands that had so often touched his face or trailed fire down his body. Something was different about them. The nails. Ever since he had known her she had torn at her nails with her teeth, sometimes to the point that her cuticles bled, and though she had been self-conscious about the nervous condition and had tried every possible remedy, she had not been able to stop.

Her nails were fine now. Smoothly rounded and well-groomed. The realization sent a dart of pain through him. Was she so contented and relaxed without him?

She raised her eyes to his again, and this time he saw a glow of eager sincerity. "It's that I've risen above my past selfishness. My pettiness. I'm not caught up in trivial things anymore. I know that life and the future are not about what I thought I wanted."

He stared at her. Trying to see through to the meaning of what she was saying.

There was a perfunctory knock and then the door opened and Everett May walked in. Alex hugged her knees to her chest and glared at him. From May's careful posture Dan thought that the man was aware of the difference in the room.

"I know who you are!" Alex said, each word a weapon of hatred for May.

May nodded. "That saves us some time then, doesn't it? Why don't you tell me who you are?" He settled onto the floor in a cross-legged position at the foot of the mattress.

"You can't trick me!"

"I don't want to trick you."

"Yes, you do! You want to twist my words around and confuse me and blind me to the truth."

"I'm flattered. You must see me as a heck of a clever guy if you think I can do that."

"Everett has just been trying to help me, Alex. I was so lost . . . so desperate to see you that I—"

"That you thought you should hire a kidnapper and make me a prisoner?"

"No."

But as he mouthed the denial he remembered Laura Ferren's warnings.

"It wasn't like that," he insisted. "I only wanted to see you. To know that you're all right. To talk to you."

"You've done that, Dan. Can I go now?"

He glanced at May helplessly.

"This is the deal, Alex. Dan is still legally your husband. He needs a chance to discuss things with you. Nuts-and-bolts stuff like is he supposed to file for divorce?"

Dan started to protest, but May's hand moved in the subtle prearranged signal that meant he was to keep quiet.

Alex leaned forward, her expression thoughtful.

"Also," May continued, "what about your daughter? Are you prepared to give up all claims to custody?"

"What would that involve?" Alex asked. "Are there papers I'd have to sign?"

"Yes. And there's the question of Dan's share of the money and the car."

"What?" Alex gave Dan a puzzled look before turning her attention back to May.

"You and your friends took all the money in the bank and the car, leaving Dan with nothing. Legalities aside, do you really think that's fair?"

"Liar!" She squeezed her eyes shut, hugged herself protectively, and began rocking back and forth, muttering an unintelligible chant under her breath.

Dan started toward her but May signaled him to stay back.

"Alexandra!" May bellowed. "Alexandra, are you insane?"

She froze and opened her eyes.

"Do you want your husband to think you've gone insane? Do you want us to call in psychiatrists or send you off to an asylum?"

She shook her head, dropped her arms, and warily took her old position at the head of the bed with her back against the wall.

"Good. Then let's pass the evening like civilized people. I've got a VCR and a television I can bring in if you'd like to watch a movie. Or we could play cards."

She looked from May to Dan, clearly surprised at this turn. "That's all I have to do? Watch a movie or play cards?"

"That's it. Your choice."

She hesitated, then frowned as though considering her options. Her indecisiveness was almost childlike. Dan had never seen her behave in such a way.

"How about the movie?" May asked.

She nodded, her expression almost grateful at having the choice made for her.

"C'mon, Dan." May started toward the door. "I need you to help me carry the television in."

As soon as they were outside the room Dan released his frustrations. "Why a movie? She was just loosening up and starting to talk. Shouldn't we keep pushing her?"

"I told you, Dan—we do it my way. Now, the first thing I wanted to do was to get her started thinking for herself, calculating, making decisions. You can bet that's been crushed right out of her since she's been with them. And I want to show her this movie. It's a comedy about family life and how families stick together. It will remind her of what the world is like outside that compound where she's been, and it should remind her of her feelings for her daughter. Maybe it will also cause her to realize that she's missed frivolous entertainments like movies. Now, if you're going to question every single move I make, things aren't gonna go so smoothly."

Dan sighed. "Okay."

"And in advance—you told me she liked cards. Well, we want to get her to play with us as often as possible."

Dan nodded. "Thinking and decision making and all that, right?"

"And nonthreatening interaction with us."

"Okay," Dan said. "It's your show."


The following evening, after interminable games of hearts and canasta and poker, another heartwarming movie, and intermittent conversations in which the challenges and questions were careful and friendly, May abruptly shifted his approach.

"Do you like being lied to, Alex?" he suddenly demanded. "Do you like being used?"

She shrank away from him.

"That's what they're doing. They're using you."

And with that Everett May launched into a heated performance that was by turns debate, sermon, and tough-love therapeutic session. It lasted for thirty excruciating minutes. Alex alternated between furious flinging of rhetoric and broken sobbing. Dan sat by, a helpless and despondent witness. Then, abruptly, May stopped.

"Let's have a soda and another movie before lights-out," he said.

It was then, while Dan was downstairs getting the sodas, that May's little cellular phone began to ring.

"Everett!" Dan shouted. He picked up the phone and ran without answering it. May had been adamant that the phone was to be for emergencies only. "Everett! The phone!"

May met him on the stairs, grabbed the phone, flipped it open, and breathlessly said hello.

The conversation was one-sided. As May listened his face changed, and Dan knew that there was something very wrong.

"What?" he asked as soon as May had disconnected.

"My son," May whispered. Then, recovering his self-possession, he said, "My son was hit on his bicycle. I have to leave immediately."

He glanced around as though taking stock. "There's plenty of supplies. I'll leave the phone, but I'm going to have to take the car to get to the airport. If I can't get back myself in two days, I'll send Julian." He checked his watch, then gripped Dan's upper arm. "You'll be fine. Keep things simple, but try not to let her know you're alone. Tell her I'm napping. Then I'm taking a walk. Tell her I'm giving you two some time together. Whatever works. If you have to admit I've gone, make it that I went on an errand and I'll be back soon."

Dan nodded. "How old is he?"

"Eight. He's in the hospital. It was a hit-and-run. How could anyone just drive off and leave a kid lying in the middle of the road?" May's calm exterior cracked and he turned away. "I've got to get my stuff," he said, hurrying back up the stairs.

"Don't worry about things here," Dan called after him, trying to sound confident in spite of the fear clutching his gut.

The rest of the evening was easy to manage. He put a movie on the VCR and she did not question May's absence. But late the following morning she finally asked, "Where's my jailer?"

"Everett is not your jailer, Alex."

"Then who is? You?"

He ignored her. "I have something for you. I've been saving it."

She didn't respond. He dropped the manila envelope onto the bed in front of her and retreated to his familiar position against the wall. Several minutes passed. She nibbled absently at a cuticle. Seeing a sign of her old nervous habit was oddly reassuring to him. Aside from anger and distress, she had exhibited an eerie lack of emotion. The Alex he knew would have ripped the envelope open immediately.

"Go ahead," he urged.

"What?" she asked as though disturbed from some preoccupation.

"Open the envelope."

She picked it up, unclipped the flap, and dumped the contents onto the comforter. It was a collection of letters and cards from Hana, written during Alex's long absence but never mailed because there had not been an address to send them to.

Alex stared down at the colorful jumble of folded papers decorated with stickers and drawings.

"They're all from Hana," Dan said, watching her carefully, hoping that the child's block-printed pleas and declarations of love would reach the woman trapped inside this nonresponsive shell.

She went through half the stack, unfolding and reading and refolding. Dan knew them all by heart. *I love you mommy. Please come home. Where are you mommy. Did you forget me. When you come home I will never be dab again.*

"She has her lowercase *b*'s and *d*'s mixed up," Alex said.

"Yes. But I've stopped worrying about little things like that since she began having so many problems with school."

"Hana doesn't have problems with school."

"She does now. Your disappearance affected her in all kinds of ways. She's been belligerent at home and withdrawn at school."

Dan thought he detected a ghost of emotion before Alex bent to finish reading Hana's notes. When she was through she gathered them neatly and slipped them back into the envelope.

"Tell Hana they were very nice."

"You should tell her yourself."

Alex had been leaning forward. Now she slumped back against the wall as though suddenly tired.

"Where is Hana?" she asked.

"At our apartment."

"Who's taking care of her?"

Dan hesitated. He wondered about the wisdom of telling Alex the truth, but decided that a bitter dose of the truth might be good for her.

"Your mother is there with her."

Alex stared at him as though he had just uttered the unspeakable.

"Valerie?"

"Yes.

"You let that woman get her slimy hands on my daughter!" Alex leaped to her feet, fists clenched and face contorted in fury. "You gave my innocent baby to that bitch!"

Dan rose to face her.

"Yes. The mother you despise is now caring for our child."

"Bastard! You fucking bastard!"

She flew straight at him, pummeling him with her fists. He took several blows before grabbing her wrists.

"Maybe I'm a bastard and she's a bitch, but what are you, Alex? You're the one who walked out without a word. You're the one who's had us worried and frightened and hurting so much that I didn't know if we'd survive. You're the one who destroyed everything and forced me to accept your mother's help."

She was still radiating fire, but she wasn't fighting, she was listening, so he let her wrists go. She didn't move back.

"Excuses," she said, flinging the accusation with contempt.

"Are you aware of everything that's happened? Do you know that your friends poisoned me when I tried to see you at that house in the Village? Do you know that I was in the hospital? That I had no one to watch Hana? That I lost my job? All this while I was gnawing my guts out because

I thought that my wife . . . the woman I loved . . . had been kidnapped by a bunch of nuts and I couldn't save her."

Alex lowered her eyes, and he found himself looking at her forehead. So close that he could have brushed the smooth skin with his lips.

"You may have reasons to despise your mother, but that woman dropped everything and flew all the way from L.A. to help. I don't know what we'd have done without her. She loaned me money and she took over with Hana. She kept us from falling apart."

Alex raised her eyes to his, and a single tear dropped from her eye to slide down her cheek.

"Don't let her hurt Hana," she whispered. "Please don't let her hurt our baby."

"Oh, Alex . . ."

Then he did what he had wanted to do from the moment he saw her walk toward the alley. He put his arms around her and hugged her tight to his chest, holding her safe and close, resting his cheek against the softness of her hair. And she didn't resist. She didn't pull away.

"I'd never let anyone hurt Hana. You know that."

She did pull back then, but only so that she could look at him.

"There are different kinds of hurting, Dan." Her eyes searched his, and an expression of quiet amusement touched her face. "You're still exactly the same. Exactly who and what I thought you were. In spite of what that evil May convinced you to do."

"Why do you seem so surprised? Why wouldn't I be who you thought I was?"

"Because . . ." She sighed. "Because no one else is. Because I'm not."

"Oh, Alex—" he began, but she put her hands over her ears, twisted out of his reach, and retreated to her position on the mattress.

She was taking it back to the standoff. Back to the blank-faced stranger. He remained where he was, arms leaden with the sudden emptiness, trying to conceal the disappointment that he felt.

Several minutes of silence passed. She appeared to have put herself into a meditative state.

"I'll go make some lunch," Dan said. "Any preferences?"

There was no answer. He pulled the key from his jeans pocket, unlocked the dead bolt, went out, and reset the bolt from the outside. In the hallway, he allowed himself to lean against the wall and squeeze his eyes shut. There was a dull pain in his belly that had nothing to do with hunger.

May had said that it usually took three days or less for the cult victim to come out of it and wake up to the world again. This was the fourth day. May had also said that he knew of cases where the victim could never be reached. What if Alex was one of those?

No. Dan shook his head and shook off the doubt. There had just been a breakthrough of sorts. He was sure that was how May would have interpreted it. So he just had to keep on and keep believing. And he had to take care of her. Right now he had to feed her.

He went downstairs to the kitchen. The morning overcast had turned into a light snowfall, and he watched the delicate drifting flakes as he made sandwiches.

When he went back to her the light was off and the room was cast in shades of gray. He put the box of food down at the foot of the bed, then moved toward the light switch.

"Can we leave it off?" she asked. "I'm sick of the bright glare. And I want to be able to see the snow falling on the skylight."

Struck with renewed guilt over her windowless imprisonment, he repeated to himself that it was a temporary necessity and for her own protection and all the other reassuring phrases that May had used so often, while he set out the lunch.

"May is gone, isn't he?"

Dan considered the lies he should tell. "Yes. He's gone."

She tilted her head back to watch the snowflakes melt against the skylight. Then she looked at him.

"Let's pretend we're having lunch together at a restaurant," she said. "One of those dingy little places in the East Village where you can sit at a table for hours and talk."

"Okay," he agreed, wondering what it meant.

She seemed suddenly different. Calm and relaxed. More herself. But no, that wasn't right, because the old Alex had not been calm and relaxed. She had been either wildly happy or nervous or worried or afraid or depressed. The woman in front of him now was peaceful.

"Do you know why I fell in love with you?" she asked.

He put down his sandwich. "I thought I'd suddenly gotten lucky."

Her mouth softened.

"I fell in love with you because you were everything I wanted to be. You were good. So good. Your goodness just shined out of you like sunshine beaming out from the sun." She gave him a sweet nostalgic smile. "I didn't know how to be good myself. And I'd never known any really good people. But I wanted to learn how to be like you. Only I was so selfish that I used to get jealous of your being kind to other people. Strangers, especially. Or people who didn't mean anything to you and were never going to mean anything to you—like that cranky old lady who lives down the hall. And I used to get so mad at myself.

"And besides being good, you were incredibly smart. You had everything sorted out so that you always saw what was right and what was wrong. I still remember how you used to read newspaper articles to me when I was in the hospital and we barely knew each other, and I'd be confused by the article. I'd be wondering who to feel sympathy for or who to be angry at or what to think. And I'd ask you a few questions. And it would really amaze me how you had this grasp of what the issues were and you had very definite ideas about the moral position."

She smiled again.

"I remember that first time I heard you call something unconscionable. It was something about people not being able to get health care or about benefits being canceled or something. I don't exactly remember. But . . . *unconscionable*! I admired you so much for having thoughts like that. I never had thoughts like that. And I'd never been around somebody whose principles were so . . . formed. People I knew were always bending and stretching the rules, taking the easiest path or the path that suited them at the moment."

She paused to eat a bite, and he thought that he should say something but he was too uncertain to speak. Was this sudden intimacy a positive sign? Was her overinflated view of him a positive sign? Would it be better if she saw him in a more realistic light? Should he catalog his faults and failings for her or keep quiet? And, most important of all, should he ask the question that he was so desperate to ask—*Do you still love me?*

"Eat," she said. "You've lost weight and you don't look so great."

"You're thinner, too." Tentatively, he reached out to stroke her wrist with the tip of his index finger. He wanted to believe that she'd been miserable. That she hadn't been able to eat.

"I was fasting for a while." She finished a sandwich half and picked up another. "I can have whatever I want now, so I'll be back to my normal weight in no time."

She hadn't been miserable. She hadn't been pining for him.

"Do you think . . ." she began, and then timidly broke off.

His heart leaped at the possibilities.

"What? What?"

"Do you think I could have a shower or a bath?"

*Take her out of the room as little as possible while you're alone,* May had cautioned. *Be very careful.*

But May had not realized how much more normal she would become in the hours after his departure.

"Sure," he said. "And there's a laundry room downstairs. I could wash your dress. I mean . . . I'll give you something of mine to wear while it's washing."

She smiled one of her old smiles then, breathtakingly brilliant and genuine. And it was almost the old Alex. So very close to the old Alex.

He put soap and shampoo, a large towel, one of his clean flannel shirts, and a pair of his jeans in the upstairs bathroom. He pried the lock off the taps and started the water running into the bathtub. Then he unlocked her room.

"It's all set," he said.

She walked down the hall beside him as though the situation were perfectly normal, but he felt awful acting as her jailer.

"Thank you," she said as they reached the bathroom.

She started inside, hesitated, glanced down at her dress, then up at him. "I'll hand my dress out . . . okay?"

He nodded and stood outside the door until it opened a crack and the dress was tossed out onto the floor. He picked it up. From behind the closed door he heard her turn off the taps. Then there was the slosh of water as she entered the tub.

She was naked behind that door. Skin glistening and slick with water. Hair wet, too, by now, since she liked to dunk herself completely when she got in.

Would she ever want him again?

He looked at the dulled brass key in his hand. How could she want a man who kept her prisoner? How could she ever forgive him?

He had not locked her in yet. Did she know that? Had she listened for the scraping sound of the dead bolt sliding into position? Was she listening now? He did not want to lock that door.

*Be careful,* May had warned repeatedly. *If anything goes wrong you'll be losing ground. Setting back the whole process. Don't be fooled. And don't try to go too fast.*

Reluctantly, Dan slid the key in the lock and turned it. The sound echoed in the empty hallway. She had to have heard it. She had to know that he did not trust her. That she was still a prisoner.

"I'm sorry," he whispered.

He hurried down to the laundry room holding her dress against his chest. While the washer filled he smoothed the dress out on the top of the machine. The fabric was a coarse cotton weave that had softened with use. It was almost white but not quite. And it had tiny flecks of brown in it. Unbleached. That was it. Like all the natural stuff at the Good Earth Store. He could not recall Alex's ever wearing such a thing, but it was hers. It was her.

He gathered the dress, crushing it into a ball, and he buried his face in the soft folds that had so recently touched her body. He inhaled the scent of her, strong and musky from days without changing or bathing, and he felt sick with desire for her.

When the washer was filled he dropped the dress inside.

He wished that there was more to do. He needed a task to focus on.

Dinner.

He would plan dinner. A special dinner. She had wanted to pretend they were in a restaurant for lunch, so he would surprise her with a restaurant for dinner, too.

He opened the freezer and dug until he found a package containing two rib-eye steaks, and he took them out to defrost. In the kitchen he found potatoes and an onion. There was nothing for salad. He went back to the freezer and located a box of frozen broccoli. It would not be a very sophisticated or imaginative dinner, but it would pass for restaurant fare. A thorough search of cupboards and drawers yielded votive candles and paper napkins with a Christmas design.

The preparations for a surprise dinner raised his spirits again. He considered what she might want to do for the remainder of the afternoon, and he filled a bag with playing cards, an album of family pictures, music cassettes, and a magazine.

"Let me know when you're ready," he called after tapping lightly on the bathroom door.

"I'm ready now."

He unlocked the door and pushed it open. Her hair was slicked back from her face. She came out shyly, dressed in his flannel shirt. The cuffs were rolled back and the tails hung down her thighs. Which were bare.

"What about the jeans?" he asked.

She shrugged self-consciously. "They were uncomfortable without my underwear."

He glanced inside the bathroom and saw that she had washed out her bra and panties by hand and they were drying on the edge of the tub.

No underwear. And those long bare legs. No underwear. And the tails of his shirt swayed provocatively as she moved. Did she know what she was doing? What message she was sending?

She wanted to play canasta and listen to music, so that was what they did all afternoon. She seemed content and comfortable, sitting cross-legged on the mattress, pondering her cards, oblivious to everything but the game. He wished he could be oblivious. But he kept noticing her bare legs and thinking about her bare skin beneath the shirt.

When it came time for him to go down to fix dinner he was glad for the escape. He got the potatoes and onion frying, then worked on broiling the steak. The broccoli was just a matter of unwrapping the frozen block and dumping it into a pot. He didn't hurry. If anything, he took more time than he needed. It was increasingly difficult for him to be with her without touching or holding her. And it wasn't just that he was sexually starved for her. It was both more complex and more basic than that. He needed physical contact with her. Anything. Everything. He felt like the little monkey with the wire mother in all those psychology films, belly filled but hungering for softness, dying for want of a touch.

The dinner was a success. She seemed pleased by the food as well as the candlelight and the silly Christmas napkins. He was glad that he had not given in to a last-minute urge to bring her down to eat at the kitchen table. They were safe together in the upstairs room, and he did not want to jeopardize that.

He told her about Hana's losing her front teeth and about Felice's promotion, keeping the conversation light, making her smile.

"This was so good," she said, neatly cutting the last of her steak into bite-sized pieces. "I haven't had steak for ages."

He started to ask what she had been eating, but he did not want her to think about her commune life. He wanted her to forget it.

She leaned over to the edge of the mattress and set her plate and utensils on the floor. He followed her lead and set his plate out of the way. She rearranged the pillows and moved so that she was beside him. Close but not touching.

"I keep worrying about Hana," she said.

"I'm sure she's fine. Valerie seems very devoted to her."

"Devoted. Right. That's Valerie. Devoted."

"Why do you hate your mother so much?" he asked.

She was quiet for a moment.

"There's so much you don't know about me. So much I kept from you." She shook her head. "I was afraid you wouldn't love me if you knew . . ."

"Oh, Alex—"

"No. Let me say everything I want to say before I chicken out." She sighed. "I never knew my father. I'm not even sure who he was, because Valerie changed her story so many times. What I do know is that Valerie took a bus from Rockwell City, Iowa, to Hollywood when she was sixteen. She worked as a waitress and went through the whole bit of trying to be discovered and become a star. She had a couple jobs as an extra and got work helping a costume designer. I was born when she was eighteen. Her most repeated story is that my father was this grade B movie producer named Robertson, but she's also claimed that she was sleeping with some really important star who wanted to marry her or that she was sleeping with some really important director who would have made her a leading lady if she hadn't gotten pregnant. She used the director bit whenever she wanted to make it my fault that she hadn't gotten the big break."

"Your fault?"

"Yeah. You know . . . she sacrificed her one chance at stardom to carry me to term. Such a self-sacrificing, devoted mom. All that bullshit. Other times—when she was telling me what a waste I was—she said that she'd only agreed to give the producer a blow job but he raped her, and then he wouldn't answer her calls when she tried to ask him for the money for an abortion."

She sighed again. "I guess . . . now that I'm older and I've seen how hard it is to make it and to be a mother . . . I guess now I could forgive her if that was all there was to it. I mean, she was young and alone and broke and completely unprepared for parenting. I could forgive her for being a lousy, manipulative, mean mother. I could forgive her if it was just that."

She glanced sideways at him, and he saw pain in her eyes.

"You don't have to say any more," he said.

"I want to. It feels good to finally tell you things. See, the really bad stuff started when I turned twelve, shot up to five-nine, and grew breasts. Suddenly men started staring at me, and my mother started treating me like I was competition. She didn't want me to meet any of her dates when they picked her up and she didn't want anyone to know I was her daughter. She'd introduce me as her little friend and her niece and her acting student and all kinds of bullshit. Then one day this gay costume designer friend of hers saw me and had a fit about how I should be reading for parts. And my mother suddenly had the idea that she'd make me the star that she had always wanted to be.

"She hauled me around and introduced me to people, and I read scripts and I was terrible. Then one day she took me to this director's office, and somehow she talked her way in and I don't know what was supposed to happen but . . ." She gave a mirthless rueful chuckle. "The guy stood behind me and told me to keep my eyes closed. Then he started making a lot of strange noises and groaning. Later, after he told me to leave, there was a big sticky spot on my coat.

"I knew something creepy had happened but I didn't exactly know what. Valerie knew, though. She knew. She dropped that coat at the cleaner's on our way home. She knew. So what do you think she did when the guy's secretary called and said he wanted me to come in again? She said sure. Fine. And she was furious with me when I didn't want to go.

"That was the first time I hurt myself. I ran outside and I climbed up onto the roof of a garage and I jumped off onto the driveway. Broke my ankle. Had a cast on for weeks and weeks. Then crutches. The whole bit.

"My mother got finally discouraged about the star idea when everyone agreed that I had zero acting talent, and I got nearly a year of peace. Then one night she had a party and this local photographer was there and he got all excited about taking pictures of me. I tried to say no but she said yes and it went okay. The guy had bad breath and he kept trying to look down my blouse, but he gave me money and took some pictures and sent them off to New York and that started my modeling career."

"You became Xan," Dan said.

"Yeah. So Valerie's been telling you things, huh?"

"Some things."

"Did she tell you that she made me go to Manhattan by myself when I was fourteen! That I got gang-raped at a party the third week I was there? That sleazy rich guys were always after me and people were constantly trying to get me to do drugs and I was lonely and miserable and scared to death? Did she tell you any of that?"

She looked at him, tears gathering in her eyes.

"I'm so sorry." He took her hand. "And I'm sorry you thought you couldn't tell me. I'm sorry you had to carry that with you as a secret."

A little smile came through the tears. "I should have trusted you more, shouldn't I?"

"Yes."

"My mother taught me never to trust anyone. Especially not her. Did she tell you she took all my money those first years? Said she was investing it for me. Right. She invested it in a nice place for her to live and a nice bank account for her to use."

"Oh, baby, baby . . ." He put his arms around her and pulled her close.

When her fingers slipped between the buttons of his shirt his heart nearly stopped.

"Danny," she whispered. "Do you still want me?"

# Chapter 11

He shouldn't. He knew he shouldn't. It was wrong. With her so confused. With him as her jailer . . .

But she looked at him with that breathless expectant look, lips slightly open, eyes wide, the darkness in them vast enough to fall into.

"Alexandra," he whispered.

"We want you, Dan," she whispered back.

He didn't hear the *we*. How could he when his pulse was a bass drum in his ears and his heart was swollen double in his chest and his cock was so hard it hurt? He hurt everywhere. Hurt with wanting her. Hurt with need. Aching like a wound. His spirit wounded. Desperate for healing.

He twined his fingers into her hair and kissed her, long and hard, so hungry for her that he wanted to swallow her whole. She put her hands against his chest and pushed him back, then unbuttoned his shirt. The faint warmth of her breath against his skin was so sweet that he felt the sting of tears in his eyes.

"We can make you so happy, Dan. Give you everything you've always wanted."

Again the words did not register.

"Take your clothes off," she said.

And he did. Hands shaking. Fighting to get everything off.

She waited till he was done. She rose up onto her knees, eyes locked on his. She raised her arms over her head and pulled the shirt off without unbuttoning it. The stretching of her body was voluptuous, and then she was naked before him and her skin was molten gold in the candlelight. With his fingertips he traced the elegant line of her neck, the curves of her shoulders, the hollow of her throat, and then, tenderly, he circled the erect buds of her nipples.

She caught his hands and drew them in, covering her breasts with them, urging him.

"It's been too long," she said. "Too long to go slow."

Which was right. Oh, God, she was right, and he flipped her onto her back and pressed against her, his hard cock against her soft belly, his hard chest against her soft breasts. His lips on hers. This was right. This was so right. This was all there was. This connection to her this joining with her this bond that made them each greater and stronger. This was the act of faith. The act of worship. This was immortality.

"I want your mouth on me, Dan. And I want to suck you. Together. Let's do it together."

"But I need to be inside you, Alex. To fill you up and feel you coming with me."

"Later," she whispered, sliding into position.

And then the hot wet sweetness took him and he fell, fell into that primal oblivion of need and need to give, of warm flesh and greedy mouths and hungry souls.

He lay there. Instead of a lazy afterglow he felt a yawning uncertainty. May had warned him about having sex too soon. Here she was, locked in a room with him, his prisoner. That was wrong. The wrong way to begin their life again.

She stretched and turned toward him, propping herself up with her elbow. It was all still there; the apricot-gold skin, the extraordinary gold eyes starred green around the pupils, the burnished mahogany hair, the angled symmetry of her face, the lean length of her body, the perfect breasts. It was all there, and yet he was afraid because she was different. She was changed.

"I love you, Alex."

She regarded him a moment, as though what he'd said was interesting. "I wish I was a man," she said. "Men are the closest thing there is to God because men bring the seed of light to create new life."

He was too dumbfounded to reply.

"Do you feel like God when you shoot your seed?"

"I feel like your lover. Your husband."

"That's because you haven't opened yourself to the truth."

Again he could not reply.

"You're lucky, because that's all you have to do is open yourself. For me it was different. Mostly because I'm a woman, but also because all my natural senses and all my primal knowledge were clogged up with garbage."

"Alex . . ."

"You used to think about God, right? You told me once that you really struggled with religious issues while you were in college."

"Yes. I still think about God. Whether there's a spiritual force, and if so, whether it's outside us or within us."

"You say things so well, Dan." She sighed. "After I had Hana I started wondering about religion, too. The whole birth thing was such a miracle and she was such a miracle that it got me worrying whether there maybe was a God. I kind of took a just-in-case approach. I didn't really believe there was an old man hanging out in the sky, but I didn't want to take any chances, so I'd go into Catholic churches and dip into that water and I'd say that little prayer to myself before I went bed . . . you know, the one about now I lay me down to sleep, if I should die before I wake . . ."

"You taught Hana to say it every night, too."

"Of course. That was the whole point. I wanted to make sure Hana was safe if it turned out there was an old man up there spying on us all." She rolled her eyes. "You won't believe this. When she was three weeks old I took her into Manhattan and spent a whole day going in and out of every kind of church I could find. Sort of introducing her. Just in case God had a favorite church."

A small laugh escaped him because it was so like Alex to be caught in the middle. Not a believer yet afraid not to believe. He remembered the time that their end of the neighborhood had had a string of fire escape burglaries. She had dismissed the danger. Pointed out how safe their building was. Later he had noticed her jewelry box outside on their fire escape. He had opened the window and retrieved the ornate wooden box and opened it. Inside were five twenty-dollar bills, her best jewelry, and a note that said "Here's everything valuable. Go away and leave us alone."

She shrugged and grinned. "I was pretty stupid about the God thing, huh? To think that there was even a possibility of this one old guy sitting on a throne in the sky."

Dan pulled the sheet up to his waist and moved several pillows into place to prop up his head and shoulders. He was uncertain where she was going and worried about saying the wrong thing. For the first time that day he wished Everett May was with him. May would know how to steer the conversation. He would know how to defuse and soothe and yet lead her out of the confusion. That was what he was famous for. And a conversation like this was what May had been aiming toward.

She seemed to think for a moment, changing as the fire caught within her—a zealot's fire—lighting in her eyes and burning with a ferocious intensity. He was riveted. He had never seen her so stunningly beautiful.

"This is what you have to get past, Dan—this God-looking-down-on-us stuff. Because it's totally wrong and limiting, and it clouds your thinking so that your inborn knowledge can't come through."

"I don't have a God-in-the-sky fixation, Alex. You know that. I'm not religious."

"Yes! That's my point. You're not religious because you're wise enough on your own to reject this ridiculous idea of a guy in the sky. But you're so hung up on rejecting that you aren't letting yourself open to what really is going on."

She sat up. Her nipples were dark in the flickering candlelight, and her rounded breasts swayed with her movements. She pulled on his flannel shirt, arranged herself cross-legged, and continued.

"There *is* a spirit guiding and shaping everything—from little blades of grass to the stars out in space. And that spirit is our creator, and it's the force that's been called God and Allah and Yaweh and all the other names people have tried to label it with. But how can you label the source of everything? How can you give it a name and a form? You can't. Through time people have been so determined to define it and categorize it—to fit it into their narrow scope of understanding—that they've gotten it all twisted around, and they've somehow confused themselves into believing that this all-encompassing force is concerned with and involved in petty human politics and power struggles. You know . . . like church hierarchies and holy wars and all that. Which would be about as ridiculous as claiming that we humans are worried about the battles that rival ant colonies are having."

She paused for a moment, focused inward as though daydreaming.

"There are things that can be known. The Source is male. It's a father force. Strong and stern and fearful. And humans are its most beloved creation because it made men in its image. Not like a shape you know. Because it has no physical form. But in the image of its essence."

She cocked her head and scrutinized him with a questioning look. "Do you understand? Because I've memorized Noah's teachings, but I've never tried to explain them to anyone and . . ."

"I understand. I also understand that these aren't your words, Alex. You're letting someone else speak through you."

What he'd meant to imply was that she'd been brainwashed, but she took it as the most positive of comments. Her entire face lit with delight.

"Yes! That's right! You're hearing him speak through me! Oh, Dan. I knew you'd understand if you ever let yourself listen. I knew you'd awaken and be given wings to rise above the rest of us."

He sighed inwardly.

"What's this new religion called, Alex?"

"It's not a religion. It's not like being a Christian or a Jew or a Muslim or a Buddhist or whatever. Those are all superficial. They have nothing to do with Him. They're just . . ." She waved her hand as though to dismiss them. "Just comfort things. You know . . . something for people to cling to when they don't exactly know what's going on and they're scared of the unknown."

"If it's not a religion, then what is it?"

"It's just the *truth*."

"And who discovered this truth?"

"I'm not sure what you mean."

"It wasn't spontaneous, was it? A roomful of people who all stood up at the same time and said 'Aha.' "

"Well . . . Abba says—"

"Abba? Is he the guru?"

"His name is actually Noah. We . . . the women and children . . . call him Abba because that's like Daddy or Papa." She smiled to herself as though just speaking of him brought her joy. "Noah is the interpreter and the messenger and the leader. He awakens those who are chosen."

Dan suddenly felt very tired. He wanted to close his eyes and block everything out. How had he imagined that she was recovered?

"Okay," he said wearily. "The group is called The Ark. And the leader calls himself Noah. Why the glaring biblical references if traditional religion is so superficial?"

She brightened again. "It's symbolic. He was guided to the name Noah because of the symbolism. The same with The Ark."

"And how does the story of Noah and the ark relate to your group? Are you catching animals and building a boat?"

"No," she said with a tinge of exasperation. "It's not literal. I told you . . . it's symbolic. We are the awakened ones, and he has gathered us and we are prepared for whatever comes, but it's got nothing to do with boats and pairs of animals and all that. It's symbolism."

His left hand was palm down on the sheet between them, and she covered it with her own. Slid her narrow fingers into the spaces between his fingers. Looked deeply into his eyes. And there was a stirring in his groin that made him want to tear his traitorous cock from his body. What was wrong with him? She was in trouble. She was possessed. She was drowning just as surely as she'd been drowning that day in the East River. Yet he was caught by the siren song of her flesh. Fortunately, she seemed not to notice. He shifted and turned onto his side, letting the sheet settle into loose folds that concealed his betrayal.

"Symbolism, Dan," she said as though reminding him of some great truth they had shared in the past. "You always said that you thought the dividing line between humans and other animals wasn't tools or opposing thumbs or color perception or memory or even the ability to feel abstract fear and grief."

"Yes," he admitted.

After hearing her parrot her new prophet's words it was disturbing to hear her shift into a summation of his own thoughts. Was that what he had been to her? A guru bearing ideas?

"You said that humans were different because of their imaginations. You also said that the price we pay for this powerful imagination is that we have intellectual and emotional hungers and we can go crazy and get bored and things."

He shrugged. "Something like that."

She grinned triumphantly. "Yes! And Noah was really impressed when I told him that. Because it's very close to the message in The Truth."

"Which is?"

"That humans are above other creatures because we were given a spiritual nature. We were given the capacity for symbolism and order. All of us were given that. And in the beginning this difference was like a foreign thing for humans because primitive people still identified so closely with the apes that they were brought up from. So the difference was something to experiment with and explore. But then as humans developed their superiority this *potential* for symbolism and order grew into a *need* for symbolism and order. But that was okay because that had been foreseen, and into every generation there were strong wise men born. Men who had wings from birth and could rise up and see everything more clearly and lead people into symbolism and order."

She smiled. "Not real wings, you know. Symbolic wings."

"And that's what this Noah is supposed to be? A leader with wings?"

"Oh . . . much more than that. He's . . . Wait. I have to back up."

She steepled her hands at her mouth, and her eyes shifted around the room as though she was searching for the right words.

"It's so hard to do a condensed version. This is sort of an outline of stuff that has to be studied and learned over a long time."

"Go on. You're doing fine."

He heard the resignation in his voice, but she seemed deaf to it.

"Well, awhile back—Noah is still trying to figure out exactly when—The Source finally got fed up with people. Humanity had become a monster. Greedy and petty and selfish and ugly. So all humans were put to sleep. Spiritually to sleep. Life still goes on as usual, but everyone's souls are sort of in comas. And Noah was chosen to find the worthy souls and awaken them."

Dan waited for her to go on, but she was studying him as though expecting a response.

"What about love?" he asked.

"Love? Love is an illusion. It started out as a symbol for the bond that souls can form at higher levels but then it got into our imaginations and we confused it into something else. The whole concept of love is really insignificant when you learn more about it."

He had to clench his jaw and swallow hard before he could speak again.

"How do men and women come together, then, if there is no love?"

"You're a man, Dan! You shouldn't have to ask that question! There's lust and attraction and all the other things that go with the mating drive. The light of Truth is in the seed. Men are the givers of seed, the conduits of Light and Truth. Women are the empty vessels waiting to be filled with Light and Truth."

"And what are women when they're not being vessels?"

"What do you mean?"

"You've implied that men can be leaders as well as seed sowers. Other than walking wombs, what function does Noah think females have in the world?"

"To serve. To help men."

Dan stared at her.

"I can see that this is an attitude problem you'll have to work on, Dan. You're not accepting enough of your maleness. And you don't understand about women. I've come to see that that was one of the biggest problems with our marriage. You didn't know your power, and because of that I didn't know my place."

Dozens of responses ran though his mind, but he was afraid that she would shut down and quit talking if he revealed what he was thinking.

"So the gender roles weren't right in our marriage?"

"Exactly."

"Explain our problems. So I'm sure I understand."

She shrugged. "It's hard to describe. Basically, you were trying to make us equals when men and women aren't designed to be equals. And you were always too softhearted and forgiving. You didn't require enough of me, or of Hana."

"So what should I have done? Should I have spanked Hana? Punished you in some way?"

"That would have helped. And you should have made rules and set limits. You should have been the ruler and the provider and the protector."

"And maybe I should have gone out every evening with my club and beaten dinner to death and dragged it home so you could skin it?"

"Noah says sarcasm is a sign of insecurity."

"Bullshit!"

"So is profanity."

"Alex . . . Alex . . ." He gripped her upper arms, wanting to shake her. To shake the lunacy out of her. "What does Noah say about abandoning your husband and child? Leaving your ruler-provider-protector and the fruit of your womb?"

She winced, but he couldn't tell whether it was from guilt or from the press of his fingers on her arms.

"It was sad that I was awakened alone. But from everything I told him about you, he said that you would see The Truth eventually and join me."

"And Hana?"

"She's a child. It doesn't matter where she is because she can't be awakened yet. I knew you'd take good care of her. So we thought it would be better to leave her with you."

"Less expensive, certainly. And less of a legal problem."

"Dan . . ." Her expression was wounded. "Noah doesn't think like that."

She regarded him sadly for a moment, then leaned forward and kissed him on the lips. Long and slow. She rose up onto her knees, letting the unbuttoned shirt fall open. Her fingers ran through his hair. He slipped his hands under the shirt and her nipples were already hard. The electricity of it sizzled through every cell in his body.

"No." He pulled away. "I can't."

"I think some parts of you can."

She flashed him an erotic, half-lidded smile, and her fingers closed around the root of his erection.

He clenched his teeth. "It's not right, Alex."

"This is more right than it's ever been for us before. Our souls are aligned now. And we join in The Truth. You have the seed and I am the vessel."

"No!"

She bent toward the head of his shriveling cock, and he grabbed her shoulders to pull her upright.

"Alex, we can't solve anything this way."

Her expression was puzzled. "What do we need to solve?"

He knew his fingers were digging into her shoulders too hard but he couldn't stop. It was all he could do to keep from shaking her.

"Everything! Our futures. Our daughter's future. Everything!"

"But it's solved for us. You see The Truth now, so we can go to The Ark together. Noah will be so glad. And we'll send for Hana. Or maybe we should go get her and take her with us? Probably. Because Valerie will be a bitch about it. She might even try to keep Hana. She's evil, you know. Not just unawakened, but evil. Noah says that one of these days she will pay the ultimate price for her evil."

He shook his head, more out of sadness than denial. Laura Ferren's words haunted him. *There's a fine line between conversion and coercion. What if she is truly converted? What will you do then? Will you try to beat that out of her? And what right do you have to do such a thing?*

He looked at the locked door. What right did he have?

Was he her savior or her torturer? What made him any different from Noah in this battle for her soul?

"Dan? What's wrong?"

He searched her face. The beloved face he knew so well. His heart was constricting in his chest. Squeezed by a giant fist.

And he knew, he knew. The knowledge gathered in his heart and brain, then sank through him, heavy and absolute. He knew that he could not keep her prisoner any longer. He could not force her to be his wife again. He could not torment her into loving him again. He knew that he had to let her go.

"Dan? You're scaring me. Say something."

"You're free, Alex. You're free."

"Yes! That's right. You do understand! Noah has freed me. And now he will free you. And Hana will grow up in freedom. All of us in harmony with the earth and bonded in The Truth and The Light, protected by The Source through Noah. Away from all the filth and crime and all the false emptiness that we call modern life. Free!"

Her eyes were shining, and he saw the vision with her—the three of them together, living on the land in a rustic but close community, growing their own food and teaching Hana themselves. Noah's preaching would be an irritant, but there were always irritants, no matter which course a person chose.

What did he have in his life that he could not walk away from?

Nothing.

Alex and Hana were all that mattered. Why not follow her into her dream? Why not be the eternal hypocrite? It was a small price to pay.

But what about Hana? What chance would she have for a normal life if she grew up in The Ark?

"Dan . . ." Alex studied him as though reading something in his eyes. "You're struggling, Dan. What is it? What are you struggling with?"

"The Ark. Going to The Ark . . ." He couldn't finish. He could not tell her that he was grappling with the idea of giving up his true self in order to hold on to her.

"But . . ." An edge of panic came into her eyes. "You're

awakened now. There's no question that you have to come to The Ark. You can't stay out in the sleeping world." She lowered her eyes. "If it's me you're rejecting—"

"No. No. I'm not rejecting you."

"Are you rejecting The Truth, then?" The panic blossomed. "Because if you reject The Truth you reject me."

A chasm broke open inside him. A fault line of profound grief.

"Fuck The Truth! Fuck The Ark! This is you and me. Remember, Alex? You and me. Us. Lovers and friends and partners. That's all I care about. The Ark can sink. The Truth can rot in hell."

She recoiled as though witnessing a hideous transformation.

"Demon," she breathed.

"Stop it, Alex."

"Demon!" She jerked and twisted and beat at his hands on her shoulders, but he wouldn't let go. "Liar! Trickster! You're trying to suck my soul away."

"Alex—"

"I'm not Alex! I am Atarah, and I curse you! I spit on you!" She spat, and the saliva landed on the bridge of his nose.

"Stop it! This is all bullshit and you know it! Deep down you know it, but you're wallowing in the drama of it. You're enjoying the drama of your own self-destruction too much to come back to reality."

"Evil demon! Give Dan back his body!"

"I am Dan," he cried, blinking hard against the burning in his eyes.

She shook her head vehemently. "No. Filthy trickster! You can't seduce my soul from me! My soul is strong. Noah is my strength."

His heart had turned to crystal and was breaking. Disintegrating. He couldn't stand it anymore. He pushed her lightly so that she fell back onto the mattress. Quickly he rose, scooped up his clothes, and headed for the door, feeling in his jeans pocket for the key as he moved.

"Demon!" she screamed.

And she flew at him and punched him in the back. Only it didn't feel like a punch. It stung. It burned.

Time stretched. Without looking up he was aware of the silent snowflakes striking the skylight and melting away in rivulets. He was aware of the air pressing against the tiny canals of his inner ear. He could hear his own pulse. He could hear her behind him and he could hear that she was holding her breath. He turned. She was stunned, eyes wide and dark, face drained of color. In her hand was a steak knife. The blade was red.

"Dan?" she said in a tiny, frightened voice. "Are you back, Dan?"

It hurt to breathe. He could feel a warm wetness running down his back. He looked at her and saw her terror and felt a great compassion. It started deep inside him and spread to fill the room. To cradle her. To forgive her. To forgive all that was human in the world. All that was weak and lonely and desperate for meaning.

"I'm back, Alex. I'm Dan. The demons are gone."

She dropped the knife.

"Dan," she whispered, breaking into a trembling smile as tears spilled from her eyes. "I'm sorry. I had to save you."

"I know."

Talking was an effort because it interfered with breathing, but he forced the words out. "I'm back now, but I'm hurt. I need you to go downstairs and get the cellular phone."

"Okay."

"It's in the kitchen. Bring it. Quick." He held out the key to the door.

She left. He pulled the top sheet off the bed and tried to wrap it around himself but couldn't. He lay back on the mattress and tried to apply pressure with a pillow. Everything was floating and distant. He felt separated from his body, from the searing pain of the wound. But there was another pain, a greater pain, that floated with him. He had lost his wife. He knew that now. She had been lost to him since that morning so long ago when he woke in the empty bed, naively believing that he would pick her up and take her to dinner and their life would go on as before.

There was no sound from beyond the door. He wondered if she had run away and abandoned him. But then she appeared in the doorway with the phone in her hand.

"Dial," he said.

She stared at him mutely.

"Give it."

He waved her forward, and she crossed the room to put the phone in his hand, her expression as blank as a sleepwalker's.

By the time he was through giving directions to the emergency dispatcher he was cold and sweating and gasping for air. He had Alex wrap the bedsheet tightly around and around his chest and prop him against the wall. It occurred to him that he might die. The thought was abstract and not at all disturbing.

Alex was on the edge of the mattress, staring at him. The blankness had dissipated, and her eyes were frightened and childlike. Hana's eyes. Hana. If he died, what would become of Hana? He stirred.

"Alex. Dress. Go down. Turn on lights."

She left. He heard her in the bathroom. Some minutes later she appeared in her dress, which she must have gone down to the dryer to find.

"I want to wait here with you, Dan. In case the demon tries to come back into you."

"No." He put as much force into his voice as he could summon. "I'm safe. Flash the porch light. Help the ambulance find us."

She nodded obediently, picked up the cordless phone from where he had dropped it, and went out.

He heard her footfalls on the stairs and he heard her say the name Noah. Whether she was muttering a prayer or speaking into the telephone he didn't know.

# Chapter 12

"You were lucky. The blade could have done much more than puncture a lung, and then surgery might not have been so successful."

Dan nodded.

"You still insist it was an accident? That you fell backward on the knife?"

"Yes."

"I've never seen an accident like that." The doctor scowled at him through her rose-framed glasses. "Neither have the police."

"It was a strange accident," Dan agreed, turning his head to look out the window at the picture postcard view.

The doctor snorted a soft humph, then began an examination, poking and prodding, peering under gauze pads. "I told the chief that I didn't think you'd be much help." She listened to his chest with her stethoscope. "You'll be out of here in no time. We should all be so healthy."

"Thanks."

The doctor started out the door, then turned back.

"I almost forgot. The nurse said to tell you that your phone has been turned on. She also wanted you to know that she's repeatedly tried that number you gave her in New York, but there's been no answer."

The door sighed shut and Dan looked at the telephone on the table beside his bed. Here he was in a hospital again with only a phone linking him to the outside world. He thought about the calls he should make. He thought about how important it was to place the calls. But he could not make himself reach across that small space and pick up the receiver. Instead he went back to staring at the ceiling as he had been doing before the doctor interrupted.

The drugs had him suspended in a pleasantly weightless, liquid state. Disconnected from his body. But he knew that his arm could reach for the phone, however clumsily. And he knew that his arm ought to do it. But if his arm did it, he would have to speak and summon the energy to answer questions. And he would have to think. He wasn't thinking now. The anonymous room with the postcard view was like a cocoon. Safe and private. No thinking—just existing. And even a voice over a wire might break open that cocoon.

He was not ready for that. Metamorphosis was for bugs and Kafka. He refused to emerge. He refused to metamorphise. Metamorphose? He felt like chuckling. Only that would have hurt, so he didn't. He stared at the white ceiling. Hiding in his cocoon. Letting the drugs float him away.

"Hello, Mr. Behr."

He opened one eye. It was the doctor. Rain was spoiling his postcard view.

"I changed your medication this morning, so you should become more alert."

He attempted speaking, but his voice was dry and crinkled like paper. He shifted in the bed and was startled by very distinct and immediate pain signals. No more cocoon. No more floating. He scrubbed at his face with his hands, looked around, and saw his lunch on the rolling tray table beside the bed. The last thing he remembered was the dawn intrusion by two nurses determined to change his sheets. Where had the day gone? For that matter, where was yesterday?

The doctor smiled in her brisk, no-nonsense manner and whipped her stethoscope from the pocket of her white jacket.

"You're doing well. If you show me that you can get up and around this afternoon, then I'll release you tomorrow."

He nodded and pushed the button to raise the head of the bed. Everything struck him at once. He was hungry. He was thirsty. He was angry at himself for having called no one in the twenty-four hours that his phone had been on.

He was concerned over the fact that Valerie hadn't answered the nurse's calls to his apartment. He was worried about his wallet and clothing, all still at May's mountain house.

When she had finished her examination, the doctor straightened and peered into his eyes.

"So, how are you feeling now?"

He had to clear his throat before he could speak.

"Alert," he croaked.

She laughed.

"I ought to warn you—the chief wants to see you again. Probably about the fire."

"What fire?"

Her eyebrows went up in surprise.

"I assumed one of the nurses had already told you. That house you were staying in burned to the ground last night. It's a big topic of conversation around town."

He was too stunned to speak.

"Chief's on a tear. First you have your strange accident with the steak knife and the woman who rode in with you disappears before she can be questioned, then there's a fire in the house you were at."

"I can't believe it. Could I have left something on or . . ."

"They're investigating it. Looks suspicious, they say. The chief is pretty certain that it was set."

He rubbed his forehead with his fingertips and avoided the doctor's eyes. Questions of who and why careened through his mind, followed by fear of the answers.

"At least we know you didn't set it, don't we?"

His surprised look made her smile.

"You haven't left this bed, so you're in the clear. That's lucky."

"Right. I'm a lucky guy."

"You are indeed. You'll come out of this with nothing but a scar. You're not in trouble with the law. And some of your things were saved from the fire because the chief had taken them for his investigation."

"He did?" Dan almost sighed in relief but caught himself. Shallow breaths were all he could manage.

"Yes. They're here in the hospital now."

He wished she would leave so that he could call Everett

May. Did May know about the house? He could not shake a feeling of guilt, a feeling that he was somehow responsible for the burning of May's deprogramming haven.

She glanced over at his tray. "You'd better eat your lunch. You had a visitor a little while ago, and she's supposed to be back soon."

"A visitor? Who?"

The doctor shrugged and moved toward the window to look out. "I didn't see her. You were sleeping, so she told the nurses she'd be back after lunch."

Gingerly he reached for the corner of his rolling tray table and guided it into position over the bed. The afternoon's offering was a white bread sandwich with a mayonnaise mystery filling, a cup of strangely orange soup, and a square of red Jell-O. He wanted to tell the doctor to leave but instead he took a bite of the sandwich, certain that she would not stand there and watch him eat.

"Try a little walk down the hall after lunch," the doctor said as she finally started toward the door. "And you might want to call the kitchen and ask for some fruit and cookies. That's usually safe."

When she was gone he pushed the tray away. A visitor. A woman. Alex. It had to be Alex. No one else even knew he was there. So she hadn't left him to rush back to Noah. Something deep inside her was still attached to him.

Alex.

He combed his fingers through his hair, shifted on the rough sheets, then sat up straight in the bed, gritting his teeth against the sharp hot pain that resulted. Alex needed him. She was probably scared to death. She had ridden in the ambulance with him, but then vanished. Since then she must have been hiding from the police and trying to get into the hospital to see him. Her staying had to mean something. But what? That she had chosen him over Noah? Or simply that she cared enough about him to wait until he could go back to The Ark with her?

The stabbing had shocked her deeply. In his scrambled memories of that night he remembered her sobbing and holding his hand. Maybe the shock of the stabbing had finally jarred her back to reality. Maybe . . .

Instantly he was infused with buoyancy and optimism.

His mind raced. He would call for his clothes and demand that he be released immediately. If they wouldn't release him, he would walk out. Then he would take her home. He would find a good counselor. Laura, of course. If Laura would have them. But she would. He knew she would. Laura would never harbor a grudge. She would help them put their life back together.

He tried to find a comfortable position in the bed. How much longer before Alex came? He wished he had his watch. Then he glanced at the phone and remembered that he still had not spoken to Everett May. Now, with the news about the house being torched, he felt an obligation to speak to the man immediately.

Dan struggled to recall the emergency contact number. May had insisted that the number be committed to memory, but for a moment, injury and drugs wiped it from his mind. Then it came to him. He gave the long-distance operator his telephone credit card number and waited.

"Window Rock Silver and Pawn," a voice answered.

"Hello, this is Dan Behr and I need to speak to Everett May."

"No one here by that name, fella. Sorry."

"No. Wait!"

There was something else he was supposed to say. He'd been so intent on recalling the number that he'd neglected May's other instruction. Now he had to struggle to dredge it up.

"I need to speak with the Pathfinder," he said, feeling like a child playing spy games. "I've lost something."

"Just a minute," the voice replied.

He heard a shuffling sound and then a series of clicks.

"Yeah. You got me," May's voice said over the static of a bad line.

"How is your son?" Dan asked without introduction, knowing that May did not want to use names on the phone.

"He's gonna be okay. Sorry about the timing."

"I've got some more bad news for you. I got hurt and had to let her go. Then there was a fire set at the cabin."

Silence.

"Who do you think . . . ?"

"I've made enemies," May said gruffly. "But I'll bet the

fire is connected to her. My son too. Could be he was hit to lure me away from the cabin. Can't talk any more now. I'll contact you at your home in a few weeks."

Dan put the receiver down, shocked by what May was implying. The man had to be wrong. Alex would never be involved with—

A light tap came at the door. His heart leaped. The hospital staff never knocked. The chief hadn't knocked. It had to be her.

"I'm awake," he called.

The door opened several inches and a face peeked in. It was not Alex's face. It was Laura Ferren.

"Don't look so disappointed," she said as she came inside.

"What are you doing here?"

She put her large purse and satchel on one chair and pulled the other chair around to sit beside the bed.

"The police found my card in your wallet and called me in New York."

"Why?"

"They were looking for answers, and they thought I might be your therapist. I told them I wasn't and that I didn't even know you were in California . . . which was true."

"I'm sorry I didn't tell you." He sighed. "You were right about so many things."

"That's not important now."

"Why did you come here?"

She studied her hands for a moment. He took in her wrinkled clothing, the escaped strands of hair falling around her face, the stress in her eyes and in her manner, and he knew that she had dropped everything and gone to great difficulty to be in that seat beside him.

"The police asked me about another number that they'd been trying in New York without success. It was your apartment number. I tried it, too. No answer at all. Any time of the day or night. So I called Felice and asked about Valerie and Hana. She told me that they were supposed to be there and that she had also been trying for days to reach them. She was terribly worried.

"I became concerned. I met Felice at your building. We talked the super into letting us in."

She reached for her purse.

"We found this letter there," she said, pulling out a folded piece of paper and handing it across the bed to him.

> Dear Dan,
>    I've been taking care of Hana for a while now and I can't stay away from my home any longer. I didn't think it mattered where me and Hana were since you are not around anyway so I am taking her home with me where she will have a nice place to live and a good school.
>    I wish you luck in what you are doing but I have no hope that Alex will ever be a good mother to Hana again. Call when you get back and we can talk about a time when it would be good for you to come visit us.
>    Take care of yourself. Hana sends her love. And I send you my promise that I will do everything I can to make up for Hana's being abandoned by her mother.
>                                                    Valerie

Dan read the letter three times, quickly at first, then slower, and then word by word, increasingly alarmed at Valerie's intentions.

"What is she trying to do?"

"That's why I came," Laura said. "I couldn't just call you on the phone and read that to you . . . not with you lying here recovering from surgery."

"She's taking Hana away from me, isn't she?"

"I'm afraid that might be her plan."

Dan's head fell back against the pillow. Why not let Valerie take her? Wouldn't Hana be better off? What did he know about raising a child? What did he have to give her? He was a jobless, wifeless failure of a man. He was an inadequate parent. Wouldn't it be selfish to hold on to her?

But what did Valerie offer? Valerie, who had ignored her daughter's pain. Valerie, who had failed so desperately as a mother. All Valerie wanted with Hana was another chance at mothering. A chance to prove that she was not the cause of Alex's wounded spirit. A chance to nurture a child successfully, thereby showing the fault had not been with the parenting but had been inside Alex herself like a defective wire or a weak spot in the grain of a board.

He fumbled for his call button and stabbed at it.

"What are you doing?"

"I'm getting out of here. I'm going after my daughter."

"You're not well yet. I'll go. I'll bring Hana back."

"Yes?" the nurse's voice said through the intercom.

"I want my clothes and wallet. I want a release. I'm leaving."

"Dan!" Laura leaned over the bed, put her hands lightly on either side of his face and locked eyes with him. "You were stabbed. You had surgery to reinflate your lung. This is serious. If you compromise your health who will be left for Hana?"

Silence.

She pulled her hands away as though his face had suddenly become too hot to touch, lowered her eyes self-consciously, and stiffly sat back in the chair.

"The doctor said she might release me tomorrow anyway."

"All right. Then wait till tomorrow. Valerie doesn't know what's going on. She'll be surprised to see us whenever we turn up."

"We?"

She stiffened and lifted her chin.

"I've already canceled the rest of the week in New York and have to be in my L.A. office on Monday. It's no trouble for me, and you may need some help."

"Thank you."

"I like Hana."

"I know. You're also an extraordinarily good person."

Her cheeks reddened, and she seemed relieved when a nurse threw open the door.

"Mr. Behr! I don't know who you think you are, but—"

"Sorry," he said. "It was a mistake. I'm supposed to leave tomorrow, not today."

The woman hesitated, regarding him with confused annoyance, then said, "Yes. That's right. Have you finished your lunch?"

"I was wondering if I could get some fruit. An apple, maybe?"

She nodded and whisked the tray out of the room.

"I'll make the travel arrangements," Laura said, rising from the chair, suddenly in a hurry to leave.

"What do you think?" Dan asked. "Should I call Valerie from here and tell her I'm coming, or should I wait until we're in L.A.?"

"I don't think you should call her at all. That would remove the element of surprise. And if you give her any notice she might decide to take Hana on a vacation somewhere."

"But I don't know her address. I'll have to call to get the address."

"I can get it."

"It's not published."

"I know how to get it. Don't worry."

Laura picked up her purse and satchel. "I'm going to find a room for the night. I'll either call or come by again this evening."

"Okay."

She started for the door.

"Laura . . ."

She stopped.

"I've lost her. I've lost my wife."

For a moment there was no response, then Laura turned her head to look back at him. He thought at first that it was a silent offering of sympathy, but he realized, after she was gone, that it had been much more complicated than that. And he wondered what she was thinking that she didn't want to tell him.

Dan was weak enough that he was glad for Laura's physical aid as well as her emotional support. She propped him up. She waited in lines so that he could stay seated. She asked the airline to let him board early, saying that she was his doctor and that he was under her care.

They arrived in Los Angeles. Laura had phoned ahead, and two of her assistants were waiting for them. They had each driven a car to the airport. One was Laura's. They guided Laura and Dan to the car in the parking area, then got into the other car and drove off. Gratefully, Dan sank into the passenger seat and left navigation to Laura. The L.A. freeways would have intimidated him even if he hadn't been recovering from surgery.

Laura got them to West Hollywood and, with the aid of some written directions one of her assistants had given her, found Valerie's address. It was a place that brought the word *cute* to mind immediately. A winding cobbled walk through small perfect plantings. A clutch of palm trees. Vines he didn't recognize draping over the doorway.

Dan knocked. Valerie opened the door, stopped, stared, mouth open and eyes calculating how much trouble she was in.

"Hi," Dan said.

He stepped in without waiting for an invitation. Laura followed.

"Daddy!" Hana cried, running into the tiny entryway to throw herself at him.

He swept her into his arms and kissed her cheek. His daughter. His child. And it struck him that she was truly his now. His responsibility. His to cherish. His to guide. No more baby under glass. No more father in the background. Her health, her happiness, her future—even her view of the world—were now in his hands.

"Aren't we surprised," Valerie said, recovering her composure. "How in the world did you find your way here without calling me for directions? I didn't think you even knew my address."

"It was easy," Dan said. "Laura knows L.A. She has an office here, you know."

"How nice. I didn't know that. Well, come in. Come in. How about a nice cold drink? I've got lemonade or Coke or root beer. All diet, of course."

"No thanks," Dan said.

Laura shook her head.

"Come sit down. Make yourselves at home."

As she talked she was leading them down a short hall. Her face was so much like Alex's face—the sharply angled cheekbones, the perfectly curved mouth—but her eyes were entirely different. Not just in their color, as he had thought before, but in the ruthless knowledge they held, in the cunning. Her eyes were the eyes of a predator. Alex's were the eyes of the prey.

They stepped through a curved doorway and into a high-ceilinged living room with an ornate fan hanging in the center. Dan froze. Every wall was covered with huge blown-up photographs. Alex's face on magazine covers. Alex posed in the shadows, her body enticing in a low-cut evening dress, her face perfection, her gaze distant, unreachable. Achingly lovely. Painfully fragile.

"Dan . . . ?" Laura said, touching his arm.

"Isn't Mommy pretty in these pictures?" Hana said. "Valerie's gonna teach me to be a model so I can grow up and be in pictures just like these. I'll be famous. Then I can have any animal I want. I can have a whole zoo!"

"Laura," Dan said evenly, "would you mind helping Hana find her things and pack them?"

"Not at all." Laura smiled at Hana and took the child's hand as Dan swung her to the floor.

"Oh, that's too much trouble for you, Doctor. Why don't you two go out to lunch? There's a nice pasta place real close to here. And when you get back I'll have Hana all packed up and ready."

"No, thank you, Valerie." He glanced at Laura. "You guys go on. Show Laura your things, punkin."

As soon as Laura and Hana left the living room Dan turned to Valerie. He wanted to harangue her. To punish her. Not only for attempting to steal Hana but for all the damage she had inflicted on Alex. But when he looked into her eyes he saw her vulnerability and her fear. He saw her furtive guilt. And he felt a great pity for her. Not only for the regrets she had to carry but for the empty life she had created.

"I don't blame you," he said at last. "But Hana is my daughter."

"You don't know how to take care of her! What are you going to do—dump her with some stranger? Bury yourself in work and ignore her? Tuck her in nights and take her for walks on Sundays and congratulate yourself on being a single father?

"Look!" She threw out her arms. "I have a nice home for her, Dan, and I have time, and there's so much I want to give her."

"She's not Alex," Dan said quietly. "This is not your second chance to do it right, Valerie."

The woman wilted. She sank into a chair, tears and mascara running from her eyes.

"I'll be a good father. I know now that I can. And I know what's important. Hana is everything to me. She's half me. The best half of me. She's all there is for me now."

"She's part me, too." Valerie's crying had slipped from the angry tears of defeat into a genuine expression of anguish. "And I don't want to lose her."

"Oh, Valerie . . ." He crossed the room to stand behind her, rested his hands on her shoulders, and gently squeezed. "You're her grandmother. I won't let you lose her. I won't let her lose you. Hana needs your love. She'll always need your love."

He looked up and saw Laura standing in the doorway, watching, hand clutched to her breast, her face filled with tenderness and compassion. And he knew that he had done the right thing.

Part
TWO

# Chapter 13

Dan rubbed tung oil into the red maple of an eighty-year-old stair banister that he had stripped, sanded, and steel-wooled to a satin finish. One room away, a wallpaper hanger shouted Greek-laced obscenities at a floor tiler, who was in turn muttering in Italian at his young Russian-speaking assistant. This was the world of Brooklyn home renovation, a loosely organized underground of the unlicensed and the illegal that was run by ambitious, hardworking men who spoke broken English. Most of the crews were family affairs, headed by brothers or a hierarchy of grandfather, son, and grandson. They thrived, advertised solely by word of mouth, and were fueled by the fact that most of the houses in Brooklyn were old enough to warrant a new bathroom or kitchen at the very least.

The boss on his current job, a wizened little man in white overalls and a snap-brim cap, hustled into the room and peered up at the gleaming banister. "What you think, Danny? When you gonna be finish?"

"Today."

"Good! Good! The people come in last night and was real happy. You fix the broken stuff so beautiful they say you gotta be a artist."

"I guess I should raise my prices," Dan said without taking his eyes from the wood.

The boss laughed. "I tell you and tell you. Your prices is good. Your prices is what the people wanna pay. But you gotta unnerstan—the only way to live and give 'em good prices is workin' quick and cheap. No more such a artist, *capish*?"

Dan smiled noncommittally, and the boss gave him a headshake and a dismissive wave, then moved on to check the progress in the kitchen, where the wallpaperer and the floor tiler were squabbling. *No more such a artist.* That was fine in theory, but the only way he could work, the only way he *would* work, was to evaluate each job and do what was best. He could not, would not, do work he was unsatisfied with—or worse, work he was ashamed of. Those days were over. Left behind at HTO. He would never again spend himself on labors that he could not take pride in.

Several hours later he straightened and stretched out his back, finished. He gathered rags and steel wool, cans and tools, packed everything into his canvas duffel bag, and scrubbed his hands with mineral spirits. Then he went to stand in the center of the dining room to view the staircase from the best angle. Two weeks ago it had been a sagging disgrace with broken balusters and a cracked newel post, and everything smothered beneath dozens of coats of chipping, alligatored paint. Now it was the heart of the house. The New York red maple gleamed, the finely turned spindle balusters were restored, and the great ball on top of the newel post was whole and smooth once again.

Dan was not making as much money as he'd made at HTO, and there was no doubt in his mind that his former co-workers there would consider this work menial, but he felt a joy of accomplishment now that he had not felt in designing cubicles for the dehumanization of corporate employees. This work tapped into skills he'd learned in childhood. Refinishing and repairing old wood pieces had been his father's hobby, and Dan had been taught the secrets of grain and density, the arts of stain and finish, in the same way that other boys were taught how to play ball or catch fish or coax music from an instrument. In addition to which, he took no work home at night and he had a self-determined schedule that allowed him flexibility and plenty of time for Hana. He glanced at the cheap watch he wore for work, thinking that he could stop for dinner ingredients before picking up Hana from her after-school program.

More than a year and a half had passed since he'd lost his wife. He no longer had days when the grief was paralyzing. He no longer had the bouts of seething anger. He supposed, if Laura had been around to analyze him, she would say he'd finally passed through all the stages of grief. By day he was almost healed, laughing easily and often, taking pleasure in his life and in his child, pleased by how quickly he'd learned to parent. Only the nights remained difficult. He lay in his bed remembering the curve of Alex's body next to his. And in dreams she still came to him, an angel of fire and heat, bringing ecstasy, bringing almost unbearable agony, replacing the intense sense of her that was fading from his waking mind.

He was set to begin an advanced degree at Columbia in the fall, and through student loans and continuing work as a finish carpenter, he thought he could get through the program without plunging them into abject poverty. After that he wasn't sure. Losing his position at HTO, scouting for another job, and surveying the current status of architecture with a cold eye had shattered all his remaining professional illusions, jolting him into the realization that his long-cherished dream of designing and building was unrealistic. There was no interest in new designs for public housing, so there was no demand for an architect to serve the needs of the poor. In middle-class housing the building contractors were cobbling together old blueprints or ordering house plans through mail-order catalogs, so architects had become redundant there. And for the wealthy, who were indeed still hiring architects to design and build, there was a social and political system, a who-do-you-know and what-clubs-do-you-belong-to system that he had not been born into and doubted that he would even be admitted to even if he wanted to try. That left corporate building—a dismal area, given the trend toward downsizing and the fact that there were still so many empty or half-finished buildings left from the boom-bust eighties. The few new corporate projects that were announced each year generated fierce competition among internationally successful architects for the commissions.

The common wisdom was that the independent architect who put visions on paper and then shepherded them into reality was doomed to extinction, and Dan knew that even getting an advanced degree would not miraculously change that for him. The stars no longer blinded his sight.

The ecstasy of youthful dreams was gone. The lightning-bolt passion was gone. But in its place was the power of self-knowledge and the certainty that he could shape his own life now. He was confident that he would study and find a direction, a specialty, in which he valued the work and in which his talents would be valued. Perhaps in preservation and restoration. And he was determined that he would not lose his bearings. He would not sell his soul for a higher salary unless he and Hana were facing starvation or eviction, and he would not sacrifice his relationship with his child for anything.

Dan rode the bus from Bensonhurst to Bay Ridge. Eighty-sixth Street was bustling. He stopped in at Richard and Vinnie's, where the white-aproned butchers who were chopping and cutting and packaging behind the tall glass case greeted him by name.

"What's for dinner?" he asked them.

"Chicken cutlets," they agreed unanimously.

While one of them trimmed and weighed the cutlets, another shaved a few slices of bologna and rolled them in white paper. "Here," he said. "Give these to Hana. Tell her she shouldn't let you come in alone."

Dan left the shop smiling to himself and walked around the corner to Star Deli, where he bought a container of freshly made tabbouleh and treated himself to a six-pack of cold beer. The woman behind the counter asked about Hana and complained laughingly about her own children. From there he went a few doors down to the Red Barn, waited while the owner spoke to another customer in Arabic, then asked what fruit the man recommended and discussed the weather while his purchase was tallied.

Hands full of bags and duffel, he started toward the Wee Care Nursery for Hana. Just walking down the neighborhood sidewalks gave him a buoyant feeling. Somehow he had taken root in Bay Ridge. This close-knit community of diverse people was home.

As soon as he stepped inside the front door of Wee Care, Hana spotted him. "Daddy!" she cried, and ran forward waving a large drawing.

She beamed enthusiasm, racing toward him in well-worn jeans and scuffed sneakers with her hair flying. No more the solemn, quiet child in the perfectly matched outfits that she'd been under the care of her mother. No more the rebellious, angry child that she'd been during the months of losing her mother and watching her father fall apart. She was now an energetic, exasperating, clumsy, sweet, endearing, mischievous, happy little girl.

He caught her and swung her around.

"Don't bend my picture!" she squealed.

They usually walked hand in hand, but today she was intent on using both her hands to hold up her drawing so he could admire it as they moved down the sidewalk.

"It's beautiful," he said, examining the lineup of green and purple figures, one giant and the rest small, all smiling, and all with electrified hair. At the bottom was something that looked like a sausage with eyes, and in the top right corner was a sun or moon with a sad face. "Can you tell me about the picture?"

She looked up at him. "It's my family," she declared. "The teacher said to draw our family."

"Ohhhh. And which one am I?"

"You're the biggest. And I'm here in the middle. And here's Felice and Valerie and Laura. I couldn't decide if I should put Mrs. Svensen in."

"I see." Dan kept his expression neutral, but inside he was hurting for her. The poor kid. She'd had to invent a family. Just one overly large daddy and a little faraway grandma weren't enough.

She giggled. "And that's Peppy at the bottom. I didn't get time to make his legs."

"You can do them later at home," he assured her. "Is that the sun or the moon up in the sky?"

"It's the moon. That's where Mommy is. She's trapped in there and she's crying because she can't come down and be with us."

"Oh." He swallowed against the catch in his throat. "Let's walk over and get some movies at Rocky's. It's your week to pick."

"Yes! I want something with real animals. Not cartoon animals."

"You got it."

She slipped her hand into his and launched into a long description of her school day. It did not demand careful listening. He wondered what she had told the teacher about her pictured "family." It seemed so pitiful to him.

Felice was still very much a part of their lives. To cut living expenses, he had decided to move out of the Shore Road apartment and had been shopping the neighborhood for a smaller, cheaper place that would allow Hana to continue at the same school. Felice heard about an upcoming vacancy in her own building and badgered her super until the man agreed to give Dan first chance. The apartment had been exactly right, and their new proximity to Felice had been a real bonus for Hana. Felice filled the role of aunt with charm and verve.

And there was Valerie. She had called Hana faithfully, kept the postal service busy delivering gifts, and had come to New York for several whirlwind visits. He trusted the woman enough now that he had even agreed to let Hana spend a few weeks in L.A. during the upcoming summer.

Then there was also Mrs. Svensen in the picture. He had taken Hana by to see her a few times, bearing sweets from Pierrot's bakery, but the old woman could not be considered "family" by any stretch of the imagination. And Laura. God. They hadn't heard from Laura Ferren in so long. She had been a frequent visitor when he first brought Hana back from Los Angeles, but a tension had developed between them and the visits had lessened. The time they spent together had become strained. And eventually she had stopped coming.

Looking back, he saw that he had been at fault. He had used her too often as an unpaid therapist to vent his grief with rather than treating her as a friend. No wonder she had tired of seeing them. He was almost embarrassed when he recalled some of the scenes when he'd been at his lowest, figuratively crying on her shoulder and asking *Why?* over and over. What a mess he'd been. Now, seeing Laura included in his daughter's portrait of a family, he regretted losing touch with her. She was someone he admired, and Hana had adored her.

When there was a break between stories Dan asked to see the drawing again. "Which one is Laura?"

Hana pointed.

"We haven't seen Laura for a while, have we?"

"No," she said sadly. "And I miss her. Felice told me to think good thoughts about seeing her and maybe it would happen."

"I've got a better idea than just good thoughts. We can call her."

"We can?"

"Sure."

"Can she come see us in our new apartment? Can I show her the animal posters on my walls?"

"I don't know how busy she is . . . but if you want to, we could invite her."

"Yes!"

The rest of the way to the video store, and then from the video store home, Hana talked excitedly about seeing Laura, finally securing a promise from him that he would call the psychologist as soon as they walked in the door.

"Is there school tomorrow?" Hana asked on the way up the apartment building's stairs.

"No. Tomorrow is Saturday."

"You said we'd go to the zoo on Saturday."

"That's right. The Central Park Zoo."

She skipped down the hallway to their apartment singing a song about monkeys jumping on the bed. As soon as they were inside she ran for the phone and handed it to him.

"Only if you take the chicken to the refrigerator," he said, holding out the plastic bag from the butcher.

Quickly she snatched it from him and ran toward their open kitchen area.

He found Laura's home number and dialed. Hana was back beside him before the connection was made.

"Let's ask Laura to come to the zoo with us! Can we? Can we?"

He held up his hand. "I'll see if she's busy."

"She won't be busy. She misses us."

"Okay. Okay."

"Did she answer yet?"

"It's ringing. Shhhh."

"Hello."

"Hello . . . Laura?"

"Is it her?" Hana whispered. He nodded and put his finger to his lips.

"Laura, this is Dan Behr."

There was a quick intake of breath and then a measured, "Hello, Dan."

"It's been so long. How are you?"

"I'm fine. How are you?"

"Terrific."

Hana tugged at his sleeve impatiently, urging, "Ask her."

"I was wondering if you were busy tomorrow? It's going to be beautiful, and Hana and I are going to see our friends at the Central Park Zoo."

The hesitation was so long that Dan thought the connection had been broken.

Then, rather abruptly, she said, "Is that an invitation?"

"Yes!" He laughed and winked at Hana. "A very special invitation. Please come."

"You sound happy, Dan."

"We are happy. And we'll be happier if you say yes."

She laughed then. "Yes."

They spotted Laura standing near the zoo entrance. She was immediately recognizable, dressed in blue jeans and a casual black linen jacket, hair pulled back from her face haphazardly on top, then rioting loose from the barrette in a curly profusion. She looked like an anthropologist from the moon, blinking in the sunlight, watching people stroll by.

"Laura! Laura!" Hana shrieked and charged forward.

The woman opened her arms, laughing, and Dan felt an odd twinge in his chest.

"Hi," he said when he reached the two of them.

"Didn't we miss her so much, Daddy?" Hana prompted, beaming up at Laura and pulling her father into the magic circle.

"We missed her," Dan agreed.

He leaned close for the polite cheek kissing and perfunctory hug and was surprised by how good it was to touch her and inhale her subtle fragrance.

"Come on! Come on!"

Hana had inserted herself between them and slipped her hands into theirs so that she could pull them both toward the zoo.

"Slow down," he said, but he was pleased at her excitement.

They went to the indoor tropical zone first, and Hana tugged them from window to window, sign to sign. There was no opportunity for conversation. Dan flashed Laura an apologetic look, but she smiled and shook her head as though to say that she was happy being dragged behind a hyperexcited seven-year-old. After the tropics they went up the steps to peer into the polar bears' domain. Hana watched with delight as one of the bears dove after a floating toy, climbed out, released it, and dove again. He was still repeating the cycle when they moved on to the red kangaroos.

"Where are they hiding, Daddy?"

Dan studied the trees and grass for the small animals. Nearby, Laura was doing the same. He glanced toward her and was stunned by how lovely she looked, standing in the golden April sun, mouth curved into the gentlest suggestion of a smile, eyes alight with a happiness that bathed everything and everyone around her—making complete strangers respond with smiles and making him respond with an undeniable sexual stirring.

He had never thought of her as anything but a friend—a rather plain friend whose femaleness was incidental—and this sudden attraction befuddled him. Where had it come from?

"You're frowning at me," she said.

"I am?" He tried to appear innocent. "I thought I was frowning at the red kangaroo."

"He's the other direction."

"That's why I was frowning. I couldn't see him."

She laughed, filling him with an incredible lightness. It began in his feet and moved upward, lifting him, making him feel as if he could leap things in a single bound.

"Can I take my sweatshirt off?" Hana asked. "I've got my dangerous species T-shirt underneath."

"Endangered species," he corrected as he helped her get the sweatshirt off over her head.

Immediately she ran back to a spot at the fence. She hadn't calmed down much, but she had at least given up pulling them everywhere at her speed.

"It is getting warm, isn't it?" Dan remarked, slipping off the jacket he'd worn.

He tucked the jacket and the sweatshirt under his arm.

"If you want to take off your blazer I'll be glad to carry it with my stash."

"No," she said sharply, and pulled the lapels of her jacket together.

Dan grinned.

"Fashion is more important than temperature, huh?"

"I'm comfortable the way I am."

"Okay," he said, somewhat annoyed with her sudden curtness.

Hana bounded back toward them.

"Monkeys now," she announced. "And then the penguins!"

They had to practically run to keep up with her. Most of the monkeys were sleeping on their island, so Hana gave them only a few minutes of her attention before spinning and racing toward the penguin house. Inside was chaos. Swarms of children were laughing and calling out, jumping up and down, running back and forth, enchanted by the creatures behind the glass. And the penguins seemed to be enjoying the experience, too. They waddled over their rocks and dove down to streak and spiral through the water, showing off before swimming up to the glass so they could peer straight into the children's faces. Laura stood at the glass with Hana, crouched slightly so that Hana could point and chatter about the birds' antics.

He moved to lean against the back wall. The penguins' side of the glass was icy bright but the people's side was very dimly lit, and both Hana and Laura receded into dark profile from where he stood. Seeing them together in semi-darkness, he could almost be fooled into believing it was Alexandra with Hana. That it was Alex who was listening so attentively to their child and sharing the delight.

The pain hit right in the center of his belly, and he

ducked out of the crowded cavelike viewing room to lean against an outside wall. He closed his eyes for a moment, knowing from experience that it would pass. Sometimes he thought of himself as having a chronic illness, a kind of retrovirus that lived in his cells and flared up occasionally. Just an annoyance, though, now. Kind of an emotional herpes. Nothing fatal, though it had seemed so in the beginning, when he had functioned solely for Hana's sake.

Hana's entrancement lasted for a full half hour, and then they were all back out in the sunshine.

"My choice now," Dan said.

Hana considered and then nodded as though acknowledging the fairness.

"What animal?"

"The seals."

He steered them toward the large tank in the zoo's central courtyard.

"You can go on up to the side, Hana. Laura and I will be sitting right back here."

Laura settled beside him on one of the stone tiers that ringed the seal tank.

"I thought you might be ready for a break," Dan said, and she smiled agreement.

They sat in silence until finally Laura glanced sideways at him and asked, "Have you heard from her at all?"

Dan didn't need to ask who she referred to. Alex was always there, hovering like a ghostly presence.

"Not a word."

"If she ever does return, she won't be the same person."

"I know that." He sighed without meaning to. "There was a divorce. I found a lawyer and went through all the legal hoops."

"That's good. You needed to do that to protect yourself."

He nodded. "Valerie's little excursion with Hana was the catalyst. I wanted to make certain that I had absolute legal custody of my daughter."

"Very wise." Laura studied her hands on her knees. "You've made a long hard journey in the last—how long has it been since she left?"

"A year and seven months." He could have pinpointed it to the day and hour but did not.

"A year and seven months," Laura mused. "It's probably seemed like an eternity."

"Sometimes. Sometimes it seems like it all began yesterday. But, except for an occasional lapse, I'm fine. I have to be, for Hana's sake."

"In nurturing others we heal ourselves . . . but I wonder if you're as recovered as you pretend."

He smiled and held out his hands. "Hey, I do an honest day's work. I coach peewee soccer and chaperon school trips. I know how to cook, clean, do laundry, and put on a birthday bash for ten little maniacs. I am such a capable, well-adjusted, and happy guy that Felice has started trying to pair me up with women."

Laura's eyebrows lifted, but she didn't say anything.

"The last two months she's been driving me nuts trying to play matchmaker. She keeps dropping by and accidentally bumping into me, always with an attractive female friend in tow, and then she goes through introductions and encourages us to talk—sort of like a parent at nursery school trying to get the kids to make friends."

"Well . . . you should be flattered if Felice thinks that all her friends would like you."

He chuckled ruefully. "That's one way of looking at it. Or she hates me so much that she can't wait to inflict the pain of dating on me." He shook his head. "I'm not ready for a romantic relationship, though, and even if I were, dating is such a gruesome prospect to contemplate."

She laughed lightly. "Felice is a very perceptive person. You must indeed be doing well if she believes you're ready to go out with her friends."

"I am doing well! I'm fine. But why does that have to mean that I want or need a romance?"

Laura shrugged, then turned away as though suddenly interested in what Hana was doing down by the seal tank.

Dan studied her a moment. In some ways she was exactly the person he remembered. Yet she seemed different from the calm, wise, compassionate woman he had known before. She seemed almost fragile. Confused, he followed her lead and focused on Hana, who was bent down with another little girl, both of them peering through the glass side of the seal tank and engaged in deep conversation.

"Look at that. Instant friends. Too bad we adults can't make connections so easily," Laura said.

"Wish we could hear the conversation." Dan smiled. "Knowing Hana, she's convinced that one of the seals is talking to them through the wall and she's interpreting the conversation for her new friend."

"You should be proud. Hana's healthy state of mind is a testament to your good fathering."

"Maybe. But I worry about her." He hesitated. "Thanks for coming today. She's been asking about you a lot. I think she's as fond of you as she is of Felice, and she needs females to feel good about."

Laura turned away abruptly. "So this was all Hana's idea?"

"I hated to be a bother . . . knowing how busy you are . . . but she's really missed you. I have, too, of course."

She rose and checked her watch. "It's getting late."

He looked up at her. The golden glow was gone. She was all business—her clear gray eyes as emotionless as a reflective surface, her mouth set into a line—and he thought that the loveliness he'd glimpsed earlier must have been an illusion. The glorious spring sunshine and the magic of the zoo and his happiness over Hana's joy must have had him bewitched for a while.

"It is late," he agreed. "Time to find lunch. Do you have any preferences?"

"Actually, I'm worried about the time. I have a lot of errands to do this afternoon."

"Does that mean you can't have lunch with us?"

She turned so that she was watching Hana instead of meeting his eyes. "I was wondering if you would consider letting Hana go with me? That way you could have the afternoon to yourself while Hana and I had a little one-on-one time."

"Oh." He shaded his eyes and looked toward Hana, trying to conceal his disappointment. He knew that the child would be enthusiastic about the suggestion, and it would be selfish of him to object. "I suppose it would be nice to have an afternoon to myself in the city. If Hana likes the idea, you've got a date."

She turned sharply from him and called, "Hana!"

After the details were worked out they walked together out of the zoo and through the park toward Fifty-ninth Street.

"What were you talking to your new friend about?" Dan asked as they were passing the pond at the southeast corner of the park.

"The prisoners who got poisoned."

"What?"

"The prisoners who got killed from drinking poisoned water because they couldn't get away to find good water. She said the zoo animals are prisoners and their water might get poisoned, too."

He swung the child up into his arms.

"That is not going to happen, sweetheart. The animals in New York drink the same water as the rest of the city does."

"But there's poisoned water in cities, too. There's people who get poisoned right from their own faucets."

"Don't worry. New York has good, safe water. The bad germs are not here. And besides that, animals can tolerate germs in their water a whole lot better than people can."

"Okay," she said, and slid from his arms to skip ahead toward a family of ducks at the edge of the pond.

"Where do these things come from?" he asked helplessly. "She doesn't watch television news, and I certainly don't read her stories like that from the newspaper."

"It just happens, Dan. Children are always aware of the big scary events in the world. Think about how all these water contamination tragedies have been in headlines and in the news bulletins. They've been a primary topic of adult conversations for weeks. You can't protect her from all that. And the fears she's developed in response are quite normal. Adults try to suppress or ignore their fears, but children express them quite freely."

Hana squatted down ahead of them and held her hand out to the ducks. She looked so small and vulnerable to him. Almost as though her motherlessness were a tangible thing.

"Do you think she'll ever get over losing her mother, Laura?"

He glanced sideways at Laura as he spoke, and he saw

the question sink into her like a well-aimed arrow. Of course. Thoughtless of him. He should have remembered that she had lost both her parents when she was young.

"Not completely," Laura answered. "It will still be hanging like a stone around her neck when she's an old woman."

"Then what can I possibly do for her?"

The agony in his question seemed to rouse the professional Laura Ferren.

"Just keep on loving her and caring for her as you have been." She looked at him for a moment and then shaded her eyes to watch Hana, compassion flowing from her in waves. "In spite of her loss she can have a full, rich life. Perhaps the loss will make it even richer."

"How can you say that?"

"Loss can open us to life. It can make everything we have more precious and intense because we're always aware of what we've lost."

"And will I reach that point, too?"

She turned her gentle, searching gaze on him. "I don't know, Dan. A parent is irreplaceable to a child. That loss leaves a hole in the heart that no one and nothing can ever truly fill. But with you we're not talking about the loss of a parent."

He was annoyed with her implication and slightly hurt by it. "So you think my loss is replaceable. You think my heart will heal over and someone else will fill Alex's place."

"Only you can decide that."

"You believe it's a conscious decision?"

"Yes."

April turned to May and May turned to June. Hana saw Felice several times a week, even if briefly, and she went out with Laura every Saturday afternoon that Laura was in New York. It became a standing date. Sometimes Dan delivered Hana to a meeting place and sometimes Hana was picked up at their apartment, either by Laura herself or by one of her assistants. With this wealth of affection and attention the child blossomed, and Dan was grateful to both women. He was also relieved not to have to be in Laura's company himself. Their morning together at the zoo had been unsettling, and although he thought of her at times, occasionally even wished he could see her, he did not want confusion in his life.

Then one day in mid-June he received a call from a lawyer in California. Valerie was dead. Hana's grandmother was dead. The news hit him like a fist. How could he tell his seven-year-old daughter that she had lost someone else? How could he tell her that the grandmother she had so recently found, the woman who had fawned over her and adored her and lavished her with attention, the woman who was the last living link to her vanished mother, was forever and irretrievably gone?

He was still asking himself the question of how when he pulled her onto his lap and made himself say the terrible wounding words. Instead of wailing or even crying, she became unnaturally still.

"Valerie is dead?" she asked.

"Yes."

"I don't want her to be dead."

"Neither do I, sweetheart."

"I'm going on the airplane to see her when school is over."

"You were going, honey, but not anymore."

"She promised."

"She couldn't help it."

"Why did she die?"

He considered trying to bring the spiritual into his explanation, but before he could formulate a sentence she asked, "Did Valerie drink poisoned water?"

"No. It was an accident. Her cigarette set the bed on fire."

"Smoking is bad for you."

"Yes."

"Did she want to die?"

"No."

"Then why did she smoke?"

"Oh, Hana . . . it's very complicated trying to figure out why people behave as they do. Maybe she just didn't believe in bad things happening."

Hana looked at him. Her expression was grave beyond her years. "I believe bad things happen."

Dan closed his eyes and held her tightly. Yes. At seven years old, Hana knew all too well that bad things happened. He had failed to protect her from that knowledge. And now he could not protect her from this new pain.

"When you die," she said quietly, "I'm going to die, too."

# Chapter 14

The plane taxied away from the terminal at La Guardia and lined up at a runway for takeoff. Hana was in the window seat, her face pressed to the Plexiglas oval. Dan was in the aisle seat. Laura was in the middle temporarily, until Hana got tired of the window. Laura had insisted on accompanying them to Valerie's funeral, saying that she had to be at her L.A. office in a few days anyway. Her concern for Hana was apparent, and Dan felt a swelling of gratitude and affection for her because of it. She had also insisted that they use the spare bedroom in her apartment while they were in town, an offer Dan had reluctantly accepted because money was so tight.

Throughout the process of check-in and boarding, Laura had distracted and amused Hana, and Dan knew that without the woman the atmosphere would have been quite different. Laura was good for Hana. And she had been a good friend to him as well.

"I brought travel games for Hana," said Laura.

"You and Felice are trying to outdo me." He shook his head and grinned. "All I thought of was a coloring book and crayons. She sent a bag of snacks. You brought entertainment."

She elbowed him playfully in the ribs.

"How is Felice? I haven't seen her for so long."

"She's fine. Did you know she won a design award?"

"No! Tell her congratulations for me."

"And she's fallen in love. With—as she put it—a guy! And a very normal guy at that."

"Good for her." Laura hesitated, gave him a sideways glance, and asked, "Has Felice found you a dream girl yet?"

"I think she's given up."

Laura feigned astonishment. "Even with all those gorgeous women from the fashion world, she can't find the woman you're looking for?"

"Who said I was looking for anyone?" he protested, keeping up the bantering spirit though he was uncomfortable with the direction of the teasing.

"You make this trip so often," he said, attempting to change the subject as the plane lifted off the runway into a blue cloud-strewn sky. "You must have enough frequent flyer miles to last the rest of your life."

She nodded. "I use a few occasionally. But I keep thinking that I'll save them for something big and wonderful."

"Like?"

"I don't know. A trip around the world, maybe."

He smiled. "That used to be a dream of mine, too. Traveling around the world. Seeing all the buildings I've heard about and imagined."

"But it's not one of your dreams anymore?"

"No." He laughed. "That was when I was young. Before I got married."

She cocked her head and raised an eyebrow. "So marriage was the end of your dreams."

"No! It was the beginning of a different dream. A dream that came true."

"Being married was a dream of yours?"

"Not marriage itself. But being with a woman like her. Having a woman like her love me."

He glanced at his daughter, worried that the child might be aware of their conversation, but Hana was riveted to the scene beyond the window, and they were speaking quietly enough that their voices did not carry over the roar of the engines. Laura's eyes flicked to the child and back to him in a way that told him she, too, had considered Hana.

They were in a cocoon of sound and movement, trapped in their seats, their heads against the backrests, turned slightly toward each other so their faces were only inches apart. There was an intimacy to it. An intimacy that was both intriguing and vaguely disturbing.

"A woman like her?" Laura said. "So your dream was to find a woman who was suicidal and deeply troubled?"

"Laura . . ." He was completely taken aback. "That's really a cruel thing to say."

She regarded him coolly without any sign of remorse.

"That," he said, suddenly angry at her, "is sick."

She didn't retreat. If anything, her composure steadied.

"I agree. It's not a healthy foundation for a relationship. And I was wondering if that's what you're waiting for again."

Involuntarily, his mouth dropped.

"I meant it was sick that you should say such a thing. I can't believe this is coming from you. You know how deeply I loved her. You know it was solid."

"Do I? I know that she was often unhappy. That she was moody and easily depressed. That she was troubled by a past that she would not share with you. What was it that you loved about her, Dan? Tell me. Were you just mesmerized by that beautiful exterior?"

"She . . ." He was so upset that he didn't know if he should or could answer, but he wanted to. It was important. There could be no doubts about his love for Alex. Regardless of the inadequacy of his answer, he could not leave the doubts unchallenged.

"I can't deny that I was attracted to her physically. I'm still attracted to her physically. God, sometimes at night she comes to me. And it's like she's really there. I can smell her and touch her and taste her. And I wake up in the darkness and her presence is so real that even after I'm awake I still feel like we're making love. I keep my eyes shut and try to keep the dream from fading . . ."

He closed his eyes and pressed the heels of his hands against his forehead to banish the sexual images. Then he met Laura's gaze again.

"But it was so much more than physical attraction. She wasn't like anyone I'd ever met. She was exotic and mysterious and sexy. And she loved me. She needed me. In my wildest fantasies I never imagined that a woman like that would need me."

Her eyes searched his, questioning, probing, prying at all the hidden crevices of his soul with an intensity that was hypnotic in its power. But even as he responded to that power there was a part of him that was disassociating and thinking about what a good psychologist she must be. Thinking about how much he admired her abilities.

"What if," she said softly, "what if I told you that I needed you? Would you see me differently?"

"Please," he said. "Don't mock me."

"I'm not. Humor me for a minute. Look at me, Dan. Imagine that I'm desperate. That I need you to save me. That I need you like I've never needed anyone before. Would that make me suddenly attractive to you?"

"Oh, Laura. I know you're trying to prove a point and work some therapeutic magic on me, but I wish you'd stop. Besides . . ." He smiled sadly. "I wouldn't be able to imagine it because you are the strongest and most *un*-needy woman I've ever known."

She put her hand to her forehead as though she'd developed a headache.

"You're a good friend, Laura. And I know you're trying to help me. But there are some things you'll never understand."

"The great mystery of love," she said with a touch of sarcasm.

"Yes. That's probably hard for a psychologist to swallow, but it's true. The great mystery of love. You can't pull it out of a hat like a rabbit. You can't touch it or hear it or see it with an electron microscope. You can't grow it in a lab. You can't infect people using bodily fluids, and you can't cure them with all the knowledge of modern medicine."

She sighed and turned to meet his eyes.

"Don't look so sad, Dr. Ferren. You're not the first therapist who didn't have all the answers."

It was night when they landed at Los Angeles International, and Dan had to awaken Hana to deplane. Laura made a quick stop at a gift shop and then they went to the baggage area, where they were met by Laura's West Coast assistant. The man ferried them through a maze of congested highways and then dropped them off at a two-story white stucco building that looked like a frosted cake. Hana had fallen asleep in the car and had to be awakened again. Palm trees swayed overhead, and a spotlight revealed a brilliant purple bougainvillea spilling over the metal railings of the second-story terraces.

Once inside, Hana roused enough to be interested in the unfamiliar apartment. She wandered about curiously while Laura showed Dan the spare bedroom and bath.

"Have you been here long?" he asked, scanning the spacious but minimally furnished rooms.

"No. The cults had tracked down the address and phone number at my old place, and they were harassing me."

"But you keep your number unlisted. And your address is unpublished."

"More than that. My number is routed through another location, my mail goes to a post office station, and my utilities are always in other people's names."

"And they still find you?"

"Oh, yes. It's the same in New York. My home has been in one location since I've known you, but I've changed offices several times."

"They're that determined to go after you?"

"Not just me. The big rich cults are after anyone they deem an enemy. Even if I've never counseled one of their people, I suppose they think that it's just a matter of time until I do. And yes, they're determined. Determined and resourceful and convinced that laws don't apply to them."

"So what all do they do? Harassing phone calls? Someone following you?"

"More. Depending on how threatened they're feeling, they've been known to sabotage a person's credit history, stir up scandals, plant drugs . . . and on and on."

"But I thought they only did that stuff to their major enemies . . . the people who actively wage war against them."

She smiled ruefully and shook her head. "That used to be true. But as the big cults have become more sophisticated and more successful with their smear tactics, they've widened their attack field. Journalists who mention them negatively are targeted. Exit counselors like myself are on the hit list, as are academics and researchers who don't see them in the most positive light."

"But Laura, aside from the big-name cults with the bad reputations, it's hard for me to think of cults in general as dangerous—to outsiders, I mean. From what I learned about The Ark, it didn't seem to have an agenda that endangered outsiders. In fact, it seemed pretty . . . ineffectual. So foolish and almost childlike in its manipulations. So . . . inane."

Laura shrugged. "The banality of evil. Don't ever underestimate a group like The Ark. Just recently—"

She stopped herself, her face registering alarm at what she'd been about to reveal.

"Patient confidence?" Dan asked.

She turned away from him so that her expression was hidden.

"That's all right," he assured her quickly. "Don't worry about it."

"Laura," Hana cried from the back of the apartment. "Your bed is so pretty! It's like a princess's bed."

Laura flashed him an amused smile and headed down the hall toward her room.

"Make yourself at home," she called as she walked away. "Food in the fridge. Several phones. Just don't give out the number or address." Then she went through a door and closed it behind her.

Dan fished in his wallet for K. R. Kirby's number. Kirby was the man who had called, introduced himself as Valerie's lawyer, and then broken the news of Valerie's death. Kirby had instructed Dan to call him at home upon his arrival in Los Angeles so that they could discuss funeral details. Dan suspected that the lawyer's interest in them indicated that a small inheritance had been left for Hana. This made him feel unaccountably guilty, but he could not deny that it would be welcome.

"Hello. This is Dan Behr calling for Mr. Kirby."

"Yeah. Yeah. Hi, Danno. How was the flight?"

Kirby's overly familiar manner in his initial call had been disconcerting, but this time Dan was expecting it.

"The flight was fine."

"Your kid doing okay?"

"Yes. A friend came with us, and she's helping to keep Hana's spirits up."

"Great. Terrific. Well, the kid will get a kick out of the funeral. It's on a boat."

Dan couldn't help rolling his eyes. Hana would "get a kick" out of her grandmother's funeral?

"Everything's set. The boat goes out at two."

"Who made all these arrangements?"

"The center. Valerie had just recently joined."

"What center?"

"The Spiritual Oneness Center. Everybody who's anybody in Hollywood belongs. I've been thinking about it myself. Even if I don't reach a higher plane, I'll make some good contacts."

"Oh."

"We've got a little problem, though."

"What problem?"

"The police want to see you."

"What for?"

Kirby, who had sounded hyperactive from the beginning, became almost manic.

"They're doing what cops do. Poking around. Looking for snail trails on the moon. Who knows. They must have had a slow week."

Dan's pulse increased, and another wave of guilt broke over him. He told himself that it was absurd. That he had nothing to feel guilty about. Hana would probably profit from Valerie's death, but that was certainly not any of his doing.

"Should I call them? Should I—"

"No. I took care of it. Told them I wasn't sure when you were getting in or where you were staying. Which was true . . . right? True. True. True. Told them they'd have to wait till morning."

"So I'm supposed to see them tomorrow morning?"

"Yeah. Did you get a rental?"

"We're staying with a friend."

"A car. A car. Do you have wheels?"

"No."

"Okay. I'll pick you up at eight sharp. We'll go straight to the station."

"You don't have to do that. I can go on my own."

"Bad idea. Never talk to those fuckers without your lawyer."

"But you aren't my lawyer. And besides, I don't need a lawyer."

Kirby snorted as though Dan had just said something ridiculous.

"Don't you watch TV, Danno?"

# Chapter 15

Dan showered and slipped naked between the cool sheets in almost total darkness. The only sound was that of his own movements. Hana had fallen asleep in Laura's bed and had been left there to stay the night.

"She looks so peaceful," Laura had said. "Let's leave her. She won't bother me."

And so the cot at the foot of his bed was empty and he was alone in the unfamiliar room. He doubted that he would sleep well. There was the police interview to think about and the funeral. And even if he did achieve sleep there was the ever-present threat of Alex's awakening him. Sometimes her intrusions were nightmares. More often she came in erotic dreams, tormenting him, causing him to wake in a sweat with the lingering touch and scent and heat of her so achingly real that he had a hard time believing she had not been with him.

He lay on his back in the bed and was surprised to feel a sweet languor steal over him. Oddly, the strangeness of his surroundings was a comfort. He felt anonymous and safe. And as he drifted pleasantly down he had hopes of a restful, untroubled sleep.

"Mmmm."

She loomed over him in the darkness. A flicker of movement, a barely seen shape. The unmistakable scent of her perfume. He was a blind man reaching for her. Blind. Love is blind. He found the small of her back and pulled her closer. Her nipples grazed his chest. The curly mat of her pubic hair brushed his belly.

"Mmmm."

The sound again. From somewhere inside him. Not a spoken sound but one that arose without speech.

"Alexandra," he whispered.

Lips brushed his neck. Movement. Warm flesh moving against his flesh. The flutter of breathing on his chest. The flick of a hot tongue on one of his nipples and then the other. A nibble at his belly button. Lips trailing down his belly. Then wet searing heat that enveloped his cock. He stiffened, arched his back, spiraled down into pure insanity, then gasped as his cock was freed.

His heart raced and he held his breath. Not daring to breathe. Desperately clinging to the dream.

She was above him again. Floating. His angel of darkness. Her breasts warm and full. Filling his hands. Firm, yielding softness beneath his fingers. Burying his face. Nipples taut. Filling his mouth. Sucking. Blissful mindless suckling. First one and then the other.

She pulled back. Was it fading? No. No. He reached out blindly, but she wasn't gone. Just shifting. Straddling him. And then he was swallowed by the hot sweet folds of flesh. Making whole what had been half. Nourishing all the parched and hungry places within him.

Faster. Harder. Spinning like a fever in his brain. Oh God oh God oh God oh God. He grabbed her arms. Pulled her down so that the weight of her swaying breasts was against him and he could feel her heart through the wall of his own chest. Her heart slamming against her ribs like a caged animal. And he knew things that he did not want to know. That he refused to know.

"Ahhhhh." He threw back his head, and the sound was wrenched from him. Burning spurting quivering explosions of red behind his eyes. Like flowers. Brilliant flowers. Coming until there was no more fluid in his body. Until he was hollow. Collapsing. Brain-dead. Praying for brain death.

He squeezed his eyes shut and spread his arms against the sheets. Breathing hard. Alex Alex Alex Alex. The name like a silent mantra. Shutting out all else until reality faded.

\* \* \*

A high-pitched beep woke him the next morning and he
jolted upright, pulse knocking, confused and disoriented.
He grabbed the travel alarm from the bedside table and
fumbled with the tiny switches until it was silenced, then,
drawing a deep breath, he scrubbed at his face with his
hands and composed himself. Six a.m. Which was really
nine by his East Coast body clock. He'd certainly had
enough sleep.

The dream.

A rush of images and sensations came over him as he remembered it. What an incredible dream.

He threw off the sheets, and faint unmistakable scents
drifted into the air.

The dream.

He stared down at the sheets, puzzled because he rarely
ejaculated in his dreams. There was usually an agony of
incompletion. This dream had been different from the others. This dream . . .

He swung his legs over the side of the bed, wrestling a
creeping uncertainty.

The dream. The perfume. The flesh. All so real. He bent
and breathed deeply of the scents from the sheets. Alex's
perfume.

Abruptly he grabbed his terry cloth robe and headed for
the bathroom. The apartment was still and shadowed, with
dawn light peeking through shutters. In the shower he
stood under needles of hot water, shutting out the dream
and cleansing himself of the darkness. When he stepped
back out into the hall Laura called, "Good morning," from
the kitchen.

His stomach lurched. He felt trapped.

"I'm making blueberry pancakes. Want some?" her
floating, disembodied voice asked.

He covered the remaining distance to his bedroom
silently and eased the door shut, pretending he hadn't
heard. But there was no escape. Inside the room he was
faced with the rumpled bed. The fading reminders of perfume and pleasure. Quickly he jerked up the bedcovers,
smoothing out every wrinkle and tucking in the corners.
He dressed in the dark pants and white shirt that were part

of his funeral suit. All he would have to add later was the tie and jacket.

"Dan?" There was a light rapping on the door.

"Yes?"

"I don't know if you heard me, but I've got pancakes ready. You just have time to eat before you leave."

"Thanks. I'm not really hungry." A lie. He was starving. "Is Hana awake yet?"

"No."

He didn't leave the sanctuary of the bedroom until it was time to go to his meeting.

She looked up when he entered the living room, reddened, then quickly dropped her eyes. She and Hana were seated on the floor, using the coffee table to eat breakfast. Cartoons blared from the television.

"Look, Daddy! We're having a picnic!"

"Well, hi there. Why didn't you come tell me you were up?"

"Laura said not to bother you 'cause you were getting ready."

He bent to ruffle her sleep-distressed hair and kiss her forehead. "I have to go talk to some people this morning, punkin."

"I know. Laura told me. She's going to take me for a walk and show me all the flowers that don't grow in Brooklyn."

He glanced up at Laura. "Thanks."

She smiled a little and peeked up at him from downcast eyes. He was the one who looked away.

"Now try not to spill your picnic breakfast on Laura's carpet, okay?"

"Okay. I'm being careful."

"I'll see you two later," he said as he walked out.

At the coffee shop where he was to meet K. R. Kirby, he sat in a booth by the window, ordered toast and coffee, and concentrated on recalling what he knew about the history of California coffee shop architecture in an effort to block out the other thoughts that were haunting him.

K. R. Kirby turned out to be a middle-aged man with a graying ponytail and a string of nervous habits. He was dressed in casually expensive clothes and wore no socks. Dan had the impression that Kirby was embarrassed to be seen in the downscale coffee shop. Or maybe that he was embarrassed to be seen with a man in a conservative dark suit.

"So, are you staying near here or what?" Kirby asked him as they walked to a red Porsche parked at the curb.

"This was convenient," Dan said, being abstruse in an effort to protect Laura's privacy.

It didn't seem to bother Kirby who plugged a disc into a CD player. The volume of the music made further conversation impossible, and Dan watched the sunny melodrama of Los Angeles glide by to a series of pulse-pounding, nerve-twanging instrumentals that were unknown to him yet vaguely familiar.

"What was that?" he asked when the car was parked and the music cut off.

"Movie sound tracks. That's all I listen to. That CD is a favorite of mine. It's a collection of car chase scores."

The police station in Los Angeles was cleaner and more modern than the station he'd visited in New York, and the police officers were more slickly polite than their East Coast contemporaries. But there was an underlying current of something that was exactly the same. He thought about it while he sat beside Kirby and waited.

"Behr?" a voice called.

"Yes."

"Through here."

It came to him as he was led into a small room with Kirby. In both police stations there was an attitude of exclusiveness. Everyone was either an insider or an outsider. Insiders were cops and a sprinkling of civilian support staff. Outsiders were the rest of the world. It didn't matter whether people were schoolteachers or dope pushers. They were all lumped together as outsiders.

The room held a small rectangular table and several hard chairs.

"Is this an interrogation room?" he asked the lawyer as they both sat down on one side of the table.

Kirby shot him a sarcastic grin. "So you do watch television," he said, then snapped to attention at the entry of two men into the room.

The men introduced themselves as Detectives Blake Trent and Justin West. They sounded so much like movie star names that Dan wanted to laugh. The reaction was fleeting, though, and immediately followed by an attack of nervousness. Miraculously, Kirby's nervous quirks vanished and he was transformed into a rock of steadiness and authority.

Detective West had Dan state his full name and address, then Trent said, "You're Valerie Vaughn's son-in-law, is that correct?"

"Yes. At least I was. Alexandra and I are divorced now."

"When was the last time you spoke to Valerie?" Trent asked.

"If you mean an actual conversation, I'm not sure. She called and talked to my daughter once a week, and I usually answered the phone and said hello to her before I put Hana on."

"Did you see her often, Dan?" Trent asked.

"Not often. She came to visit us . . . let's see . . . I guess it's been four times over the past nine or ten months."

"Do you come to Los Angeles often?"

"No. This is only the second time I've been here."

"Is there a point to this?" Kirby asked.

West hit himself in the forehead with the palm of his hand. "Where's my mind today? I didn't ask who wanted coffee. Or tea."

"I'll have Lemon Zinger," Trent said.

West turned to Dan and Kirby.

"You guys still haven't gotten an espresso machine, have you?" Kirby asked.

"No," West answered apologetically. "But we've got a cappuccino mix that's pretty good."

"I'll try that."

"Dan?"

"I'm not really—" Dan began, but he was cut off by Kirby, who said, "He's a coffee drinker."

"The stuff from the pot or the cappuccino mix?" West asked him.

Dan sighed. "From the pot."

The whole charade was annoying Dan, and he, too, wanted to know what the point was.

After a friendly distributing of drinks, Trent suddenly turned to Dan and said, "Where were you last Tuesday, Dan?"

Dan shrugged. "I worked till four, picked my daughter up at five, and spent the rest of the evening at home."

"You can prove that?" Trent demanded. "Other employees will vouch for your being on the job?"

"Sure."

"Anyone who saw you at home that evening besides your daughter?"

"I'm not sure. Wait . . . I think Tuesday is the night we walked a friend's dog for her."

Trent shot his partner a resigned frown.

"What's this all about?" Dan asked, looking from one detective to the other. "I thought Valerie's death was an accident."

The two detectives exchanged a look that obviously contained a wealth of communication, though Dan couldn't read it.

"Let's say it was a suspicious accident," West conceded.

"No kidding!" Kirby exclaimed. "You mean this isn't just routine fishing? You really think Valerie was murdered?"

"It was a suspicious accident," Trent said firmly, repeating his partner's phrase. "And she didn't die alone. We're releasing it to the press today: a male body was discovered with her."

"Who—?" Dan began, but Kirby gave him a sharp kick under the table.

"Burned?" Kirby asked.

"Yes. We haven't been able to identify him so we're asking for the public's help."

"Were they both in bed?" Kirby pressed.

"No."

"Well . . ." Kirby stood. "That's it, then. My client certainly couldn't have made it out here and back from the East Coast last Tuesday, could he? Maybe your unidentified stiff caused the accident."

West smiled. "We'll be checking with Dan's employer and his dog-owning friend."

"Naturally," Kirby agreed.

"It could have been a paid job," Trent said, tossing the line off casually but casting a laser look at Dan.

"Are you suggesting—" Dan began.

Kirby cut him off with, "If that's all, guys, then we've got a funeral to make it to this afternoon."

"Maybe we'll see you there," West said affably.

Kirby took hold of Dan's arm and turned him toward the door in a clear signal to keep quiet and leave. The arm grip continued until they were out of the building.

"They've got nothing," Kirby said, finally releasing him.

"I want to know what happened to Valerie," Dan said. "I want to know if it really was murder."

"What's the difference? They've got nothing on you. That's all we need to worry about, so just blow it off and enjoy the sunshine."

"Blow it off? First of all—I'm upset by anyone thinking that I would kill another person. Secondly . . . we're talking about the possibility that Valerie was murdered! Doesn't that have any effect on you?"

"She's dead." Kirby shrugged. "If there was, like, a drooling maniac with a smoking gun, then, sure, I'd be all excited about it, but it's, like . . . who knows? Life is weird. Stuff happens. Why put yourself on a downer with negative thoughts, you know?"

Dan stared at Kirby a moment, furious—what about justice? what about Valerie's rights? what about society's duty?—but he turned from the lawyer without speaking, not just because he realized how fruitless it would be but because a fear was dawning inside him and it was a fear he was not ready to give voice to. Could this have a connection to Alex? To The Ark? Everett May's son had been the victim of an unsolved hit and run. The burning of the deprogramming house remained unsolved. Now Valerie's death by fire was also unsolved and suspicious. Could it be possible that May's paranoid suspicions were well founded?

* * *

When Dan finally arrived back at Laura's apartment there was just enough time for him to grab a quick lunch before the car came to take them to the boat. Laura and Hana had already eaten and were dressed for the funeral. The child was pensive and subdued.

"She's been asking about death," Laura whispered.

But there was no opportunity to discuss that or anything else out of Hana's hearing. During the ride Laura kept the conversation light even though it was not light-hearted, and she managed to engage Hana in a game spotting license plates. Dan was grateful to her. His experience with the police had shaken him, and it would have been difficult to shove that aside and amuse his daughter.

The more he considered their suspicions the more distressed he became. He wondered what other lines of investigation they were pursuing. He wondered what they knew about The Ark. Certainly they had to have looked into Alex's whereabouts and learned that she was living in a cult. What else had they learned?

"Oh, my . . ." Laura breathed.

Dan came out of his mulling to see that they were being dropped at a party boat. Balloon bouquets decorated the railings, fluttering and dipping on the sea breeze, and there was a large banner that read GOOD-BYE VALERIE.

They walked from the car onto the dock and stood, staring.

"I thought it was going to be one of those Neptune affairs," Laura said. "Very dignified, with ashes to scatter and a flower for each mourner to throw overboard. This is ludicrous."

Hana slipped her hand into Dan's. "This isn't a real funeral, is it, Daddy? Maybe Valerie isn't really dead. Maybe somebody tricked us."

Dan picked up Hana.

"I'm sorry, punkin, but Valerie is dead. This is a funeral. It's just a different kind of funeral. Maybe it's like a party so people won't feel so bad."

"But I still feel bad," Hana insisted.

"So do I," he said, sending Laura a helpless look.

"That's right, honey," Laura said. "We still feel bad, and that's normal."

"Who's responsible for this?" Laura asked him under her breath as they moved forward.

"Some New Age center she was involved with. Kirby said she wanted them to arrange her funeral and burial."

"What New Age center?"

"Something about oneness. Kirby said it was big with Hollywood people."

"Oh, no . . . not that."

"There they are! The star attractions!" Kirby shouted from the top deck of the boat. "Come on aboard."

Dan exchanged a horrified look with Laura but dutifully carried his daughter up the ramp and onto the boat.

A crowd of people attended, all of them trying to be sleek and sexy, all of them dressed too casually for the occasion in Dan's opinion, and all of them too interested in the snacks and open bar. The boat set anchor several miles from shore and tinkling wind chime sounds came over the loudspeakers. The crowd quieted expectantly. From below deck a man ascended, long white hair pulled back from an almost ethereal face, flowing robes a shade of pale blue, hands posed in an attitude of prayer. He continued up the next set of stairs to stand on the deck above, where he leaned over the rail and opened his arms in a benevolent gesture.

"Join with me," he invited, and Dan realized that the man had to be wearing a hidden microphone for the softly spoken words to carry so well.

Dan lifted Hana and held her close. All around them, rapt faces were turned toward the speaker.

"Is that Jesus?" Hana whispered.

Dan chuckled under his breath. "Maybe an L.A. version," he whispered. Then he quickly added, "No, sweetie. He's sort of like a minister or priest."

"Shake off those negatives!" the man sang.

"No more negatives," the crowd chanted.

"Get high on life!"

"High on life," came the chorused reply.

"You *can* have everything you want!"

"We *can* have everything we want."

"It's all yours if you follow the teachings!"

"It's all ours."

The man held up his hands to signal silence, bowed his head a moment, then went into a strange singsong speaking rhythm.

"We'll miss Valerie. If only she'd come to us sooner she might have been saved. But what's done is done. She tried to cross her troubled waters, but the negatives got her before she could reach the safe shore."

He stopped as though he'd heard something.

"Valerie!" he cried. "Is that your spirit I feel?"

Suddenly the man crumpled to the deck. Two muscle-bound young men appeared and lovingly carried him away.

"Who was that?" Dan asked a woman standing close by.

She eyed him as though he'd just failed to recognize Abraham Lincoln's statue. "That was Rory Bountiful. He rarely makes appearances outside the center anymore, you know, but he always speaks at the funerals of people who've put the center in their wills. It's kind of a point of honor with him. Even in this case, when Valerie disappointed him and left most of her money to relatives."

A female voice filled the loudspeakers, and Dan looked up to see a woman from the crowd speaking about Valerie, her fellow "co-seeker." She was followed by several men and another woman. All of their reminiscences of Valerie somehow ended up sounding like testimonials for the center. There was no body, no coffin, no urn of ashes—nothing to connect the event to the reality of a death.

The assemblage was invited to "set free" the balloons, and two artificially large-breasted platinum-blond sisters sang a slightly altered version of "You Light Up My Life," a song that was announced as capturing Valerie's effect on people, then the boat headed back toward shore.

Once all the activities were over and attention was focused on finishing the food and drink, Dan finally had an opportunity to speak to Laura privately. He held Hana, who had fallen asleep with her head on his shoulder, and huddled with Laura in the cove of a stairwell on the upper deck.

"Who are these people?" he whispered.

"This is one of the most successful emerging cults on the West Coast."

"No! I mean, I know it's a scam, but the members lead separate lives, so how is it a cult?"

"Control. Absolute leader domination. A sole purpose of enriching the leader and the group." Laura glanced around as though afraid of eavesdroppers. "People are lured into attending free sessions, then once they're hooked, they're charged increasing amounts to achieve higher planes of understanding. They're programmed to believe that their lives will be worthless if they don't continue. They sign legal agreements and pledge assets. I'm surprised they aren't set up to get Valerie's entire estate."

Dan shook his head, utterly saddened. "What is wrong with people? Is everyone going mad around us?"

"On the contrary. I think that everyone is desperately searching for sanity, for something to save them from the lunacy and the confusion. It's a scary, complicated, disturbing world, and people are lost in it."

"But how the hell does any thinking person get conned into believing that a bozo like this Rory has any answers?"

She smiled sadly. "They want to believe. When they look at Rory Bountiful they don't see Wally Batts, the computer geek who used to design soft porn games—they see a messiah who looks like our childhood images of Jesus. When they listen to him they don't hear a pathetic social failure who has to sing to keep his stuttering under control—they hear a prophet."

"But how did he get started? I thought cult leaders at least had to have a little charisma."

"Wally came in the back door, so to speak. He designed some successful software, an elaborate mystical porno extravaganza that developed a big underground following. From there his accountant built him and the organization into what it is today. The accountant had Wally completely overhauled before presenting him publicly— hair consultants, plastic surgery, public relations, and image counseling . . . the whole bit. Then Wally was displayed but carefully kept inaccessible so his mystique could be maintained."

"So here's where we're hiding!" K. R. Kirby declared, peeking around the corner. "Come on, kids. The boat is docking, and since you're my only audience for the reading of the will I think we'll just do it over dinner."

Laura and Kirby sat on one side of the table, Hana and Dan on the other. They all had overpriced plates of food, and only Kirby was enjoying it.

"This is the deal," Kirby said. "One quarter, right off the top, goes to you, Danno. She wanted it that way because she said her daughter had taken some money from you and also because she wanted you to be able to make a nice home for the kid. The rest of the estate is to be divided into three equal parts. A part goes outright to the center. The other two go into trusts. One is for Alexandra Vaughn Behr if and when she proves she's left The Ark. Should Alexandra not claim the money it eventually goes to Hana. The other trust is for Hana. Monies can be drawn from Hana's trust for a whole list of things like education and orthodontia. The entire trust reverts to Hana when she turns twenty-five."

He bent to his briefcase and pulled out a sheaf of papers. "That was the summary, now this is the official version." And he began reading.

"I have to go to the bathroom," Hana said as soon as he was finished.

Dan started to rise, but Laura waved him down, stood, and held out her hand. Dan watched them cross the room together, turned and realized Kirby was staring after them as well.

"You two have something going?" the lawyer asked.

"No," Dan said too quickly. "We're just friends."

Kirby grinned. "I go for smart, uptight, successful women. They're such a challenge. So if you don't have any claims on her . . ."

Dan did a silent five-count. "How large of an estate did Valerie leave?" he asked.

"Not a fortune, but nothing to sneeze at either." Kirby resumed eating and spoke around mouthfuls of food. "After the condo is sold and everything is liquidated and Uncle Sam gets his cut, I expect you're looking at about a hundred thousand."

"So each share will be a quarter of that."

"No. The hundred thou is an estimate of your share."

Dan shook his head. "Where did she get so much money?"

Kirby shrugged. "I avoid asking questions like that."

But Dan knew how she had come into so much money. Alex had earned it modeling and Valerie had taken it from her. Knowing that made him question the justice of it all. Technically, the money should all be Alex's. But Alex had let The Ark steal his money. And Alex certainly ought to be required to contribute something to her daughter's support if she had anything to contribute. He wondered if he was just rationalizing to make himself feel justified in accepting the gift.

"What happens if I decline my part?" he asked.

Kirby stared at him. "I'm not sure," he answered finally. "But why would you want to screw up the works like that? If you don't want the cash for yourself, you could at least use it to make life nicer for your kid."

Hana came skipping back to the table. "The bathroom has special towels that kill germs, Daddy. Here." She passed him a wet square of paper that was like a baby-wipe. "It kills the AIDS virus on contact."

Dan glanced at Laura, who rolled her eyes and held up her hands. "Aren't you glad Hana can read now, Dan? She read everything in the bathroom."

"So . . . want me to forget you asked that?" Kirby said.

"Yes," Dan answered quietly.

They were back at the apartment by eight. Dan bathed Hana and put her nightgown on, brushed her teeth, and trimmed her paper-thin nails.

"Can I sleep in Laura's bed again?" Hana begged.

Before Dan could answer, Laura's voice called, "It's fine with me."

He concealed his annoyance from his daughter, wishing Laura had let him make the decision. But then he knew, deep down, that Laura had spoken up because she did not want the child to sleep in the cot at the foot of his bed. He did not know what he himself felt about that.

"Want to play Go Fish until bedtime?" he asked his daughter.

"No. I want to color."

"How about reading? I could read your new book to you."

"No, Daddy. I want to color in the horse book Laura gave me."

"Okay," he agreed.

He helped her get settled at the kitchen table with her horses of the world coloring book and her giant-size box of crayons. She was quickly absorbed, the tip of her tongue signaling extreme concentration.

He had no more excuses. He had to talk to Laura.

Hana did not even look up when he left the kitchen. Laura did not look up when he entered the living room.

"Working?" he asked as he sat down across from her.

"Yes." She took off her stylish wire-framed reading glasses and dropped them on the papers that littered the coffee table. "I was just going to make some tea. Want a cup?"

"No. Wait. Don't go."

She had started to rise but sank reluctantly back onto the couch.

Dan studied his hands a moment. He moved from the chair to sit on the couch with her so that he could lower his voice and be certain that Hana didn't overhear.

"I dreamed I was making love with Alex last night. At least I thought it was a dream. Or I wanted it to be a dream."

"Was it a good dream?" Laura asked softly, her eyes riveted to his.

He took a deep breath.

"Yes."

"Then why are you questioning it? As long as the dream

is good, for everyone, why should we examine it during wakefulness and possibly destroy it?"

"But . . ." He searched her face. "I don't understand."

"Who does?" she said with a sad, wise smile.

# Chapter 16

The lighted clock numbers read 3:00 a.m. He was wide awake. Even so, there was a dreamlike quality to her appearance. One minute he was alone in the darkness and the next, with only a whisper of movement, she had slipped into the room.

It was definitely Alex's perfume. He had not imagined it or wished it so. It was so. And it was so easy to pretend. He had not had sex with a woman since losing Alex. More significantly, he had not been sexually intimate with any woman but Alexandra since their first time together, more than seven years before. Every erotic impulse, every fantasy, was somehow connected to her in his mind. Just her. He closed his eyes, shut out all but that intoxicating fragrance and the warmth of the woman slipping beneath the sheets next to him. And it was Alex. For him it truly was Alex.

She was less rushed this time. Her hands roamed slowly over his body as though she were memorizing it. Then she tugged at him, turning him over onto his stomach, and she explored his back, the backs of his thighs, his calves and ankles. The wet tip of her tongue traced his spine, making him shiver. She nipped at his buttocks, then slipped a hand between his legs to caress his scrotum.

He flipped over and pulled her under him, her back pressed into the bed. Using a slow, deliberate hand, he followed the contours of her body as though he were molding it from clay. Then he tasted the hollows and crevices and all the secret places.

When her quick shallow breathing became a soft series of moans he opened her with his fingers, felt the delicate folds pouring out a welcome, and then he slid in.

Wrong! Wrong! Wrong!

The words flashed somewhere in his brain but he ignored them. Because it didn't matter if it was wrong. The dream was good. There was no harm in dreaming.

She wrapped her legs around him, digging her heels into his clenched buttocks. And she moved with him, moved against him, thrusting her breasts against his chest, thrusting her pelvis, pulling him deeper, urging him to go faster. Harder. Faster. The juices of her desire bathing him in absolution.

And he came with a shudder that racked his body like death. He came and hated himself for it.

The next day was Saturday, and they took Hana to Disneyland in Anaheim. It was a hazy day, bright with sunlight refracted from particles of pollution. Dan could not meet Laura's eyes, and he was glad for the necessity of sunglasses. Behind the dark lenses he could hide his confusion.

They spoke of the immediate—"There's the parking area over there" or "Do you want to eat now?" Or they spoke to and through Hana. Their conversations were careful and measured. As though they were both balanced on a tightwire, each depending on the balance of the other to maintain the act.

At the amusement park they spun in teacups and caroused in pirate ships and cruised into the jungle. Floating through a small world, Dan remarked that he felt a diabetes attack coming on, and Laura laughed. The moment frightened both of them. They retreated into a protracted silence that made Hana ask if they were mad at her.

The odd thing was that when they were pointedly ignoring each other, they seemed like a real family to Dan. He thought they must look very natural together. A family of three. With the parents either angry or so bored by their years together that they had nothing to talk about. He thought about this as he followed Hana into a castle, and he wondered what the day would have been like if Alex had been there instead of Laura.

He thought of Alex laughing. Of Alex tossing him one of her sideways glances, full of sexual promise. He thought of Alex taking his hand and looking at him with those incredible eyes. So vulnerable. Trusting of him alone. But then he thought of how Alex would have been worried about the sun and fussing over Hana, smearing her face with six-hour sunscreen every thirty minutes. And she would have complained about the amusement park food. And she would have complained about the lines. And she would have managed to make Dan feel that he'd failed them by taking them to such a place.

They would not be having fun if Alex were there.

As soon as the thought was formed he felt that he had committed a horrible act of betrayal. It had been good! They had been happy! He forced it all down and away, into one of his mind's closets, and he slammed the door, determined not to let Hana's day be ruined by her father's brooding.

Suddenly Hana dashed to the picture of a princess from some animated film. She studied the picture and then, almost as though she had sensed his inner turmoil, she turned to him.

"She looks like Mommy," the child said wistfully. "She's as beautiful as Mommy."

"Yes," Dan agreed.

"Don't you wish Mommy was here with us, Daddy?"

He caught a glimpse of Laura's stricken expression before she turned abruptly to study something on the opposite wall.

"This is the place for wishes, isn't it?" he said evasively. "I think this is a wishing castle."

"Oooooo," Hana breathed, her eyes lighting with awe. "What do you wish, Daddy?"

He sighed. "I don't know, punkin. I don't know what to wish for anymore."

That night he lay on his back, waiting in the darkness. Wanting and ashamed of that want. Stunned by his own dishonesty.

There was a lock on the bedroom door. He could get up and lock it. He could shut her out.

But there were so many tangles and knots in it now. And he had more than himself to consider. He did not know why she had begun their twisted game. Out of pity for him? Out of a casual boredom? Out of lust? Out of simple convenience? Or was there something deeper?

Did he want to know?

No.

That was the bald and shameful truth. He wanted her to come to him in the darkness. That was all he wanted. He wanted release from understanding and compassion and logic and pain and moral questions. He wanted to cast off his intellect and his soul.

A sound. The familiar whisper as the door was opened and closed. The subtle air change as she moved toward him through the blackness. He opened his mouth in a silent shout of joy, closing himself to what he was and had been, falling into sweet oblivion.

She knelt on the bed beside him and poured warm scented oil on his chest and belly. Pools of oil that dripped onto the sheets. He strained to see and could make out her form, or at least it seemed that he could. She was putting oil on herself. Slathering it on her breasts and belly.

He heard the soft chink of glass meeting wood as she reached to put the bottle on the bedside table. Then she straddled his thighs and her hands were on him, sliding in the oil, spreading it across his skin. Slicking it over his hard cock.

Greedily he reached for her. Her warm slippery soft flesh. The slick globes of her breasts.

He wanted to ease her toward him, and he put his hands on her back for purchase. Immediately she jerked, knocking his arms away. There was a moment of mutual hesitation. Then she grabbed both his wrists and yanked them up, stretching his arms over his head, stretching her own arms. And she held him there as though he were a prisoner while she moved on top of him. Her breasts slid over his chest. Her belly slipped and slid against his. She writhed and slithered against him, breathing warm moist air into his ear.

Then she let go of his hands and slipped down, taking his oiled cock between her breasts. Moving, sliding, squeezing until he thought his head might explode.

He sat up, pulling her with him so they faced each other,

and in one swift motion he hugged her to him and swung them both to the edge of the bed, and he stood, holding her, and she clung to him. She wrapped herself around him. Then she lifted her hips and settled, taking his cock into her. And she rode him in the darkness, sliding up and down while he held her, with his muscles straining and his jaw clenched, fighting the need to come.

She stiffened and moaned. A series of tiny contractions fluttered from deep within her. Then his knees trembled and his heart quaked in his chest and he lost himself. He was not Dan Behr, not a man not conscious not human, not a separate entity but a sizzling electric burst, an energy a force a power, the power of primordial creation.

They fell onto the bed together sideways, still joined. She started to move away but he held her tightly to him. His arms were wrapped around her shoulders. His face was buried in her hair. Masses of kinky fine hair. Not like Alex's at all. He let go with one arm and put his hand against her forehead. Brushing the hair back. Stroking the smooth curve as he stroked Hana when she needed to be soothed. Then he traced her eyebrows with his fingertips. He touched her closed eyes. He slowly ran a finger over her lips.

Only when the back of his hand grazed her cheek did he realize she was crying.

"Laura," he said, shattering the silence and the dream.

And she tore herself from his arms and ran from the room.

The alarm woke him at sunrise. He lay there in the bed, breathing in the fragrance of the oil and their joining. The darkness was gone. He was himself again. Dan Behr. But he didn't know who that was anymore.

He stumbled slightly on his way from the bed to the shower, brain foggy from too little sleep.

"Got to get it together," he ordered himself as he waited for the water to warm.

They had to be at the airport in four hours, and he hadn't begun to pack yet. He ducked under the needle spray and let the water wash his fuzziness away. Pack. Wake Hana. Do breakfast. Get her ready. And hope that the freeway demons weren't out causing traffic jams that morning.

He dressed hurriedly and went to the living room to gather Hana's scattered possessions. There was no sound from Laura's bedroom. They were both still asleep.

It occurred to him that she had probably set her alarm to correspond with his schedule, just as she had on the previous mornings. It would go off soon and he would be trapped in the quiet morning with her. What then? Would his leaving bring about a painful scene? Would she suddenly want to dissect their nights together? Would she ask how he felt about her?

He could not face it. He could not face her. Cowardly though it might be, he wished he could sneak away without seeing her at all. He wished he could take back the tenderness he had shown her last night, because it felt false to him now. What had he been thinking?

They had had sex. Several times. Always at her instigation. So be it. Things like that happened to people. They were both consenting adults, and they were both hungry and no harm had been done. But then he had crossed the line into affection and destroyed the balance. Why?

He wasn't ready for a relationship. Sometimes he felt that he might never be ready. It was Alex he still dreamed of. It was Alex he still wanted. It was Alex he still loved. Wasn't it?

Quickly he slipped into Laura's bedroom, crossed to her bedside table, and switched the alarm button to OFF. The room was heavily shuttered and deeply shadowed. Hana was curled up in a ball on the opposite side of the bed, her two favored fingers resting against her bottom lip, ready if she needed the comfort of sucking them. Laura was on her side, facing Hana. Her hair was loose, and he realized that he had never seen her without it twisted up or pulled back or plaited into a braid. The hair made him smile. It was wild and unruly. A cloud of hair that floated and curled in lavish profusion over the pillow. He thought of her fighting with it each morning, stabbing the pins into place with a determined set to her mouth. And then as the day wore on, battling the escaping tendrils, tucking and repinning and smoothing in a futile effort to maintain control.

How strange it was that so many women found their inner and outer selves difficult to reconcile. Alex had loathed her own beauty so much that she had at times wanted to destroy herself to be free of it. Perhaps she was an extreme example, but he could remember his mother frowning at her own reflection, and he had witnessed the unhappiness and the obsessing and the cosmetic binges and the crash diets and the surgeries of his female acquaintances through the years, all of them searching for something that would change that person they saw in the mirror. Something that would make their exteriors match their interiors. Or was that it? Maybe he had it wrong. Maybe their dislike of the outside reflected a dislike of what they felt inside. Or maybe they were hiding. Seeking camouflage. Or maybe all the psychobabble was right and women were crazed from the blitz of media images featuring unattainable female perfection.

Then again, maybe the answer was different for every woman. Laura was certainly different. Except for her hair battles and the crazy sexual game she'd started with him, she seemed to him as strong and stable and well-adjusted a woman as he had ever known.

Quietly he turned to go. Laura moved, flinging one arm out of the covers, and he saw that there was something different about the skin on the back of her upper arm and on the small portion of her back that was revealed. In the dim gray light it was impossible to determine exactly what he was seeing. But there was something. He had the urge to touch that skin. Then he remembered putting his hands on her back during lovemaking and having her knock them away. And he thought of how she always wore long sleeves and high necks.

He sighed and slipped away from her bedside, intending to leave, but her bathroom door was open and something compelled him inside. The room held a faint scent that was distinctly different from the perfume Alex had worn. He eased open the mirrored cabinet. The shelves there held common products. He shifted and examined the contents of the cabinet above the toilet. There he found lotion and powder and bath oil and perfume, all in a matching fragrance that was light and vaguely familiar from being around her. Only one bottle was different. Right in front. One tiny bottle that he knew well.

He picked it up, opened it, and sniffed. Alex. Oh, God, after she was gone he had sprinkled that on his pillow on particularly cold and lonely nights. When the supply she'd left behind was gone it took an effort of will not to buy more.

Alex's perfume. Of course Laura would have seen it when she was looking through Alex's things and hoping to counsel her. But why would the woman have remembered such a detail? And, more important, how long had she owned this tiny bottle and what had she intended when she bought it?

There were too many questions. And he had a plane to catch. He put the bottle into his shirt pocket and slipped out.

With the suitcase zipped and a cold breakfast arranged on the table, he went to Laura's door and knocked.

"Wake up, ladies. I'm putting the toast into the toaster in two minutes."

As soon as he heard the low murmur of their sleepy voices he went back to the kitchen and poured himself another cup of coffee.

Hana appeared first, bright-eyed and fully alert as only children can be just two minutes after waking.

"Are we going on the airplane today, Daddy?"

"That's right. We're leaving for the airport in just a little while."

"Did you call the airplane and tell them I don't want one of those disgustible kid's meals?"

"I called them. They said they'll make you a fruit plate. And the word is *disgusting*."

"With bananas and apples?"

"Probably."

"With grapes?"

"I don't know, punkin, but it will be better than a hot dog, right?"

He looked up and saw Laura leaning in the doorway. Her hair was clipped up haphazardly, and she had thrown on a long wrap robe. She looked confused.

"I meant to be up," she said. "I thought I turned on my alarm."

"Sit down." He pulled a chair out for her and another for Hana. "The toast is on its way."

Hana did not move. She hugged her kangaroo and frowned.

"What's wrong?" Dan asked, controlling his impatience.

"I don't want to go home on the airplane."

"Why?"

"I didn't visit Valerie yet."

Dan drew in a deep breath. "We can't visit Valerie, sweetie. She's dead."

"I don't want her to be dead!"

"No one does, Hana. We're all very sad about it."

"Is Mommy sad?"

"I'm sure she is."

"Valerie is Mommy's mommy."

"Yes."

"Are Valerie and Mommy dead together?"

"No," Dan answered, hardly able to get the word out.

"Hana," Laura said, "is Kangaroo going to ride on the plane with you?"

"Yes." The child brightened and slid into her seat. "Kangie likes fruit plates."

Dan plucked the stuffed animal from her arms and held it up. "Mmmm," he said in a squeaky voice, "I love food and I'm going to gobble up Hana's breakfast if she doesn't eat it first."

Hana giggled and took a bite. Then she looked at Laura.

"Are you coming on the airplane, too, Laura?"

"No, honey. But I'll be back in New York in a week, and we'll do something special."

"I want to make a puppet."

"Then that's what we'll do. We'll find a book on making puppets and we'll do it."

Hana smiled happily and bent to her cereal. Laura seemed more than a little disconcerted by having slept longer than she'd intended and by appearing at the table in her robe. She, too, concentrated on her cereal. As soon as Hana was finished eating he wrestled her to the bathroom for the tooth-brushing and cleaning up that she always resisted. He had stopped wondering why she wouldn't cooperate because he had decided that her tenacity was a

virtue of sorts. Or at least it would be in adulthood. Someday. If he could grit his teeth and stand it that long.

When he finally finished with Hana he told her to check
under beds and in corners for forgotten animals, and he
carried their suitcases out of the bedroom and toward
the front door. Laura was dressed and standing in the living room.

"I know you'll probably try to turn this around somehow so that you can blame yourself," she said, hands
clasped tightly together as though she were giving herself
strength. "But you have no responsibility. And, despite
what some people think, pleasure is not a crime."

He stood, suitcase in hand, feeling cornered even though
her words were freeing him completely.

"The car should be here any minute," he said. "I think
Hana and I should go on out, because we won't be able to
see him or hear him honk from in here."

"Yes," she agreed. "You miss everything from where I
live."

Each night after returning to New York he lay awake in
the darkness staring up at the ceiling. California was a long
way away, and so were the dreams. Now they seemed like
something he had imagined. Erotic fevered fantasies.

Though he was back in his own bed, he slept fitfully and
woke several times each night, certain that he'd heard the
soft movements that signaled her coming to him. He got
out the little bottle of perfume he had taken, and he sprinkled the fragrance on his pillow as he had when he first
lost Alex. He wanted to resurrect dreams of his marriage.
He wanted to think of Alex. But the scent of that perfume
stirred confusing images. It was linked now to the darkness in Laura's apartment.

The more he considered what had happened, the more it
disturbed him. He did not believe in casual sex. That was
an oxymoron. Sex was not casual. Maybe sometimes it
was a weapon or an act of vanity or a gift or a plea or a cry
of loneliness or a desperate yearning for connection, but it
was never casual. How could it be? It was the heart of existence. It was the essence of life.

While he was not above having a sexual thought or two

when confronted with an attractive female on the street or in a magazine, he had a strong personal need for sex with meaning. It seemed empty otherwise.

So why had he done it? He was not in love with Laura Ferren. He was not infatuated with her. He had not had one sexual thought about her before. She was a good person and a solid friend. That was all. And now their friendship had undoubtedly suffered major damage. But then, that had been done the moment she first slid into his bed, because even if he'd resisted, their easy relationship would have been dealt a blow.

Which made him angry at her. What had been her motive? Why had she started this?

The questions gnawed at him. He could not stop thinking about it. And at night, determined as he was to put it behind him, memories of those dark dreams haunted him. Finally he decided that the only hope of easing his turmoil and the only hope of salvaging any part of their friendship was to confront her. To be direct and honest. And to come to an agreement with her.

On Saturday morning Laura called to make her arrangements with Hana. Hana had been expecting the call and pounced on the phone at the first ring. Dan stood, watching her and listening, his palms suddenly damp.

"Hi, Laura! I knew it was you," the child said happily. Then, "Okay," and again, "Okay." Her face lit. "Yes! Yes! Okay. Here's Daddy."

Hana held out the receiver to him. He hesitated, his pulse accelerating. He wiped his hand on his jeans and took the phone.

"Hi, Laura."

"Hi, Dan. Has she been upset at all during the week?"

"You mean about Valerie?"

"Yes."

"Off and on, but we're coming to terms with it."

"Good. Well, I've got the afternoon planned, if that's all right with you. I found a puppet theater that does a workshop after the show, teaching kids to make their own puppets."

Dan laughed.

"What? What's funny?"

"Nothing. It's just that I can't believe how you always come up with the perfect thing, regardless of how busy you are."

"It's not that hard, really. And I enjoy everything as much as she does."

Silence. It fell suddenly between them and then it grew and stretched. What he wanted to say to her could not be said over the phone, and the not saying of it required all his attention.

"I—" he began.

"I—" she began.

"Listen—"

"Go ahead. You first."

"I just thought . . ." He cleared his throat. "That maybe I could take you two to dinner somewhere after your puppeting."

"Fine," she agreed softly. "Could you drop Hana by my office at noon?"

"Fine," he said, and wondered why in the hell he had suggested dinner. That sent the wrong message. It set the wrong tone. And they wouldn't even have a chance for private conversation with Hana right there listening. Now he was committed to looking at her across a table and engaging in polite chitchat when all he really wanted to do was get the serious discussion over with and then go back to normal.

They met at Frontiere in Soho. Hana was buzzing about the puppet show and her own lopsided creation, a hand puppet of a lobster that she had named Walter. Her voice for Walter was low-pitched and contained the ho, ho, ho's of a street corner Santa Claus.

Dan avoided looking at Laura and studied the menu. When he read the entrees the first thing that jumped out at him was a lobster special. Quickly he turned the menu over, and as he did so he realized that Laura was just reading the special and he glanced up and met her eyes and they both grinned.

"I want dinner, too," Hana announced in Walter's voice, waving the lobster at Dan's face.

"Okay, Walt," he said. "What do you like?"

"Ice cream."

"Well, you should help Hana eat a good dinner then, because if she does there will be ice cream for desert."

"Okay, okay, okay," Walter agreed.

"Can I go show Walter those flowers over there, Daddy?"

Dan followed her pointing finger. "Yes, but use your restaurant manners, no running, and come right back here when you're finished."

As soon as the child was out of hearing distance Laura leaned toward him.

"I've got something to tell you, Dan." Her expression was serious and troubled. "We have to talk later. Without Hana."

Everything thudded and clutched in his chest. He managed a nod, thinking he was the one who was supposed to have said that.

"How do you want to do it?" she asked.

He shrugged, feigning a nonchalance he did not feel. "However's easiest."

"We could go from here to my office. Charlene, my assistant, lives right downstairs in the building. Hana could visit her while we talk."

"Maybe we should just put this off," he said, suddenly grasping for reasons to postpone. "I couldn't ask someone to accept a surprise visit from a seven-year-old on a Saturday night. I'm sure Charlene has other plans for her evening."

"No. I asked her earlier. She has no plans and she's delighted."

"You asked her earlier? What, you decided what would happen and then manipulated me into going in the assigned direction?"

She regarded him with a puzzled look.

"Is there something wrong, Dan?"

"No. What could be wrong? It's all set. We go to your office and talk."

Laura's current Manhattan office suite had begun life as an apartment, and it had the requisite cubbyhole kitchen, a small bedroom that was the working office where she had her desk and computer and files, another larger bedroom that functioned as her assistants' office, and then a spacious living room, to which she had added doors so that it could serve as her consultation room. This was where she spent time with people.

"Could I get you some tea?" she asked as she showed him into the consultation room. "I'm afraid we're out of coffee."

He accepted because it gave him a chance to settle and collect his thoughts. He wanted to be clear about what he would say to her and how he would phrase it.

The room was pleasantly appointed in a bland way, designed to put people at ease but not to distract them. The lighting was low and intimate. He crossed to the seating arrangement, a couch and two upholstered chairs with a slim coffee table in the center. He didn't want to sit on the couch because he was afraid she might think he wanted her to sit next to him, so he chose a chair. It was comfortable. Soft without swallowing him. No doubt it had been chosen to scientific specifications by Dr. Laura, the perfectionist.

"Hmmm," he said under his breath. "Do I detect a little hostility here?" He crossed his legs, rested his chin pensively in his hand, and imagined a prone patient on the couch. "How do you feel about that?" he asked. "Does it make you angry?"

"What?" Laura said, coming through the door with the tea.

Not just two cups of hot tea plunked down on the table, as he would have done, but the whole business with the tray and milk and sugar and dainty little paper napkins.

"I was just playing therapist," he said. "Want me to practice on you?"

He was nervous and he realized it, and he also realized that he should shut up before he said something really dumb. So he sipped the tea and burned his mouth.

She stared down into her cup for a moment, then looked up at him.

"I've been agonizing over this," she said. "I've started

to say something to you several times and stopped myself, but now . . . I feel that I can't wait any longer."

"Listen," he said, suddenly in the grip of terror. "Sometimes it's better to leave things unsaid."

She frowned and shook her head.

"No, you need to hear this."

"How do you know what I need to hear? You're the one who said we should leave it as a dream. What if that's how I want to keep it? What if—"

"Dan . . . this is about Alex."

He stared at her. He felt for a moment that he might suffocate or that his heart would stop.

"Alex?"

She nodded, then sighed heavily.

"I started counseling a woman about a month ago. Let's call her Jane. She was referred to me after she was brought to the attention of one of the cult watch groups. I had a very difficult time getting started with her because she was so extremely terrified and paranoid."

"This woman . . . Jane . . . She's not Alex, is she?"

"No. Of course not. I would have told you immediately if that were the case." Laura picked up her tea, cupped it in her hands a moment, then set it back down on the table without drinking.

"This woman had been found in a river. In spite of serious injuries complicated by hypothermia, she survived. The question now is, how credible is she? She's incoherent at times. She shows signs of paramnesia—distorting and confusing her memories. And her paranoia has a decidedly delusional component."

"Laura . . . how does this connect with Alex?"

"She was a member of The Ark, Dan. She says she tried to run away, was caught and tortured, then somehow escaped. We don't know how much of it is based on reality. Her injuries could have a variety of causes, and she tells conflicting stories about how she ended up in the river. But she was most definitely with The Ark."

"Oh, God." He cradled his head in his hands.

"I know it's disturbing for you. I wrestled with myself over whether I should tell you or not. But then, when she said she knew Alex, I realized that I had to tell you."

Suddenly he wanted to scream *No!* He did not want to hear any more. He wanted to put his hands over his ears and run from the room. But he sat very still.

Laura twisted a napkin and bit the corner of her lip.

"Jane claims to have been one of the leader's many wives."

"Noah's wife?"

"Yes. She says she ran away after she couldn't get pregnant, because she was afraid Noah might decide she was inferior."

He shook his head in appalled disbelief.

"And she told me that Alex, who's been renamed Jael, is becoming very important. She's now Noah's most favored wife. She's been chosen, as Jane put it, to be the supreme vessel for Noah's seed."

He sagged into the chair. Feeling nothing. A great swallowing nothing.

"I'm sorry," Laura whispered.

He breathed for a while. In and out. Listening to the sound of the air. And eventually he felt something. It was as though a string had been clipped inside him and he was set free. Like the balloons at Valerie's absurd funeral.

He drew a deep breath. "Can I talk to this woman?"

"Absolutely not. I'm already betraying her confidence by speaking to you this way."

"Thank you. For telling me."

She nodded and leaned back in silence to drink her tea. He studied her. She was wearing black jeans and a long-sleeved silk blouse in a bluish gray that was nice with her eyes. It was a very daring outfit for her—the tailored woman of beige and brown. There were other differences as well. Her nails were polished. And instead of the hard geometries that usually hugged her earlobes she wore long filigreed earrings that brushed her neck when she moved. She looked good. When he first met her he had thought of her as plain. Now he realized that the plainness had been a choice for her. When she cared to she had an off-beat attractiveness—a sort of Victorian lady meets the East Village.

"Laura," he said, and she flinched.

"I thought you had brought me here to talk about . . ."

There was no good way to finish the sentence, so he let it hang. She knew what he was trying to say.

Her cheeks colored and she lowered her gaze.

"Damn," he said. "You're supposed to be a pro at talking through emotionally charged situations."

"Not when they're my own," she admitted.

Without any conscious effort he moved from the chair to the couch. He looked into her eyes. Gray eyes but with a hint of blue today. Not the startlingly beautiful, haunted eyes that Alex had. But eyes that a man could drown in nonetheless. Full of such complexities. Intelligence. Compassion. Great kindness. Gentle humor. And now a vulnerability that was tinged with both hope and fear.

"Why did you start this? Was it out of pity? Were you trying to shock me out of being so stuck on Alex?"

She smiled ruefully and shook her head.

He waited. She kept her gaze down. He heard the quick intake of her breath and felt her tense as though she were going to begin, but then she released the breath and gave a small shake of her head. "It's hard," she whispered.

"I need to know."

She nodded. "Don't look at me, all right? Can you close your eyes while I tell you?"

"Okay." He closed his eyes.

Again the intake of breath. "I was"—another breath— "physically attracted to you from the first moment. There I was in your home to help your wife. And I was stricken with this whole-body cliché. A real *coup de foudre*. Only I don't believe in first-sight lightning strikes. It's something I've always counseled against trusting. And I was furious at myself for being so unprofessional.

"I thought it would go away. I used excuses to see you as often as possible, not just because I was thinking about you but because I was convinced that familiarity would cure me. But it didn't. And then I began to get attached to Hana, and that made things even worse.

"I had fantasies about taking Alex's place—not that I believed I could ever really fill the place of such a beautiful and desirable woman—then I hated myself because there was this little voice deep inside me saying, 'I hope Alex never comes back.'

"It was agony for me when you were gone with Everett

May, not knowing what was happening, worrying that you would fail, but realizing that I would lose any chance with you if the deprogramming were successful. Then suddenly you were in the hospital and you needed me and I had a new purpose in your life. I wasn't just there to try to help you get your wife back anymore. She wasn't coming back. And you were suffering. Hana was suffering. You both needed me.

"So I cut back on my client hours and spent as much time as possible with you. But then, gradually, I became disgusted with myself. It didn't matter that Alex was gone for good—you were still in love with her. And you didn't really need me, and there I was hanging around like some kind of masochistic idiot. And so I forced myself to stop. I quit being there for you. I immersed myself in my practice."

She gave a rueful laugh. "But hope springs eternal, and every single day I would wake up thinking maybe . . . just maybe . . . that would be the day you called. That would be the day you realized you missed me.

"Then one day it happened. You called and invited me to the zoo. I was . . . ecstatic. I thought . . . Well, whatever I thought was laid to rest when I realized that it had been Hana who missed me. Not you. You hadn't thought of me at all. I was nothing to you.

"So I licked my wounds and determined to keep up a relationship with Hana, because, in truth, I had missed her, too. I wanted a child in my life. Then Valerie died and I was terribly worried about Hana and my scheduling made it easy for me to go to L.A. a few days early and . . ."

There was a pause. "I didn't consciously plan to get you alone in my apartment and seduce you. At least I don't think it was a conscious plan. Although I *had* bought the perfume in the airport gift shop. I went in to pick up a gift for one of my assistants and I saw that perfume and I remembered it from studying Alex's things and I just . . . bought it.

"And suddenly everything converged. I was in the dark of my own apartment with you so close. So close. Dreaming your sexual dreams of Alex. And I wanted you so badly that it felt like something I might die of. And I thought and thought. I thought about how the few sexual experiences I've had in my life have been . . . unsatisfying. I thought about being thirty-two and never having known real passion—about the possibility that the chance to know passion might not come again for me. And I thought about you. . . . What could it hurt to give flesh to your dreams? What could it hurt to give respite to your agony? And there was Hana, sleeping so conveniently in my bedroom. Everything was perfect.

"I promised myself that it would be just once. Just one time in the darkness with Alex's perfume, slipping into your sleep so that you would never be quite sure if it was part of your dream."

Another pause.

"But I broke the promise. I couldn't stop. I lost control and I ruined everything."

Silence.

He opened his eyes without asking for permission. She looked utterly humiliated, head down and tears in her eyes.

"Laura . . ." he said softly. Words. Words. Nothing was adequate. He couldn't think, so he tried to speak straight from his heart. "I don't know where to go from here. I don't know what's right or wrong. What's kind. What's cruel. What's insane. What's possible.

"I feel . . . I don't know how to explain it exactly. It's as though the Alex I loved is dead, and the rational part of me knows that, but I can't seem to stop loving her. I'm afraid I might never get over her. I feel as though I'll never love anyone else. So . . . it seems dishonest to get involved with you. I feel like I would be cheating you. But . . . Look at me . . . please?"

She raised her eyes to his, and the pain in them squeezed his heart.

"But I'm also feeling very selfish, because something has happened. It's like you've mended a broken piece inside me. And now you're inside me. And I want to be with you. Not just in the darkness. Not just in dreams."

She seemed stunned.

"If you don't feel the same way, Laura . . . if you want to forget anything ever happened . . . just say so. Tell me honestly. We need to stop pretending with each other."

"Dan," she breathed.

And in his name he heard all the answers.

He cupped her face in his hands and smiled. "Do you realize that we've never actually kissed?"

# Chapter 17

They had a blissful month of happiness before the next nightmare began. Laura cut short her time in Los Angeles. He didn't ask how. Twice, on Friday nights, Felice invited Hana to sleep over so Dan and Laura could have two whole nights of adult togetherness. Then Laura came back from three days in L.A., and he knew she was troubled from the moment he saw her.

She came straight to his apartment from the airport, and the three of them went out to dinner. Dan knew from her manner and from the expression in her eyes when she looked at him that this was about The Ark and Alex.

"That woman you called Jane—you've just seen her in L.A., haven't you?"

"Yes." Laura sighed and reached to stroke Hana's hair. "I'll tell you later. When we're alone."

Dan could not help being impatient with Hana's customary bedtime stalling. His nerves were on edge, wondering what Laura had learned that could be so much worse than what they already knew. Finally, after a snack and a story and several drinks of water, Hana was tucked in with her animal friends and they were free to talk. He sat down in the living room and waited, knowing that she had to tell it at her own pace and in her own way.

"Not much progress has been made with Jane. In fact, she's regressed. I'm working with a psychiatrist, and even together, with drug therapy and inpatient care at a topnotch facility, the woman is slipping. I don't know if she'll ever be able to function in society.

"It's so difficult to get through to her. To communicate with her. She rambles and hallucinates. Everything she says is disjointed, and she mixes fact with fantasy and with diatribes that must have come from The Ark's leaders. That's why it took so long for us to realize . . . to see the enormity of the thing.

"You have to understand, she's very hard to follow. We just recently decided to try a new approach—studying the audiotapes of her sessions. Really going over them and taking notes and trying to fit together all the nonsensical bits and pieces.

"Finally, we worked out the patterns and started in the right direction. And suddenly I saw that Jane was not talking about just her own torture and mistreatment. She was talking about the torture of others. She was talking about murders. And she was talking about crimes the cult had committed against outsiders."

"The unawakened," Dan breathed.

"Yes."

"Do you think she's telling the truth?"

Laura gave a sigh of deep frustration. "I think there's enough truth to be chilling."

She left her chair and began pacing. "But it's so hard to judge! For instance, she says The Ark was responsible for all those water-contamination incidents! That they were practice for something planned in the future. When we questioned her, though, she didn't know any details beyond what's been released to the public—so are her stories true or just paranoid fantasies triggered by what she's heard in the news?"

"My God, Laura, there's got to be someone out there who has knowledge of The Ark. Someone who could corroborate or discount such bizarre accusations."

"Actually, that's another disturbing element to the puzzle. I've never counseled anyone from The Ark before. That's not unusual, given the numbers of cults that have sprung up within the last ten years. But I've asked my colleagues, and none of them has ever counseled an ex-Ark member either. I've checked with all the various organizations that monitor cults and hate groups. Not one of them has ever been contacted by a person leaving The Ark.

"So what conclusion does that bring me to? Is The Ark such a wonderful nurturing group that not one single member ever tries to leave, or are Jane's claims true—that anyone caught trying to leave is condemned as a traitor and disposed of."

"What are you going to do?" he asked.

She stopped pacing and gripped the top of her head in her hands as though the anguish was causing physical pain.

"I told this woman to trust me! I swore to her! I promised that I wouldn't repeat anything she told me or reveal anything about her—even her existence!—to the law or the media or to any of the cult watch organizations. She was so terrified of The Ark and she believed . . . still believes! . . . that the only reason she's alive is that she's hidden so well that The Ark assumes she's dead. And she's convinced that to step out of hiding and be, as she called it, 'one little escaped rat trying to sink the ark' would seal her death warrant."

The pacing resumed.

"I was so focused on her . . . on her crisis condition . . . And it's not unusual for exiting cult members to be obsessed with secrecy in the beginning of treatment. That's a common phenomenon that they usually come out of as their sense of security increases."

Dan caught her wrist as she passed, stopping her circuit. "You weren't wrong to make the promises, Laura."

"But it's wrong to break them!"

"Don't break them."

"I have to. The Ark must be investigated. If even a few of her allegations are true, then this is an incredibly dangerous cult."

"Surely the federal authorities are already aware. Couldn't you just leak a little information to them without compromising her or becoming directly involved?"

She shook her head vehemently. "The Ark has kept such a low profile that it's way down at the bottom of everyone's caution list. This Noah is very clever. He's been maintaining an innocuous facade while building his membership and his assets. Even now, according to Jane, only his warrior counsel knows his full agenda."

"But what if none of her stories are true? What if you stir up all this trouble and betray your patient and none of her stories are true? What if The Ark threw her out because she was nuts?"

"Then I'll have made a serious error in judgment. I'll have compromised myself and my practice. And if the authorities aren't careful with this woman . . . if they destroy the fragile balance she has left with all their probing and questioning . . . then I'll have that to haunt me for the rest of my life, too."

"Don't do it, Laura. Turn this over to a colleague. That psychiatrist you mentioned. Let him take over completely. Bow out of this now."

She smiled sadly at him. "I know this scares you. You've already lost so much to The Ark. But do you really want me to take the coward's way out? You wouldn't if our positions were reversed. And if I ignore this and then The Ark goes on to harm people—I'd be responsible."

He took her arm, pulled her down onto his lap, and cradled her.

"You can't protect me from this, Dan."

He held her tighter.

"Put aside this relationship for a moment, Dan. If this was just you. Just you who this woman had told her stories to. What would you do?"

"But it's not me, Laura. It's you!"

"And I should have less of a moral responsibility? I should have less of a conscience?"

"No."

"So tell me honestly, Dan. What would you do?"

He tried to think of a way around it, but could not.

"I'd try to stop them," he admitted. "Any way I could."

She put her arms around his neck and kissed his forehead.

"Yes. And that's why I knew you'd support my decision."

She sighed as though a heavy weight had been lifted from her, then she kissed his mouth, long and slow. He unbuttoned her blouse and kissed the lovely swelling of flesh above her bra. Quickly she slipped from his arms and stood. One side of her blouse hung open, revealing a tantalizing view of white lace over a rosy nipple.

"Come on," she said, taking his hand. "Straight to the bedroom."

He resisted. "Hana's out cold. Let's be wild and do it right here with the lights on and the blinds open."

She laughed. "You belong in Los Angeles instead of New York."

"All right. We'll close the blinds."

"I can't relax . . . with even the possibility that Hana might wake up and—"

"Okay. Okay. Behind the bedroom door. But a light stays on."

"Dan!" Her voice was still playful but with a stubborn edge.

He stood and put his hands on her shoulders.

"How long are we going to be lovers before you trust me?"

"What do you mean, trust you?"

"To see your back."

She tried to pull away, but he held her.

"At first you didn't even want me to touch it. Right?"

Reluctantly, she gave a small nod.

"You kept knocking my hands away and I kept putting them right back until you finally gave up. Right?"

Another small nod.

"And nothing terrible happened, did it? My penis didn't shrivel. I didn't run away shrieking in horror because the skin on your back felt different. So why can't you trust me to see you?"

"I can't. No one has seen it."

"Then it's a first you can give me," he teased gently. "A virgin back."

"No. Dan, don't ask me to—"

"To what? This is not a request for S and M, Laura. I'm asking for something that is perfectly natural. I want to see you naked. I want to feast on your body with my eyes."

She frowned. "My back was burned, and it's awful to look at. It's disgusting. Revolting. I don't want to be revolting to you."

"So because of this irrational fear, I'll never get to see more than your outline in the dark while we're making love?"

Her expression indicated that she was worried.

"I guess we could have a light or candles if I stayed on my back the whole time," she offered tentatively. "That way it would be against the sheets. But you'd have to promise that you wouldn't try to move me. Or to look."

"No."

He spun her around, yanking her blouse off her shoulders. She cried out and tried to run, but he held her. He pinned her arms at her sides and pressed his cheek against the shiny, discolored flesh that began just beneath her shoulder blades. He brushed his lips over the scarred knobs of her spine. She stopped struggling and sobbed quietly.

"There," he said, turning her gently to face him. "It's over."

He kissed the tear tracks on her cheeks, kissed the hollow of her throat, kissed the erotic dip of her cleavage.

"I've seen your scars and I still want you just as much."

"You do?" she whispered.

"Feel this," he said, guiding her hand toward the front of his pants. "What does that tell you?"

For Hana's last day of school Dan planned a dinner that featured Hana's favorite foods. He was expecting Laura to be in New York and he invited Felice as well. Felice was early and full of fun. Laura was late and was drawn and distracted throughout the evening. He knew, without her having to say it, that her mood was related to Jane and The Ark, and he suspected that her dreaded contact with federal authorities had occurred that afternoon.

Felice left and he put Hana to bed. Laura's distress was such that he wasn't certain whether to press her into a discussion or to keep silent and wait.

"Well," he said, settling onto the living room couch, "that's it. Another year of school over. She's getting so old."

Laura had been roaming around the apartment, idly straightening things. Suddenly she stopped. "I need a walk."

"Okay. I'll see if Felice can come back for a while." He reached for the telephone.

"No." She put her hand on his arm. "I need to go out alone."

He knew that it was childish to feel hurt, but he did.

"Fine. Don't go down to the water by yourself, though. Be sensible."

She gave him a look of such affection that he felt the glow of it go all the way through him.

"I'll be careful," she promised.

He watched her walk out the door, disturbed suddenly, and angry with himself. This was all so dishonest. Why did he continue with this committed but uncommitted relationship? Where could it possibly lead? Why had he allowed himself to be trapped into this pretense, this honey-coated web spun through lies of omission, feelings unspoken, doubts kept silent? He had no intention of marrying her. He did not love her.

He wanted to love her. He wished that he returned the feelings he knew she had for him. But he knew what love felt like, and this wasn't it. He simply did not feel the intensity that he had felt with Alex. It was just not there. With Alex he had felt a desperation, a gut-wrenching need. His emotions had rocketed and plunged. He had known agony and despair and torment punctuated by great ecstasy.

In contrast, he could be separated from Laura for days, missing her without any desperation. His guts didn't twist when she was angry with him or he with her. He never tortured himself with worrying about whether she was attracted to other men. He never agonized about the depth of her feelings for him. What he had with Laura was companionable and sexually fulfilling. But it was not the soaring, all-consuming love that he had known with Alex—the love that still burned inside him like hot coals buried in the ashes. He did not love Laura Ferren. And the longer their involvement continued the more painful and difficult it was going to be to break it off.

Though he wished to escape the examination of his feelings, questions haunted him. Why did he still love Alex? Why did he still yearn for her? Was it her he wanted, or was it the relationship itself that he could not get over? Was it love that burned inside him or was it a hunger for that lost love, a lust akin to an addict's hunger for opium? Or was it just the memory of such a love that was still burning? He couldn't pretend these uncertainties did not exist. He couldn't lie to Laura or to himself.

He tried to occupy himself with reading until she returned. When he heard the key in the lock he felt relief at knowing she was safe, but dread at the thought of seeing her.

She seemed restored and more at peace as she sat down beside him on the couch.

"Boy, it's hot in here," she said. "You don't realize how hot until you get out."

He put the book aside, hating himself because he found it so hard to say what ought to be said. "This apartment doesn't catch the breezes from the water like my old place. I've got every window open and there's no air movement at all."

"July first is just days away," she said, fanning herself with a magazine. "This place is going to be unbearable." She glanced at him, and he knew what was coming.

"Maybe you and Hana should stay at my apartment for a while," she said tentatively.

"This place would be fine with an air conditioner," he countered. "Maybe I'll let Valerie buy me one of those energy-efficient window units."

"I wish you'd stop saying things like that. The money is yours now, not Valerie's."

"It will always be Valerie's. She just can't use it anymore."

"Why do you feel so guilty about taking it? She left it to you because *she* felt guilty about her daughter's stealing all your money."

"Alex didn't steal it," he bristled defensively.

"Okay. The cult stole it."

"Not exactly," he countered stubbornly.

"Yes! Exactly! That's what cults do. They steal lives. They steal children. They steal money. They steal dignity and self-respect. They steal souls!"

He turned away from her, filled with unreasoned anger.

She was silent for a long moment, then said, softly, "You've never asked me about the cult I was in."

"I didn't think you wanted to talk about it."

"I don't. And I'm grateful to you for not asking. But I'm . . . I don't know why but it's preying on my mind tonight, and I want to tell you. I need to tell you."

"Okay."

She stared at the face of his grandmother clock as though searching for a beginning, "I guess my father was hungry for beliefs," she finally said. "He wanted to be caught up in something glorious and mystical." She smiled sadly. "He loved those nice young Mormon missionaries who came around, and he always had time for the Jehovah's Witnesses at the door. I think he flirted with joining both, and maybe the only thing that kept him from it was that he couldn't make up his mind. Then he heard a charismatic tent preacher and he was hooked. We all became born again.

"That infatuated him for a while. But it didn't hold him. He got restless again. And somehow or another he came into contact with a man who claimed to be a prophet and who called himself The Seer. The Seer came to our house for dinner. He had a bushy beard and he wore robes and a sort of turban on his head. I was eight years old and not paying too much attention to adult affairs, so I don't know exactly how my father was sucked in so completely. But in a very short time he'd given everything we owned to The Seer.

"My father kept his job, but every other part of our life changed. We moved to a house just outside San Francisco that was full of The Seer's people. It was a huge old house, poorly maintained, and overcrowded. My father slept with the men. My mother slept with the women. And my younger brother and I slept with the other children, end to end on the floor in sleeping bags. There were no locks on the bathroom doors—or on any doors, for that matter. The kitchen was run like a mess hall, with certain people assigned meal duty. More than thirty people lived in that house. And there were some commuters, too—cult members whose work was far enough away that they couldn't live in the house but who attended special events and spent the weekends with us.

"Our lives were governed by rules. Some rules came and went according to The Seer's current messages from on high, but the big things were inflexible. We had to read assigned passages in the Bible every day and then go through lectures and tests in the evening. This was a requirement for both adults and children, but it also counted as our home schooling. We couldn't attend outside school because that was the devil's workshop. Certain foods were evil. Certain colors were off-limits. Bathing was controlled. Books had to be approved. Newspapers and magazines were strictly forbidden. Permission had to be granted for sex, and the methods and positions were proscribed. And, most confusing of all to me as a kid, my mother had to go with any man who got permission to 'use her.' That's what they called it. The men asked to 'use' women, and the women had no voice in it.

"Punishments were all spelled out. Snacking between meals warranted the loss of a meal. Having money and not turning it in for the communal good earned a whipping. Disobeying one of The Seer's direct orders got you twenty-four hours in the punishment closet for the first offense and increased time for further offenses."

She shook her head.

"My father was a willing and eager believer, and my mother, who was a timid woman and truly devoted to my father, just followed along behind him like a sheep to the slaughter.

"Things fell apart when the child welfare people started poking around. I was ten, going on eleven, then. They didn't like the bruises on our backs and bottoms, and they didn't like the fact that our only textbook was the Bible. They came to the house over and over. And The Seer became increasingly agitated over it. He'd keep us up at night ranting about their being the devil's handmaidens.

"Finally a pair of social workers appeared one morning waving some kind of an order. Most of the men went ahead and left for their jobs, but The Seer asked my father and two other men to stay until the devil's handmaidens were finished.

"The social workers herded us into a big bedroom without any of the cult's adults allowed to be present. We were scared. We'd been warned that we'd be hauled off to jail and locked up forever if we said the wrong thing. It's crazy when I think back, because I can remember being terrified of those two women, and yet they were trying so hard to be kind to us.

"At that time there were nine kids ranging from three to

twelve years old. We'd had a few kids older than that, but they had run away by then. The social workers talked to us all for a while. Then they zeroed in on the two oldest girls—one eleven and one twelve. They kept asking them about their initiations into womanhood. And their purification by The Seer.

"I hadn't reached that milestone yet, but I was very aware of it looming. We all knew about purification. At evening lecture The Seer sometimes talked about what a burden all that purifying was for him. The thing is, though, I didn't understand what actually happened. The mechanics of it were never discussed.

"Only females needed to be purified, because they were naturally unclean. They needed it when they were being welcomed into the fold. And then they had to have boosters after they'd had their period, and after they'd had nightmares indicating that they were harboring filthy thoughts, and after they had any kind of emotional outburst—again, a symptom of filthy thoughts—and they needed it if they were ever away from the house and had contact with the forces of evil—say, an optometrist or a dentist.

"That was for the adult women. For little girls there was a big initiation thing. When a girl got her period for the first time she was made to stand in front at evening lecture and beg for forgiveness for having fallen from grace. Then she had to sleep in the adult women's room for the duration of her bleeding. As soon as the bleeding was finished she was taken to The Seer's and stayed there, in the purification room, for as many days as The Seer deemed necessary.

"The Seer lived next door to the communal house, you see. His place was supposed to be so full of mystical vibrations that it was dangerous for lower beings—in other words, anyone but The Seer—to spend very much time there. Women who went over to cook and clean always hurried so they wouldn't absorb harmful levels of vibrations, and women who went over for cleansing rituals were careful to stay only in the purification room, which had mirrored walls and ceilings to block the vibrations.

"The girls who started their periods and went through

the ritual were given little angel necklaces to wear." She snorted in mock amusement. "Shades of David Koresh, huh? With his Stars of David to mark the little girls who had started their periods and were ready to bear his divine offspring."

Dan put his hand over hers, but she didn't seem to notice. She was too deeply caught in the pain of her past.

"So on that day the social workers took the two older girls away. It was horrible. The girls were kicking and screaming. The police came, and they were pushing everyone, shouting and shoving and cursing. And those two girls were carried out in hysterics.

"As they were being taken out, one of the social workers, a young woman who can't have had very much job experience, threatened The Seer. I still remember it so clearly. Her jacket was torn. One of the girls had kicked her in the mouth and her lip was bleeding. And she shouted at The Seer. Shook her finger in his face and told him that the girls were being taken for medical exams and he better have a damn good lawyer because she knew what had been going on with his purifications.

"As soon as she was gone The Seer declared an emergency. Someone asked if the men who'd already left for work should be called back or if the commuters should be called, but The Seer said there wasn't time. He said we were under direct attack from the legions of the devil. The phone cords were ripped from the walls to prevent evil spirits from coming through. The electric wires were cut outside the house. My father and the two other men who had stayed went out and nailed boards over all the windows and over the back and side doors. Then they came back inside and angled big nails through the edges of the front door into the doorjamb.

"When we were safely sealed in we lit a circle of candles in the meeting room and we sat down to chant and pray. That went on until we all got hungry and tired. The smaller children started whining. The Seer told some of the women to make instant lemonade, a drink that was reserved as a treat because we ordinarily weren't allowed refined sugar.

"There was knocking at the front door. Normal at first and then very loud, like pounding.

"The Seer told us to blow out the candles, and I remember how spooky it was in that shadowy room. It was like twilight but different. Tiny cracks of sunlight showed where the boards came together over the windows, and for some reason even those little slivers of sunlight were frightening. It was a total nightmare. My little brother scooted closer to me and I held his hand.

"The Seer stood and raised his arms. He was weeping.

" 'The devil's legions are at the door, my children! We have to fight our way to heaven! We have to save our souls from their eternal damnation!'

"Big pitchers of the lemonade were carried into the room. The Seer said he was going to bless the drink with divine power because each of us needed to be strong to resist the evil. And he whispered to my father. And my father helped him stir something into each of the pitchers. Then paper cups were filled and passed out. My father brought ours. He handed them out to my mom, and to me, and to my little brother. Then he smiled and patted us on the head.

"We were all thirsty. My mother finished hers right away, and when my little brother asked for more she had nothing to give him. I was always slow and had barely sipped mine. I took one more small sip and then gave it to my brother.

"I don't know what they put in the lemonade, but it didn't take long to act. People started weeping and moaning and wandering around. Some of them shouted at invisible opponents. Some of them went to corners and stared at the dustballs. My mother was smiling and catching things out of the air. My little brother started to shake, and his eyes glazed over.

"I was scared because I felt a little weird, too. Everything had fuzzy edges and the boards in the floor were like ocean waves. But I wasn't out of it like everyone else because I hadn't ingested very much of the drug.

"Voices boomed from outside the house. *'This is the police. Open the door.'* And The Seer went wild. He was ranting and raving and shouting about us saving ourselves.

"My father tipped over big red cans and liquid ran

everywhere. It smelled bad. I don't remember knowing that it was gasoline. My brother started jerking and twitching, and he collapsed and the liquid got all over him. I tried to pull him up but he knocked me backwards so I got it all over my back.

"It was terrifying but I remember being very calm. I tried to talk to my mother; she paid no attention. And I remember thinking that I should get my brother upstairs and we should change our clothes.

"I tugged at him until I finally got him on his feet, and we made it across the room and up a couple of steps. Then he sat down and went into a daze and I couldn't get him to walk anymore. I was several steps above him, pulling on his arms, trying to drag him up the stairs, when suddenly there was this horrible explosion of pounding and smashing. Cracking wood and shattering glass. And screaming. Everyone huddling around The Seer, piling up in the center of the room. My father with another red can, splashing everyone. Splashing himself. And then there was this moment of stillness. And the sound of a wooden match scratching . . ."

She buried her face in her hands, took several deep breaths, then shook her head.

"My memory stops there. Like the film ran out in the camera. I know I must have seen the fire. I know I must have seen my brother burn. I was told later that the fire had roared up the stairs so fast that I couldn't have outrun it. And I must have been conscious when it hit me, when my clothing caught fire and the gas on my back ignited. But it's all a blank."

Another deep breath.

"And I hope that blank is never filled in."

Dan took her in his arms and held her for some time in silence. Then she stiffened and pulled away.

"I've gone through all the investigators' files and I've studied The Seer's cult from a professional perspective. He was a seminary dropout turned hippie turned used car salesman turned drug supplier for a rock band and then finally turned prophet. His egomania was really pretty modest—satisfied by being the center of a small, innocuous group. He was fairly lazy about recruiting, and he didn't bother claiming that he had a 'new way' that everyone should follow.

"He was practical, too, balancing control versus finances. He never managed to score any wealthy converts, so he chanced sending the men off to jobs in the real world for the sake of a steady flow of income. And he came up with his commuter program as a creative means to bring in extra funds."

She shook her head.

"He was a small man. He never wanted to be Napoleon, just the local mayor. He was content with being absolute and all-powerful only to his meager little band. He was content with a house for his followers, a house and a few luxuries for himself. Enough women to keep sex exciting. A few little girls to add spice. In my research I can't see that he was ever interested in End Time or Armageddon or any of the Judgment Day scenarios. I think he just snapped when he thought that everything was going to be taken from him.

"A small, insignificant little tyrant. Yet twenty-two people died. My whole family died."

Dan waited to be certain that she had finished, then he asked, "Did you ever see any of the other survivors?"

"Yes. I tracked them down after I was finished with my training. Not one of them had been able to reassimilate into society. In some ways they had died in the fire, too."

He looked at her and felt a great swelling of emotion. How had she survived? How had she found the inner strength to become the wise and compassionate and generous person she was?

"I practically lived in the children's ward of a hospital for two years, having operation after operation and endless physical therapy. I was schooled by the hospital tutor. I was pampered and indulged by the medical staff—and taught, too. When I was up to it, they sometimes let me go on rounds with them, and they taught me medical terms and simple procedures. During the brief intervals when I didn't have to be at the hospital I got to stay in the homes of various doctors and nurses. And eventually this one doctor, Violet Ferren, took me in permanently.

"She wanted to adopt me, but she was afraid to try. Being single, and over fifty, and having had a rather colorful past as a warrior on the feminist front lines—she was afraid that the courts would deny the adoption. And that going through the process would only call attention to us and create the danger of my being taken away. When I was eighteen I asked the court to let her adopt me, and we made it legal."

She smiled sadly.

"Everything that I value about myself, I owe to Violet. I wish she was still alive."

He tucked an escaping tendril behind her ear.

"Violet is alive in all the good work you do with counseling. Violet is alive in all the kindness and guidance you give Hana."

"Oh, Dan . . ." Tears filled her eyes, and she smiled. "You are the sweetest man I have ever known."

# Chapter 18

It was the hottest Fourth of July on record, and Dan was regretting his promise to attend the big Macy's fireworks display on Manhattan's East Side. Though it was now evening, the heat was still reflecting from the baked pavement in humid blasts.

"They're supposed to have a new color this year," Laura said.

"What?"

They were standing in a crowd of people at the base of an on-ramp to the FDR Drive, waiting to be allowed onto the closed roadway.

"The brothers who do this every year. They're some of the top fireworks people in the world, very inventive and innovative, and they've developed a way to add another color this year."

"I didn't know there were colors missing."

"Sure. Some are really hard to do. Some can't be done at all. That's why there's so much basic gold and silver."

"Well, I appreciate artistic fireworks as much as anybody, but surely there's a more pleasant way to see them than this."

A uniformed officer up on the roadway waved to his counterpart at the barricade. The crowd around them began to stir.

"Get ready," Laura warned.

Dan picked up the small cooler full of drinks at his feet and prepared for the charge up the ramp. Hana had gone with Felice to pick up something at her office. In matching red, white, and blue sequined baseball caps that Felice had made, they had struck out together, spirits high, with plans to get ice cream and then meet Dan and Laura on the FDR between eight and eight-thirty.

"Remember, Daddy," Hana had said. "Get us a good watching spot. Felice says it has to be past the Seaport 'cause that blocks some of the low ones.'"

"I'll remember," Dan had assured her. Then, with a sarcastic smile, "Thanks for the tip, Felice."

Now, in the midst of a stampede, burdened with the task of claiming a "good watching spot," he wondered how he had let himself be talked into any of it. With Laura, he hurried down the empty stretch of wide, elevated highway that edged the East River. The crowd was boisterous and aggressive but not at all unpleasant. Just beyond the group of buildings that formed the Seaport they found an area against the back of the highway that allowed an unobstructed view of the sky over the river with the bonus of a concrete wall to sit down and lean against without fear of being trod on. They arranged the old blanket Laura had brought to sit on, staking out a big enough space for the four of them, and then spent the next thirty minutes explaining to people that they weren't being hogs but were saving space for two more. The fireworks show wasn't scheduled to start until sunset, so there was a long time to wait. Dan concentrated on studying his surroundings. It seemed very strange for the usually busy FDR to be swarming with people rather than cars, and he thought that part of the general festive mood was due simply to the fun of being up there on the highway.

The crowd settled, and he watched vendors hawk glowing bracelets and balloons. He watched children playing tag among the leaning or sitting or reclining or strolling adults. He watched young couples with their arms entwined. He listened to the music booming from the huge portable loudspeakers, part of a live radio broadcast that was being staged somewhere nearby, though out of his sight. For the most part he avoided talking to Laura. He had come to a decision. He thought that they should end their relationship. He could not monopolize her affections any longer. It was too selfish and dishonest. She was at a point in her life where she desperately wanted to be married and have a family, and he was not ready for that. He was afraid he might never be ready. So he had to let her go. Painful as it might be, that was the simple truth.

"It's eight," Laura said, looking down at her watch. "I hope they can find us."

Dan got up off the blanket. "You stay here and hold down the fort. I'll look around for them."

He wandered slowly back toward the on-ramp, scanning for the flashy ball caps. When he was opposite the Seaport he looked down over the side of the highway and saw a milling, celebratory crowd, mostly younger people, probably the overflow from the various taverns that ringed the area. Then he saw a flash of red, white, blue, and he had to smile. There were the hats. Bobbing along in the mass of humanity. Felice's outrageous caps. He could have spotted them from an airplane window.

He watched the flash of sequins as they progressed through the jammed plaza. They had probably gone into one of the Seaport establishments for their ice cream, and they were just now weaving their way toward the on-ramp.

There was so much movement that he didn't see anything wrong until it happened. Suddenly there was a disturbance. A startled ripple with the flashing hats at the center. Then the crowd opened around a figure on the ground. Felice! Felice sprawled like a broken puppet with the cap still on her head . . . And Hana? He searched frantically. Where was Hana? People were kneeling around Felice, but none of them was a child-sized figure in a red, white, and blue cap.

"Hana!" he shouted, but his voice was swallowed by the cacophony of sound.

Felice hurt. How? And Hana . . . God, she must be so frightened. He started along the wall, threading in and out of groups, trotting at first, then running, never taking his eyes off the scene below.

"Watch it!" people called after him in annoyance.

Suddenly he saw a winking of sequins at the edge of the crowd. And he saw Hana's small figure being carried by a man. Carried as though she was unconscious or hurt. The man was rushing. Rushing her somewhere. And then the man turned at the corner of a building and disappeared, followed closely by two other men.

Dan fought his way through the crowd, unmindful of anything but his daughter. A policeman tried to stop him. Dan broke free of the man's restraining hand.

"My daughter," he cried as he continued on. "I saw them taking her away!"

The cop ran behind him, talking over his radio.

"She's okay," he yelled from behind Dan. "Slow down, buddy. They say she's okay."

Dan slowed down enough to hurry beside the officer, who went a ways with him, then passed him off to another officer, both men assuring him that the injuries were minor and that he needed to calm down. When he reached the plaza there was an ambulance taking Felice away.

"The lady's gonna be fine," the officer in control told him. "They're taking her in because she's a little woozy from being knocked down, so if you want to ride in with her—"

"But what about my daughter?" Dan demanded. "How is she? Why didn't they take her in the same ambulance?"

"What do you mean, your daughter? We've got this one injury here—"

"No! No! My daughter was with her. In the same kind of cap. Felice fell and a man carried my daughter away. I saw it all from up on the highway."

The policeman evaluated him for a split second, then started yelling into his radio, yelling at the other officers around him, yelling for the crowd to move back.

"Show me!" he ordered, and they ran together with a uniformed cadre trailing after them.

Dan's heart was pounding. His adrenaline was rushing. Thoughts were screaming through his brain. It was all a mistake. There had obviously been two ambulances. Hana had fallen, too. The police just did not know what was going on.

As soon as they rounded the building where he'd watched the man disappear with Hana they were alone on the sidewalk. There was no view of the fireworks from that street and it was empty. No merrymakers. No ambulance. No man holding his daughter. Nothing. Except a red, white, and blue cap lying on the pavement, the sequins crushed by the tread of a heavy foot.

* * *

Dan sat in a chair in his living room. It was somewhere near three a.m. There was a small light on, but it would not have mattered if it had been dark because he was not aware of anything in the room. He kept seeing the abduction over and over. The bright hats bobbing through the crowd. The sudden ripple of movement, like a lake surface disturbed by a falling stone. And in the center of that movement were the bright hats. Only it had become just one hat.

Then the sighting of his child's limp form in the arms of the anonymous man. Anonymous evil. The man rounding the corner, followed by two other swiftly moving men. Somehow he should have been able to stop it. Somehow . . .

Laura came out of the bedroom wrapped in a robe. Her eyes were swollen from crying.

"You got up again," she said.

"I couldn't lie there. It's worse lying there."

She padded barefoot across the room.

"Want some tea or something?"

"I don't care."

She nodded and went to the kitchen nook.

They had spent hours with the police. While Dan went over and over what he had seen and answered questions about his life, Laura had raced to her apartment to get pictures of Hana so they could be distributed. They had been shown the statements of the three witnesses who had realized something bad was happening and who had helped Felice and been willing to stay around and talk to the police. And then the flurry of activity ground to a halt because there was nothing more that anyone could do. They were told to go home and stay by the phone in case there was a ransom demand.

"Here," Laura said, handing him a tall glass of iced cranberry tea.

He knew it was cranberry by the color, but when he drank he tasted nothing.

"They wouldn't listen to me," he said. "After I said that her mother might be involved—all they wanted to do was look on it as a custody dispute."

"The FBI kidnapping experts have been called in," Laura

said. "They're experienced with abductions. They'll . . . have ideas."

"I don't need ideas! I *know* who took my daughter! I know that The Ark has her! And the forceful kidnapping of a little girl by a dangerous cult does not qualify as a custody dispute!"

She rubbed his shoulder and held her cold glass against her forehead.

"I'm sorry," he said. "I didn't mean to yell at you."

"I know."

"Why don't they go ahead and call? Why can't we get this over with? How long do they think I need to talk to the lawyer and get them their money? I'm ready with it all. Hana's trust. My account. Everything is ready to transfer to them, so why don't they call?"

She took his glass from his hand and put it on the table. She pulled his head against her belly as though she wanted to shut out everything in the world for him. But he didn't let her. He tilted his head to look up at her.

"You think it's worse, don't you? You think they want more than Valerie's money."

She bit her top lip and looked away from him.

"Say it. Tell me what you think."

She looked down into his face.

"I think Alex has decided she wants her daughter. And if she has influence with the leader, as we've heard she has, I think that she asked to have her daughter brought into the fold."

Oh, God, he'd thought that, he'd had that darkest of thoughts, but to hear it spoken aloud, to hear Laura express it with such resigned assurance, made him sick with fear. Made him sick with anger. Made his heart and his brain and his gut reel with unendurable pain from somewhere deep and terrifying and his chest wouldn't work and his breath was strangled in his throat and his tears burned to ashes in his eyes before he could shed them.


"Please sit down."

They were in an office. The man in the white shirt and tie was a federal agent named Wilson. He looked and sounded too much like a normal businessman to give Dan any confidence in him. Dan wanted to see a uniformed SWAT team. He wanted action, not talk.

"This is very sensitive," the agent said. "We do agree with you that your daughter was taken by the cult. But since her mother was no doubt the instigator this does come into the realm of a custody snatch, and we feel confident that the child is in no immediate danger."

Dan opened his mouth to protest, but the agent held up his hands and said, "Let me finish before you jump in." He straightened the knot of his tie. "Even before Dr. Ferren supplied us with her information on The Ark, we had an information-gathering operation in place, and we don't want to jeopardize that. After that operation is complete, then we can formulate a plan for reclaiming your daughter."

Dan leaned forward slightly, ignoring the restraining hand Laura placed on his arm. "So you want to leave my daughter in there with those maniacs while you gather evidence, and I'm supposed to console myself with your assumption that she's being treated well and your assurances that you can safely remove her before all hell breaks loose. Does that sum it up?"

"It's delicate," the agent admitted. "But let's examine the options. From what we've already learned about The Ark—which is, by the way, calling itself The Arm and The Ark now—they have enormous resources. If we went there and banged on their gate, demanding your daughter, do you think they would hand her over? Absolutely not. If we stormed the place with a warrant, do you think they would meekly lay down their weapons and surrender her? Absolutely not."

Dan sat back in his chair.

"What do you mean by resources?" he asked glumly.

"Our data suggest an arsenal of arms. And a highly disciplined, highly trained force."

Dan stared at him, stunned. "But why? What are they planning?"

"We don't know yet. We projected the scope of their resources from money trails and the movement of both arms and scientific equipment."

"How could you people have missed all this for so long?"

The agent frowned. "It's a nasty world out there, Mr. Behr. Hate has mutated. In the old days it was simple. You had the KKK running around stirring up trouble against people of color. That was bad, but in hindsight it was nothing. We lopped off the head of the KKK and what happened? All these little offshoots popped up. White supremacist groups like the Aryan Nations, the Posse Comitatus, and the Order took hate and violence to new levels, claiming that not only were whites chosen and superior but also that our American democratic government had no right to rule free white men. That kind of thinking changed the whole ball game because it meant that there were no restrictions. Violence didn't have to be confined to brutalizing the other races anymore. All manner of crime could be justified as guerrilla resistance to federal terrorism."

"The Order is the group that committed all those big armored car robberies, right?" Laura asked.

"Right," Agent Wilson said dryly. "Four million dollars' worth. They're also responsible for gunning down a radio talk show host in Denver and dozens of lesser-known crimes."

"Are you trying to say that The Ark is actually one of these supremacist militia groups?" Behr asked.

"The answer to that is complicated. What happened is that all this bigotry and supremacism interbred with religion. The best example is Christian Identity. Its message is that whites are the true children of Israel and that white men are God's chosen. Jews and people of color are Satan's spawn and beasts. With that message it created a hate-mongering fundamentalist religion that it merged with the militia ideal by saying that America is the new Jerusalem and the Constitution was handed down by God to the white Christian founding fathers. Which means that its followers don't have to obey anything that isn't in the first ten Amendments and the Articles of Confederation. Nothing else the government does or says has any legitimacy. Therefore, white Christian men are the only true sovereign citizens of the United States, and they have a religious duty to put the government, women, nonwhites, and non-Christians back in their rightful places through whatever means possible."

"You still haven't answered me," Dan reminded him impatiently. "Is The Ark a supremacist militia group?"

"No. It's something new. You see, it used to be that cults were distinctly different from this kind of group. Cults were abusive of members, but there was only the occasional violent group . . . and that violence was confined to actions against members or members' relatives—or to thrill violence like the Manson family's spree. There was no terrorist or extremist or seditionist component to cult violence.

"But there's been another mutation. If you look at the top leaders in the supremacist groups, they're all cult-type figures—authoritarian, charismatic, egotistical—so you always had the same kind of guys at the top of both groups. And these top guys were all peddling belief systems. Now what's happening is that cult-style groups are being formed by leaders who've repackaged supremacist ideas in New Age jargon, added a dose of religious fatalism, and are employing militia techniques to train and arm."

The agent looked from Dan to Laura and then back to Dan. "We believe that The Ark could be a Jim Jones–style cult but with some kind of a militia agenda."

"And you're just now getting around to investigating it?" Dan asked incredulously.

Stiffening, the agent said, "We try to be diligent, but we have many crosses to carry. There are a lot of groups out there, and we can't possibly keep track of every one. And even if we did have the manpower and resources, how do you think the public would feel about us snooping around and infringing on citizens' rights, infringing on freedom of religion, every time there was a whiff of suspicion?"

Dan rested his elbow on the desk and cradled his forehead in his hand. "You're going to war with these people, and my little girl is caught in the middle of all this."

"You *can* get her out safely?" Laura asked the agent.

"We'll have intelligence to analyze very soon. Once we have it, we will determine a course of action."

"This course of action you determine . . . will we be notified at all? Or will we just hear about it on the news like everyone else?"

"This is a very sensitive and highly confidential operation with the safety of personnel involved."

"So what you're saying is that you've got spies or whatever and you're more worried about them than about my daughter."

"Mr. Behr . . ."

Dan pushed out of his chair, ignoring Laura's warning glance. "As Hana's father and the person who has the most concern for her safety, do I have any input at all?"

"This is about more than your child, Mr. Behr. While we are very committed to bringing her back safely, we also have to consider the grave danger that this group poses to the public at large. I know this is difficult for a parent to hear, but—"

Dan wheeled and stalked out of the office.

"Dan!" Laura called from behind him.

He slowed just enough for her to catch up.

"Dan, what good can it do to antagonize that man? What possible—"

"Don't," he cautioned her. "Just don't."

After hours of agonizing and soul-searching and arguing with Laura, Dan sat in her apartment staring at the wall as she fixed lunch. The phone rang. She answered it and, with an odd look on her face, handed it to Dan.

"Hello."

"Hello, Dan."

Alex. It was Alex.

"Hello, Alex." He felt that sudden sharp centering that comes with impending danger.

"She's with me, Dan. I wanted to tell you. So you wouldn't worry."

"Thank you. But I knew."

There was a shuffling and a muffled "Here . . . say hi."

"Hi, Daddy."

Hana's voice sounded thin and wavery with fright. He tried to keep his reply reassuring.

"Hi, punkin. How are you doing?"

"I miss you."

"I miss you, too. But you missed your mommy for so long and now you get to be with her, don't you?"

The shuffling again, and Alex came back on the line.

"That was nice, Dan."

"Oh, Alex, couldn't you have found a gentler way? That must have been terrifying for her."

"Mmmm. Like when your goons snatched me? Or is it okay for me to be scared?"

"I'm sorry. But that's in the past and this is now, and we have to do what's best for Hana."

"I am. Even though you were taking good care of her, I couldn't leave her out in the cold any longer. She's safe in The Ark with me now, under Noah's protection until she's old enough to awaken."

"I can't stay out here alone."

"But you've got your own personal psychologist to take care of you," Alex said, taunting him with her knowledge.

"That's nothing," he said, "but how did you . . . ?"

She laughed, sounding superior and buoyed by his denouncement of Laura. "Noah's all-powerful, Dan. There's nothing he can't find out."

"And how did you know I'd be at this number?"

"We tried your apartment first. But this was better. Noah thought the police might have your apartment phone bugged, so I wouldn't have been able to say more than a few words to you if you'd answered there."

"I can't stand this, Alex. You and Hana are all the family I have. I'm a dead man if I lose both of you."

"I tried to get you to come with me to The Ark, Dan. Noah was ready to accept you, but you turned away. You denied your place."

"I was . . . filled with conflicts. Like there was a war going on inside me."

"The battle for your soul?" she asked. "The demon inside you at that evil house?"

"Yes. But the battle is over and the house is burned."

"Noah destroyed that house to drive away the evil and to teach May a lesson."

Her voice was challenging, daring him to disapprove of Noah's judgment. His thoughts raced. If he could persuade her of his interest . . .

"That's good," he said, in praise of the house's burning. "Noah was right."

"He's always right." She sighed. "I wish you had come with me, Dan."

"As soon as I was free of that house, and well enough to think again, I wanted to go with you, but you had already gone. You abandoned me to the cold."

"Oh, Dan . . ."

"Don't leave me out here alone, Alex. Please."

"I'm not your wife anymore," she warned. "I can never be your wife again. I'm Noah's consort."

"I've learned to live without a wife. But I still think of you as family. And Hana . . . Hana is my blood. Please, Alex. If you have any kindness left in your heart for me, please . . . forgive me. And ask Noah to forgive me. Don't turn away."

She hesitated, and he knew that he had hooked her.

"I'll talk to Noah," she said abruptly. "You'll be contacted with his decision."

Dan replaced the receiver and stared down at the phone. "She believed me. She bought it all."

He looked up to see Laura standing in the doorway, face white and eyes wide. Standing there as if frozen.

"What was the object of that?" Laura asked.

"I'm going in there to get Hana."

"No. No. You have to leave it to the authorities. You can't enforce the law on your own."

"If I have an opportunity to do this, I'm damn sure jumping at it. I'm not going to sit here helplessly and wait for the day I can watch the federal invasion force on television while it turns The Ark into another Waco or Whidbey Island with my child in the middle of it all."

Laura exhaled a forceful breath and glared at him.

"So you think they'll open the gate for you and you'll swoop down like an action hero and carry Hana to safety?"

"No. I'll go in as a believer. And I'll wait for my chance."

"Oh. And they will be fair and civilized with you, of course. They won't torture you to test your loyalty or maim you or terrorize you or decide that you're a fake and murder you."

"I can handle whatever happens."

She laughed in a bitter acid bark. "How caveman of you,

Dan. How fucking testosterone ignorant! If they kill you, what happens to Hana?"

Her anger and uncharacteristic loss of control only calmed him. Made him more certain.

"I can beat them, Laura. I can fool them. You just heard how easy it was with Alex."

"Alex is a convert. She's a drone. She's been conditioned to believe bullshit. You won't convince Noah. Noah is the source of all this. It's his show. And from what we've learned about the man, he is not a raving lunatic leading his followers into his delusion. He's cold and calculating. He has an agenda. He's not going to fall for your act like Alex just did."

"Maybe you're right. But I think I have an edge. I got the impression before that Noah was encouraging Alex to recruit me. There was something about me that interested him."

"Great. So he wants you. That means he'll get you in there and really focus on you. Really concentrate all his efforts on indoctrinating you. After all you've learned about cults and about psychological manipulation . . . are you so arrogant that you believe yourself immune?"

"I can fight it, Laura. Just like certain prisoners of war have been able to keep from being broken when all their comrades succumbed. I'll study the psychology of it. You can help me! What better teacher could I have than you?"

"This is getting better and better. Now I'm not only supposed to understand this insanity and agree to it—you want me to help."

"Yes. Because you see what's right. Because you love Hana. Because you care about me."

"I love you!" she cried, speaking that most loaded of phrases for the first time. "I've loved you since I met you." Tears welled in her eyes and streamed down her face unchecked. "And now I'm going to lose you. I'm going to lose you and Hana both."

He felt a momentary urge to comfort her, but he pushed it away. Resisted it just as he would resist whatever emotional manipulations Noah had waiting for him. He looked at her, felt sympathy for her, but felt his own strength grow in response.

"I could call Agent Wilson and tell him what you're planning," she threatened. "He'd stop you."

"But you won't do that. And, deep down, you want me to go get Hana."

She compressed her lips and clenched her fists in an agony of frustrated anger. "One of the most captivating aspects of your character is your devotion to your daughter. But now that devotion is going to get you killed."

"But you understand that I have to go?"

"I don't understand. But I know that you will."

# Chapter 19

Three days later Dan had still not been contacted. He didn't know what to do. He had spent every moment near a telephone, ignoring an invitation to meet with Agent Wilson again, ignoring Laura's constant and repeated arguments. That morning, sick of listening to Laura, he had walked out of her apartment while she was still asleep and taken the train to Bay Ridge. Now at his own place, he was sitting as he had been for days, next to a telephone—willing it to ring—while he read about mind control and psychological torture.

The phone rang and he lunged for it.

"Hello!"

"It's me, Dan. Why did you leave without saying anything to me?"

"You weren't awake, Laura."

"You could have written a note."

He sighed heavily. "When I went out I thought I was just going for a walk. Then, while I was walking, I decided that we needed a break from each other."

"Dan—"

"I don't want to fight with you anymore. You can't change my mind and I won't discuss it anymore."

She was silent for a moment, then said, "Okay. Okay. No more." Another silence. Then, in a small voice, "Will you come back? Or if you want me to, I could come there after my last patient this afternoon."

He sighed again. "I don't know what to do. Alex did call me at your place before, so maybe I should stay there. Maybe they're still worried about this phone being tapped."

"It's up to you, Dan. I'll be glad to come out there if that's what you want."

"No. Let me think about it. When are you through with your last patient today?"

"Four o'clock."

"I'll call you by then."

"Okay . . ." she said, and he knew that she wanted to say that she loved him, but after that one revelatory outburst she had not repeated the phrase.

"Talk to you later," he said, and hung up.

He went into Hana's room and sat on the bed. He had straightened her possessions, lining up her animals in regimented rows, but now everything was too neat and it felt cold and sterile to him. He wandered through the rest of the apartment. And it suddenly struck him that his pleas to Alex had had a truth at their core. He could not go on in life with this gaping hole in his heart. If he lost his child permanently he might as well be dead.

By noon he could no longer stand to be in the silent rooms and he regretted leaving Laura's telephone—the phone they'd used to contact him before. He called Laura's office and told her assistant that he was going straight to her apartment and would be there the rest of the day. Then he turned on his answering machine and went out, heading for the subway.

The air was heavy and hot. Waves of heat undulated over the pavement. He thought of the hundreds of walks he had taken down that same sidewalk with Hana skipping beside him. Running ahead, then running back to him. Filled with boundless energy. Asking if they could stop at Star Deli or run in to Mr. Chin's or go to Sally's for hummus and "peter bread." *Please, Alex,* he whispered to himself as though praying. *Please don't let anyone hurt her. Please take good care of her.*

He barely noticed a dirty white van that pulled up to the curb ahead of him. As he drew even with the van the doors flew open and three men leaped out and grabbed him.

"What—"

But he was already inside, sprawled on the floor with a boot heel against his back.

"Noah sent us," the booted man said.

Dan's heart thumped against his chest wall and his underarms ran with sweat. He didn't know what to do or say. This was not what he had expected.

"Looks clear," a voice said from the front. "We caused no blips on anyone's radar screens."

The boot lifted, then toed Dan in the kidney.

"You've been friendly with the Feebs," the voice from the front accused.

"I met with them one time. I had to. When you guys came for my daughter you made it look like a kidnapping to everyone. The FBI was called in as a matter of routine, and then they dragged in other branches."

Hands grabbed his shoulders and roughly pulled him up into a seat. He saw that there were four men altogether. The three men who had jumped out and the driver. He could not fully see the driver's face, but the man appeared to be similar to his comrades. All of them were white and clean shaven, with average haircuts and faces that held no hint of a threat. All were dressed in jeans and casual shirts. There was not one thing about them that would have caused him alarm, and he found that chilling.

"I was expecting a call," Dan said.

"How do we know he's not lying about the Feebs?" the driver demanded nervously.

The voice was familiar.

"How do we know, huh?" the driver demanded again, addressing his question to the front passenger and looking sideways as he spoke. From this better view of the face Dan realized that the driver was the man who had held the gun to his head at the house on Vanzant Street.

"What did Noah ask you to do on this assignment?" the front passenger said to the driver with a cool air of authority.

"Drive," the driver admitted sheepishly.

"Did he ask you to think or to help me make the decisions?" the cool man said.

"No."

The man turned his body and focused on Dan.

The leader, Dan thought. Clearly the leader of this little band.

"Are you ready, Behr? Do you embrace Noah and forsake all of the sleeping world?"

"Yes," Dan said, wishing his voice sounded steadier. "I do."

"Give me your wallet."

Dan handed over his wallet. The man examined the contents. He pulled out Dan's bank card.

"Where's the teller branch?" he asked.

"On Third. In the Seventies."

"Exact directions, please."

"Turn right just ahead. When you hit Third Avenue go left."

The driver stayed with the double-parked van. The other three men went in with him, the leader at his side, the other two walking behind. He was worried that the lunchtime crowd of customers would annoy the leader, but the man stayed calm. He smiled at the customer service representative who asked if she might show them how to use the express machine for their transaction.

"No, thank you," he told her nicely. "My brother is making a cash withdrawal."

This was not ominous, Dan assured himself as they inched forward in the snaking line. This did not mean that they were going to take his money and leave him dead in an alley. This was routine. Noah wanted cash up front. Hadn't that been true with Alex as well?

When they reached the window, Dan told the teller that he wanted all but a dollar from both his savings and checking accounts.

"These are premium accounts," the teller warned. "If you let the balance fall for more than a few days you won't get the good interest rates anymore."

"I know," Dan told her. "But I found a car I can't live without."

She left her station to check something, and the leader whispered, "Good job, but why leave the dollar?"

"I guessed it would be less of a hassle if they thought I wasn't closing the accounts."

The leader smiled. "Nice, Behr. Nice."

After several delays and two withdrawal forms to sign, Dan was given an envelope containing slightly more than twelve thousand dollars in cash. Valerie's money. She would be infuriated if she knew.

As soon as they stepped out of the bank the leader took the envelope. "You renounce this money, Daniel Behr? Do you gladly offer it up to the greater good of The Ark?"

"Yes. I renounce the money."

"There was supposed to be more," the booted man said from in back of him.

"I have more," Dan offered quickly. "It's in mutual funds, though. Not through the bank."

The leader nodded. "We'll let Noah worry about that."

"Okay, boys," he said once they were back in the idling van. "Let's head home."

"To The Ark?" Dan asked in surprise. "We're going to The Ark now?"

"That's right."

"Can I stop by my place first? Pick up a few things?"

"You've forsaken this world, Behr. There's nothing you need from here."

"Have I forsaken clean underwear and a toothbrush?" he asked, and immediately regretted the crack.

But the leader laughed and waved the envelope. "We'll buy you whatever you need as we go. The Ark provides."

They traveled at a fast pace, stopping when they needed fuel and once at a drugstore, where the booted man went in and came back out with a small bag. There were no snacks or drinks in the van, something Dan thought of as routine on any long motor trip, and his stomach kept reminding him that he hadn't had lunch before he was pulled off the street. On one of their gas station stops Dan suggested buying cold drinks and pretzels from a line of machines. All four men stared at him as though he had proposed the unthinkable.

"We don't eat between meals," the leader explained. "That weakens a man."

"How does that weaken?" Dan asked, thinking that it would be better for him to sound curious and ready to learn than to mutely accept. But he couldn't help feeling a measure of sincere curiosity.

"We're not your teachers, Behr."

With that there was a silence that lasted several hours.

They didn't talk to each other. They didn't listen to the radio. In fact, there was a gaping hole in the dash where a radio obviously used to be. He wondered what they thought about. He wondered if conversation was also a weakness.

Around seven that evening they pulled into a roadside diner for dinner. They were given a table adequate for five, and the men sat without hesitation, as though there were rules as to who sat by whom.

"You're here," the leader said to Dan, indicating the chair beside him.

Dan had the strangest feeling sitting there with them. He felt like he was in military school. They all sat very straight and conducted themselves with an almost formal discipline. After they had ordered their food, but before taking even a sip of the water that was their only beverage, they raised their right hands like jurors being sworn in and said softly, "In Truth."

Dan was torn between an urge to laugh at them and an urge to get up and run away. They were ridiculous. They were fascinating. They were frightening.

He had never been in the company of extremists or radicals before. No doubt these men were kindred spirits of the various stripes of terrorists who haunted the headlines. No doubt they were akin to the skinheads and the militia followers and the men who were so busy planting bombs in Europe. But he had the disquieting thought that they might also be related to the U.S. military and men who wore police uniforms and even Agent Wilson.

And he thought about how strange and absurd so many common rituals would seem if they were not familiar—military salutes and Scout pledges and the pledge to the flag and grace before meals and the gestures that accompanied so many religious faiths. Was the raised hand and the "In Truth" truly absurd or was it only unfamiliar?

When their plates were delivered Dan realized that each of the other men had ordered exactly the same thing. Only his plate was different. He wondered if he had committed a minor sin by selecting roast chicken over roast beef. Nothing was said, though. And he got no look of censure as he had when he'd ordered iced tea.

"This is surprisingly good," he said after he'd eaten a few bites. "Or maybe I'm just hungry."

They all looked at him and then back down at their plates.

"We eat only to survive," the heretofore silent man from the back of the van told him.

"We're not his teachers," the leader said as though scolding the man, and Dan heard an undertone of scorn in the word *teachers*. "We are warriors."

The hair rose on the back of Dan's neck.

They traveled through the night without stopping to rest, the driver switching off with the two men in the back so that each could have a turn at sleeping. And how they could sleep. Dan was amazed. No blankets or pillows. No complaints about cramped positions or neck aches. They seemed to fall asleep at will, sleep soundly, and wake up refreshed and instantly alert. Dan suspected that he was exhibiting another weakness with his shifting and turning and inability to sleep, but he could not emulate them.

At dawn they stopped for gas and took turns in the station's bathroom, carrying shaving kits in with them. Dan was given the drugstore bag when his turn came. He went inside the cramped room, opened his bag, and found a toothbrush, toothpaste, shaving supplies, deodorant, a small bar of soap, and a nail clipper. The booted man had tried to anticipate every grooming need.

He performed an awkward morning routine, trying not to touch too many surfaces in the grimy bathroom. While shaving he suddenly caught his own eye in the mirror and stopped. There he was, covered with shaving cream, traveling in the company of warriors from a secret society, heading cross-country to an armed hideaway. It was as though he had fallen into the frames of a child's action cartoon. But then he continued shaving and slipped with the razor. The red blood that blossomed in the white fluff was very real.

Colorado was breathtaking. He had never been in the state and he was awed by the great natural diversity he saw. The rolling windy plains that gradually rose to a land of buttes, then soared to a wall of mountains with peaks at fourteen thousand feet. He assumed that they were going to travel through Colorado on their way to California and the compound near Calder where Alex's ill-fated deprogramming had occurred, but when they pulled off the highway at a lookout point, the booted man suddenly whipped a black hood over Dan's head and pushed him to the floor of the van.

"Relax," the leader's voice ordered. "This is a security precaution. Don't let the hood bother you. Just close your eyes and breathe naturally."

Dan rolled onto his side. His pulse was racing and, though his breathing was not at all restricted, he had the panicky sensation of impending suffocation.

He told himself that his hands were free and that he was not being threatened in any way. He told himself that the cloth of the hood was not impeding the flow of air. He told himself that lying on the floor in blackness was no different from taking a nap. And eventually he was able to calm all his physical reactions. Eventually he did slip away into something like a nap. And he dreamed of Laura. He dreamed that she was boarding a ship for some unknown destination. They stood on the dock together and kissed, then she joined the crowd going aboard, turning back to wave and smile at him once before disappearing.

When he woke he remembered the dream vaguely and then let it go. His shoulder ached from bouncing against the hard floor of the vehicle. His legs were cramped from being bent. He was thirsty. He had lost all track of time and his imagination was running amok, conjuring surreal tableaux wherein he was traveling through time, surrounded by companions whose human faces had fallen away to reveal monsters.

"How much longer?" he asked aloud.

He heard the leader's voice say, "He's awake now. Yes. No problems. We're approaching the boundary now. About to switch." And he realized that the man was speaking into a cellular phone or a radio.

"We're there, Behr, but the hood has to stay on a little longer. Relax."

"I thought the compound was in California."

"That was a temporary location while we built here."

The van stopped. One of the men near him in the back got out. After a minute the van eased down a short incline, and it seemed to him that they had driven inside something. The van stopped again and the engine was cut. Hands pulled him up and out. Led him across a paved surface. Sounds echoed. They were definitely in an enclosed space. A garage?

"You can sit up the rest of the way," he was told as he was guided into another vehicle. Smaller. He hit his head and his elbow. But it didn't have the low-slung design of a sedan. One of those hybrid Jeep-like vehicles maybe. This was confirmed when their travel resumed and it was clear from the jolting and jarring that they were riding in something designed to handle rough terrain. They bumped and bounced for a while, then traversed a smooth stretch. Finally the vehicle stopped, and the black hood was abruptly jerked from his head.

He squeezed his eyes shut against the blinding rush of sunlight. The vehicle's doors were opened. He heard new male voices giving the "In Truth" greeting. Arms reached for him. He stumbled out, blinking and squinting.

Faces loomed before him. Some curious. Some dismissive. Some openly suspicious. None were familiar. None were female.

He wanted to ask for Hana, or Alex, but decided that it would be best to keep his mouth shut.

"This way," the leader said. "You have an audience with Noah."

Dan followed, with the other men from the van right behind him. He had a general impression of being in a small valley high in the mountains. The air was thin and fresh. There was a group of buildings situated against a vertical slope of mountainside. Two standard metal storage buildings. A big barn. A smaller barn. Several long houselike buildings with porches. Except for the prefab storage units, everything was constructed of weathered logs and beams, and the effect was somewhere between rustic mountain lodge and old-fashioned ranch. From somewhere nearby he heard the whine of power tools.

They crossed to one of the long buildings, went up the

steps to the porch and then inside. As he entered he noticed that there was a small metal plaque beside the door, a painted label in the style of the military. It said HEAD-QUARTERS. Inside he found himself in a wide central hall-way that ran straight through to an identical entrance on the opposite side of the building. White walls. Plain plank flooring. No staircase in sight, though there was clearly a second story. The hallway had three doors on the right and three doors on the left. Each of the doors had a label. He saw CLOSET and TOILET and OFFICES before being led into AUDIENCE ROOM.

He entered the audience room with his escort and stopped. The sight that greeted him was both startling and somehow completely expected. At the opposite end of the room the standard ceiling suddenly soared open to the sec-ond story, creating an abbreviated cathedral that rose right up into the roof's peak, where two large skylights had been set. At the second-story level was a white door. It hung there in the smooth whiteness of the wall and from it de-scended a white staircase. With the sun pouring in through the skylights the effect was not unlike glimpsing the door to heaven. At the foot of this staircase was a raised plat-form draped in purple bunting. Centered on the platform was a striking oversized chair with carved claw feet and arms that ended in carved lions' heads. And everything was bathed in celestial light. It was a brilliant feat of de-sign. A kid in muddy playclothes would have looked im-pressive stepping out of that door, descending those stairs, and assuming that chair.

Dan waited nervously for Noah to appear. When nothing happened he relaxed enough to take further note of the room. It was approximately twenty by thirty, with win-dowless white walls and plank flooring. The walls were hung with handloomed tapestries that seemed to depict stories, though he would have had to study them closer to know the themes. Besides the door through which they had just entered and the white door at the top of the stairs, there was also a door near the corner on each side wall. One was labeled WARRIORS. The other said SANCTUM.

At floor level there were two chairs flanking the throne.

Otherwise the room was empty. Just a big open space in which to feel intimidated and self-conscious.

He glanced to either side at his traveling companions. They were all tense.

The WARRIORS door opened and two men in light gray uniforms emerged. Both wore gunbelts. Without the slightest acknowledgment of the visitors, they strode directly to either end of the platform and stood at attention.

A loud gong sounded. The men beside Dan stiffened to attention, staring up at the white door.

"No-ah! No-ah! No-ah!" they chanted.

The gong sounded again and the door slid open.

# Chapter 20

Suddenly he was there. Noah. The man who had seduced Dan Behr's wife and stolen his child. Noah. Dressed in long gray robes with a purple mantle, standing very straight, head high, gazing upward. Noah. Right there. To hate in the flesh.

"No-ah! No-ah!"

Slowly, Noah's eyes lowered to his audience. Then he descended the stairs. At his pretentious chair he stopped and extended his right arm as though blessing them.

"In Truth!" the men shouted enthusiastically, raising their right arms in the standard greeting.

Noah sat in his chair and regarded them in silence. There was no doubt that the man had a presence. His dark brown hair fell to his shoulders in waves from a center part, very much like portraits of Jesus from Dan's childhood. His craggy, slightly pocked skin seemed to speak of hardships endured. His eyes were haunting. Riveting. Electrifying in their intensity.

"You did well by bringing this man to me," he said in a deep vibrato. "Were there any difficulties, Zelek?"

"No," the leader said.

Only now he had a name. Zelek.

"Is there something troubling you, Gareb?" Noah asked the driver.

"No . . . I . . . um . . . I just don't trust this guy. How do we—"

"You question my judgment!" Noah thundered in a display that brought all the great biblical screen epics to Dan's mind.

"No! No!" The driver fell to his knees and groveled. "Forgive me. I'm still learning the wisdom of silence."

"You're confined tonight, Gareb. The rest of you will have the reward of a night of comfort. Go now."

They disappeared quickly through the door marked WARRIORS.

Noah fixed the beam of his stare directly on Dan. "Your stubbornness has caused me inconvenience, Daniel."

Dan didn't know how to answer or whether he should answer, so he kept quiet.

One side of Noah's mouth curved into the faintest of smiles. "I see you already know the wisdom of silence."

Dan maintained his silence and the smile increased.

Abruptly Noah stood, moved to the end of the platform, and descended. Then, in long swift strides he went toward the door marked SANCTUM, calling after him, "Come, Daniel."

The sanctum was a simply appointed but comfortable office with a beautifully made desk, two leather chairs, and a leather couch. On the desk was an arrangement of fresh flowers. Had Alex arranged them? There was a window on one wall. Dan noticed that the window did not have a shade or blinds but rather solid shutters that folded back against the wall. There was a door marked TOILET. Dan automatically pictured the floor plan in his mind, noting the wasteful plumbing design.

"Sit, Daniel." Noah waved expansively at one of the chairs as he settled behind his desk.

Dan sat. Never in his life had he hated anyone as he hated this man. Never had he wanted to do real harm to another human being, but he thought that he could unflinchingly aim a gun at this man and pull the trigger.

"You want to kill me," Noah said, startling Dan. "I'm glad to see that. I can't respect a man who has no anger. No fight. That's one of the great disasters of this age—that men have been diminished!" He slammed his fist against his desktop. "Reduced to sheep who bleat understanding and forgiveness and tolerance when they should be standing up for what is right and condemning what is wrong!"

Noah leaned forward slightly, eyes burning into Dan's. "You believe I have wronged you. Therefore you are justified in your anger. You would be worthless as a man if your heart was accepting and embracing me now.

"Your task is to temper that anger with wisdom and to learn about our mission here so that you can truthfully examine yourself and discover whether there were indeed grievous wrongs done you or whether the crime . . . the dishonesty . . . is lodged deep within your own heart."

Noah extended his hands, palms up, across the desk.

"Can you do that, Daniel?" he asked with fierce sincerity. "Are you strong enough to question yourself . . . your belief systems . . . the entire fabric of your existence? *Do you have the strength?*"

Dan realized that he had been holding his breath, suspended, hanging in paralysis as the deadly silk of Noah's words encircled him.

"I have the strength," he said, adding to himself that he had the strength to hold on to his hate. He had the strength to hold on to a clear vision of right and wrong.

Noah smiled. "You are a fine man, Daniel. You were never meant to languish in obscurity." He erupted from his chair then, and was at the door before Dan could react.

"Joab! Joha!" he called as he opened the door. "Show Daniel his quarters and give him clothing. In thirty minutes bring him back to me."

"When will I see my daughter?" Dan asked, unable to restrain himself any longer.

"When the time is right," Noah said. There was a steely edge beneath his patient words.

A sharp steely edge, Dan reminded himself. He had to be very careful. Very, very careful.

Under the watchful eyes of the two J's Dan took a cold shower in a room where everything was white ceramic tile. No mirrors. No windows. Three toilets squatted against one wall with no enclosures for privacy. A long gang urinal. Three sinks. And there was the shower, a metal pole set into a drained depression in the center of the room. Three drizzle-style shower heads were arranged around the top of the pole so that three bodies could gather around the pole at the same time. It reminded Dan of the bathroom/dressing room at his childhood public swimming

pool, right down to the lack of hot water taps. To heighten
that impression one wall had a grouping of square cubby-
holes and hooks, each with a number. Towels hung on the
hooks. Grooming implements were stored in the cubbies.
He had been told that he was eleven, and he saw that his
drugstore bag from the van had been stuffed into cubby
number eleven.

He finished drying, then wrapped his scratchy little
towel around his waist and was led down the hall to a dor-
mitory room and assigned the top bunk of a bed. The room
was within the area marked WARRIORS, and he didn't know
whether that was a good or a bad sign. There was no one
else about in the living quarters. Apparently The Ark toler-
ated no shirkers who lounged on their beds or dallied in
the bathrooms during the day.

At the foot of his neatly made bed, where he had left his
dirty clothes, he found clean underwear, a faded pair of
jeans in his size, and a coarse gray cotton pullover shirt
with a tie neck and elastic at the wrists. It was obviously
homemade, and when he got it on and tucked into his
jeans, he felt as if he needed a cape and a sword.

Dan was about to attempt conversation and ask which
man was Joab and which was Joha when the men's eyes
widened in horror.

"Get that towel off the bed!" they ordered in unison.

Dan snatched up the wet towel. One of the men took it
from him and marched out of the room.

"We, uh, didn't notice you had it on," the other man admitted. "Towels are not to leave the bathroom. They stay
on your hook except for when you're using them."

"Okay," Dan said. "Do they ever get washed?"

"The women put clean towels on the hooks every
Saturday."

"What do I do about clean clothes? I don't have anything with me but the one shirt and pants. Should I—"

"The Ark provides." Joab or Joha turned and pointed
to the end of the room. "You put your dirty stuff in the
hampers. One for underwear, one for shirts, one for
pants. You open those closet doors and there's shelves
with clean clothes all stacked according to sizes. Try to

wear everything at least a couple of days. Washing wastes water."

"Okay." Dan couldn't shake the feeling that he had stumbled into military summer camp.

"I'm sorry, but I didn't catch whether you were Joha or Joab," he admitted.

"Joab."

"Is that your last name?"

"We have no last names here."

"Then is Joab a name Noah gave you?"

"Joab is my warrior name. The name I was given when I earned my place."

"I see. And Zelek and Gareb?"

"Those are warrior names, too. The names of mighty men."

"What do you have to do to earn your place as a warrior?"

"That's for Noah to say."

Dan nodded, then surveyed the room, aware that he was making Joab edgy and that he needed to change the subject before the man remembered the wisdom of silence.

"What else should I know?" He glanced around him at the neat rows of bunks. "I guess we make our beds every morning."

"No. That's women's work. All you've got to remember is that you're eleven." He indicated the numbers on the metal bed frames. "See. Your bed is eleven." He bent and pulled a shallow metal locker from beneath the bed. An eleven was stenciled on its top. "This is yours, too."

"Do I keep my shoes in there?"

"No. Shoes go underneath the foot of the bottom bunk. Your locker is for any other stuff you might have, like something Noah gave you to read or maybe glasses or medicine or your extra ammo. 'Course, you're not a warrior, so you won't have a gun."

"Is one of these bunks yours?"

The guard jerked his head toward the front. "Three."

"Is this all for warriors?"

"That's right. Warriors only."

"Then why am I sleeping in here?"

"Noah wants us to keep a close watch on you."

Dan was led back to a very different Noah. The flowing locks had been smoothed back into a neat little tail at the nape of his neck. The robes had been shed for a charcoal-gray shirt and pants of a crisp uniform twill. The shirt had epaulets at the shoulders and was striking in that it was simple yet so obviously a fine piece of clothing. Around his neck Noah wore a gold medallion hanging from a dark purple ribbon. His footwear was black cowboy boots in some exotic leather.

"You saw the headquarters building," Noah said, taking long energetic strides that made Dan work to keep up.

They were crossing from the headquarters to the other long building. The two guards with the J names were in lockstep behind them. As they walked they passed Ark members—women hanging laundry, men pushing wheel-barrows filled with compost, women carrying baskets of freshly picked vegetables, and everyone looking happy. Everyone sang out the In Truth greeting with joy. It wasn't what Dan had imagined at all.

"That's the women's and children's quarters and the dining hall," Noah said. "It's very similar in design to the building you were in. Sadly, the overcrowding there is terrible. We need a new dining hall so that we can use the entire building for living space."

Dan wanted to shout "Stop!" and race inside to look for his child, but he kept in step with Noah and passed the building by.

"Behind the women's quarters are most of our generators and water-treatment equipment." He waved toward a cluster of tower-mounted propellers high up the side of the mountain. "We have a wind farm that creates such surpluses that we've never had to resort to our emergency gas-powered generator. Though we do actively conserve the electricity, of course, as everyone should. Eventually we hope to have enough solar panels installed to have hot water available also."

The compound reminded Dan of a small, rustic college campus. They walked along neat pathways surrounded by manicured rectangles of green. He saw additional Ark members, and all of them were smiling and eager and busy.

"Two of those metal buildings are equipment storage and one is for the helicopter."

"Helicopter?" Dan asked in amazement.

"A necessity, I assure you. In our remote location it's essential for emergencies and useful in many other ways as well. We often do airlifts, trucking materials or equipment up as far as the roads allow, then chaining them under the chopper and flying them the rest of the way."

He pointed. "The concrete block building over there is for goat milking and dairy processing. That small barn is for the sheep and goats."

They rounded a building and Dan was surprised to see a number of large military tents.

"The tents are temporary men's quarters. We're growing out of our facilities."

The whine and drone of power tools had become increasingly louder as they walked, but instead of reaching a building site Dan was led between two tents and toward a moderately large glass greenhouse, clearly constructed from a kit, but a very good quality kit. The glass was fogged with moisture, and Dan could make out nothing inside except a jumble of green growing things.

"Here we are," Noah said. "Our first stop."

He led Dan into the humid hot air. There was a woman working at a bench in the back, putting seedlings from a flat into individual pots.

"Jael," Noah called softly.

She turned.

"Abba! What an honor. And Dan!"

It was Alexandra, cheeks flushed with the heat and hair aflame in the sunlight streaming down through the glass roof. She was still in a shapeless dress, but this one was bright purple instead of the unbleached white she had worn before. The color was beautiful on her. She was beautiful. Achingly lovely. His heart constricted in his chest.

"I'm so happy!" she said, using her cotton apron to clean the soil from her hands.

She took several steps toward Dan, then glanced at Noah. Noah's nod was subtle.

"Dan," she said again, then hugged him lightly in a very sisterly fashion that did not allow anything but their arms and shoulders to touch. "Welcome."

"Would you show us your palace, Jael?" Noah asked in a manner that was both courtly and teasing.

Her eyes went to Noah, and she smiled shyly and made a little curtsy. The adoration in her gaze made Dan physically ill.

"It's probably not interesting to anyone except me," she said. "But over here is where I get all the tomatoes going, and those shelves are for other vegetable seedlings that will be transplanted out into the garden. The back is all exotic flowers. Have you seen our big outdoor garden yet, Dan?"

"He'll see everything in time," Noah assured her.

"It's the most magnificent garden!" She looked around, eyes aglow with a depth of contentment and joy that Dan would not have believed possible. "Not as wonderful as the greenhouse Noah built me . . . but then, nothing could be that wonderful."

She bent her head in supplication. Noah lifted his hand, and she clutched it eagerly and kissed the back of it. "Thank you for honoring me, Noah."

"In Truth," he said.

"In Truth," she responded, raising her eyes to him as though he were the most magnificent and precious sight she had ever beheld.

He spun on his heel and banged out the greenhouse door, heading toward the large barnlike structure. Dan followed and caught up, a sick devastation sinking through him. He had never seen her so happy. Without him she had been remade into a completely different person. A beaming, rapturous, untroubled person—her soul cleansed of every past hurt and horror. A person he didn't know. And though his rational mind had been prepared for this, though his intellect had accepted this possibility long ago, his heart had still held hope. But hope for what? he asked himself angrily. Hope that she would still be an emotional wreck? Hope that she wasn't really happy? Yes. Exactly. He had hoped the worst for her because then he might have had a chance to win her back. He had hoped the worst for her because then she might have seen him as her salvation again, just as she had in the beginning.

So who was the evil figure in her life? Was it Noah? Or was it him? Suddenly all the hatred that had boiled inside him for this man evaporated and he was left feeling a vast emptiness. He tried to resurrect it with thoughts of Hana. The man had stolen Hana! No. Alex had wanted Hana. Alex had missed her daughter. It wasn't right that Hana had been taken, but neither was it a sin to be laid on Noah's head.

Dan glanced back at the greenhouse. "I thought her Ark name was Atarah," he said.

"It was. Atarah—because her beauty was like a crown jewel. But when she triumphed over her kidnapping and returned to us I saw that she had much more than beauty to offer. She was given the name Jael. A proud, brave name. 'Most blessed among women is Jael.' Jael killed Sisera, Israel's mighty enemy. Do you know your Christian history?"

"I'm afraid not."

"It's an inspiring story. She lured him into her tent and drove a peg through his head while he slept."

Noah stopped and looked up at the large barnlike structure.

"What do you think of our assembly hall?" he asked.

It was one of the most clumsily designed and crudely constructed buildings Dan had ever seen. If it hadn't been so large he would have called it a shack.

"It's a disaster," Dan said, his anguish making him careless. "It looks like it was designed and built by a kindergarten shop class, and I doubt that the roof will withstand one winter snow load."

Noah's face darkened with anger, either from the harsh assessment or the directness with which Dan had spoken, and for a moment Dan thought that he might be in big trouble, but then the man recovered his composure. He signaled his stunned and threatening guards to relax.

"You are even more than I hoped you would be," Noah said in a voice that was just above a whisper.

His eyes burned into Dan and he moved closer, as though intending a kiss or the thrust of a short-bladed knife. He stood that way, toe to toe and eye to eye, for a long heart-stopping moment. Then, he gripped the back of Dan's neck with one hand, and with the other he pressed hard against Dan's chest.

"Don't you feel it, Daniel? You have always belonged here. I knew it from the moment Jael told me about you— about your passion for design and building, about your passion for life."

"If you wanted me so badly, why did your guy poison me and threaten me with a gun when I tried to get into the New York house?"

Noah frowned. "I was out of the country at the time, meeting with followers in Australia, and I'm afraid Gareb badly mismanaged that entire episode. He was punished and demoted afterward and has only recently earned back his full warrior status."

"None of this makes sense," Dan said. "Why didn't you just come to me and tell me what you needed? Why didn't you just explain the situation? Maybe we could have worked out a deal."

"Awakening is a personal journey that cannot be forced or forged through deals. You had to make the journey at your own speed."

"But . . . you coax others along with your speeches and your meditations and your retreats."

"We give the message to those who are seeking it. Would you have willingly attended any such thing? And if you had attended would you have listened?"

Dan struggled with his inner turmoil.

"Relax," Noah said. "Let the past fall away and look to the future. You have a fire in you. I need that fire. Give it to me . . . give it to Truth and to The Ark and you shall inherit the earth with me!"

Dan stood very still, meeting those laser eyes, his heart thumping beneath the hand. He didn't realize he was holding his breath until Noah abruptly withdrew his hands and turned away. When he did Dan sucked in air like a drowning man. His knees felt almost too shaky to walk on.

"You'll see your daughter now," Noah said, opening the door to the crude assembly hall. "Shhh," he cautioned, and motioned for Dan to follow.

The building was raw and cavernous inside with a skeleton of beams overhead where an ill-considered start had been made at framing a second floor. At the far end hanging canvas tarps screened off a corner. The faint music of children's voices came from behind those tarps.

Dan glanced sharply at Noah, then proceeded forward. Hana. He wanted to shout out her name.

Noah put a restraining hand on his arm. "Careful. You'll frighten them."

Dan hurried forward and saw through a gap between the tarps that a group of children were having school. They were all faced away from him, sitting cross-legged on a mat. At the front was a tall, gentle-looking man wielding a piece of chalk at a portable blackboard. He hesitated when he saw them, but Noah gestured for him to continue.

"Can anyone tell me who Pythagoras was?" the teacher asked.

Hands shot up.

Dan studied the backs of all the heads as a wrong and then a right answer was offered. When he spotted Hana his heart leaped into his throat. There was his child. Safe and near. Relief flooded through him, and he had to wipe his eyes against a sudden excess of moisture.

Noah pulled the tarp open wider then and gestured. The teacher paused.

"Hana," the teacher said quietly, smiling. "You have a surprise."

Hana got up and turned, her small face furrowed in puzzlement. She saw Noah and smiled shyly. Then she saw her father.

"Daddy!" she called in her high sweet voice.

She ran to him, and he swept her up into his arms, burying his face against the side of her neck, inhaling her, hugging her, choking back tears.

"I missed you so much, punkin."

"I missed you so much, too, Daddy, and I don't ever

want to be gone from you again. Why didn't you come sooner?"

"I'm sorry, punkin. I didn't know how to get here."

"Oh."

"The Ark is hard for some to find, Hana," Noah said.

She smiled brightly. "But you found it now, Daddy, so all you have to do is never ever go away. You're gonna like it here so much! There's animals! Baby goats and little fluffy chicks. And I get to help feed them."

"Why don't you go back to school now, Hana?" Noah said. "I'll finish taking Daniel on his tour. Then he can meet you when class is over and you can take him to see all the animals."

Excited, Hana wriggled out of Dan's arms. "Can he feed the animals, too?"

"The feeding is your responsibility," Noah told her gravely, "so you'll have to decide whether he can help or not."

"Okay, Abba," she said.

Still smiling, she slipped back between the tarps and returned to her place in the class.

Dan stared after her. "I'm . . ." he began, but could not finish.

"You're amazed to find how well she's doing," Noah said.

"Yes," Dan admitted. He drank in the sight of her narrow shoulders and neatly braided hair one more time, then drew in a ragged breath and turned to follow Noah out.

"How can he teach so mixed an age group?" Dan asked as soon as they were back outside.

"This is the same type of classroom that American pioneers sent their children to. You'll be surprised when you see some of our results. The older ones encourage the younger, and our teacher works to see that everyone is challenged."

"Those were pretty sophisticated math concepts on the blackboard."

"Yes." Noah smiled. "And we have eight-year-olds who think they are games. You see, we respect children's abilities and their desire to learn. We don't patronize them or coddle them, and we don't waste their time with foolish agendas that try to teach things like self-esteem and social skills. Self-esteem comes through achievement. Social skills are absorbed through interactions in the community. School is for learning skills that won't be learned any other way."

"They don't have much of a facility," Dan said. "Can't we build them something better?"

Noah beamed and slapped him on the back. "Daniel. Daniel. Daniel. The Truth is in you."

Uncertain what to make of that, Dan followed without further comment. The construction noises increased again, finally reaching a crescendo when they arrived at a framed-in structure swarming with workers. Most were using hand tools, but in the quiet of the mountains the noise was magnified. The moment Noah was spotted everything stopped.

"In Truth!" called the collective voices of the men, dropping tools and lumber to raise their right hands.

"In Truth," Noah replied, extending his arm. "Carry on. Don't let my presence slow you. Your work here is vital."

He turned his attention back to Dan.

"This will be the new men's quarters," he said, shouting as the noise level resumed. "It's crucial that we have the men indoors before winter."

Noah led him through the construction chaos, talking as they went. "Both the women's building and this one are just variations of the headquarters building, because those are the only blueprints we have. We tried to build the assembly hall—as you so astutely noticed—without any architectural plans."

Dan's gaze roamed over the half-framed skeleton. The inefficiencies and poor utilization he'd seen in the headquarters building were being magnified here in their efforts to modify the design for a different use.

"I don't suppose you have any praise for our work here either," Noah said with a touch of rueful amusement.

"Well . . ." Dan surveyed the activity around him. "I have to give your crew credit. For a bunch of guys who clearly don't know what they're doing—they seem to have a lot of enthusiasm."

Noah regarded him a moment, then suddenly turned

from him, thrust his arms into the air, and shouted, "Silence!"

All around them the whir and whine of tools stopped. Men froze in position, their faces bathed in expectant reverence.

"My people!" Noah said, leaping with agility onto a stack of plywood so that he would have a stage. "A man has been sent to us! A man with the skills and the knowledge to guide us in our building of a glorious homeland!"

He leaned over slightly and extended his hand to Dan. There was absolute silence. Dan could feel hundreds of eyes on him.

"Come, Daniel. Join me."

Pulse racing, Dan took the outstretched hand and climbed onto the plywood. Noah did not release his grip. He tightened it. Crushing Dan's hand in a powerful vise.

"Do you join us, Daniel? Will you build from your heart here? Will you give us your fire?"

Dan scanned the faces around him. The age range was somewhere from seventeen to fifty, and he knew that many must have known hard knocks in their lives, yet somehow they were all endowed with an openness that verged on innocence. As though The Ark had given them back their innocence.

Where was the evil here? He could not see it. The Ark made people happy. It gave them purpose and meaning. It restored them. It educated the children. Yes, the warriors carried guns, but why wouldn't they feel besieged by the attitudes people on the outside had about them and the lies that were being spread?

"Yes," Dan said. The word came out as barely a whisper, and he had to clear his throat and repeat it. "Yes," he said firmly and clearly.

Noah raised their joined hands and faced the men. A cheer went up. "Yes!" Noah thundered. "This is a time for building! A time for creating! And Daniel the builder has been sent to us! Daniel the builder gives himself to you and to the glory of this homeland we are raising in the safety and purity of these mountains! The Source provides! The Ark is blessed!"

The men stomped their feet and chanted, "No-ah! No-ah! No-ah!"

Noah continued to hold up their joined hands, rotating slowly to face every man in the crowd. Then, suddenly, in a deep ringing voice he called out, "Dan-iel! Dan-iel!" and there was a tiny instant of surprised silence and then the men took up his chant. "Dan-iel! Dan-iel! Dan-iel!"

# Chapter 21

It was so easy. So easy to lose himself in the work and the routines and let the days slide by, one after another, until he lost the urgency that had fueled his need to save Hana, until he lost his need for escape. What was there to escape from? Hana was happy. And every morning when he woke he was filled with a sense of purpose, an eagerness to meet the challenges of that day's work.

What was there to complain about? The air was fresh and there was food to eat. His daughter had quality child care and schooling. He had clean clothes and clean sheets and none of the minor annoyances of life on the outside—traffic jams and subway snarls and grocery store lines and a checkbook to balance.

He asked for supplies and they were produced. He asked for books and they were acquired. One evening he had become so immersed in a design problem that he had not heard the bells and had broken the sacred rule of appearing promptly for dinner. But instead of censuring him, Noah had had a meal sent to him. Noah had even excused him from assembly so the work could go forward at a quicker pace.

Dan felt more valued and more challenged than he had ever felt in his outside employment. He felt a passion for this work. A glowing sense of accomplishment. And he felt needed. He felt the appreciation and admiration of everyone in the compound. He felt . . . good. And he saw absolutely no sign that Noah was engaged in any great evil. Yes, the man was clearly amassing power and probably wealth, but if that was a crime then all the executives in the world would have to be punished. Yes, Noah used some wrongful methods to achieve his ends—the taking of Hana being an example—but in the court of wisdom and common sense, had any real crimes occurred? Despite the overbearing warriors with their sidearms, Dan saw no hint of crimes committed or planned, and all the suspicions he had had before, all his dark speculation about accidental deaths and suspicious fires, seemed now to be ridiculous. And the federal authorities' paranoia about The Ark—what was that based on? Inflated rumors and wild stories from disgruntled former Ark members. He was certain now that the "information gathering"—however it was being accomplished—would yield only minor infractions of the law.

And although he did not agree with many of Noah's teachings, he found it hard to condemn them. Were they any worse than the teachings of many organized religions? Yes, there was a certain amount of subjugation and manipulation, but wasn't that inherent, to one degree or another, in all religions? For that matter, wasn't that inherent in every type of organization? How could anyone sit in judgment of The Ark and still be an advocate of freedom of religion or freedom of choice? And how could it be said that the all-encompassing nature of commitment to The Ark was worse than the commitments that most religions required of their devout followers? How about the lifetime one-hundred-percent body-and-soul commitments workers often made to all-encompassing corporations?

The big question was whether The Ark harmed people, and from what he had seen there was no harm being done. Quite the contrary. People seemed to be flourishing. How many of the healthy, active people around him would be homeless or jobless or facing some dark emotional abyss if they had not joined The Ark? Painful though it was to admit, his own wife had found contentment and peace within The Ark. The Ark had made her whole. The Ark had succeeded where he had failed. So, although he still thought the group's methods of recruitment were callous or just plain wrong, although he did not fully condone the tyrannical control Noah had over people's lives, although he was uncomfortable with the strict definitions of gender roles—The Ark seemed to him an almost positive and certainly benign group, not unlike other idealistic communes that had mushroomed in various periods of history.

And as to his own involvement, when he considered it at all, he had come to think of himself and Hana as on a mountain vacation. Visitors at a summer camp. A really wonderful creative summer camp where there were no calendars to chart the days. No newspapers to bring intrusions from the outside. It was very much like the sleep-away Scout camp he'd attended when he was young. There he had had the same feeling of complete and utter removal from anything that happened outside the camp's borders. Except for occasional homesickness, which diminished daily, there had been no thoughts of the greater world. Every moment from dawn to evening had been filled with routines and activities and rules and campfire singing and a grand sense of camaraderie, and at night he had been too exhausted to do anything but sleep. His life at camp had become the norm, the reality. So much so that the bus ride back and the sight of all those waving smiling families had been a shock. Like being jolted out of a dream. This, too, was a dream. And how could it hurt to dream for a while?

His first priority was to revise the plans for the men's quarters and get that building up. For an office, he was given a corner of the warriors' lounge, a special privileges area for the warriors that was across the hall from their sleeping quarters. There he put together a makeshift drawing board and desk, and applied himself to revising the blueprints for the men's quarters. He worked on the plans daily from early morning till lunch. After lunch he held carpentry classes for the building crew. The men knew nothing beyond the basics, which surprised him until he became acquainted with them and learned that they were almost all city people, raised in rentals or in homes where there had been no opportunity to help Dad with projects.

All the men were serious about learning, but three of them emerged as stars: the dour but hardworking Nathan, twenty-seven years old and powerfully built, a former lifeguard who had lost his wife and baby to the crossfire of a territorial drug lords' dispute; the shy and eager-to-please Caleb, a gawky nineteen-year-old who had grown up in foster homes; and the quietly steady Jacob, forty-four, a former supervisor with twenty years on the job whose company had been taken over and sucked dry by speculators. Nathan, Caleb, and Jacob. He made them his job foremen, each with a specific crew of workers to be responsible for. And then there was Mark, a former electrician's assistant in his twenties, short and with the appearance of a Mafia enforcer but who had joined because he thought the world was too uncivilized and brutal a place. Mark was his foreman in charge of both electrical and plumbing. As the time approached for the resumption of building on the men's quarters, Dan felt their eagerness and enthusiasm, and he took pride in the well-honed force he had trained.

In spite of his heavy schedule he carved out a piece of every afternoon for Hana. They spent most of their time together with the animals. Mary, a stout fortyish woman with a sweet voice who had been a lingerie clerk and an alcoholic in her previous life, coordinated the nurturing of dairy goats and laying hens and finely fleeced sheep. When they didn't go to help Mary with the animals they went to the huge garden that was presided over by Peter, a wiry energetic man in his thirties who talked about the plants as though they had personalities and who always used the pronoun *we*: "We like to hoe carefully here because the corn has shallow roots and doesn't like to be poked." He seemed the type of quirky and dedicated horticulturist who ends up with a gardening show on public television, but he was actually an ex-convict who had served time for forgery.

After his afternoon visit with Hana, Dan would return to the plans, take a break for dinner, and then work through till bedtime. The warriors were unhappy with his presence in their private lounge. They never gave voice to their

complaints, but each time he came into the room all who
were present on the array of couches and chairs got up and
left. He was not one of them and they made that clear,
falling silent together and casting each other glances. The
membership of The Ark saw the rest of the world as
outsiders—the unawakened—and saw themselves as the
chosen. But inside The Ark, the warriors' circle consisted
of the most elevated of the chosen.

He caught pieces of their conversations sometimes,
when they passed by in the hall, or when he was in the hall
and moving too silently for them to be alerted. What he
heard reminded him of the athletic teams and fraternities
he'd had contact with. There was a sternly maintained
chain of command, but it was underscored by camaraderie
and boyish competitions like towel fights or impromptu
wrestling matches. They operated with a different set of
rules and standards than the rest of the membership was
held to, and they all had an unconcealed sense of superiority that went beyond their function as the compound's
protective and policing organization.

He came to understand them as volatile men. The sort of
men who were looking for chances to use their strength
rather than their wits, men who preferred violence to other
solutions. The sort of men who found excuses not to cooperate with cease-fires and bombing moratoriums. The
sort of men he had always distrusted and avoided. And he
thought that Noah was doing the world a favor by harness-
ing their hostilities and anger and barbarism into a useful
service.

His continuing occupation of their lounge created tension to the point that Noah finally took the unprecedented
step of assigning Dan his own room, a modestly sized
space that was to function as a combination office and bedroom, thereby offering Dan the freedom to work late into
the night if he chose. It was still within the warriors' quarters but on the other side of the bathroom, and so it was
somewhat separated from their living and sleeping space.
Dan's private room was an unheard-of luxury, and it
stirred deep warrior jealousies even though they were
happy to move him out of their lounge.

Their jealousy did not bother Dan because he had already learned to cope with their hatred, a collective emotion that sprung from Noah's instant acceptance of him and Noah's granting him such unearned stature in the compound's hierarchy. He had the feeling that the warriors were tolerating his presence in their midst in the same way a circus tiger tolerates the presence of another animal in the act—always waiting for the day when the trainer will step out and leave them untended together. It was a strange situation, unsettling, yet with a certain fascination for him. To be safe among the tigers was exhilarating. And he found himself increasingly less wary and more curious. Their fierce loyalty to Noah and their almost childlike acceptance of Noah's authority were mystifying. What did Noah offer these men that bound them so tightly to him?

All volatile men, yet with extreme differences in their personalities. Zelek, cool and socially polished; Gareb, ill-tempered and ill-advised; Joha and Joab, automatons; Ira, a blockhead; Ammiel, a cunning weasel; and others whose varying character traits were becoming familiar to him even though he had not learned all their antiquated biblical names. How had Noah attracted such disparate men and shaped them into a cohesive force? What kept them satisfied?

But Dan did not dwell on these questions, because the days flew by in a flurry of work while he mapped out revised plans for the men's quarters and got his newly trained crew to work on the building. And each evening after dinner, walking through the fully framed and plumbed and wired structure, inspecting the progress in the lavendered mountain twilight and feeling the substance of it, the reality of this hulking mass that he was breathing life into, he was filled with a great surging contentment, so heady and sweet it was almost sexual.

This was a fantasy come true. He was everything—architect, contractor, head carpenter ... everything. And what was the cost? He had to toss off "In Truth" greetings and nod at references to The Source. He had to put up with a constant lurking warrior "shadow"—a bodyguard Noah had insisted that he have, though he could not see where the threat might come from and suspected that the warriors were assigned as much to spy on him as to guard him. And he had to sit through the occasional assembly in which Noah raised the rafters with his impassioned vision of the new world they would all create together. He had to get final approval of everything from Noah, which sometimes was annoying because Noah was in and out, buzzing off in the helicopter to visit the other compounds. But those were all small prices to pay for a dream. Because that was exactly what he was receiving in exchange for his cooperation. Which made him wonder about the warriors. They had gone into harness as their price. But what dream had so captivated them? What was it they wanted so badly?

Dan straightened and rose from his drawing board, stretching out his back, rotating the stiff muscles of his neck and shoulders. It was almost time to meet Hana, and he wanted to go by the building site first. The crew had been especially driven to complete the men's quarters because it was to be their home and they were tired of living in tents. With Noah's permission they had worked extra hours and raised the building in an unbelievably short time. Nathan, Caleb, Jacob, and Mark had learned to manage the crews so efficiently that Dan was able to turn his attention to the next project.

The next project. To describe it as such did not convey what it meant to him. This was big. Challenging. The most daring design he had ever undertaken, and all his from the first joining of pencil to virgin paper. And it was not destined just for paper. This vision would be realized in concrete and wood and stone.

Noah had originally asked for a simple dining facility, but Dan had dreamed a glorious new assembly hall that was connected to dining room and kitchens. It would be a huge, versatile building. A building of exquisite proportions and infinite uses. A building that would glorify The Ark and Noah. A building that Dan could pour his soul into. And Noah had said yes.

For weeks Dan had hunched over his drawing board

each day, and at night he'd buried himself in books on food service kitchen layouts and electrical engineering for large multiuse buildings and plumbing specifications for restaurants. He consulted at length with Ruth, the brusque but efficient ruler of The Ark's kitchen, a thirtyish Culinary Arts graduate who had been gang-raped one night after working her shift in a swanky L.A. restaurant and who lived at The Ark under the protection of a white dress—making her off-limits to all men. Through Ruth he learned the workings of a commercial kitchen.

Dan wished that he had access to outside experts, but Noah dismissed all his concerns that he might not be capable of putting together the mechanical end of the project. "I have absolute faith in your resourcefulness," Noah said over and over. The other thing that Noah would not consider was the purchase of a computer. Dan made several arguments in favor of one, citing the helpful programs available and the cost-effectiveness of computer information, but Noah was adamant. No computer. Books were fine, but he would not allow the purchase of a computer. "Did the Egyptians need computers to build the Pyramids?" he demanded. "Did the people of Chartres have computers when they built their magnificent cathedral?" Dan was disappointed but he was not surprised, given the back-to-the-earth philosophies that Noah espoused. And he felt a sort of grudging admiration for Noah's adherence to principles.

And in the end Noah's faith had not been misplaced. Somehow Dan had managed to design everything, systems and all. Now they were ready to break ground for the new building. The initial materials had been ordered and delivered, and everything was set to go. All that was left to do on the men's quarters was the interior finish job, and he could leave one crew of men to complete that while everyone else went to work on the new building. He could barely contain his elation. This was it. His own masterwork. Fully formed on paper and soon to rise under his guidance.

He left his room and started down the hall toward the warriors' lounge. As he approached the lounge, he heard

Zelek's voice saying something about a mission in Los Angeles. Silence fell when the men spotted him, and Zelek rose, apparently Dan's assigned shadow for the afternoon. Since it was Zelek, one of the few warriors he had ever managed to have a conversation with, Dan waited for him to catch up rather than heading out and having the man follow.

"So," Dan said casually, "I've been to Los Angeles, too, though I didn't get to see any of the missions or other historic buildings. Just Disneyland."

Zelek shot him an odd look.

"What was it like?" Dan asked.

"What?"

"The mission you were talking about. It wasn't Capistrano, was it?" Dan searched his memory. "Or is that even in L.A.?"

"If you've seen one mission you've seen them all," Zelek said.

Dan laughed. "That's right. Buildings don't impress you, do they?"

"I guess there's got to be a certain amount of them in the world, but the earth is being destroyed with too much building—and with filling the wetlands to have more room for suburban sprawl and with clear-cutting the forests so we have wood to use and with polluting the water with the by-products of manufacturing all the artificial crap that goes into our buildings."

"Well, I do think that there's a lot of environmental abuse and that we need to retool our policies with an eye to the future, so I'd have to say that I agree with you."

"There's no agreeing or disagreeing. There's only The Truth."

Dan nodded as he always did when any jargon was spoken. Then he changed the subject with, "I heard the chopper early this morning. Was that Noah returning?"

"No. He's not due till tomorrow. That was a supply shipment."

"Any building materials?"

"I don't know. You'll have to ask Abel."

*Ask Abel.* That was the standard response. Poor harried

Abel was in charge of procurement for the compound. He ordered whatever was needed, from soap to steel beams, kept track of supplies on hand, and took care of the compound's money transactions and records.

Dan thought about how beautiful the day was with the sun warm and the air fragrant from the rich scents of growing things. He thought about how little he'd seen of the mountains. Almost nothing beyond the defined boundaries of the compound.

"I think I'll take Hana on a long walk today," he said. "I'd like to see something other than animals and rows of vegetables."

"That's not advisable," Zelek said shortly. "There are security devices around the perimeter."

"But you'll be along. Can't you just guide us around them?"

"The layout is known only to Noah and Ammiel."

Dan walked the remainder of the way in silence, considering this news and aware from Zelek's tone that he should not ask any further questions on the subject. But the questions hung in his mind. What kind of security devices? And what exactly had Zelek meant by "That's not advisable"?

Dan's good mood had flattened, and when they reached the building he conducted his inspection without enthusiasm. He set down his clipboard of notes and papers and went through the structure as usual, with his hands free so that he could touch and test, but his heart was not in it. Security devices. Some kind of alarm system? He had always assumed that—if worse came to worst—he could simply take his daughter and slip away. It was a shock to realize that he could not just leave. And Zelek's warning made him suspect something more ominous than a routine security system. Booby traps? More poison like what he'd encountered on the fence at the Manhattan house? In his first days at the compound Noah had assured him that all the nastiness at the Manhattan house had been Gareb's doing. Noah had regretfully explained that Gareb had been overzealous about his protection assignment. But now, well acquainted with Gareb, it struck Dan that the man was not capable of thinking up the poison idea, much less acquiring the exotic chemical.

He retrieved his clipboard and went to meet Hana.

"I'm tired, punkin," he told her. "Let's just walk to the stream today and watch the water."

Zelek kept them in sight but did not intrude. Even so, Dan found himself irritated by the warrior's presence. How long did he have to be at the compound before he could move about on his own?

"How about a giggle fest?" he teased, tickling Hana's neck with a long blade of grass as they settled on the grass beside the stream.

She did not giggle or join in the tickling game. "I've got bug bites," she said, sounding very subdued. "I don't want to play tickle."

"Oh. Okay. What did you do in school today?"

"I took a test, and the teacher says I'm almost ready to graduate."

"What kind of a test?"

"Reading words and math."

"Do you mean graduate to another level?"

"Graduate to the girls' school."

"What's that?"

"That's when you get to be with all girls and you don't have to do reading or math anymore. You get to learn special things like canning and sewing and cooking. The teacher said we'll get to make doll clothes."

"That can't be right, Hana. The teacher must have meant that you'll get to have extra classes—in addition to your regular math and reading."

"No, Daddy—" She clapped her hand over her mouth.

"What's wrong?"

She lowered her eyes and mumbled, "I'm not supposed to call you Daddy anymore."

"Why?"

"It's not fair because some of the kids don't have daddies. Besides, Noah is our father."

Dan's blood turned cold. "Who told you this?" he demanded, grabbing hold of her arms more tightly than he meant to.

Her mouth trembled but she did not pull back or cry or even complain.

He let go immediately and rubbed her arms. "Who told you not to call me Daddy?" he asked her gently.

She hugged herself as though afraid of him and said in a small voice, "Mommy told me. She said Noah is my Abba and I don't need any other daddy."

Dan turned away to conceal his anger from the child. Damn Alex—Jael. He could see what she was trying to do. She wanted him out of the picture. She wanted her cozy little family to consist of just herself and Hana and Noah.

"Do you think I'm bad?" Hana asked fearfully.

"No, sweetie." She had never asked him any such thing before. Was her mother responsible for that, too? "Don't worry," he assured her. "I'll talk to the teacher and I'll talk to your mother. It will all be fine."

He held her hand on the way to the women's quarters, where he said good-bye to her at the door. Then he spun around, heading toward the greenhouse, intending to have it out with Alex. To demand that she account for herself. And to ask why Hana was behaving oddly.

"Where are you going?" Zelek called, clearly puzzled by the change in routine.

Dan stopped and waited for the man to catch up.

"I have to talk to Jael."

Zelek frowned. "Do you have permission?"

"I need permission to talk to her?" Dan asked incredulously.

"From Noah," Zelek confirmed.

Dan swung toward the greenhouse, frustrated and angry. He clenched his fists. Both his hands were empty. "Damn! Where's my clipboard?"

"You must have left it by the stream," Zelek said, his gaze cool and measuring.

Dan stalked to the stream with Zelek close behind. The clipboard was on a rock. He grabbed it and headed for the assembly hall site, too agitated to go back to his room and work. At the site, he sat down and pretended to take notes so that Zelek would fade into the background again and leave him alone. He flipped through the pages beneath the clip on his board. The third leaf down wasn't a page at all. It was a paper napkin. Someone had used a pencil to print a message on it.

How much longer are you going to let them fool you?

# Chapter 22

The note stunned him. Who wrote it, and why? It had to be a resident of the compound. No one could or would sneak in and out of the place to leave him a note. And since his arrival the only outside visitors had been two men in thousand-dollar suits who came in and out by helicopter a full week ago. It could not have been one of them, because he'd used the clipboard every day since.

The note had to have been written by someone who lived in the compound. Possibly someone he knew. Had the federal authorities somehow managed to get a spy into the place despite Noah's careful background checks? Was that what the agent had meant by "an information-gathering operation"? Or was there an unhappy Ark member trying to stir up a rebellion?

Or . . . was it perhaps a test? Something engineered by the warriors or by Noah himself to see whether Dan could be trusted? If that was the case, then he should turn the note in. But if he turned the note in and it wasn't a test . . . if it was genuine . . .

All through dinner that evening Dan found himself studying the faces of the men at his table, but no one made eye contact. Who was it? Was the note writer watching him now? Was he afraid of what Dan might do? Or was he waiting to crucify Dan for not taking action?

Beth, who always served his table, leaned close to spoon potatoes onto his plate, and he studied her face, searching for a sign. She and the other servers were the only women in the room. The current dining area was far too small for the whole group to eat at once, so they had meals in shifts, men eating first and then the women and children. He rarely came into contact with any of the women. A woman would have a difficult time communicating with him except by secret notes. But how could it be a woman? The federal authorities wouldn't send a woman into a possibly dangerous situation, would they? And he could not imagine a woman as the leader of a revolt. And if it was a trap it would be warriors involved, not a woman.

He picked at his food without appetite. *How much longer are you going to let them fool you?* Was he being fooled? Maybe not fooled, but he had certainly been blind to what was happening with Hana. She was being taken from him. He saw that now. He thought about how long it had been since he'd had dinner with her or read her a story or tucked her into bed at night. He had been so absorbed in his work and so infatuated with his elevated position that he hadn't considered what a different experience Hana was having from his own. This wasn't a summer camp for her. This was a total indoctrination by her mother. He was glad now that he hadn't had the opportunity to argue with Alex over the "daddy" issue, because it would only have put her on her guard.

How was he going to get Hana out of The Ark? He had grown comfortable enough with Noah that he thought he could eventually announce that he was leaving and that would be that. But Alex was not going to let Hana go. She would fight, and she would enlist Noah's help.

He would have to get to Noah first, before Alex suspected that he was planning on leaving. Noah might be an egomaniac, but he was also a pragmatist. He could be dealt with. Dan decided that he should be direct. Tell Noah that the courts had given Dan full custody of his daughter and, though he didn't want to make trouble for The Ark, he would if it became necessary. Then he would offer a deal. He would promise to complete the assembly hall if Noah promised him and Hana safe passage out as soon as the hall was up.

With that plan in his mind he could neither work nor rest that night. He lay on the narrow bed in his dark, cluttered bedroom, berating himself for his stupidity. He should have known what Alex was capable of. He had the scar where she had stabbed him. Finally he slept, but he was tormented by a long involved nightmare. Hana fell through a crack in the earth and he went in after her to bring her back from the underworld. Noah and Alex-Jael were there, sitting on thrones beside a wide black river that danced with tongues of flame. Holding his daughter's hand, he ran and ran through the strange and threatening crystalline darkness, pursued by demons, always in sight of the opening to the upperworld but never quite able to reach it. And beyond that opening, bathed in white light, was Laura Ferren's face. "Don't look back!" she called, but he had already turned.

Noah returned the next morning, and Dan put in a request for an audience. He was told that Noah was extremely busy and that he would be summoned whenever Noah could fit him in.

Nervous, he tried to conduct himself normally. He went to Abel's office in the headquarters building to ask about the steel order. Abel, a prematurely balding little man of indeterminate age, was in the middle of an argument with Ruth about food supplies. It occurred to Dan that it was the first time he'd heard a woman argue with a man since he'd been there.

"Here!" Abel said, fishing a file from the cabinet and slamming it down in front of Dan. "Look up whatever you need to know."

Dan flipped through the receipt and order forms. They went back just about two years. That was apparently when Noah had started building in the Colorado mountains. But the amount of concrete and steel that had been purchased did not make sense. The new assembly hall would have a steel frame, but all of the existing buildings were wooden or concrete block structures. What had all the steel been used for? And though there were some basements, that did not account for the enormous amount of concrete purchased.

"Where did all this steel and concrete go, Abel?" he asked.

"How should I know?" Abel said impatiently. "Nobody tells me what things are for."

Gareb, who was Dan's shadow for the day, came in then

to say that Noah had sent for him. Dan hurried to the audience room, where Noah was holding an official session. A line of Ark members waited outside the headquarters building for the chance to present requests or complaints, reminding Dan of the petitioners who used to go before the kings in medieval times.

"Daniel!" Noah boomed when Dan was escorted into the room. Noah was seated in his ostentatious chair and was wearing his full regalia of robes and purple mantle. "How is my builder? I hear you were troubled by something yesterday."

The question caused a warning light in Dan's mind. He looked up at the enthroned and berobed man. He glanced around the room at the warriors who were present. And he knew that it would turn out very badly if he tried to present his deal for leaving. He needed to see Noah alone and informally. Yet he also knew that Zelek had reported his being upset and he had to say something or be seen as holding back.

"It's nothing serious," he said. "I just wondered why it is that I'm not allowed to speak to Jael without your permission. Is it something I've done?"

Noah smiled. "Daniel. Daniel. Always assuming the burden, aren't you?" Regally, he adjusted the sleeves of his robe. "We have a lot of rules here. They may not always seem fair or just to a man like you, but what you have to remember is that they weren't made with you in mind. They were created to keep life at The Ark smoother and more orderly for everyone.

"The rules against male-female socializing were designed to teach work-related discipline. You have to remember that many of our people come from troubled situations and have not developed the sort of work ethic you yourself possess. They have to learn. And if we are to have the compound ready for a hard winter everyone must spend their time working rather than socializing."

"I see," said Dan, keeping his tone light. "So does that mean I can speak to Jael in the evening after work hours?"

Noah smiled apologetically. "Since Jael is my wife, that involves another set of rules. No one is allowed to speak to my wife without permission. That may sound extreme, but

I assure you it's necessary for her protection. Otherwise people would be constantly trying to get advice from her and asking her to pass along requests to me, and she would never have a moment's peace."

Dan nodded.

"What was it you wanted to speak to her about?" Noah asked, a little too casually.

"About Hana." Dan searched his memory desperately for a safe subject. His pulse was elevated. His armpits were damp. All his confidence in his position with Noah had somehow evaporated, and he felt threatened again. "I'm worried about Hana's having so many bug bites."

Noah shook his head and grinned in amused tolerance. "Daniel. A man of your talents has to learn to leave such things to the women. Your time is valuable."

Dan pretended to consider this. "It's a habit, I suppose. From when I had all the responsibility."

"But those days are over, Daniel. You're part of the whole here. And there are others who will gladly shoulder those responsibilities so you can concentrate on what's important."

"I'll try to remember that."

"Good! Good! Now, why is it you seem so tense today?"

"I . . . I guess I'm nervous about the assembly hall. We start construction in three days and I'm worried that I've forgotten some detail or made a mistake."

Noah leaned forward slightly and studied Dan intently. Dan's heart thumped in his ears.

"I'm very pleased at the progress on the men's quarters, Daniel. Your dedication and your passion for your work move me greatly. Tonight at assembly, after my communion with the people, I'm going to call you to my side so I can honor you for all the work you've done. And I think it's about time for you to have a reward."

Dan tried to appear normal and busy all day, but his thoughts were in turmoil. He saw now that he had been a fool. That Laura had been justified in her fears. Noah had seduced him and he had not been strong enough to resist. The glow was gone. He was no longer under Noah's spell, and he saw everything clearly.

He kept to his routines and spent his usual amount of time with Hana. Only now when he was with her he was sickened to realize how many changes had escaped his notice. Her bright smiles were vacant. She no longer skipped ahead. The mischievous gleam never entered her eyes. Little by little her spirit was being crushed. He dared not ask how. For all he knew she had been trained to report every word he said.

When he told her good-bye she sighed sadly, and his chest ached. He had failed her. He had to get her out and away from Alex-Jael as soon as possible. But how? How? Noah would never agree to his leaving before the assembly hall was built. It dawned on him that he could send Hana out alone if he had to. Laura would take care of her. So he would make a deal with Noah—he would build The Ark's assembly hall only if Hana was sent out to live with Laura. If Hana was safely out, he would stay as long as necessary. He would do whatever Noah asked. That would be his deal.

He made it through dinner, then went to his room to wait for assembly call. Sitting at his drawing board, he stared at nothing, his thoughts circling around Hana and how he would present the deal to Noah. He must have seen it for several seconds before the meaning of it registered. The corner of a napkin was visible at the edge of the papers on his clipboard.

He lunged for the board.

Have they told you about the Cleansing yet? Be careful.

Again it was one of the rectangular white paper napkins that were on every table in the dining room. The printing was in pencil again, and it was crude, or maybe just rushed. The point of the pencil had torn the thin paper in places.

He shredded the napkin, then wadded it into his fist and carried it to the bathroom to flush down the toilet as he'd done with the first one. When had it been slipped onto his board? He'd been so preoccupied with his thoughts that it might have been there all day. The Cleansing. He had never heard that term. Was it like baptism? Even as he posed the question he knew that it had to be something more ominous. He wished that he could find the person writing the notes, because he wanted to shout "Stop!" He didn't want to know any more. He just wanted to get his daughter out.

Standing beside Noah on the assembly stage before the entire population of the compound filled Dan with self-disgust, but he managed to get through it. He had no idea what reward Noah planned for him, and he was relieved that no presentation was made at the assembly. Apparently the reward would be given to him at a later time.

With the robotic Joha as his escort, he walked back to the headquarters building. He stepped into his room and lit a candle because electricity was allowed only while he was reading or working and he intended to do neither. When he turned, he was startled by the sight of a naked woman lying across his bed, asleep.

He stood gaping.

She bolted upright as though frightened. "I'm sorry," she said in a small, timid voice. "I didn't mean to fall asleep. I left it dark so I could surprise you and then I just closed my eyes for a minute . . ."

He didn't recognize her, but then, he only knew a few of the compound's females.

"What are you doing here?" he asked.

"I'm here to reward you."

Her long loose hair fell across her face and hid her expression as she leaned back on her elbows and arced her back provocatively. Her body was firm and golden in the single candle's glow. Her breasts were high and pointed. The curves of her stomach and hips cried out to be touched.

As if reading his mind, she lay flat and ran her hands over her body. She parted her legs slightly and slid a hand down to caress herself, softly thrusting her pelvis in response to her own touch.

Dan was transfixed. And he was instantly hard. *Hard cock, soft brain,* he reminded himself. But it was one of the most erotic displays he had ever personally witnessed, and somehow the fact that this woman was a stranger to him made it even more so.

"I'm yours, Daniel. All night long. Whatever you want to do."

"This is crazy," he said, more to himself than to her.

She stood on the bed, displaying her body for him, pirouetting and touching herself.

He doubted that he would have made the decision to go forward, but he didn't need to. She stepped off the bed and came to him.

"It's such an honor to be your reward," she said, sinking to her knees in front of him, her hands busy at his fly. "You're a great hero, Daniel." Her fingers closed around his erection. "And I will always treasure this day."

"Wait a minute. Wait a minute!" he said, gently pushing her hands away. Tempted. So very tempted because it felt almost normal in this otherworld that was The Ark. But however immersed he had become in this place there was still right and wrong, and it was wrong for sex to be a reward, for a woman to be assigned as a reward. And there was Laura. Tenuous though his relationship with her was, it nonetheless tugged at his conscience.

The woman tilted her head back to look up at him, and her hair fell away from her face; the nearby candle illuminated her features fully.

"My God! How old are you?"

"Fifteen." Her bottom lip trembled slightly. "Don't you like me?"

"Who sent you?"

"Abba." Uncertainty made her appear even more the child. "I'm your reward. I'm a virgin, so it's a really special reward. Did I do something wrong?"

"Get dressed," he said, turning away from her to rearrange himself and leaving the room as quickly as he could.

At night the back door of the headquarters building was secured, and there was always a guard on duty at the front door, so he couldn't avoid being seen. He took a deep breath and tried to appear casual as he went out. It was Gareb on duty at the door.

The man smirked. "Boy, she got you off fast. She must've been good, huh?"

Dan started out without answering.

"Wait! Where you going?"

"The new men's quarters. I thought of something I need to check."

Gareb's face betrayed a series of mental calculations. "There's no warrior assigned to you tonight. They figured you'd be busy in your room."

Dan shrugged. He could tell that Gareb was wrestling with whether to call someone.

"Here." Gareb tossed him a flashlight. "No hurry, huh? You've got her all night long, right?"

Dan ignored him and clicked on the light as he headed away from the building.

He hadn't realized she was a child! Shame swept over him for having been tempted at all. And the shame grew, encompassing him. How had he been so blind to the abuses going on around him? Women as rewards—as things to be used. Children as sexual objects. It made him sick to think what else he might be condoning just by his willing presence there. As he walked the shame turned to rage, and by the time he saw the dark shape of the new men's quarters he wanted to take a sledgehammer and destroy it.

This disgusting world was what Alex had brought their daughter into. And he had compounded the crime by blithely allowing her to stay. What horrors had she been exposed to? How much did she know about fifteen-year-old girls as rewards? How much had her mind been poisoned? Had they already taught her that her only value was in becoming either a servant or a sexual object? Or a combination of the two? What a fool he'd been. Playing right into Noah's hands. Blindly accepting the Ark's surface appearance without bothering to look deeper.

He stalked up to the windowed side door leading into the new building. The flashlight beam flared on the dark glass and caught his reflection there, stopping him cold. He stared into that face. Seeing it as if it belonged to someone he'd known years in the past. He had not seen his own reflection since arriving at the compound. Since he'd fallen into this evil rabbit hole and forgotten what normal was. Forgotten what right and wrong were.

He continued inside the building. The smells of new wood and joint compound and caulk filled him with a bittersweet pain. This was his creation. A building that he had brought to reality. Yet he had built it for *them*. This was the temptation he had not been able to turn away from. This was the seduction he had willingly sacrificed his soul for. To design. To build.

What a fool he was. What a weak and foolish man. Another puppet dancing at the end of Noah's strings. Seeing what he wanted to see and turning a blind eye to the rest. Sleeping through the rest.

Noah with all his talk of awakening. This was awakening! This sudden piercing agony of realization. This was awakening! Right now! All the rest had been a trance. A sleepwalk. A denial of both reality and self.

He leaned against a wall and clicked off the light, letting the darkness envelop him. There were no sounds. The building was lifeless. Heartless. Malevolent. He had consorted with the devil and created a monster. Suddenly he had to be free of it, and he ran for the door, stumbling over unseen obstacles, falling once. And then he was outside. Free of the monster, but not really free. Far from free.

He bent to catch his breath and then walked to a half-buried boulder that the children used for their safe spot during tag. He sat. Laura filled his thoughts. How seldom he had considered her during his time away. How frantically worried she must be.

With his eyes closed, he conjured her face. Her eyes. Her smile. He felt her strongly inside him. Her wisdom. Her compassion. Her strength. And he saw that she had been there all along, waiting for him.

Laura.

There, too, he had been a fool.

He felt as if he were suddenly viewing the whole of his life from some high place and he could see every hill and valley, every wrong path taken. He saw the destruction of his father's life—dedicated to saving a woman who didn't want to be saved—and he saw the repeat of that in his desperate need to save Alex from her inner demons. It was as though the tragic duet between his father and mother had been imprinted in his genes. And he wondered if his mother's self-destructive and self-absorbed nature hadn't been . . . What was the word they always used? *Enabled.* His father had enabled his mother to avoid taking responsibility for herself and for her actions. And after his father's death he had, as a teenager, stepped right into the same role.

And he saw that Laura had been right when she'd accused him of not knowing how to love an equal. Of waiting for a woman in distress. Needing a woman in distress before he could open himself enough to forge a solid connection. She'd been right when she told him that his ability to love had been tangled with his need to be needed. To be the gallant knight. To be the savior.

He had only been fooling himself when he'd believed that he and Alex had a modern marriage of equals. He hadn't known how to partner with a strong, independent woman. Somehow, deep down in the most unconscious primitive part of him, had been the feeling that this pattern of desperation and salvation was the only deep and truly experienced love.

And it struck him, with a bitter self-disgust, that he was like Noah. Noah also needed to be the savior, the provider, the champion and the redeemer. On a much grander scale, to be sure, but the germ of it all seemed closely related.

He cradled his head in his hands, feeling small and defeated.

No!

The power of that word reverberated through him. No. He was not defeated. He was ready to fight. And not just to save his daughter. Hana was his first priority, but he was also ready to fight for his own survival.

But how? What was he against Noah and the warriors? There was no way to get a message out to the authorities, and he did not even know who his note-writing ally was, much less whether or not the person had any resources.

He would fight with his wits. He would be clever. Deceptive. He would use the advantage he'd gained by becoming Noah's pawn and fool. And he would start by learning everything he could. Was there a guard all night at the women and children's building? How long could Hana disappear during the day without someone looking for her? And what exactly was the security around the perimeter?

So much time had passed without his being alert. Without his studying their weak points. But he had no more time for self-recrimination. From that moment forward he would be a man with a single-minded purpose. Nothing would get by him. No opportunity would be missed.

He saw the circle of light from a flashlight bobbing through the night toward the dining hall and he knew that someone was out looking for him. Without turning on his own light, he hurried silently back toward the headquarters building.

"Where's Ira?" Gareb demanded as soon as Dan reached the door.

"I don't know. I didn't see him."

"He went out to look for you."

Dan shrugged and handed over the flashlight. "We must have missed each other."

With a frown Gareb stepped aside to let him pass. Dan opened the door to his room, filled with the strength of his renewed determination. He froze when he heard sobbing, then realized who it was.

"Why are you still here?" he asked, lighting the candle.

She was curled up in the center of a now-disheveled bed, her whole body shaking. He looked around for her dress but didn't see it, so he pulled off his shirt.

"Put this on," he said, holding it out to her.

She sat up awkwardly, the sobs turning to ragged gasps as she slipped into the shirt and hugged it tightly around her. When she moved he saw that there was blood smeared over the white sheets beneath her.

"What is this?"

Fear blossomed in her eyes when she looked up at him, and his heart ached for her. He sat down beside her on the bed.

"What's your name?" he asked gently.

"Elizabeth."

"You don't have to be afraid of me, Elizabeth. Tell me what's going on."

She lowered her eyes, swallowed several times, then raised her eyes to his again.

"I was waiting . . ." she said, the words punctuated by dying sobs. "And I thought it was you. I'd blown the candle out so you wouldn't have to look at me . . . in case you left because you thought I was ugly. And I heard this noise of something heavy dropping on the table. It sounded like when the guards take off their guns at the pleasure rooms, but I didn't connect that really. I'm only connecting it now. And then he was on top of me. He put one hand over my mouth and I could hardly breathe and he shoved his thing into me . . . and it hurt." The sobs tore through her chest again. "It hurt."

"Who! Who raped you?" Dan was gripped by a murderous blast of rage.

"Gareb."

He leaped from the bed, but she caught his arm.

"No!" she wailed. "I'll get in trouble."

"Elizabeth! You were raped. You are the victim."

She looked at him as though he was speaking nonsense. "That wasn't rape. He's a warrior and I'm just a lowly vessel. I'll get in trouble because your reward is ruined."

Dan sank back onto the bed and put a hand to his head, holding on to sanity, holding on to practicality, reminding himself that he had to play by their rules.

"Okay, Elizabeth, you're right. I won't go confront Gareb. But I think you and I should talk to Noah tomorrow and tell him I was cheated and report that Gareb left his guard post and broke rules."

"I can't go! I'm a female. Girls can't report warriors."

"Isn't it our duty to report that a guard left his post?"

"As a female my duty is to leave things like that to you."

Dan sighed. "Okay. Why don't you go back to your own bed now? I'll walk you past Gareb."

"I can't. I was told to stay with you until morning."

He sighed again. "Let's get some sleep, then."

Quickly she scrambled off the bed and onto the floor, using her hand as a pillow.

"Get back up here," he said.

She sat up and cocked her head in puzzlement.

"I order you to sleep on the bed with me, so blow out the candle and get up here."

She smiled.

It was an awkward dance of elbows and knees, stretching out together on the narrow bed, he on the outside facing away from her and she closest to the wall. When it was accomplished and he had started to relax he suddenly felt her hands.

"No. None of that," he said, more gruffly than he'd intended.

"I don't please you?" Her voice was childish and pathetic in the darkness.

"You please me. And you tempt me. But I've had a revelation tonight and I'm going to stay celibate until I understand it."

"Ohhhh." She was very impressed. "But you can't go too long or you'll be poisoned by your seed dying inside you. Abba says that the greater or mightier a man, the more boundless his seed and the bigger danger there is if he doesn't release it. A hero shouldn't be celibate too long."

"I'll be careful. You know what would please me?" he said, feeling a twinge of guilt for using her. "I'd like to talk. Talking would help me relax and fall asleep."

"About what?" she asked, sounding puzzled, as though it was almost inconceivable that he would want to hear anything from her.

"Whatever. Just . . . talking. I was wondering about the Cleansing."

"What? Do you mean the laundry?"

It was clear to him that she had no idea what the Cleansing was. "Yes. Do you work in the laundry?"

"No."

"Okay, well, tell me about living here. I've been so busy building that I haven't had time to absorb what's around me. You can start with yourself. How long have you been in The Ark?"

"I can't talk about that. It brings out negativity in me."

"Okay. If you don't want—"

"Well . . . I guess . . . if the talking is what pleases you . . . I'm obligated to answer."

He waited, letting her make the decision.

"I was eleven. My dad . . . I mean, Elias . . . sent a plane ticket to me in Arizona and promised my mom I'd be back in three weeks. I flew to San Francisco, where he'd been living, and he picked me up and drove me straight out into the mountains. He told me he'd joined a really special group and we were going to stay with them. That's when I joined. That's how long I've been in."

"So you started out at the California compound and then came here?"

"Yes."

"Did you ever get to see your mother again . . . or even talk to her?"

"My mother is unawakened. She doesn't matter."

"But I'll bet you think of her and miss her."

"I try not to be weak."

"All of us are weak sometimes."

"Not Noah! Not you! Not the warriors!"

Dan sighed. "I don't know an Elias."

"He's . . . He was one of Abba's first circle of warriors. Now he's a martyr to The Truth."

"He's dead?"

"Yes. On a mission."

"A mission?" Instantly he knew. That was the sort of mission he'd heard Zelek and the warriors discussing. Not a historic Spanish church but an assignment.

"A secret mission to make the world safe for The Ark."

"Do you know what happened to him?"

"No. He went with Ira and Zelek to Los Angeles, and he didn't come back. I thought he went to another compound at first, but then Noah had a martyr ceremony and I found out. They said he got burned and he died out there."

A dark suspicion reared in Dan's mind.

"How long ago was this?"

"I don't know. It was before the warriors went on the mission to bring you back. Not a long long time before, but before."

Elias. Her father. He had been burned during a mission in Los Angeles. Something had gone wrong, and he had been burned. Was he the corpse at Valerie's? Yes. Dan was certain of it.

The Ark had sent warriors to murder Valerie.

"I can't talk about that anymore," she said. "I'm feeling really negative."

"Right. I don't blame you." Suddenly he thought of Bibi Khadra. Would this girl know her or know of her? When he escaped he wanted to be able to bring Ben Khadra information about his daughter.

"Do you know anyone named Bibi? She'd be about twenty now. Pretty, with dark hair."

"No. But anyone who doesn't have a proper name is rechristened by Noah and the old name is never spoken again."

"So she could be called anything now."

"Yes."

What information could he safely get from her? He thought for a moment then asked, "Do you have a lot of friends over in the women and children's building?"

"I have brothers and sisters. I have guides."

"How many children are there in that building?"

"Ummm . . . thirty, I guess. Nobody's allowed to have any new babies for a while. Except Jael, of course. Jael is growing Abba's baby."

Dan felt a resigned sadness at this news, but nothing more. No great swell of emotion. Not the slightest twinge of pain. Not even anger. And that absence of feeling was incredibly good. He was free of her. He was totally and completely free of her.

"Are you asleep?" she whispered, rousing him from his thoughts.

"No. I was just thinking. About my daughter, Hana. Does she know Jael is pregnant?"

"Everyone knows. We had a celebration. It will be the first of Abba's seed to take root here."

Dan suppressed a sarcastic comment. "I'm surprised Noah has only one wife."

"He doesn't! Before Jael there were two other wives here. Bathsheba died bringing forth his child—she turned out to be weak and unsuitable as a breeder. And after that, Susanna, his other, became very strange. One night she disappeared, and Abba says that demons probably carried her off."

"Susanna. She was the one who designed the Audience room, wasn't she?"

"Through Noah she had many talents."

Susanna. Was she the disturbed and brutalized escapee Laura referred to as Jane?

"Maybe she just decided to leave," Dan suggested. "Maybe she went back to her family on the outside."

"No one leaves The Ark," the girl said as though this was not only unthinkable but terrifying.

"Not ever?"

"People go to other compounds and the warriors go on missions, but no one ever leaves."

A cold fear ran through him.

"Could you—" he started to ask.

She said, "Wait." Whether to herself or to him he wasn't sure, but he waited.

"I just remembered something. When Bathsheba was trying to give birth she was screaming out things. Possessed things. We could hear her all the way down the hall. And the nurse kept shouting instructions . . . 'Push, Bathsheba,' and 'Hold it, Bathsheba' . . . and Bathsheba started crying out 'Baby, baby.' That's what I thought anyway. Even though it didn't make sense the way she was saying it. Now I wonder if she wasn't crying 'Bibi. Bibi.' Wanting the nurse to call her by her old name."

Dan collected himself for a moment and drew a deep breath.

"Sounds like it's dangerous being Noah's wife."

"Abba's wives have to be the bravest and the purest because evil is always trying to attack him through his wives."

"Does Noah have wives and children elsewhere?"

"Oh, yes! It's Abba's duty to father the future."

"Where are these children?"

"At the other compounds. With his wives."

"California and Australia?"

"I know them by name but, except for the Shelter here and the Garden in California, I don't know where they are."

"So we've got the Shelter, the Garden, and what else?"

"Shining Mountain and the River."

Four compounds. Did the authorities know that? Elizabeth yawned, reminding him that time was short and he had to focus on his particular concerns.

"Why did you come here from California?"

"Most everyone from there was moved here. Only special people stayed. Along with women to serve them and comfort them. And Noah's wives. He has to have wives at every compound."

"What kind of special people?"

"The people who work in the underground rooms beneath the buildings."

"What do they do there?"

"Very secret things. It's not for us to know."

He could tell from her mounting unease that he had to change the subject immediately.

"I've never asked Noah how many people live here. Do you know?"

"No."

"How many women are there in your building?"

"Lots." She hesitated. "Let's see . . . I'm counting sleeping rooms and bunks in my head . . . Maybe two hundred? Maybe a little less."

"Do the children sleep separately from the adults?"

"Until age twelve. There are two big children's rooms. One for boys and one for girls."

"Does an adult stay in the room all night?"

"There's always a woman sleeping in a bed near the door."

"And are there guards inside, too?"

"No. No men are allowed inside unless they're staying in one of the pleasure rooms."

"Is there a guard outside the main door all night to protect you?"

"Always. Why are you asking me these questions?"

"Because I want to make sure you feel safe over there."

"Oh, I do. The Ark protects."

"I'd like to go to a pleasure room one day," Dan said, setting up his next series of questions. "Have you been in the pleasure rooms?"

"For training." Then proudly she added, "I've had a lot of training in pleasing men. Not just from the guides but from Abba himself. I wish you'd let me suck your seed from you. Abba says I'm really good at it."

Dan swallowed his revulsion and tried to block out the thought of Noah in the pleasure rooms teaching the fine points of a blow job to young girls. The man was not just evil. He was worse than that.

"Who gets to go to the pleasure rooms?"

"Warriors and some top workers and special people— like you—can request nights there. Then they get rewards, too. Regular workers can't use the pleasure rooms, but there are certain celebration days when workers can have any woman in a gray dress. Those days get crazy because women will be trying to do their daily chores and keep having to stop and lift their dress." She yawned again. "There's more. And there's new rules and new covenants all the time."

"If I went there . . . to a pleasure room, would I get to stay all night?"

"Sure."

"And would I get to choose who pleasured me?"

"Most men don't get to, but I'm sure Abba would let you choose."

"Could I chose you, Elizabeth?"

"I think so. I mean, girls under twenty are reserved for the warriors and Abba only, but you're like a warrior."

"Reserved, huh?"

He felt her nod. "From twelve to your first use as a vessel you're a virgin in training. Then you go to reserved. From twenty to thirty-five you can be a breeder, but you have to qualify to be a breeder and some don't. The ones who don't skip right to being comfort women."

"What does a comfort woman do?"

"She gives comfort every way she can, with food and cleaning and receiving seed . . . everything."

"Receiving seed, huh?"

"The seed of the workers. So it won't be spilled on the ground. So our collective strength won't be weakened. So the men's strength can fill the women and give them long lives. Even the seed of the lowliest man brings light and truth to a woman."

And it dawned on him that the dresses were important.

He'd been aware of the different colors without considering their meaning. But then, he had had very little contact with the women.

"So," he said, "little girls wear brown dresses. And the kind of whitish beige is . . ."

"VITs . . . virgins in training. Reserved wear the rose-pink. That's what I'll get tomorrow. Breeders are green. And comfort is light gray like the men's shirts."

"This is absolute? All females must participate?"

"You can ask to declare chastity. But Abba has to give permission, and he doesn't do it very often. The grown-ups in the off-white dresses are the chaste ones . . . like Ruth, who runs the dining hall, and Rebekah, the head nurse, and Deborah, who runs the laundry, and Judith, who cooks for Noah . . . they've all chosen the white."

"And purple is for Noah's wives."

"Yes." She sighed. "I'd like to wear the purple someday."

# Chapter 23

The next morning Dan asked to see Noah. Joha was on duty outside the sanctum door. Dan had finally gotten it straight, which robot was Joha and which Joab.

"He's got an important visitor inside," Joha warned, "but I'll tell him you're here."

Dan had heard the helicopter's departure the day before and its return just after dawn. He had not bothered to speculate about its meaning because it came and went so often, bringing in supplies or bearing Noah away for days at a time. It was unusual, however, for the helicopter to bring in outsiders.

"Daniel!" Noah's voice called from behind the partially opened office door.

Dan was waved in. When he entered the room he saw a small gray-haired man in a white lab coat filling a syringe. Noah was sitting on the corner of the desk with his shirt off.

"Come in! Come in, Daniel. You can be first after me to get the inoculations."

Dan watched the needle plunge into Noah's arm. "What is it for?" he asked.

"It's Dr. Joseph's magical cocktail. Joseph is the wizard."

Noah hopped off the desk and pulled his shirt back on. "This is the man I was telling you about, Joseph. My master builder, Daniel."

The doctor, if indeed that's what he was, inclined his head toward Dan. His manner was curt and dismissive.

"What's it for?" Dan asked again.

The doctor was already opening another disposable

syringe. As he filled it he answered. "Immunization against several common diseases that adults fail to get booster shots against, and a vaccine against a family of diseases that no one in the world has even heard of yet."

"Roll up your sleeve, Daniel, or take off your shirt. Don't be hesitant."

Dan was hesitant. If he hadn't just seen Noah receiving a similar shot he would have been convinced he was being murdered. As it was, he thought there was a good chance that something weird was being shot into his body. But there was no way to escape without making Noah angry or suspicious or both. He pushed up his sleeve and stared at the panel of labeled buttons on the wall behind Noah's desk. It was over in seconds.

"If no one has heard of these diseases, why do we need immunity against them?" Dan asked.

The doctor glared at him, but Noah smiled enigmatically. "We are making history, Daniel. We are on the threshold of a new world."

Noah walked the white-coated man to the door, saying, "Ira has it set up on the lawn. Two of the women with nurse's training are there, and people are assigned to line up in shifts. Get it all started and then go to the clinic for your normal procedures."

"Everyone in the compound is being immunized?" Dan asked as the door closed on the doctor's departure.

Noah sat down at his desk, his eyes never leaving Dan's face.

"The formulations are safe for children, Daniel, so don't be concerned for Hana."

Dan nodded. "Is that guy an actual doctor?"

"Not only is he a physician, he is a brilliant researcher—shunned by the established medical community but embraced and funded by The Ark."

In an effort to conceal his surprise and curiosity, Dan turned his attention to Noah's desk—and was even more surprised, because he realized that one of the objects there was a small telephone. Not cellular but connected to a cord.

"You have a phone?"

Noah laughed. "For emergencies only. I had the line installed before the compound was a quarter finished, and it cost dearly in both funds and aggravation. I hated to have to do it. But cellulars and radios have their limitations and are security risks."

He bent to unplug the phone from the wall behind him, and Dan saw the small outlet, not actually hidden but very unobtrusive. Slowly Noah coiled the cord around his hand, regarding Dan as he did so. He slipped phone and cord into the bottom drawer of his desk and locked it with a key that he then placed on his desktop and ignored.

Dan wondered if the whole display was some sort of loyalty test. He could not believe that Noah had left the phone out by mistake. The man did not make mistakes.

"You wanted to see me, Daniel? How was your reward last night?"

"That's why I'm here. To make a formal charge."

"Go on."

"I was concerned about a detail in the finish work, and I couldn't enjoy myself until I checked on it, so without having touched her, I left Elizabeth to wait for me and went out to the dining hall. Gareb was on duty at the door."

"Yes. And I understand you went without waiting for a warrior to accompany you."

Dan nodded. "Gareb seemed eager for me to go. When I returned I found out why. There was blood all over my sheets. I demanded that the girl tell me what had happened. Gareb had jumped on her in the dark, thinking that I'd already taken her virginity, and I suppose thinking that his little extra wouldn't be noticed by me. So I was cheated and his post was unguarded."

Noah's eyes burned and the cords in his neck stood out and his cheek muscles hardened. He leaped from his chair and stormed to the door, shouting.

Two alarmed guards burst in with guns ready.

"Take Gareb to the punishment pit. I'll be there shortly."

As soon as the men were gone Noah turned back to Dan, completely composed. "You were right to come straight to me with this, Daniel. We must all be our brother's keeper, doubly so when that brother requires guidance and discipline."

Calmly Noah settled behind his desk.

"When will you start our great building?" he asked.

"Within days. I need to clear my head first, though, so I thought I'd organize a few small repair projects. For instance, this building has some rotting windowsills and a loose stair tread. With your permission I'd like to look over the women's quarters, too. I'm sure there are similar problems there."

Noah nodded approvingly. Then he steepled his hands and glanced out the window. "So you suddenly became celibate in Elizabeth's arms last night?"

The bottom fell out of Dan's stomach. Elizabeth must have reported to Noah the moment she left him. But she must have told an edited version, because Gareb's crime had certainly been news to Noah. All Dan could do was bluff and hope that she hadn't reported anything to Noah that was too damaging.

"I was angry!" Dan said, slapping his palm down against the desk. "And I was offended. I was expecting a virgin and what I got was Gareb's sloppy seconds."

Noah's eyes narrowed. "What was the celibacy about?"

Dan shrugged, his heart skipping. "She's young and she was upset about failing me. I didn't want to traumatize her. Ruin her enthusiasm or give her performance anxiety."

Laughter burst from Noah's lungs. "You are owed," he said. "If there was another virgin ready right now I'd call her here immediately." His eyebrows lifted slightly. "Usually only first-level warriors can take part in a warrior punishment, but part of your repayment should come from Gareb's flesh. I'll send for you when we begin."

Dan spent the next several hours dreading the summons. Though he detested Gareb, and had been ready to tear the man apart with his bare hands during the night, he did not want to participate in Noah's planned punishment. He tried to keep busy inspecting the headquarters building and assigning repairs.

It was Ammiel who came for him. Ammiel was the least seen but most senior of the guards. If anyone could be called Noah's second in command it would be Ammiel—though, by physical standards, he was the least formidable of the guards. Short in stature, with narrow shoulders and a slightly concave chest, he had unblinking reptilian eyes and a habit of slinking around on the fringes of things. He was in his late forties and had reportedly served in Vietnam. Dan assumed that was accurate, because the man was a top-notch pilot.

Ammiel led him to a building that he told Dan had been the very first structure to rise on the compound. It had started out as Noah's quarters and was now serving as the clinic. It was there that the women with nurse's training treated a variety of injuries. Dan had been inside only once and that had been to carry in a teenage boy with a nail through his foot. The place had impressed him as clean and efficient. Supplies had been stacked neatly on open shelves. He recalled being amused to see an entire case of birth control pills—amused because the men and women seemed to have so little contact with each other. But now, following Ammiel through the clinic and seeing the supply of pills again, he was no longer amused. He was sickened. Instead of offering the compound's women freedom from the worry of conception, those pills were just another form of control, a tool to further dehumanize the females.

"This way," Ammiel said, leading Dan toward the center of the open room.

All twelve cots in the room held sleeping men covered by white sheets and blankets. A nurse watched them from the back. She was wearing white for chastity. Dan wondered if any of the younger girls like Elizabeth ever stopped to consider that the women with any influence at all—the nurses and the head cooks and the top laundress—all chose chastity over sexual servitude. Didn't that send any messages?

"What happened to all these men?" Dan asked Ammiel. Oddly, though the population of the compound contained only a scattering of minorities, the men lying on the beds were nearly all non-Anglos.

The nurse heard his question and quickly turned away to busy herself with a task.

Ammiel had knelt and was tugging at a trapdoor in the wooden floor. "Take hold," he ordered.

Dan bent to help. "What's wrong with all these men?"

"They're sleeping."

"But . . ."

The trapdoor opened to reveal a concrete staircase to a basement. Ammiel started down. Dan looked around at the sleeping men again, and Ammiel said, "Care to join them?" He chuckled like a weasel cartoon character, then motioned Dan to follow with a brusque, "Pull the door shut behind you."

In the concrete basement there were iron rings in the walls and other metal things that Dan did not want to notice or consider. Gareb was chained naked to a pair of rings, hanging so that only his toes were touching the floor. Dan focused on Noah. Behind him were Zelek and Ira.

"Hello, Daniel," Noah said. "In answer to your question, the men upstairs are volunteers in an experimental program that Dr. Joseph is conducting."

"What kind of a program?"

"Chemical sterilization."

A chill went down Dan's spine.

"They hope to be more worthy and more focused once they are free of that aspect of human weakness."

Dan nodded, but he couldn't stop himself from asking, "Why those particular men?"

Noah gave him a measured look. "The Ark accepts many for service, but not all are suitable for breeding." He turned then. "We shall begin," he said solemnly.

The warriors dropped to their knees and Dan followed suit.

Noah opened his arms wide and threw back his head. "Witness!" he thundered. "This most trusted of men! This warrior! Breaks his oath for the third time! What is our duty here?"

"Guidance and discipline!" the kneeling men responded.

"You are guilty of leaving your post, Gareb. You are guilty of stealing a reward that had been earned by another. What say you?"

Gareb's shaking rattled the chains slightly. "I am

guilty," he cried. "I am weak! I am untrustworthy!" Tears slid down his face. "Guide me, Noah. Cleanse me with discipline."

Everyone rose. Ira stepped forward, and Dan saw that he, too, had tears running from his eyes.

"In Truth, my brother," Ira said, and touched his palm to Gareb's forehead.

Each of the other warriors went through the same ritual. Daniel looked to Noah.

"No, Daniel. That is for warriors to brother warriors." Then he wheeled abruptly and ordered, "Turn him!"

Two of the men flipped Gareb so that he dangled with his face to the wall. Noah stepped forward with a whip and lashed it across the naked white back. A bright red welt sprang up before the whip could fall again. Three times Noah struck him. Gareb's body jerked each time, but he made no sound. The whip was passed to Ammiel, who wielded it with obvious relish. Gareb's stoic silence dissolved into whimpers. Each of the other men in the room took a turn with the whip, each administering three lashes. Gareb's back opened in diagonal bleeding lines and the whimpers turned to cries.

The whip was passed to Dan.

"Three," Noah said, eyes locked on Dan, darkly challenging.

Dan's gut twisted and sweat poured out of him. No. He couldn't. He couldn't. He looked down at the whip in his hand. He could not torture a helpless man. He looked up. All eyes were on him. Waiting. The ferocity of Noah's gaze was terrifying.

Hana, he thought. For Hana. For escape. He couldn't falter now. He couldn't lose Noah's confidence.

He stepped forward quickly and raised his arm. One. Two. Three.

"Ammiel!" Noah snapped, and Ammiel lunged forward to pour a dark brown, pungent-smelling liquid over Gareb's back.

A familiar smell. A hospital smell. Betadine? It was over, and now they were going to minister to his wounds. It was over. Thank God. It was over.

"Turn him," Noah ordered, and Gareb was flipped to face his torturers once again.

His face was white. His eyes were bulging out of the sockets. Ammiel darted in once again, this time pouring the liquid over Gareb's genitals. Gareb's sphincter let go. The smell of human excrement filled the room, overpowering the smells of sweat and chemicals.

Dan turned his face from the sight, caught Noah's movement from the corner of his eye and turned back. Before his reeling brain could understand, before his sweat-soaked limbs could react, before the horror could sink into him and be comprehended, there was a flash of steel. And blood. Bright flowing blood. And Gareb's terrible screams. And Noah cutting, tearing something free, a bloody mass, a testicle, the man's testicle.

"It is done," Noah announced, dropping the testicle into a chalice. "Daniel!" he called sharply. "Open the door for me and follow me out."

Mechanically, Dan obeyed. He followed Noah up the stairs into the clinic. Doctor Joseph was sitting on a chair in the clinic reading through a file.

"Bring him up," Noah called down the stairs. Then, to the white-coated doctor, "Your emergency case is ready, Joseph. Please do all you can. Try to save the remaining testicle. And, of course, I'd appreciate your saving my warrior."

Noah went to a sink and began sluicing the blood from his hands. Dan bolted. Away from the blood. Away from the cots filled with neutered men. He made it outside and around to the back before he doubled over and vomited.

When there was nothing else left to come up he leaned against the rough wall. Noah had come after him in time to witness the whole display. Dan expected to be reprimanded for his weakness, but Noah was smiling, clearly pleased.

"You conducted yourself well in there, Daniel. You could earn your way into the warriors' circle one day."

He clapped Dan on the back. "There are seasoned warriors who've never had to witness the third discipline."

Dan swallowed against the bitterness in his throat. "What's the fourth discipline?"

Noah laughed. "I like your sense of humor," he said. "I could see it from the beginning, and I've been so glad that we didn't have to eliminate it. I don't get many loyal followers who retain their humor."

Dan forced a smile.

"Take the afternoon off," Noah said. "Relax and gather your energies."

"Thanks," Dan said, the bile rising in his throat again, "but I think I'll keep busy."

He wandered around the compound, carrying clipboard and tape measure, pretending to inspect windowsills and doors while he gathered ideas for escape. He thought about stealing one of the heavy all-terrain vehicles, buckling Hana into a seat, and driving like hell until he got somewhere. But the route out was barely a road at all. What if he ran them off the mountain or got them stuck? What if he didn't get them completely away? The punishment for attempted escape could very well be death. The helicopter. If he could get one of the guns, might it be possible to grab Hana and then force Ammiel to fly them out in the helicopter? The more he considered the helicopter the more promising the plan seemed. But how could he get a gun?

As he moved about he left his clipboard untended frequently, setting it down and then returning for it as though absentmindedly, hoping that his secret communicant would find the chance to slip him a note. Joha, who was his shadow for the day, seemed not to notice. But then neither of the J's—the robot warriors—ever seemed to notice much. It was no wonder they hadn't achieved upper-level status. He thought about the men who had been at the punishment. Did Noah intentionally keep his top circle of warriors small or was it hard to find just the right combination of evil aggressiveness and loyalty?

Finally, just before dinner, he retrieved his clipboard and found a note. This one was carefully printed in small letters.

The Cleansing is a plan to release a highly contagious lethal virus that was developed in a lab at the California compound. Noah is vaccinating his chosen against it now. I haven't been able to contact the outside to warn them. We must get this information out.

# Chapter 24

Dan felt like a wild animal caught in a cage, pacing helplessly in circles against the bars but unable to find a way out. He couldn't eat or concentrate on work. A day passed and then another. At night he lay in his bed, so sickened and fearful that he felt almost feverish. He could not block out the images from the torture room. He could not stop thinking about the Cleansing. When was it supposed to begin? Now he had not only his daughter to worry about, he had the fate of unsuspecting people on the outside as well. When he dozed off he had terrible nightmares and woke up crying out warnings.

He thought constantly of escape. He had to get out and warn people. He had to get Hana out. He could not bear the thought of what might happen to Hana if he should fail to save her. But he had explored so many ideas and still not come up with a good plan. The location of the arms room had eluded him, and he had no confidence in his ability to overcome and disarm a warrior. How was he going to get a gun? And, to further complicate his plan, the helicopter kept leaving. He had to find a way to know in advance when it would be there.

He agonized over who the secret note writer was. Would the person help him? Did the person have any escape ideas? Why didn't he or she make direct contact? Was the person a planted spy or a disenchanted Ark member?

And what about the federal investigation? How much of this horror had the Feds uncovered? How long before they acted? And when they did act, what would that mean? With a group as dangerous as The Ark, they could very well launch a full-style invasion. And if that happened he had no doubt that Noah would respond with open warfare. The entire compound would be a battle zone.

By the third day following the torture he was still trying to present an outward calm but was inwardly frantic. The enormity of Noah's evil reverberated through him constantly. And, like a naive architecture student faced with the first major project, he was becoming increasingly aware of the difficulties he faced in designing an escape. It wasn't just the gun and the helicopter. Hana's accessibility was a problem.

Under the guise of building inspection he had managed to see inside the women and children's quarters, and he thought that if he was in a pleasure room there for the night, it would be possible to sneak down the hall and get to the children's room in the dark. The question was, how could he possibly pluck a sleeping Hana out of that roomful of children and one adult and carry her out past a guard without alerting anyone? And then, even if he did accomplish that, he would be faced with the task of going into the warriors' quarters after Ammiel. Unless he could find out when Ammiel was on duty at the door all night.

He had always visualized a nighttime escape so that the compound would be quiet and dark, but he wondered if a daytime plan might be better. If he could already have the gun concealed under his clothes, and if the helicopter was there, and if it was Ammiel's day to shadow him then he could meet Hana for their afternoon visit and . . . It occurred to him that a distraction might work for him. If he could get all the elements in place and start a fire, perhaps?

Just before lunch the helicopter arrived, with Ammiel flying and Ira in the front passenger seat. When it was shut down two hooded passengers were helped from the back. A man and a woman. No one had been brought in hooded since Dan's own arrival. This implied that they were complete outsiders.

After the hoods had been removed and the two had steadied themselves and the man's black western hat had been retrieved from the back of the helicopter, they were led toward headquarters. Dan wondered if they would get the full treatment as he had when he first arrived, with Noah in his robes in the audience room. But then Noah stepped out of the building to greet them.

"Mr. Conrad," Dan heard Noah say.

"Cody to you, my friend," the man insisted, taking off his hat and holding it to his breast in an old-style gentlemanly gesture. "And this is Rina."

The woman's smile was spoiled and sensual. With his expensive western clothes and her sexy sundress, they looked as though they were on their way to a dance.

"We'll do business in my office over lunch," Noah announced. He turned and, catching sight of Dan, he waved. "Stay close, Daniel, and be ready to join us. I need your expertise."

Apprehensive, Dan sat down on the headquarters' porch steps to wait. He leaned against one of the solid posts that supported the porch overhang, trying to appear casual. Inside, his thoughts were churning. What did this mean? Ira and Zelek hovered near the front door, exchanging glances, eyes glittering with unspoken excitement. Who were these visitors? Clearly they were not new converts. What business were they doing with Noah?

Unable to sit still any longer, Dan got up and went to the door.

"Noah didn't summon you yet," Ira said, puffing out his chest as though expecting an argument.

"I'm going in to my room. You can find me there."

Ira frowned, but Zelek gave Dan the nod to go inside. In the main hallway, just outside the door to the audience room, was a door marked TOILET, the "public" bathroom for the headquarters building. There stood the woman in the sundress. She was arguing with the two J's. Joha seemed his usual implacable self, but Joab's immobile face was flushed with anger.

Dan intended to hurry past them, but Joha called out, "Daniel!"

Reluctantly, Dan approached the threesome. The lower-level warriors such as these two had gradually come to accept Dan's position with Noah and grudgingly viewed him as somewhat of an authority figure. He could see that they wanted his help with this troublesome "unawakened" woman.

The woman turned immediately to him and demanded, "Who are you?"

"Daniel is the builder and he has wisdom," Joha said.

"Oh, yeah . . ." She regarded Dan with an exasperated expression, and he saw a flicker of something in her eyes. A sharpness. Perhaps just sarcasm, but it revealed that she was not the airhead she first appeared to be. "A regular hero, huh . . . just like Paul Revere."

"Yes," Joha said firmly. "So speak respectfully to him."

"They're treating me like a prisoner," she complained to Dan.

"Noah gave permission for her to use the toilet," Joab reported. "She's finished. I was just trying to take her back in."

"Drag me back in, you mean. Don't put your hands on me again, creep." She looked at Joha. "And you! What'd you have to jump in for? Think your buddy isn't man enough to handle me alone?"

The red in Joab's face deepened to purple.

"Let me take her back in for you and stand duty at the sanctum door," Joha offered his fellow warrior. "A swap of duties. Noah won't mind."

Joab was just nodding yes when Noah's voice intruded.

"Joab! Bring Daniel!"

Joab set his jaw and pushed the woman forward. Dan followed. Joha looked for a moment like he might try to accompany them, but then he turned and went back to his post at the back door.

When Dan entered the sanctum Noah was at his desk; the man, Conrad, was seated across from him. The remains of sandwiches and fruit were on the side table. Dan sat down in a chair and the woman moved sullenly to sit down on the couch. There were black-and-white photographs on the corner of Noah's desk. The photographs were of weapons. Rifles and grenades and machine guns and bazookas. And land mines. Was that what they used for perimeter security?

Conrad was an arms dealer. The realization neither surprised nor shocked Dan.

The woman fished in her purse and came out with a cigarette and a black plastic lighter.

"No smoking in here," Noah told her curtly.

She sighed, dropped them back into the purse, and pulled out a stick of gum.

Noah opened the large right-hand bottom drawer of his desk and pulled out a laptop computer, the telephone, and a modem. "I want to do the deal right now, and then I want you to talk to my building expert, Daniel," he said as he was connecting wires and getting his equipment set up. "I want to find out what it would take to build a bunker."

"What kind of firepower does it have to stand up to?" Conrad asked.

"Everything."

"How 'bout we take a walk and you show me where you want this and then Daniel and I can discuss details."

Noah hesitated, glancing down at his booted computer. "All right," he said.

They filed out of the sanctum, passing Joab on guard at the door.

"Joha!" Noah called down the hallway, "lock the back door and leave it. Go to the helicopter shed, find Ammiel, and bring him to me."

Joha hustled to obey, exiting through the front door ahead of them. After the last of their group had left the building, Ira fell into step behind them. Noah and Conrad walked ahead and the woman settled in beside Dan. He could not focus on Noah and Conrad's conversation. He felt like he was in a box and the walls were slowly moving in to crush him.

"Ira!" Noah called, kicking at the ground. "Where's that stake I drove?"

Ira hurried forward. The woman, beside Dan, stumbled and fell. Automatically Dan bent to help her up. When he took her hand there was something in it. "Get this to him," she said under her breath. Then, jerking away from him indignantly, she began slapping at her skirt.

"Look!" she wailed. "Grass stains on my dress!"

"Calm down, Rina," Conrad said.

"I have to go back to the bathroom," she demanded. "I have to get these stains out before they set."

"I could have the dress run through the laundry right away," Ammiel suggested.

"Absolutely not. This is a Giacometti original. I'm not letting some laundry ruin it. I'll sponge it out myself."

Noah gave a tight nod, and Ira scurried to Rina's side. "I'll walk you back to headquarters."

Dan stood, frozen, the unknown object clutched tightly in his hand. He couldn't look at it or acknowledge it in any way. He couldn't even drop it without calling attention to himself—and probably incriminating himself in whatever she was doing. All he could think about was that he wanted to be rid of it. Whatever it was, he was certain that he should not be caught with it. And what the hell had she meant by "Get it to him"? Get it to whom? The spy, probably. The note writer. But who was it?

"Daniel!" Noah called, "come over here!"

Dan thrust his hand into his pocket and released the object there. It was cylindrical and wrapped in paper.

Ira returned. The business of the bunker continued. Dan heard Noah explain that he had built the clinic building in a bunkerlike manner, with lots of concrete block and gunports to shoot through, but that recent reading had convinced him that he wanted something more substantial. He asked for Dan's opinions. Words came out of Dan's mouth. He didn't know where they were coming from because he knew nothing about bunkers and couldn't concentrate on what he was saying. Had the woman been sent by the federal authorities? Why had she demanded to go back to the bathroom? What was she up to? He tried to keep offering problems and thoughts about the bunker because he suspected that she'd had a reason for leaving, and he suspected that the longer Noah was kept busy the better it would be for her.

Suddenly there were shouts and Joab was waving from the headquarters door. Noah took off at a run with Ira close behind him. Conrad reluctantly followed.

Dan took the opportunity to duck away, cutting around several buildings till he came to the old outhouse that was left from before the installation of the water system and the sewage lines. Hands shaking, he pulled the object from his pocket. It was the black lighter she had flashed in the office. She had wrapped it in a note.

We've got Noah on weapons and drug mfg. Team standing by. No hurry. Get a progress report to me to take out if you can. If not use best judgment on beacon timing. Depress red button on bottom for ten seconds to activate when you're ready for company.

He set the note on fire, then dropped it down the hole. The lighter worked fine. There was nothing false about it. Just that round red plastic button on the bottom that would probably summon every armed fed in the nation if he pressed it.

She must have planned on giving the lighter and note directly to her cohort, but for some reason she'd been unable. Or maybe her plans had changed.

He stared at the red button. *Team standing by.* Pressing the red button would call in an invasion force. Noah and his warriors were heavily armed, and they weren't going to go peacefully. No one would be safe. Pressing that button would start a small war. He was sure of it. And there would be no safety zone for the innocent. Not for Hana and himself. Not for Elizabeth and all the other children. Not for the hundreds of unarmed and confused men and women around him. Even if he did figure out who the spy was, did he want to turn this beacon over to him? He slipped the lighter into his pocket and rushed to headquarters to see what was happening.

They had the woman in the central hall. Ira held one of her arms and Joab held the other. Her lip was bleeding. Big slow drips dropped onto the front of her sundress. There were red marks on both her cheeks. She didn't look at Dan as he came in.

"You will tell us," Noah said in a menacingly friendly tone. "If not here, then we can go somewhere more persuasive."

"Tell us who you work for!" Zelek shouted into her face, striking her as he spoke.

Noah seemed to notice Dan then. "This demon bitch is a spy, Daniel. She was caught transmitting information from my computer. Fortunately, she didn't have time to send much."

Ammiel came running in, panting, gun in hand. "I just shot Joha! He was tearing up the helicopter engine!"

Noah's face contorted in cold fury. The woman went white as paper beneath her heavy makeup. She did not look in Dan's direction at all.

Conrad stepped out of the hall bathroom, swabbing his face with a wet towel. "I'm telling you, Noah, you've got to get me out of here. I can't be involved in any of this."

Noah wheeled, ripped the gun from Ammiel's hand, and shot the arms dealer full in the face. The man slumped to the ground, urine and blood running from beneath him.

"Take her to the clinic," Noah ordered.

Dan followed them but stayed toward the back. Joha shot! It had been Joha all along. Joha the robot man. He'd been the note writer. Now she had no one to help her. No one except him. He gripped the lighter in his pocket. He had to do it. He couldn't not do it. They would kill her. They would most certainly kill her. With a deep breath he moved his finger into position. He held it there. Up ahead she was being jerked along, stumbling, fighting them, not showing any fear. He pushed the button and counted to ten.

That was it.

He slowed until he was well behind, and then he ran to look for Hana. He nearly bumped into Alex-Jael.

"Daniel," she cried. "Why are the warriors running everywhere? Where are you going?"

He looked at her, the woman he had loved so deeply, the mother of his child, and he could not pass her by.

"Something bad is happening," he said, grabbing her shoulders. "They caught a woman spy, and I'm afraid we're about to be raided. You need to warn everyone and find somewhere safe to hide."

"The tunnels," she breathed, her hands moving protectively to the bulge of her unborn child and her eyes widening in fear.

"What tunnels?"

She shook her head. "They're secret."

"I have to know," he insisted. "Noah wants me to help everyone so I have to know."

"Under the ground. There's two tunnels connecting the basements of the assembly hall and the helicopter hangar and the clinic. They join under headquarters, and that's the start of the main finished tunnel."

"Where does the main tunnel go then?"

"Into the mountain. It's an old mine in there. Noah had it all reinforced and filled with supplies and—"

"Show me the entrance in the assembly hall. Now!"

She ran in spite of her swollen belly. The entrance was a trapdoor concealed in the floor. He had to move chairs to get to it. When he finally had it open he flicked the lighter and held the flame over the blackness. He noticed for the first time that a small red light was flashing from within the depressed button.

"What are you doing with a lighter?" she asked. "And why is it flashing like that?"

"It's not important," he said, lying on the floor so he could lean down in for a look.

"This isn't good, Alex. There's no shoring or anything."

"But when you get to the main tunnel it's concrete," she assured him. "They just didn't get all the rest of this done yet."

Concrete. Concrete. He should have guessed what they were up to. He leaped to his feet.

"Where's Hana?"

"Exercise time should have started. She'll be out—"

But he was running before she was finished.

Hana was near the rock. Doing calisthenics in a circle with some other girls under the guidance of a teenager in a rose-pink dress. She stepped out of the circle to speak to him.

"Daddy . . . I mean, Daniel," she said. "I'm not allowed to see you till it's visiting time."

He squatted down so that he could speak to her face-to-face.

"Hana, this is very important. Very important. I need you to stay right here at the rock until I come back for you. Will you promise me you'll do that?"

"Okay."

"Don't go anywhere else. I'll be right back for you."

Then he raced to the clinic, heart pounding wildly. He had no gun. No weapon of any kind. Everything was locked up or in the hands of the warriors. He entered the clinic quietly. It was empty. No patients. No nurse. He crept across the room to the open basement door and crouched to listen.

"Let's cut a titty off!" he heard Ammiel suggest.

Terror and adrenaline raced through him in equal measure. He gripped the lighter and swung down onto the stairs.

"Daniel," Noah called. "Come. You've earned a turn here."

She was naked and bloody, on her stomach—tied so that she was bent over a table. Her eyes were closed, but he could tell she was breathing.

"Come on and stick it to her," said Ira, wiping off his still tumescent penis and gingerly tucking it into his pants. "We're teaching her what a real man's seed feels like."

"No thanks," Dan said, telling himself to stay cool. Rape could be survived if she was strong-willed. And she had to be strong. She had to be a tough person or they wouldn't have sent her on this job. The main thing was to keep her alive and unmutilated. Why in the hell had they sent a woman? But then . . . if she'd been a man she would already be dead.

"He doesn't like sloppy seconds," Ammiel commented, laughing his weasel laugh. "And this is fifths."

"Noah," Dan said, holding out his hand with the lighter balanced on his palm. Surely the signal had been received by now. Surely he had waited long enough. Any longer and she would have been dead.

Noah took the lighter without comment. He studied it, turning it in his fingers. The red light was still flashing.

"Where did you get this, Daniel?"

"I found it on the ground near headquarters. It's hers, isn't it?"

"Yes."

Noah dropped the lighter to the floor and crushed it with his boot heel.

"Do you think that was a signal?" Dan asked.

Ammiel suddenly looked up at the ceiling. "They're on their way," he said. "The evil legions are coming to destroy us."

"What should we do?" Dan asked.

Noah grabbed Ira's gun and put it against the woman's temple.

"Wait!" Dan put his hand on the gun but didn't try to move it. "Couldn't we use her for a hostage? Maybe buy some time to get through the tunnels?"

Noah lowered the gun and regarded him with one of his penetrating stares.

"What do you know about the tunnels, Daniel?"

"I'm a builder, not a fool."

Noah maintained the stare for a long moment. "Yes. And you belong with me. You'll go into the tunnels with me." Then he turned to his men and ordered, "Get her up. Take her to headquarters and tie her to a porch post at the front door. They won't open fire with her in the way. And Ira, sound the drill alarm."

"I'll go get Hana and Jael," Dan said.

"Good." Noah's voice became a rapid-fire staccato. "Joab! Here's the key to the weapons room. Start arming the saviors as soon as you've tied her. Ammiel! You know what to do. All three. Make it fifty minutes."

Dan bolted up the stairs and caught up to Ira.

"What is the drill?" he asked.

"You're not authorized to know," Ira said.

Dan grabbed the front of his shirt. "This is *real*! People are going to die here. Now, if I'm to carry out Noah's orders I have to know what the drill is."

Only after he released the man did he realize that Ira had had his finger on the trigger of a gun pointed straight at his belly.

Ira frowned a moment, then lowered the gun. "Warriors and probationers go to headquarters, where they're to acquire extra weapons. Everyone takes shelter except the Saviors, who are armed and sent to the clinic to hold off the attack. I don't know where you fit in."

# Chapter 25

As Dan ran for his daughter he had the deep suspicion that he had not been told everything. That even with all the evil he knew about, there was still more. That perhaps the evil Noah embodied was infinite.

The compound had an air of curious expectancy due to the unusual behavior of the warriors, but there was no panic and no sign that people had been alerted to danger. Why hadn't Alex spread the warning? Then, just before he reached the rock, an alarm began blaring out of a speaker on the assembly hall. The little girls at the rock stopped their jumping jacks and turned to run.

"Wait!" Dan caught up to them. "Where's Hana?"

"Jael took her," the girls chorused before darting toward their quarters.

Frantically, Dan scanned the compound. People were running everywhere now. But oddly no one was running toward the tunnel entrances. They were all heading for their quarters. Swarming into them like bees into their hives. The women and children into the long older building and the men into the brand-new building that they had just moved into.

Dan spotted Elizabeth.

"Elizabeth!" he shouted as he ran to catch her. She stopped and waited for him.

"We've got to hurry, Daniel. There's punishment for not obeying drills."

"This isn't a drill, Elizabeth! The authorities are coming. With guns and God knows what else. I've got to find Hana!"

"She probably went with Jael."

"Into the tunnels?"

The girl's puzzled expression solidified his fears.

"You don't know about the tunnels, do you?" He looked up at all the running people heading dutifully into their quarters, where they would not be protected at all. "No one knows, do they?"

She was looking up at him with frightened eyes, and it came to him that she was his child, almost as much as Hana. She had been given into his care somehow.

"What does Jael do during the drill?" he demanded.

"She takes five chosen women to headquarters to support Noah and the warriors during the battle." Right. That was the lie. Noah had it set up so that his wife and five of the most desirable women would escape into the tunnels with him.

"Come with me," Dan ordered, grabbing the girl's wrist.

"I can't! I'll get in trouble if I'm not in my quarters by the time the alarm stops."

"I'm speaking with Noah's power!" he shouted. "And I order you to stay with me!"

He pulled her beside him as he raced toward the headquarters building. They were almost there when he heard a few far-off explosions. The perimeter land mines! Explosions that were hurting people. And then a buzzing. A droning. And the sky filled with the thumping and roaring of helicopters and the wind whipped and a voice boomed out over a microphone: "Untie the woman on the porch and drop all weapons! This is a direct order from—" The chatter of automatic weapons sounded from the gun ports at the concrete clinic, and one of the helicopters veered crazily and smashed to the ground in a flaming ball.

He stopped. Shocked by the crash. Suddenly overwhelmed by the horror and violence.

"Hurry!" screamed Jael. She was crouching just inside the door of the headquarters building, watching for him. Hana was clinging to her dress. "Hurry, Daddy!"

Hana's terror gripped him and he bolted for the porch. He leaped up the steps, past the naked woman bound to the porch post. Her terrified eyes followed him above her gag. "I'll be back," he promised as he passed her, still holding Elizabeth's wrist, though she no longer needed to be pulled along.

As he entered the hallway, Jael ran ahead into the audience room, calling, "He's here!"

Hana flew at him. He released Elizabeth to scoop her up, closing his eyes a moment and squeezing her tightly as she clung to him and sobbed into his shirt collar. The double doors labeled CLOSET stood open, and Dan saw an opened false back and a room filled with weapons, night scopes, gas masks, other tools of war. They had been there all the time. Right under his nose.

"Come on!" Jael called from inside the audience room.

He caught a glimpse of Ammiel rushing in from outside as he responded to Jael's call and took the two girls into the audience room. He expected Ammiel to be right behind him, but the man stayed behind in the hall.

Inside the audience room, near the entrance to the sanctum, was a cleverly constructed trapdoor, made so that it blended in with the pattern of wood planks in the floor. Noah was standing beside it. His eyes took in Dan, then Elizabeth. He frowned, impatient and irritated, but then he relented with a nod. "All right," he said, "but I'm allowing you to bring her only because I favor her, too."

Ammiel appeared then, agitated and sweating. "All set," he announced, consulting his watch, the only watch Dan had seen during his entire stay at the compound. "Men in thirty-two. Women in thirty-nine. Here in forty-five."

"Good." Noah smiled. "I hope that gives our visitors enough time to get here." He sat down on the edge of the tunnel opening. "I sent Ira and the other women ahead. Ammiel, you come with me. Zelek, you're in charge of Jael. Daniel, you're responsible for the girls." Then he dropped down into the tunnel and Ammiel followed immediately.

Holding Hana, Dan turned and ran for the hall.

"Dan!" Alex cried.

"Go on!" he called back. "I need a flashlight and a gun. Just go on and I'll be right behind you!"

"But Hana—"

"You heard Noah. The girls are my responsibility."

He put Hana down in the hall. Elizabeth had followed him and he pushed the girls together. "Crouch down against the wall! Don't move! Not for anyone!"

Then he ran into the weapons room, pocketed two flashlights, and wrested the bayonet from a rifle. He rushed out onto the porch, into the hellish bursts of noise and flame, and he cut the woman loose.

She ripped off her gag and together they dived back inside the doorway.

"I'm sorry," he said, aware that it was inadequate but needing to say something.

She shook her head, then closed her eyes and hugged herself, her body racked by shudders.

"Rina . . ." he said softly, then, "Rina!"

Her eyes jerked open. They were wide and blank. She looked around as though lost. Her gaze snagged on Hana and Elizabeth huddled together on the floor in stunned horror. The sight of the girls seemed to reach her, sparking something in her eyes. She drew in several deep breaths and transformed herself into a crouching, sharp-eyed professional.

"Weapons?" she said, and he knew immediately what she wanted.

"There's guns and clothes in this building," Dan told her. "I don't know how your people plan to get you safely out of here, but I'm not trusting them with my daughter's or Elizabeth's life."

"What choice do you have?" Rina demanded.

"Noah has an escape tunnel. I'm going, too. I'll figure out how to get free from him after we're safely away from all this."

Rina's shoulders sagged. "It wasn't supposed to go down this way," she said.

"Come on, Dan!" he heard Alex call frantically.

"I'm coming!"

The woman had spotted the open door to the weapons room and darted down the hall toward it. Dan pulled the girls to their feet. He leaned over slightly to swing the petrified Hana into his arms and caught sight of something odd. On the floor, hidden slightly by the open door of the weapons room, was an object.

Holding Hana, he crossed the floor to it. Even without ever having seen such an object he knew immediately what it was. And suddenly Ammiel's announcement made sense. "Men in thirty-two. Women in thirty-nine. Here in forty-five." Because what he was looking at was a bomb.

A bomb. That's what Noah was talking about when he said that he hoped his visitors had time to get there. He hoped the authorities got caught in the blast. But even if they didn't, everyone else was to be sacrificed. All of his loyal followers were to be blown to bits while Noah and his chosen survivors fled secretly to safety under the ground.

Dan couldn't let it happen. But how was he going to stop it? And what about the girls?

Alex was wringing her hands and standing just beside the entrance to the tunnel when he rushed the girls back into the room. Zelek was beside her.

"Hurry!" she cried.

"Go on," Dan told Zelek. "Climb down and I'll hand Jael and the girls to you."

Zelek climbed down. Dan set Hanʹa on the floor. Alex held out her arms to him in preparation for descending. He took hold of her and pulled her close.

"Did you know?" he asked softly.

"What?" She looked at him with those beautiful softly starred eyes.

"About your mother?"

"That she died from her filthy smoking habit? Yes. I knew."

"How about the bombs?"

Her smooth brow furrowed. "Bombs?"

"Come on!" shouted Zelek from below. "They're way ahead of us."

Just then Rina burst in wearing one of Noah's long gray robes and holding a machine gun. Alex screamed and the woman pointed the weapon at her, shouting, "Freeze! Hands over your head!" Dan shielded Alex with his body and pushed her down into the hole, hoping Zelek would break her fall.

"Dan!" Alex cried as he slammed the trapdoor back into place and moved to stand on it. There was pounding from below.

"Get out of my way!" Rina ordered, discharging a burst of fire into the wall, then leveling the gun on him.

"What are you going to do?" he asked. "Go into that tunnel and capture them all by yourself?" The pounding beneath his feet had stopped.

"Out of my way! Those bastards! I'm killing those bastards."

The gun shook as she started to cry.

"Don't go to pieces now, Rina. You need to stay tough. There are bombs. Those bastards you want to kill deserve it, but hundreds of people are going to die. Little kids. Men and women who've never held a gun or threatened anyone. Noah is sacrificing them all. He's got bombs set to go off in the quarters."

She frowned at him in confusion. "You're not going down into the tunnels?"

"I can't. Not knowing about the bombs."

He could see her mind clicking. Suddenly she lowered the gun.

"I don't know anything about bombs," she said, "except that novices shouldn't try to disarm them."

"We have to get everyone out, then."

"Jesus! To where? Those psychos holed up in the torture building are firing at everything, and with this mess I can't guarantee that my guys will do any less."

Dan gripped his head in his hands. "The telephone!"

She seized his meaning immediately and they both rushed to the sanctum. The computer was gone but the phone was still there. Immediately she began dialing.

"I don't know how long it will take to get through to the right people," she warned.

He closed the heavy wooden shutters over the window and called the girls into the sanctum as Rina spoke a few sentences and then screamed, "I know they're busy with an emergency situation. I'm in the middle of it! All right . . . just patch me through to someone!"

"Stay over here," he said to the girls, indicating the inner wall. "Rina is your friend. She's going to be talking on the phone. You stay here till I come back. Or . . . you do what she says."

"What are you going to do?" the woman asked with her ear to the phone.

"I'm going to warn everyone in the buildings."

She looked incredulous. "How? With all that firing from the clinic you won't make it. And if you do . . . how can people escape from the buildings when their own men are out there shooting everything?"

He considered this as he raced for the weapons room. He knew nothing about firearms but things were familiar thanks to years of movie watching. He grabbed a wicked-looking small machine gun, two grenades, and an extra flashlight. Then he rushed back to the trapdoor and opened it.

He could hear Rina on the phone, arguing with someone. Then suddenly she appeared in the sanctum doorway with the phone cord stretched and her hand over the speaker.

"Where are you going?" she demanded.

"Backwards," he said. "If the tunnel goes from the clinic to headquarters, then I should be able to follow it from headquarters back to the clinic. I'll stop the firing and then get the people out."

The tunnel was dark and cool and smelled of earth. He clicked on the light and moved as swiftly as he could in a hunched position, picturing the layout of the compound, knowing that the first trapdoor he came to would lead into the helicopter shed and the second would be into the clinic. He found it easily. Because it led into a basement it was a vertical door. He opened it and was inside the torture chamber. Above him he could hear the intermittent discharge of guns. A jolt of intense fear struck him and he wondered what he was doing there. He didn't believe in killing, he didn't believe in violence, yet there he was. Could he point a gun at another human being and squeeze the trigger? Could he pull the pin on one of those grenades?

Heart slamming against his rib cage, he crept up the stairs and opened the trapdoor a crack. It would be easy to simply roll a grenade inside. But then he heard their frightened voices.

"Should we keep firing, Nathan?" There was a muffled sob. "Why is this happening?"

He knew them! The "saviors" Noah had assigned to fire blindly from the clinic's gun ports were men from his building crew.

He pushed the door open farther, shouting, "It's Daniel!"

The firing stopped.

"Daniel?" a voice called.

"Yes. Noah sent me. I'm coming up."

They all stared at him as he climbed out. The faces were so well known to him. Nathan and Caleb and Jacob and several teenagers whose names he didn't recall. Every one of the men in the room had worked with him on the building.

"What's happening, Daniel? Are we winning or losing?"

"It's over. They've surrendered."

All the men except Nathan cried out and dropped their guns, some sinking to their knees in relief.

Nathan was frowning and still clutching his machine gun. "If they've surrendered then why are those men out there?"

Dan moved to a gun port and looked out. A phalanx of men was visible on the outer edge of the clearing, moving slowly behind a metal barrier.

"Noah has it under control," he assured them, praying that Rina had established contact. "We've got to hurry. There's a tunnel leading out of the basement. Leave your weapons and follow me. You'll be safe."

Dan went back down the stairs into the torture room. Caleb started down after him. Shy, puppy-eager Caleb, who had never known anything but foster homes in his nineteen years and who thought he'd found a real home in The Ark.

Suddenly Nathan yelled, "No! We're the Saviors. Our mission is to stay here until Noah releases us."

Caleb stopped, his lower body on the stairs and his head and shoulders still in the room above. He looked down at Dan longingly then back up.

"I don't want to die here, Nathan!" Dan heard someone in the room above cry out and there was the sound of footsteps, as though everyone had decided to run for the stairs and then Caleb looked back down at Dan and his face exploded. Shots and screams sounded above, and then quiet. Then a single set of footsteps.

"Daniel."

It was Nathan's voice. Nathan had butchered them all for Noah, sacrificed them all for The Ark and for Noah's lies and Noah's vision, and now he was after Dan. To kill again. And he would not stop killing, not until he was unable to pull the trigger.

Dan jerked the pins from both grenades and lobbed them upward through the trapdoor and into the room, then he turned and lunged into the tunnel. He ran blindly. When the concussion hit, clods rained down on him and a portion of the tunnel behind him collapsed. He curled into a protective position, fearing that the entire tunnel would go. But it didn't. So he ran on. To the end. The entrance to the assembly hall. And from there outside. Into an eerie silence with the clinic flaming and the helicopter wreckage still smoldering. He ran to the men's quarters because it was closest.

He burst in through the door shouting. There were men crouched everywhere, some covering their heads and some muttering to themselves.

"Get up! Get out! There's a bomb in here!"

No one moved.

Dan ran to a man he recognized. Mark, the electrician. He grabbed the man by the shirtfront and shook him. "There's a bomb in here! Get everyone out!"

"We'll get in trouble if we leave before the all clear. It's a bad punishment to leave during drill."

"This isn't a drill!"

The man stared at him as though he were speaking in a foreign tongue.

Dan backed away. It was hopeless. The children. He had to at least get the children out.

He turned and ran out, headed to the women's quarters. No one was in sight. He raced to the sleeping rooms and found them huddled together in groups, some crying, some praying.

"Out! You have to all get out of this building. There's a bomb in here. Noah wants you to get out." They stared at him. A few moved, but it was clear they were uncertain.

"There's been no all-clear siren for the drill," a small voice said.

He pointed the machine gun at them. "Out now! Round up the children and bring them."

It worked. They stirred. Slowly at first and then more

rapidly, surging toward the hallways and right up to the front door. But he could not get them to step outside.

"This building is going to blow up in just minutes. You'll all be killed."

"How do we know you're not possessed by a demon?" asked the very levelheaded nurse he had seen in the clinic.

Minutes. Minutes. That's all he had left. Minutes before all these people died. He pushed his way through them to the door and ran for headquarters. Ran till he thought his heart might explode. Pushing himself. Pumping his legs. He heard the crack of a gunshot. Then the air was filled with staccato firing again. Something slammed into his thigh and he fell.

"No! No!" he heard Rina screaming. And then she was bending over him in those ridiculous robes.

"The drill alarm . . ." He clutched her shoulders and pulled himself up.

"What are you doing?" she cried, but she supported him as he moved forward, blackness crowding his vision, shaking his head to fight it.

Up the steps and across the porch. Into the sanctum. There it was among the labeled buttons on the wall behind Noah's desk.

"What?" Rina asked again.

He lunged forward, leg dragging, and he slammed the switch to On. Just before he passed out he heard the blast of the drill alarm sound through the compound, signaling the all-clear.

# Chapter 26

He dreamed of Laura. He dreamed that he was dead. He opened his eyes and saw a face.

"Hello."

He blinked several times to bring the face into focus and finally recognized Rina, though this was not the Rina with the teased hair and the chewing gum. This was a polished and professional Rina.

"Hello, Rina."

"It's actually Katrina."

"Okay." He swallowed against the dryness in his mouth. "Where am I?" But then he saw that he was once again in a hospital and he tried to laugh. "It's a good sign."

"What?"

"The hospital," he said, meaning it as a joke. If he was in the hospital then he wasn't dead.

She smiled. "I think you're a little woozy from the anesthetic."

"Hana!" He was suddenly, sharply aware.

"She's fine." Katrina put her hand on his arm. "And so's Elizabeth. They're right downstairs with Laura."

"Laura is here? You know Laura?"

"Yes. She was the one who pushed for getting an agent—me—into the cult to check on you." She hesitated. "I'm supposed to call my boss and the doctors the minute you wake up. And I could call Laura . . ."

"Wait. Please. How many people got out?"

"Most of them. It was amazing. They filed out into the open like little automatons as soon as you hit that buzzer. But there was so much flying debris when the blasts came; some people were killed by it even though they were outside."

He closed his eyes for a moment. So many images. So much blood and brutality.

"Did they catch him?"

Her face clouded. "There were explosions inside the mountain. Teams went in but the tunnels are sealed now with tons of rock. He's got to be underneath it . . . but nothing could be verified." She glanced toward the door nervously. "I shouldn't really tell you any more until you've been debriefed."

"Did they catch any of them?"

"The man and the five women who went into the tunnels ahead of Noah. They were caught coming out of an opening on the other side of the mountain."

Conflicting emotions warred within him. To wish Noah dead meant that he was also wishing Alex dead. And could he, now that the nightmare was behind him, could he, from his position of safety and normalcy, could he wish anyone dead? Even Noah? He studied the oversized form of his leg beneath the blanket.

"Where am I?"

"This is a secured facility. We're keeping your survival a secret for now."

"A secret?"

"Until the raids on all the compounds are complete. Just as a precaution."

He tried to think through the ramifications of that but it required too much mental energy. "I had surgery, huh?"

"They sewed muscles and veins and whatever back together and a plastic surgeon patched up the chunk that was missing."

"Chunk?" he winced and reached for the pitcher of water beside his bed.

"Let me," she insisted. After she had poured the water she held it out to him, chewing on her bottom lip, eyes darting away from him and then back. "Dan . . . I didn't report it."

He looked at her quizzically.

"What happened before you came down into the torture room. I couldn't. If I tell them it changes me, it changes everyone's perception of me, it changes my life. This way it's a nightmare that I can learn how to forget."

He handed her his glass and lay back, closing his eyes for a second.

"I don't know what you're talking about," he said. "I guess I'm still too woozy. I don't know what happened to you before I got down there."

She sucked her lips in and blinked hard. "Thanks."

The debriefing lasted for hours. They pried every kernel of memory from his brain and then packed up their tapes and notes in preparation for leaving. He was exhausted by then but demanded answers. That was when he learned the full story. Joha, who was really Agent Vance, had survived. He had been found near the disabled helicopter, had been rushed to surgery, and was now in serious but stable condition.

They told him that Vance had been in place for three months when Dan arrived at the compound and had not had contact with the outside for thirty days. The mountains had caused problems with his communication device from the beginning and then it had completely failed. Several attempts had been made at sending in a contact agent but all had been unsuccessful. When Vance infiltrated The Ark it was assumed that a man with his training would be able to slip out of the compound at will, but that had not proved to be true. It had also been assumed at that time that they were dealing with fairly basic crimes—illegal weapons and suspected manufacture of controlled substances.

Vance had revealed his martial arts training and become a warrior to be closer to Noah and gain information. He had also sought warrior status so that he could eventually be given a mission and a trip out of the compound with the opportunity to give a full report and get new orders. Everything he had seen and heard confirmed for him that The Ark was involved in the expected paramilitary-style legal violations.

That changed when he was promoted from a probationary warrior to a full warrior. He became a member of the inner circle and was entrusted with Noah's true goals. He learned that underneath all Noah's rhetoric was the belief that humans had run amok on the earth and that there had to be a brand-new start. A "cleansing" that would drastically reduce the earth's population and leave Noah and his warriors in control.

In pursuit of his goal Noah had investigated many types of mass extermination. He'd experimented with the manufacture of drugs, intending to taint them so that addicts were killed in large numbers. This had not proven practical, but he had made vast sums of money selling designer drugs. He then experimented with poisons, using several prison water supplies as tests. That and Sarin, the same poison gas that the Japanese cult had made famous, were both promising but not ideal. There were too many problems with the dispensing of the poisons.

Then Noah was stricken with the purest and simplest of plans. Nature could do the cleansing. Nature was more fierce and uncompromising than any human act could ever be. With just a little help from Noah, nature could wipe out all the unsuitable humans on the earth in one mighty plague. And—a few disgruntled scientists and a lot of money later—he had the perfect biological weapon: a virus that spread rapidly; a virus that no one except his chosen would have immunity against; a virus that killed its host in record time.

When he learned all this, Agent Vance became desperate to get out, but he was not senior enough to be chosen for the mission to bring back Dan and there were no other missions in the immediate future. He tried several escape attempts and came very close to being caught. He had no idea when a contact agent would manage to penetrate compound security and he carried this terrible burden of knowledge, aware that the agency had no idea of the enormity of Noah's ambitions, aware that if he failed to get the truth out, or if he was killed before he could get it out, the world might not be warned in time.

Because he was in the inner circle he was present at conversations about Dan. He knew the whole story and he knew that Noah had never been certain about Dan—that Noah was using Dan and had great admiration for him but that he did not trust him. Vance watched Dan. He sent a note to test him. And then, because he was desperate, he decided to try making Dan his ally.

In the meantime the agency had arrested Cody Conrad for illegal arms dealing and learned that the dealer had done business in the past with Noah. They used Conrad to set up a deal in which Katrina would go along as a contact for Agent Vance. Katrina was only supposed to make contact with Vance and slip him the emergency beacon. The agency team that was put in place had been assembled with plenty of equipment but with a long-term siege in mind, not an immediate attack.

Katrina knew all about Dan Behr and the kidnapping of his child, but she did not know if Noah had managed to brainwash him. As soon as she was inside the headquarters building she saw Vance on guard at the back door, so she asked to use the bathroom in the hall and she staged an upset with Joab to get Vance's attention and signal him as to her identity. When Dan appeared they were in the process of trying to get rid of Joab so that they could speak freely. Through codes Vance indicated to her that Dan was trustworthy, but they did not get an opportunity to exchange information before she and Dan were both called into the sanctum.

Then Noah's booted computer was left alone in the sanctum and the opportunity was too perfect for her to ignore. She knew she was pushing her luck. She couldn't get to Agent Vance, so she slipped the beacon to Dan for safety, then she set herself up to go back into the sanctum and pry into the computer. The very first file she opened had information on poisoning water supplies and details about the prison experiments. This was big. This was urgent. And the modem was already connected for her so she initiated a transmit. And then was caught.

The rest Dan knew.

After they were all gone he lay alone in the quiet room and replayed the story in his mind. He had always believed that evil was a distinct and identifiable thing. Even with all that was recorded about the banality of evil he had still thought that the truly big and all-encompassing evils of the world would stand out. That he would be immediately aware and on guard. Ready to fight if necessary. Ready to stand up for what was right. Yet, there he had been, in the midst of it, and he had been blind. Noah's evil had been so great that it was nearly incomprehensible. It was the stuff of myths. The stuff of Revelations. The stuff of horror and science fiction. And yet, the man had been close to him . . . had gripped his hand and looked into his eyes, and he had had no instinctual sense of that evil. He had had no gut recognition.

Was that a fault or a lack of something deep within him? A personal failing? Or were all people susceptible to the seduction of evil, just as they were susceptible to Noah's mutant deadly virus?

Laura came in while he was napping. He woke to find her sitting beside the bed.

"Hi," he said.

"Hi," she answered.

He felt awkward and uncertain.

"I'm sorry. I know you went through hell worrying."

She smiled, mostly with her eyes, absolving and understanding, filling him, purifying him, lifting him from the darkness and bathing him with light.

"It's all over," she said.

But it would never be over. Didn't anyone see that? If Noah was gone there would be another Noah. Because evil was inherent. Noah had not started out evil; the evil had grown within him. And the possibility of evil was in everyone, waiting like the tiny germ of a cancerous cell, waiting to blossom and devour everything good and healthy. That was why people found it so difficult to recognize and confront evil, because it was natural. Because it was familiar. Because it didn't descend in a gray miasma or burst into view with fiery breath. Evil was always there, beneath the good, beneath the normal, within the heart of every person, waiting for power to spark it to life, waiting within the heart of every politician or business tycoon or religious leader. Always there. Waiting.

And he saw that he had come to a crossroads in his life. Could he put everything behind him—not just his descent into the underworld and the visions of suffering and death that had been seared into his inner eye but also his former self; the Dan Behr who needed to be the savior, who needed desperation in order to feel passion, who was so dazzled by extreme physical beauty that he had never learned to see the allure of inner grace? Could he begin anew, scoured clean and ready for a different history?

"It's not over," he said. "But I think that knowing . . . understanding and accepting . . . gives us the best weapon to fight it."

A great regret came into her eyes, and he realized that she had tried to protect him from learning what she had known all along. And he saw with a sudden burst of clarity that the difference between his relationships with Alex and Laura was like the gulf between a cult and a religion. One was nurturing and generous and freeing. The other was self-serving, greedy, and enslaving.

"Would you consider getting married?" he asked.

"In general or to you?"

"To me."

"I don't have to consider it." She grinned. "The answer is yes."

# Chapter 27

Good times and bad times followed in Dan Behr's struggle to put the past behind and make a new life. He was determined to be happy, and most of the time he was. But the memories were there. The knowledge was there.

He took a new apartment with Laura in Bay Ridge despite the fact that both of them would have to commute to Manhattan. Bay Ridge was home for Hana, and it still felt like a haven even though Dan knew that there were no real havens.

Once in a while both he and Laura were called in to consult on the investigation of a new cult. To his dismay he was considered an expert now, even though he was honest about how close he'd come to falling permanently under Noah's spell. He didn't want to have anything to do with cults, but he knew that he had to. Because now he truly was one of the awakened, and so he had to be a sentinel. He had to protect those who didn't or couldn't see.

After a simple wedding the three of them took a vacation together and then settled into a routine, he at Columbia, Hana in second grade, and Laura with her practice. On Hana's eighth birthday he awoke early feeling particularly good, particularly grateful to be alive. He slipped out of bed without waking Laura and went to the kitchen to make a surprise breakfast of raspberry pancakes—Hana's favorite.

As he prepared the birthday breakfast he thought about his daughter and how quickly she was growing up. Love for his child filled him. He worried sometimes that he might not be able to protect her from all the evil that he now knew was out there in the world waiting. But the evil had always been there. He just hadn't been aware. Now he knew. Now he was on guard. And he would protect her and teach her to protect herself. Just as worrisome were the other challenges he faced as a parent. Could he nurture her and guide her through the world without letting himself or any outside force extinguish her unique spirit? Could he teach her gentleness and cooperation yet still nourish her fierce independence and her stubborn inquisitiveness? Could he raise her to be strong and centered and at ease with herself? Could he raise her to be a woman like Laura?

The thought surprised him, but he realized that it was true. He would consider his parenting a success if his daughter grew to be a woman just like Laura.

The phone rang. He answered it only to hear the click of a hang-up, which didn't surprise him because it was probably a wrong number. They never got calls that early in the morning.

When the pancakes were almost ready, he nuzzled Laura awake and then they went together to wake the birthday girl. Hana was pleased with the attention.

They were seated at the table when the phone rang again. Laura went for it this time.

When she came back, she shrugged and said, "They must have dialed a wrong number because there was someone there but they hung up. Who makes phone calls at seven in the morning anyway?"

The phone rang again when Laura was in the shower and Dan in the bedroom. He headed out to the living room to answer, feeling a twinge of annoyance now and ready to tell someone off. Hana had already picked it up. She was listening intently, her expression rapt.

"Who is it, punkin?" he asked, assuming that the call was for him or Laura since Hana's social set did not use the phone yet.

Her eyes lifted to him, but she didn't answer.

"Hana . . . is it Felice?" That was the only person she had phone conversations with, and they were usually conversations that preceded a request to speak to an adult.

She still didn't respond to him. She just stood there. Entranced.

"Hana!"

A chill passed through him, and he grabbed the phone

from her and put it to his own ear. Breathing. Soft breathing with a sort of catch in it, as though the person were crying.

"Who is this!" he demanded.

Immediately there was the click of the disconnect.

"I think it was Mommy," Hana said sadly. "She must miss me on my birthday."

# ACKNOWLEDGMENTS

The people to whom I owe the greatest debt are those I have promised not to name—the cult victims who shared their pain with me. Thank you all for your help and your trust. And thank you to the professionals who offered insight but asked to remain anonymous.

My gratitude goes also to those I am privileged to name:

Francisco (Frank) Rodriquez of the University of Oklahoma, who was so generous with his personal experiences and research.

Detective Danny Massanova of the NYPD and his gracious commanding officer, Lieutenant Andy Eanniello. And New York's finest—Ray Pierce of the Criminal Assessment and Profiling Unit.

The American Family Foundation and Marsha Rudin at the International Cult Education Project.

The now defunct (sued into bankruptcy) Cult Awareness Network.

Joseph Szimhart, who has courageously devoted himself to helping others free their minds and souls from cults.

Priscilla Coates, formerly of the Cult Awareness Network, who has worked so tirelessly as an advocate for cult victims.

And of course Audrey, who is so entitled, Aaron, who makes wishes come true, and Michael, who keeps it all real.

If you enjoyed *Thief of Souls*, you won't
want to miss Darian North's stunning new
thriller about a woman who survives the worst
kind of brutality, only to lose her beloved son
as a consequence of the secrets she's tried
to keep from him. Thus begins this powerful,
disturbing, complex, and deeply provocative
novel, as a woman's love for her son must
override her fear of the world, and the
inner courage she discovers is the
greatest gift of all. . . .

## *VIOLATION*
### by Darian North

Turn the page
for an exciting early preview. . . .

A Dutton hardcover on sale in September

## THE PAST

She fought him, pleading and screaming when her mouth was uncovered, scratching when she could and even biting. Terror had stripped away seventeen years of music lessons and manners, scoured away the cultured layers of female behavior, and seared away eons of human civilization, paring her down to one basic need—survival. But the pain eclipsed even that. It howled in her head, banging and clawing at her skull from the inside so that instinct failed, reducing the primitive signals in her brain to neural electrical storms.

Now and then a wisp of thought drifted in.

*Is he gone?*

But the thoughts were almost without meaning because her brain could neither analyze nor record them.

*Am I dying?*

Consciousness slipped. Then she was aware of movement and fresh explosions of pain as she was carried outside and laid on the ground. Her cheek brushed remnants of bone and fur where feral dogs had torn apart a rabbit some weeks earlier. She smelled soil, grass and dry weeds, the faint musk of decay. Her eyes were open to the moonless sky, and the penetrating darkness made her shiver. Pinpricks of light stared down at her. The earth soaked up her blood. And her last conscious human act was a dawning of recognition, an acceptance. She was alone. Like the rabbit.

## THE PRESENT

Spring. Finally. A day to banish the chill of a long snowy winter and rainy April, sky a crystalline blue, sun coaxing everything to life and penetrating muscle and bone so that he too was touched with renewal, transformed into someone less morose and more energetic than the thirty-seven-year-old wreck of an ex-cop that he was. He had been inspired to run sprints or do bench presses but, having access to neither track nor weights, he had settled for backyard destruction. His object was a large dead thing. His weapon was an ax. And to accompany the effort he had carried out the portable CD player loaded with supreme versions of Tchaikovsky's Fourth and Fifth Symphonies.

He chopped. The sun and the music fueled him. He was a powerful, blissfully mindless machine. Rhythmic, strong, and smooth. After a while his muscles began to burn and a dull ache marked the path of the bullet through his back. It was good. Very, very good. One of the best days he'd had in a very long time.

But such a thought begs to be doused in cold water so he was not surprised when the doorbell sounded faintly over the music. His swing faltered and the fine mood was broken. The bell rang again. Ignoring it, he tried to recapture his chopping rhythm. There were no drop-in acquaintances in this life he'd made and he was not in the market for magazines, cookies, or religion. Packages could be left on the porch. Eureka was still a place where things could be left on porches. So let them ring, whoever they were, and then let them go away.

Some minutes passed and he thought he had escaped.

"Jack! Are you back there?"

Something between a groan and a growl rumbled in his throat. Just what he needed. A surprise visit from the remora.

The boy appeared at the corner of the house, apparently having wrestled his way through the collapsing side gate. Newly thirteen, he was awkward and uncertain, bearing a defensive mantle. Everything about him—ragged clothes, lank sandy hair, slouched shoulders—was designed to convey an attitude of disregard. He was a poster boy for "I don't give a shit," yet his eyes said just the opposite. And it was the kid's eyes that held Jack, that kept him from crushing the boy's attentions and that kept him from saying "Get lost" now.

Scanning the yard the boy came up with a toneless "Wow." It was not complimentary.

Annoyed, both by the disturbance and by the fact that the kid had obviously decided he could waltz in uninvited, Jack lowered the ax blade, turned down the music, and gave the kid a serious scowl. "You aren't cutting school, are you?"

"Early dismissal today," the boy answered, toeing the earth with his worn athletic shoe.

"Don't they have a bus on early dismissal days?"

The boy shrugged. "I didn't get on it."

Damn, the kid was irritating. Jack mopped his forehead with

his shirtsleeve, catching a whiff of the scotch that had put him to sleep the night before. What did the kid want from him, anyway? Did he think he could blow off the bus and then con a ride?

"How are you getting home?"

Again the shrug, this time indicating that getting home was not a concern. The kid had a million shrugs with subtle meanings, but all were rooted in indifference. A giant all-encompassing indifference. He was the king of indifference. Well, two could play that game. Jack hefted the ax and attacked the gnarled base of the monster again.

After a long wordless stretch the boy finally said, "That was a really old rhododendron."

A rhododendron. It was just like David to know that. The boy was a walking encyclopedia on the natural and scientific, though he seldom chose to reveal that side of himself.

"Did you kill it?" the boy asked.

"No. Why would I kill it?"

Another infuriating shrug.

Jack chopped. He continued to hack at the dead monster until his arm muscles cried for relief and each swing was forced out of sheer willpower. As long as the boy was there watching he could not allow himself to quit.

"When you were a policeman, did you learn a lot about lying?" the boy asked suddenly.

Jack let his swing fall flat and the ax head thunked into the ground. He was so relieved at the excuse to stop that he was not irritated by the question, but he frowned anyway, just for the sake of appearance.

The boy hunched into himself and looked down so that his hair fell forward and obscured half his face. "I mean, did you have to know why people lied and what the lies meant?"

What the hell was this about?

"That was part of the job," he answered carefully. "Sure. Recognizing lies . . . deciphering lies . . . outsmarting liars. A detective needs a Ph.D. in BS." And, he added to himself, a detective needs to be the best liar of all.

The boy nodded as though this confirmed what he had already believed, and Jack saw that he was struggling. There was something big on David's mind, some major problem just beneath those shrugs, and he was dangerously close to dumping the problem right there in Jack's backyard. Great. He'd

had to put up with the kid tagging after him when he was doing the landlord-handyman routine and he had even put up
with having the kid *help* on weekend projects but he was not
going to let a drop-in-anytime habit develop and he sure as
hell wasn't about to start playing child psychologist.

He squinted up at the sky as though he could read the time
there. "I need to get this finished," he said. "Don't you have
homework or something?"

He might as well have said, *What's the trouble, son?* the way
the boy the looked up at him, brow furrowed in determination
and facial muscles fighting against a display of emotion.

"Why would someone lie about everything in their past—
where they're from and where they went to school and even
who they were married to and everything?"

Jack sighed and considered the question, apprehensive
about where it led. "The person could be hiding. Or they
could be ashamed. Or they could be evil scum." He mopped
his forehead again. "A lot depends on who's doing the lying."

In a voice so low that it barely carried, the boy said, "It's
my mother."

Christ. Didn't they have school counselors for this kind of
thing? Jack leaned the ax against the pile of amputated limbs.

"What makes you think she's been lying?"

Another shrug.

Jack's own mother had been far too sensual and flamboyant
for him when he was young. During adolescence he had become fervently convinced that he was adopted and had spent
nearly a year trying to persuade his brother and the twins. And
this kid certainly had a reason for maternally inspired denial
because Thea Auben was a genuine pain in the neck and even
loonier than most women. But then again, she'd always
seemed like a pretty good parent.

"You know, David, detectives working a case can get a
feeling, a gut instinct, and it can really grab hold of them—
but that doesn't mean it's always one hundred percent right.
Sometimes it can be dead wrong."

"This isn't like that," the boy insisted. "I mean I have
had—" shrug—"feelings and questions. Stuff I wondered
about and couldn't understand. But this is all true stuff."

"Factual, you mean? Based on concrete evidence?"

A nod.

Jack frowned, clicked off the music, and started toward the house. Halfway across the yard he glanced back. "You coming?"

He led through the back door into the mud room. While he washed, the boy studied the rack of fishing equipment along the far wall.

"Interested in fishing?" Jack asked, glancing over his shoulder as he toweled off his arms.

The boy's answering shrug caused Jack's irritation level to shoot upward. "You like fishing or not?" he snapped.

"Never tried it," the boy admitted grudgingly.

Jesus. No wonder the kid was a mess. Here he was living in the heart of redwood country where the fish practically jumped out of the cold clear-running streams to take a hook, and he'd never been fishing. What a crime. He thought about how he'd learned to fish under the watchful eye of his father, how he'd been given a special kid-size rod and reel at around the same time he was given his first pony saddle. This boy had not had such opportunities. His father had died before he was born. And there were no uncles or grandfathers taking up the slack.

"I suppose you haven't had lunch."

"I'm not hungry."

"Me either, but it's past lunchtime and we're going to eat."

He moved through the kitchen and the boy's eyes followed him. That was where the hunger was—not in the belly but in the eyes. If he could only avoid those eyes.

"You planning to give me a hand here, or just watch?"

"What do you want me to do?"

"Get glasses. Find something you want to drink. Pour me tea out of that pitcher in the refrigerator. And be careful. Don't move any cards."

The boy stared down at the lines of cards and the pages of tallied scores on the kitchen table.

"That's solitaire, isn't it? My mom plays solitaire on the computer."

"Solitaire on the computer?" Jack shook his head at the thought, thinking about the feel of the cards as he lays them out, the snap if it's a new deck, the slickness beneath his fingertips. None of those satisfactions would exist on a computer. "What does it do," he asked, "show each hand like a picture?"

"Yeah. It's just up there. You click and it's instant."

"But you miss laying out the hand, creating the pattern, seeing the numbers and the connections as they fall. . . ."

The kid looked at him as though he'd suddenly started talking about receiving alien radio waves through his teeth.

"Here." He handed the boy a paper plate barely supporting a hot microwaved burrito.

They ate standing at the kitchen counter. Jack hoped there would be no further discussion of lies or mothers, and there wasn't. The boy focused on his food in complete silence, eyes downcast and shoulders hunched. Which was fine because Jack had had enough adolescent angst or whatever it was. He consumed his burrito without tasting it then watched the boy take one slow, resigned bite after another.

"All right. What evidence do you have?"

The boy exhaled as though he'd been holding his breath. "There's no record of my mother being born where she says she was. There's no record of her going to school where she says she did. She doesn't exist in any data bases. And there are no birth or death records for my father, either. Or a record of their marriage."

Jack was momentarily taken aback. "How did you come up with all this?"

Another shrug. "Research. I got a book called *The Computer Detective*. It's pretty easy."

"Does your mother know what you've been doing?"

"No."

"You've come up with all negatives. You have an absence of evidence rather than evidence."

"So?"

"You have no proof of anything. All you know is that you can't find the data. That usually indicates a problem with the investigative techniques."

The boy's expression was openly skeptical.

"From what I understand about computers, one tiny glitch, even a misspelling, can throw everything off."

"Yeah," the boy agreed reluctantly.

"You could ask your mother why you can't find the information."

"No!"

Jack studied the kid's face, wondering whether the note of panic was the result of secrets kept or pride threatened. "What got you started on this anyway?"

"I . . ." Red crept into the boy's cheeks and he immediately looked down. "I was talking to a friend and he got me thinking." He shrugged. "I was already bothered by stuff. I mean my mom never wants to answer my questions and she's always changing the subject or trying to distract me. And when I think back to stories my grandma told me—they don't make sense."

"Like what?"

"Just stuff she said when she was in the hospital."

"Your grandmother could have been mixed up. Sick people get confused."

"Yeah, but there were lots of other things . . . little things. And why don't we have more pictures from before I was born? Why don't we have pictures of my dad. We have one old beat-up picture of him in this group of guys where you can barely see his face."

"Again, that's an absence of evidence. It doesn't prove anything."

"Maybe. But it's weird."

"Not necessarily. Things get lost during moves or destroyed in fires and floods. Then again, some people are savers and some aren't. You won't find much memorabilia in my house, but that doesn't mean I'm lying about my past."

"You don't lie, you just won't talk about it."

Jack threw his plate in the trash, ignoring the remark. "I think you're jumping to conclusions." He held up a hand, ticking off points on his fingers as he went through them. "You could have a problem in your computer search methods. Your grandmother could have been confused and disoriented when she was sick. Keepsakes could have been lost or destroyed. And . . . if you look at it from your mother's point of view . . . Could be she's trying to avoid the past because she doesn't like to be reminded of your father's death."

The boy responded with a one-shouldered unconvinced shrug.

"Let face it," Jack said, attempting to lighten the conversation. "All adults are a little weird."

"My mother's majorly weird."

Jack got out the pitcher of cold tea for a refill, thinking of Thea. From what he had seen he might have described her as a control freak or a neatnik but he wouldn't have described her as weird. She had books alphabetized by author and canned goods alphabetized by contents, her son's medical and dental checkups on the calendar months in advance, and a magnetic grocery list on the refrigerator with the items listed according to the aisle they were on in the store. He had never glimpsed the inside of her bedroom but he would have bet big money that the linens matched and the bed was made every day. But then, maybe all that was weird to a thirteen-year-old. No. David had neatnik tendencies himself so that wasn't the source. Yet, in spite of his defending her to her son, he has sensed something underneath all that organized efficiency and shy reserve, something elusive, something that had intrigued him from the beginning, pricking at his cop's instincts as well as his male ones. Could there be a deep dark secret surrounding David's paternity? Could the boy be prying open a real can of worms?

It occurred to him that he should probably give Thea some warning as to her son's state of mind, but he couldn't imagine having such a conversation with her. She was distant and aloof, definitely beating him in the eccentric recluse game. He knew her only through the comments her son made and from seeing the way she lived in his house. In truth he barely knew her at all. It almost seeemed he'd had a clearer understanding of her on the day they met.

*"Mr. Verrity? I'm Thea Auben and this is my son David. The realtor said yours was the only available rental in the area that might be close to what we're looking for."*

*"What are you looking for?" he'd asked, silently cursing the real estate woman because the last thing he wanted was to rent to a helpless, needy single mother. He could just imagine her calling him out to change lightbulbs and empty mouse traps, or engaging him in long late night discussions because she had no one else to talk to.*

*"We want a good solid house that's away from town but not so isolated that it's a problem for David to get to school," the woman said. "With a view of the forest."*

*"Are you sure you want to be out so far? There are apartments for rent in town. Close to everything. Your son could walk to school."*

*"No," she said emphatically. "We want to be out."*

*"Are you new to Eureka?"*

*"Yes. From Sacramento. But we've always wanted to live near the redwoods, haven't we, David?"*

*The boy nodded. His eyes were as measuring and cautious as a veteran homicide detective's.*

"*I haven't been here long either,*" *Jack admitted.* "*My uncle and aunt were long time residents. The house I'm renting out was theirs.*" *As he spoke he studied her with a cop's eye.*

*White female. Average height and build, with the kind of face that gave witnesses trouble because there was nothing irregular about it, no one feature that demanded notice. Hazel eyes. Brownish chin-length hair that was clean and shiny but otherwise left to go its own way. Clear skin with a slightly tanned appearance; maybe her natural complexion? Basic jeans and T-shirt. No major cosmetics use. Probably late twenties to early thirties, though there was a quality she had—a shy reticence, a wary self-consciousness, a nonspecific anger— that made her seem closer to her son's age. All told she was a fairly unremarkable woman, a woman he wouldn't have looked twice at in a bar or in one of the flashy hangouts he used to frequent in L.A., yet there was something compelling about her, something that stirred his protective impulses.*

"*We just lost my mother,*" *she exchanged a glance with the boy and it was clear that their grief was still raw.* "*We've come here to make a new start.*"

"*To stay,*" *the boy said with a determination that spoke of previous disappointments.*

*Jack looked from mother to son. They appeared more like brother and sister, both in age and in behavior.* "*I don't know how much the realtor told you, but the house is on the Avenue of the Giants, and it actually sits behind a shop—one of those places that was built to sell souvenirs to tourists.*"

*She bit the corner of her lip and cast a doubtful frown at her son.*

"*I've got the shop leased to two women who've started a sort of artists' cooperative, trying to sell area art along with the souvenir junk, and I've got to warn you, the shop could be busy during the summer. Avenue of the Giants has been known to have actual traffic jams during high tourist season.*"

"*But the house is behind the shop, right?*" *the boy asked.* "*People wouldn't be coming to the house first or anything. . . . I mean, the real estate lady said that from the road you wouldn't even know there was a house back there.*"

"*That's right,*" *Jack admitted.* "*But that means there's no neighbors to watch out for you. There's nobody close by to lend a hand. And in the winter when the shop is closed you're pretty isolated back there."*

He waited while the mother and son exchanged a wordless communication.

"But the school bus can always get through on the highway, right?" the boy asked.

Jack nodded. "I guess I should also warn you that the two women who run the shop are . . . well, they've got what you might call an alternative lifestyle. And their friends—all the artists who'll be bringing art and hanging around the shop— they're all pretty unconventional. It could get a little wild. I don't know if that bothers you."

"Why would that bother us?" she asked as though angry at the idea of anyone being bothered by it.

Damn. Wasn't there anything he could say to discourage her? "That's a good attitude if you're going to live around here. Humboldt County is a real magnet for alternatives— witches, ganja growers, mountain-man wannabes who live out in the trees without electricity or plumbing, ecology radicals who would kill a person to save a tree, and timber executives whose goal is to clear-cut the world. They're all here."

"And ex-policemen," the boy said, eyeing Jack for a reaction.

Jack vowed to throttle the motor-mouthed realtor next time he saw her.

"But I thought this was a safe place," the woman said with alarm, and he knew that at last he'd struck a chord. "We read that there was very little crime here."

"Oh, let me tell you—" Jack said, winding up to exaggerate the crime rate and toss in a few lurid accounts of territorial bloodshed among the marijuana growers and the danger to hapless hikers who left the trails and strayed into forbidden fields, but he made the mistake of meeting the kid's eyes for a moment and then he couldn't. "It is pretty safe for the average person. I guess the wackos balance each other out."

The woman hesitated a moment before asking, "Can we see the house, then?"

"It's a twenty- to thirty-minute drive from here. Are you sure you're interested?"

"There was nothing else," she said wearily.

*He hesitated. "Okay. You can either leave your car here and ride in mine or follow me."*

*"We'll follow," she said quickly.*

*He started toward his car, then turned back. "Winter is different here than in Sacramento."*

*"We know. We researched it."*

*"We research everything," the boy said.*

*Jack sighed. He glanced at their car. It was in rough shape and he suspected that everything they owned was packed into the trailer.*

*"Did the realtor tell you the rent?"*

*"Yes."*

*They looked so tired and vulnerable, yet they weren't pitiful at all. The woman had dignity. He'd always been a sucker for dignity.*

*"Well . . . that's negotiable," he told her though dropping the rent would mean no profit.*

*"If we like it we won't argue with you about the price," she said. "I'm sure it's fair."*

*"No. The realtor has it listed wrong. Your rent would definitely be less. Definitely less."*

That had been the previous June. Just short of a year ago. At first he'd kicked himself for the momentary bout of insanity that caused him to rent to a single mother and lower the rent as well, but she had turned out to be the perfect tenant. She asked for almost nothing and had even tried to discourage him from the maintenance and repairs he'd felt compelled to do, preferring to live with problems rather than have him intrude on her privacy. The woman had proven herself to be stubbornly and relentlessly self-sufficient. Self-contained. The phrase popped into his mind with amusing irony. It referred to the oversized camper units that some tourists vacationed in. Self-contained units. Meaning they had their own batteries and generators and water supplies and whatever. That was Thea. She needed no outside help, no outside energy for her closed little world to function. And he had to admit a certain admiration for her. She had achieved what he aspired to.

In fact when he considered his own situation—with property owned so that he was guaranteed freedom of habitat; with money coming in through disability, pension, and trust payments so that he need never work or expose himself to a workplace community of colleagues or customers again; and with no dependents or pets at all—he should have had the recluse's advantage. Yet he had blown it by moving from his uncle's place and buying himself a house on the edge of town with neighbors in sight. And what did he choose to do with his no-colleagues, no-forced-fellowship, no-dependents time? Mornings he usually went to the donut shop and afternoons to the coffee shop, sitting alone, but still within a circle of humanity, and at night he occasionally found his way to one of the area's dank bars to sit silently amongst other pathetic male patrons in the smoky darkness and hit on women he'd never look twice at under a forty-watt bulb. Some recluse he was.

Thea on the other hand had managed to erect an invisible barrier around herself even though she worked, had to rent her home, and had the responsibility of a child. She ran some kind of computerized service out of her living room, bypassing the whole workplace scene, and according to David, she conducted the business so that there was never any face-to-face contact with her clients. And she sure wasn't a regular at any of the local hangouts. From what he has seen she spoke only when spoken to by shopkeepers, bank tellers, and other unavoidable members of the community, causing some people to think her shy and others to label her as anti-social.

He knew from David that she hadn't made one friend. Whenever she drove to town, whether it was for groceries or to see a movie, she was with the boy. Her entire life seemed to revolve around her son. But this was where her carefully fortified, perfect little existence faltered and revealed the erosion of the mortar. Though she was a hovering and involved parent there was something wrong. Something off. The kid was all mixed up and cruising toward an emotional train wreck, and her handling of the boy had Jack thinking that she needed to go to one of those shrink sessions where everyone learned to shriek obscenities and hit each other over the head with foam bats.

"I don't think your mother would intentionally lie to you about the past," he said, lying to the boy.

The kid appeared to struggle with his thoughts a moment. "What if my father is really alive? What if she's been hiding me from him, keeping me from having a father. I see stuff like that in the news sometimes where parents hide kids."

"That's pretty hard to believe."

"Okay then, you try," the boy challenged. "Just try to get her to tell you things about the past and about my father. Make her tell you his exact name and where he was born and died. And then you call up some of your cop friends and ask them to check."

"Hey, I'm not in on this! I'm not suspicious of your mother and I'm not grilling her. Neither should you. Instead of acting like an adolescent jerk and coming up with all this bullshit you should be helping her, making life easier for her, showing some gratitude for all she's done to take care of you."

The boy reacted as though he'd been slapped and his eyes brimmed dangerously with moisture.

"You just want me to go away and leave you out of it! You don't care what's wrong or what's true as long as it doesn't bother you! You don't care what happens to anybody!"

With that he spun and slammed out the door. Jack stood for a moment, staring down at the careful rows of his ongoing solitaire game. Fine. Now he was rid of the kid and he could get back to work. He dumped the boy's half-eaten burrito in the trash and headed back out to the yard. Back to digging out the monster rhododendron. He picked up his ax, stared at the mangled base of the plant, sighed, threw the ax down and went into the house for his car keys.

"Damn, damn, damn," he muttered as he started his battered green Bronco.

The boy was a fast walker. By the time Jack caught up to him the kid had made it almost to the highway. Windows down, he pulled up alongside.

"David . . . come on . . . get in."

The boy continued walking as though Jack was not there.

"Come on. I need to go out to the place anyway. I have something to talk to your mother about."

With a wounded yet measuring look the boy turned and glared at Jack for several seconds. Curiosity finally won out over pride. "What are you going to talk to her about?"

"Business."

"Promise you won't tell her—you know—all the stuff about my father. I mean, you could try to find out things from her but just leave me out of it."

Jack sighed, then grudgingly agreed. "But it's only for now," he added. "It's not blanket immunity."

With a sheepish grin the boy opened the passenger door and climbed in.